DANCING
WITH FLAMES

DANCING WITH FLAMES

A Dragon's Breath Novel

Susan Illene

ISBN-10: 1535368306
ISBN-13: 9781535368308

Images obtained for the creation of this novel's cover were licensed for use from Teresa Yeh photography and Jeff Brown Graphics. Design by Claudia McKinney at Phat Puppy Art.

DEDICATION

To the marigolds that return every spring, long
after those who planted them are gone.

1

BAILEY

Traveling down city streets in a post-apocalyptic world could come with all sorts of challenges—testing my driving skills being one of them. There were cracks and potholes in the roads that I couldn't always avoid, causing my truck to bump along with jaw-rattling annoyance. Damaged vehicles, fallen trees, and downed power lines also made regular appearances that required careful maneuvering to get around.

Then there was the hazardous trash, debris, and broken glass littering the pavement that seemed to flourish now that there was no one in charge of picking up the refuse anymore. Even if you got past those obstacles, you still suffered from the smell. In some areas, the strong odor coming from the rotting food and human waste was so overpowering it could make you gag. I hadn't realized how valuable government

SUSAN ILLENE

services were until they were gone—and unlikely to ever come back.

How had we reached this point in the span of four months? Another dimension had collided with ours, bringing numerous natural disasters and fire-breathing dragons with it. Oh, and let's not forget magic, because why not? It had been used by sorcerers to banish dragons in the first place, after all.

Who would've guessed some of those mythical creatures we grew up hearing about might have actually been real? I'd never dreamed civilization could come crumbling down so fast, or that I would have such an important role to play in the new era that arose after it. Times were dark, but I suspected they were about to get even darker.

"Look out!" Conrad yelled from the passenger seat of my truck.

I slammed on the brakes as a frantic, middle-aged man with short, graying hair dashed onto the road fifty feet ahead and waved his arms. His blue-collared shirt was covered in sweat, his jeans worn and dirt-encrusted, and wild desperation filled his eyes—not a good combination. Conrad and I scanned the area, searching for any signs of an attack. It wouldn't be the first time we'd been ambushed while driving through town.

"See anything?" I asked Conrad.

He frowned. "Nope, no one."

Not necessarily a good sign—they could be hiding. Through my open window, nothing moved aside from a black cat sitting on a porch across the street. It stared at us with disdain, flicking its tail. This neighborhood appeared cleaner than most and only had light structural damage. Other than a few burned down homes and a crater in the middle of the street ahead, it was still habitable. A strong sign people lived nearby, though none other than the one guy had revealed themselves.

The beleaguered man came over to the side of my truck, gasping for breath. I grabbed my pistol from the console and pointed it at his chest. "Don't come any closer."

"Please," the man said urgently, lifting his hands high. "I have to talk to you."

I narrowed my eyes. "What do you want?"

"My name is Keith Barbour, and I live a few blocks from here." He nodded toward the east. "I'm looking for the dragon slayer. Are you her?"

My gaze hardened further. "Why do you ask?"

I had only taken down a handful of the beasts since my first kill a month ago. Sure, a few people were always lurking nearby to witness my battles, but I hadn't realized how fast word would spread. Norman—a suburb of Oklahoma City—had lost over half its population in the last few months from people either dying or fleeing town. Those who remained stayed out of sight unless they wanted to be seen. The ones who did show their faces for long, well, they tended to have less than altruistic plans in mind. I had learned to trust no one outside my close circle of friends.

"I heard on the radio there's a dragon slayer in town. Hank said it's a woman driving a black truck and wearing some kind of weird leather get-up." He cocked his head at me. "How many of those with that description you think are driving around here? Though, I did expect you to be…uh, bigger."

Damn Hank and his need to report everything.

The description was close enough, though our only surviving radio announcer had probably said more. I was part Cherokee Indian, part Malaysian, and part white. That combo gave me straight, black hair, brown eyes with a slight slant to them, and perpetually tan skin. No one could ever quite nail my features down, so most people just described me as mixed. I was used to getting comments on my petite size, though. Nobody thought I would have the strength to kill something five times bigger than me—sometimes the dragons were even larger than that—until they watched me do it. Little did they know super-human strength came with the job.

"Keep an eye out," I ordered Conrad.

"Don't worry." He grinned, holding a shotgun he'd grabbed from the backseat. "Ain't nothing gettin' by me."

He was a guy I knew from college before the apocalypse, but we hadn't become good friends until after all hell broke loose. The dark-skinned nineteen-year-old was a few years younger than me, but he'd come in handy more than once in dangerous situations. Nobody had my back more than he did, which was good since I slayed dragons as a profession now and ran into trouble rather often.

I lowered my pistol a fraction and addressed Keith. "So what do you want from me?"

Some of the tension in the man's shoulders eased. "A dragon took my neighbor's five-year-old son a few days ago. It's been back every night since, showing up around sunset looking for more of our kids. We've been keeping them hidden in an underground storm shelter, but when the beast can't get to them, it tears up our neighborhood instead. We've tried shooting at it—" he paused to shudder, "but it's like trying to stop a tank with a pellet gun. The dragon just kills anyone who gets in its way."

This was different than any other story I'd heard. Dragons attacked and burned humans on a regular basis with horrifying results, but they had a reason for that—even if it wasn't a great one. They were angry about getting banished to another dimension for a thousand years. Over there, they had lived in a barren land with not much in the way of food sources. It had been a struggle to survive for all that time. When they returned four months ago, they came back with a terrifying vengeance—despite the fact it was sorcerers who had sent them away, not us. But humans got the blame as well since we stayed on Earth while they suffered in *Kederrawien*, the dragon dimension where they came from.

Regardless of the animalistic nature of the beasts, they were much smarter than people assumed. Most humans didn't have a prayer of taking one down without major firepower, such as rockets, and the element of surprise. Acquiring either was almost impossible at this point. The military had stopped their air strikes months ago and Oklahoma—as well as much of the country from what I'd heard—now had to fend for itself.

A small number of dragons had a taste for human flesh and would prey upon people for food rather than animals, but they always targeted adults—more meat on their bones. This was a whole new angle for them to seek out children, and a rather unsettling one if it was true. Not that dragons snacking on anyone sat well with me, but I'd had to adjust to a lot of horrible things since their arrival. Death took on a whole new meaning when you faced it every day.

"You're sure they're after your children?" I asked, skeptical.

"Yes." Keith nodded. "Heard about some other neighborhoods havin' the same troubles, too. There's been at least a few kids taken in the last week or so. We think the dragons can smell 'em."

I closed my eyes, mourning the lost children. There was no way they could have survived dragons taking them. All the beasts had to do was hold and carry them for a few moments before their skin would begin to get scorched. Dragon bodies were way too hot for humans to touch, which was why you did not want to be captured alive by them.

Taking a deep breath, I opened my eyes again. I couldn't let the dragon take any more children. I had planned to spend the day gathering food supplies. All the grocery stores had been picked clean, but there were a few gardens planted before the apocalypse that Conrad and I had found growing unattended. At least twice a week we went to pick any ripe vegetables to bring back to our neighborhood. We also had some fruit trees we checked on frequently. When you had almost thirty mouths to feed and winter approaching, you spent almost every spare moment looking for ways to survive for as long as possible.

"We're going to need to take a look at your neighborhood," I said, resolved to commit my day to this. It was for a good cause, and it would be worth it, but I had a feeling more and more people would be seeking me out now that they knew what I could do.

Relief filled the man's eyes. "Oh, thank God. I'll show you the way."

"Is it me, or is it hot?" Conrad asked.

He crouched next to me where we took shelter under a pavilion. We'd set up a lure in the large open park next to Keith's neighborhood with the hope of drawing the dragon away from people. I would need plenty of room to maneuver while fighting and Conrad would need a place to hide once it got started. Only one of us was impervious to fire.

"Yeah, too hot for late September." I scrunched my nose. "This bait idea of yours better work. I can still smell it, and it's at least two hundred feet away."

Conrad had gotten the grand idea that the best method to draw the dragon to us was to put out the rotting carcass of a dead possum we'd found on the road. The rancid stench would overpower the hungry dragon's senses and bring him toward the park. Their kind might prefer bigger meals, but they liked easy ones even better. We had hung the roadkill from a tree branch where flies now buzzed around it. I had developed a strong stomach, but I still tried to avoid looking at the poor animal too closely.

"I got a cousin who hunts alligators down in the Louisiana bayou—or at least he did," Conrad paused. For a moment, the pain of not knowing what became of his family flashed into his brown eyes, but then he shook himself. "Anyway, he used to swear by this trick. I figure since dragons are sort of like reptiles, it might work."

"Let's hope so," I said, wishing my sense of smell hadn't become keener since I completed the rite of passage that all born slayers had to perform. Basically, it involved killing a dragon and eating its heart. And yes, it tasted like chicken.

"It's coming. It's coming!" Keith screamed from across the street. He stood on his porch and pointed toward the north where a green dragon approached low in the sky, soaring not more than fifty feet above the rooftops.

I gestured for him to take cover and lifted my crossbow. Conrad had already raised his. We'd been training on them for weeks with Aidan—a dragon shape-shifter who'd become my secret ally against the pure dragons—but this was the first time I'd actually put my new weapon to use in live combat.

Sweat beaded atop my forehead as I waited for the creature to come closer. Its body was about the size of a juvenile elephant, and it had wide, leathery-green wings that spanned at least twenty feet. The closer it flew, the faster my heart pumped and the more my instincts drove me to attack. I was a slayer and my sole purpose in life was to kill the fire-breathing beasts who threatened humans.

The dragon soared lower over Keith's neighborhood, and I held my breath. Was it searching for the children? The wind shifted, and the creature's head turned toward the park. It had caught the scent of our bait. I gripped my crossbow, holding it steady though every fiber of my being wanted to forget the plan and dash across the field. The dragon was coming. Just a few more seconds and it would be close enough. I didn't have Aidan here to help this time. If I was going to pull this off, I had to make sure I had the advantage.

As soon as the dragon flew into the park, I let loose my zaphiriam bolt, made of a special black metal with red veins that could pierce dragon scales. It was also impervious to high heat and fire. The bolt clipped the edge of the creature's left wing, not even slowing it down. The beast probably thought a bug hit it.

"Damn it all to hell." I was *so* going to ask Aidan for a different range weapon.

No matter how much I practiced with the crossbow, it didn't feel as natural to me as a sword. Aidan had mentioned that not everything would come easily, even as a slayer, and that some weaponry wouldn't be a good fit for me at all. It was a matter of trying different things until I found the ones that worked.

Unfortunately, pistols and rifles weren't an option since lead bullets hardly fazed dragons. We couldn't replace them with zaphiriam because the metal was too hard to make effective ammunition. The accuracy wouldn't be as high, and it would wear out the gun barrels too quickly. Aidan couldn't manufacture bullets in his clan's forges anyway since his skills were limited to blades, such as knives and swords. For everything else, he relied on the weapons makers at his fortress to craft what he needed, but dragon shape-shifters didn't use firearms, so we were out of luck there.

There was no help for it now. The beast had landed next to the tree with the bait. This would be the next best chance to take it down while it was distracted with food. I dropped my weapon and leaped to my feet.

"Bailey, hold up," Conrad hissed, aiming his own crossbow.

"Hurry!"

As the dragon chomped down on the hanging bait, Conrad let loose his bolt and nailed the beast in its belly. The creature let out a loud roar, dropping its food.

"Got that bastard!" Conrad grinned up at me. "Now that's how it's done."

Of course, it would work just fine for him, dammit. I patted him on the head. "Good job. Now, stay down."

I took off running, pulling my sword from its scabbard as I sprinted across the park. The dragon's red eyes zeroed in on me. It started thumping my way like an enraged bull with its wings half-open for balance and steam puffing from his nostrils. A normal person wouldn't go near it. I, on the other hand, couldn't have stopped myself from attacking the green dragon if I'd tried.

Every instinct called for its death. I craved it like a junkie who needed her next fix. My blood raced, strength poured through my muscles, and time almost stood still as I got closer. The dragon lifted one of its stubby forearms, ready to swipe me with its sharp talons. I put in a final burst of speed, slid across the ground, and sailed straight underneath it—narrowly missing the swipe of its claws. Holding my sword above me, I slashed into its chest with the jagged edge. The blade skimmed across the scales before digging deeper. It cut into tissue and caught on a rib. My body's momentum jerked to a stop, and I twisted until I'd freed the weapon.

With a guttural cry, I stabbed upward. The sword slid into the dragon's stomach and hot, dark-red blood splattered over me. The beast let out a deafening roar that would ring in my ears for years to come. It swung its body back and forth, dragging me across the grass. I held onto the hilt like a lifeline as the blade ripped through the creature's gut.

The dragon's movements steadily slowed as it bled out and lost strength. Above me, it shuddered and groaned. If I didn't want to be crushed, I needed to get away fast.

At the last second, I yanked my sword out and began rolling away from the creature. It swiped at me with its talons, slashing across my right arm and igniting a searing burn. I scrambled onto my knees to get clear. I'd only made it a few feet away when the beast fell heavily to the ground and rolled onto its side. The dragon weakly angled its head up enough to let out a mournful cry, but it wasn't as loud as the first.

I ignored the biting pain of my wounds and leaped to my feet. The beast was heaving now, struggling to lift itself back up. I couldn't let that happen. The dragon had wounded me, and targeted innocent people. I narrowed my gaze on its swollen belly and lifted my sword with the tip pointed downward, aimed at the beast's heart.

Just before I made the thrust, a flash of movement from the corner of my eye distracted me. Another dragon approached. Its wings beat furiously, and it sailed across the park at top speed. Before I could readjust the sword for a proper defense, the red beast crashed feet-first into my chest, knocking me to the ground.

2

AIDAN

A high-pitched roar broke the still air, loud enough for anyone in the area to catch it. Aidan winced at the female dragon's wail for help. It wasn't intended for him specifically, but he couldn't miss the desperation in her call. She followed the roar with a telepathic plea for someone to save her, using an open method any dragon could hear.

Aidan stiffened as soon as he heard her give her name—Matrika. She was the leader's daughter for the Shadowan *toriq*, or "clan" as humans called it, and she was beloved by her kinsmen. It came as a surprise to him that she'd come alone this close to the edge of Taugud territory, considering the tensions between his toriq and hers. A few responses came back to her, but those dragons were too far away. No matter how much they hurried, they wouldn't reach her in time to save her. Aidan had every intention of ignoring the call, despite being in close proximity, but Matrika sent another telepathic plea saying she was being attacked by a slayer.

He knew of only one person that could be—Bailey.

Aidan launched into the air and flew hard toward the female dragon. Her cries were growing weaker by the second until he feared she'd be dead before he even got there. The slayer didn't realize who she was battling, or the trouble it could cause her. Bailey would kill Matrika, not realizing three more of the female's clansmen were on their way. She didn't have the skills or experience to fight that many dragons at once. Even if Bailey left the scene quickly, they'd still track her back to her human neighborhood. She and all her friends would be dead before the sun set. It was one thing to slay a lowly dragon, but the upper hierarchy required more planning and precautions to succeed without retaliation.

He reached the park and found Bailey lifting her sword for the final strike. Unable to risk losing a moment, Aidan flew at full speed. With one final beat of his wings, he surged forward and pushed his feet into her chest, knocking her to the ground. Bailey let out a choked cry. His talons had punctured her skin, but it couldn't be helped. This was the only way to stop her in time—the only way to save her from what she was about to do.

Aidan landed a few feet past the slayer and roared at Matrika to flee. The female dragon gave him a surprised but grateful look and struggled to her feet. Bailey scrambled back up, reaching for her sword.

Aidan swung around and knocked his tail into her legs. She landed face-first, catching a mouthful of grass and dirt. He'd trained Bailey to watch for dragon tails, but she'd been too focused on Matrika to notice. Somewhere in the back of her mind, she must have known he wasn't her true enemy and calculated him as a lesser threat.

The female dragon lifted into the air, flapping her wings ungracefully. She didn't fly fast, and it was clear she was in pain, but at least she was getting away. Aidan felt mixed emotions as he watched her go. He wouldn't have minded seeing the Shadowan clan's princess die, but not at the price Bailey would have to pay. Aidan would do what he must to protect the slayer—even if she hated him for it.

Bailey dove toward him with her sword raised, screaming obscenities. She did not have control over her instincts, and as the only dragon now available to attack, she couldn't help coming for him. Aidan side-stepped, narrowly avoiding the strike she aimed for his head. Then he leaped on top of her and pinned her to the ground. Bailey struggled against him. She managed to free one arm and punched him in the snout.

Pain tore through Aidan's nose. It was a sensitive spot for dragons, and the slayer knew it. If he were to get through to her, he'd have to change to his human form. As Bailey continued to beat her fists on his face and chest, Aidan allowed his inner flames to flow outward and engulf him. The grass around them burned until nothing remained except dirt. The slayer herself wasn't affected by fire, and she wore the black camrium attire he'd given her. It was impervious to flames as well.

He took one more blow to the head before his change was complete. Bailey's struggles subsided as the fire died down and she could see his face. For most dragon slayers, even his human form wouldn't stop them from attacking, but he had held her close for two days during her transformation process. Partially so that she would get used to his scent, and partially because he wanted to help her through the painful transition in any way he could. She'd completed her rite of passage with the ability to see him as an ally and not an enemy. It was only his dragon form she couldn't tolerate yet, though he'd been working with her on that as well.

Bailey glared up at him. "Why did you stop me? I was a second away from killing it!"

"Matrika has summoned every dragon in the area." Aidan stood and helped the slayer to her feet. "I know of at least three who responded, and they are heading this way now."

Bailey threw her hands up. "So why not let me kill her first, and then we could go?"

"I'll explain that later." Aidan picked up the slayer's sword and held it out to Conrad, who'd just run up to them.

The young man glanced at it without taking the blade. "Man, what the hell?"

"Take it," he said, forcing the hilt into Conrad's hands.

"It's Bailey's," he argued.

"Give that back to me." The slayer attempted to maneuver around Aidan.

He caught sight of several humans coming from their homes across the street. They spoke amongst each other, no doubt debating whether to join them in the park or not. That was the absolute last thing they should do.

Aidan checked the sky. It was still clear, but it wouldn't be for long. "You must get these people back inside. The dragon is a princess among the Shadowan, and they will come to avenge this attack on her."

"But she isn't dead," Conrad argued.

Aidan's inner dragon growled. Three dots had just appeared in the sky to the north, alerting him and the beast within him that they had minutes to spare before it would be too late and they'd have a major battle on their hands. He drew from *shiggara*, a mystical place where he could store a small number of useful items. A flask appeared in his hand. He removed the top and poured *stinguise* juice—a foul smelling concoction not unlike that of a skunk—across the ground where Bailey and Matrika had battled. He didn't have time to fully remove the slayer's scent since she'd fought in too large an area, but it would hide his and Conrad's.

Bailey covered her nose but didn't say anything. She'd seen him use the stinguise juice after other battles she'd fought and knew its purpose. Aidan gave her a grim look. If she was going to keep attacking dragons

17

on her own, he would have to give her a bottle to keep with her.

Conrad took a few steps back. "That stuff is rank."

"Yes, but it will keep the Shadowan from looking for you."

Aidan glanced at the sky, alarmed to find the dragon shapes growing larger in the distance. He took hold of Conrad's shoulders, turning him so that he could see the looming threat. "Get the humans to safety. Their lives are in your hands."

The young man swung around. "What about you and Bailey?"

"I must take her away and hope the dragons follow us until we can lose them, but that will only work if you are not here to draw their attention."

Conrad nodded. "Got it, man."

"Are we going in my truck?" Bailey asked, giving Aidan a confused look.

"No, leave it here. We will go the faster way."

Bailey dug into a pouch on her leg harness and handed over a set of keys to Conrad. "Which way?"

The dragons would be here in two minutes. The time for discussion had ended, and Aidan couldn't wait any longer. He let his fire consume him so that he could return to his beast form.

"Wait, you can't mean *that* way." Bailey backed up a few steps. Through the flames, he could see her anguished expression. Any minute, her instincts would take over, and she would want to kill him again. He knew she wrestled with the guilt of that, though she tried to hide it from him.

As his body shifted into a much larger form, he watched her wrap her arms around herself and shiver. She squeezed her eyes shut, delaying the inevitable for as long as possible. Once the flames died down, though, she scented the beast, and her lids flew open.

Aidan didn't hesitate to leap into the air, wrap his scaly arms around her body, and sail into the sky. He didn't like carrying people and certainly not in this way, but he kept a tight hold on her. Bailey struggled at first, attempting to wiggle free. Once he climbed high enough, she stopped. Self-preservation took over, and even her slayer instincts saw that breaking away now would only result in her death.

He dared a glance back and spotted the three Shadowan dragons still far behind. Aidan had a safe lead on them, but with the extra weight in his arms he couldn't fly at full speed. They would catch up soon. The only option he had was to fly directly to his territory and hope none of his brethren saw him carrying Bailey. There would be no easy explanation for what he was doing with her. Other than his cousin, Donar, none knew Aidan had allied himself with a dragon slayer. If they saw him carrying her in his arms, they would know she could not be a normal human. Only a slayer could tolerate his scorching heat for long without burning.

Aidan crossed the invisible line where the shapeshifter territory began and looked back. The three dragons were already turning around. For now, they were safe. Should the Shadowan return to the park and pick up the slayer's scent, though, they would be able to recognize her if she crossed paths with them in the future. The only thing protecting her now was that they must assume Aidan planned to kill her himself.

It would be some time before Bailey could return without risking drawing the Shadowan's attention. He headed toward his secret lair, his gaze scanning relentlessly for any sign of his clansmen. Aidan prayed to the dragon goddess, *Zorya*, that his path would remain clear.

3

BAILEY

I was going to slay the dragon holding me the moment my feet safely touched the ground. My entire body thrummed with the need to fight, to kill, but through my rage I recognized my situation. Falling would be bad, very bad. I might be more durable than the average human, but I didn't think I could survive a hundred foot drop. Even if I could, it would hurt like hell and the resulting injuries would leave me unable to defend myself.

A shudder ran through me when I glanced down. Not just because the houses and streets below appeared too small, but also because of what gripped me so tightly. Arms similar to a man's—except with red scales—and fingers with long black talons were wrapped around my chest. The creature was strong, very strong. The massive chest radiated heat behind me like an inferno, and his heavy muscles rubbed against my back. This red dragon wasn't as large as the green one I'd just fought, but he was fast to have captured me so easily.

Somewhere in the back of my mind, it registered that he was familiar. Someone I had known for months, but while he was in this form, I couldn't make sense of it. All I could think of was the need to free myself and shove a blade through his heart. Watch him die, as all dragons should. In the deep recesses of my soul, this bothered me, but I couldn't clear my head enough to understand why.

In the distance, I caught sight of another red dragon in the air. I stiffened at the same time as the beast holding me let out a low growl. The other beast flew a course straight for us. I estimated my chances of winning a fight against both of them while up this high in the sky.

Not good. Not good at all.

The dragon flared his red, leathery wings to slow down. The one at my back relaxed a fraction and made a throaty, rumbling noise that sounded suspiciously like a greeting. Wonderful—they were friends. I'd kind of hoped they'd do my job for me and kill each other, assuming they took their battle to the ground first.

The two beasts flew beside each other for the next few minutes as we soared in an easterly direction past the outskirts of Norman and into the countryside. Ranches and farms dotted the land. There were no vehicles on the roads, and aside from a herd of cows, nothing moved below. It was eerily peaceful.

I clutched the beast's arms as he dropped lower, almost skimming the tops of the trees. It was getting late, and the sun would be setting soon. How I'd get home without my truck this far from town, I didn't know, but I'd worry about that later. First, I had to kill the two dragons and hope I survived. A glance at my empty scabbard told me this wasn't going to be an easy battle without a weapon. Maybe I would die, but I'd take at least one of them down with me.

A small empty field appeared up ahead. Though I'd never seen it from above, I recognized it and the two-story house sitting at the far end. This was where I'd trained to become a dragon slayer. The one holding me and his flying buddy had been the ones to teach me. They kept a weapons stash inside the house and all I needed to do was get to it. These fools might have been the ones to train me, but that was their mistake.

I braced myself as the dragon dipped toward the field. To my surprise, he dropped me mid-air. I fell about six feet, hitting the ground hard and rolling several times across the high grass. As soon as I stopped, I scrambled onto my knees and watched as the two dragons continued their flight to the edge of the tree line. It was only then that they landed.

Pushing off the ground, I dashed toward them. *Kill, kill, kill* ran through my mind like a mantra. The very sight of them colored my vision with rage. Their snouts billowing steam, their red scaly bodies flexing with hard muscles, and their long tails with spikes on the ends swishing back and forth—all of it grabbed my attention and drove me to attack.

They tucked in their wings, and their bulky bodies went up in flames. I didn't worry about that. The fire wouldn't hurt me, and they were more vulnerable while some kind of metamorphosis altered them. In the midst of the flames, they transformed into what looked like demons. I put in another burst of speed, closing the distance. Just fifty more feet and I'd be on them. I caught sight of a sharp stick on the ground directly on my path and slowed briefly to grab it. Gouging their eyes out would be a good start. They'd still be able to hear and smell, but at least it would give me some kind of advantage.

Just as I made it to the last dozen feet, the flames covering their bodies subsided. Men who mostly resembled humans—except for having yellow snake eyes—stood in the dragons' place. Both had short black hair, olive skin, and toned muscles.

Seeing them like that, I slowed my steps and dropped the stick. My rage ebbed away like the tide going out to the sea. I recognized Aidan, the leaner and lither of the two men. He had been the one who carried me here and organized my training. The other one was Donar. He was a big oaf and Aidan's cousin. They were my two shape-shifter allies that I'd failed to recognize in their dragon forms—at least on a conscious level—and wanted to kill. God, I hated how little control I had over myself when my slayer instincts took over. It was like I became a different person.

I started to apologize, but then I remembered what led me to this place. Aidan had dragged me here against my will. I narrowed my gaze on him. Just because I didn't feel the need to kill him anymore didn't mean I wasn't still angry about what he had just done.

"Are you out of your mind? First, you stop me from killing that dragon, and then you carry me back here, knowing what it would do to me." What if I had tried to kill him mid-air? Sure, he had been smart enough to leave my sword with Conrad, but he had no guarantee I wouldn't have fought him anyway.

His lips set in a grim line. "I apologize for that, but it was necessary."

His voice rolled over me, the accent so foreign, and yet, a little on the sexy side. When I'd first met him, I'd been a little too intimidated to think much of it, but after months of getting used to him, I'd grown to love his deep timber. It could distract me if I wasn't careful.

"No, it wasn't necessary." I crossed my arms. "You should have let me stay there and protect those people."

He lifted a brow. "If I had done as you suggest, those dragons would have attacked the humans as well. Would you truly prefer to have their deaths on your hands?"

I closed the distance between us and poked him in the chest. "Not if we fought them. You and I against three aren't the worst odds."

"It would be if they called for more help," Aidan said, glaring at my finger until I dropped it. "Matrika sent an open summons that any dragon could hear. I had no way of knowing if she spoke privately with any others in her toriq. If more of her kinsmen had come, you would have had no choice except to fight them until you were dead. I could not risk that." A hint of strong emotion came over his eyes and he shuddered.

And there it was—the sign he cared more deeply about me than he wanted to admit.

"Fine, we had to get away, but you should have let me kill Matrika first. She's been taking human children and harassing that neighborhood every night trying to get more kids. That was the whole reason I was there—to protect those people from her."

He shut his eyes and expelled a breath. "I'm sorry to hear that, but even if I'd known, I would not change what I did."

"Can we discuss this inside?" Donar asked, casting a wary glance at the darkening sky. "If I heard Matrika's call for help from farther away than Aidan, it is likely others in our clan did as well. It is not a good idea to be out in the open should they fly over this place."

That was one of the reasons why Aidan and I only met to train in the afternoons. His clan members usually didn't stray far from the fortress until evening—dragons did the bulk of their hunting at night—so the risk of being noticed was lower when the sun was high.

"Yeah, let's go in," I agreed, heading across the field toward the two-story house.

It had white siding, a red brick fireplace jutting from the side, and a covered porch running the full width of the front. My best guess was that the place had probably been built in the 1920s or 1930s. Someone had kept it in good condition before Aidan took it for his private lair. There were no obvious signs of disrepair, and the siding appeared to have been replaced within the last few years. We had no idea what happened to the owners, but they hadn't shown up since I started coming here a few months ago.

We entered the living room. It was cozy with wood floors, brown leather couches, black end tables, and a huge flat screen anchored above the fireplace. Every time I saw the television I remembered how much I missed watching TV shows and movies. These days we only had generators for electricity, and what little power we could get from those (when we had the spare fuel to run them) had to go to more important things like our vehicles. Modern entertainment was a luxury we couldn't afford. Maybe one day we'd push the pure dragons back enough to rebuild and start over again.

That was part of the reason Aidan and I had agreed to work together. His clan wanted peace and safety as much as the humans did. The shape-shifters' first step was to claim enough territory that they'd have all the resources they needed to survive and a buffer zone between them and the pure dragons. I was secretly helping Aidan with that. His clan didn't have a problem with humans and even let some of them live in their fortress, but a slayer like me was a different matter. We were supposed to be enemies, not allies. Aidan might have been able to think farther ahead and see the advantages of working together but not the rest of his people.

In exchange for my help, he had promised to take me to my family's ranch in Texas once we secured his clan's territory. I had tried getting there on my own right after *D-day* (when the dragons first invaded), but a giant chasm had opened up across the southern end of Oklahoma. To reach home now, I would have to drive hundreds of miles out of my way to get around it. That wouldn't be easy, considering I'd have to forage for fuel along the way, avoid dragons, and try not to get attacked by human gangs. It was just too dangerous to take the risk right now, and building up my slaying skills would only help that much more once I did return to Texas.

I only hated that I had to wait so long before I could leave. It could take up to a year for me to complete my end of the bargain with Aidan, and anything could happen to my family during that time. Though I managed to talk to my mother and stepfather regularly through a satellite phone, I worried about them. Dragon attacks were just as bad where they lived, southwest of Dallas, and they couldn't fight the beasts the way I could.

Then there was the fact that I had two older stepbrothers and one younger half-brother who were at that age where their courage was greater than their ability to calculate risks. Every time I checked in with my family, I braced for the news that one of them had gotten hurt or killed. So far they hadn't, but I figured it was only a matter of time. My stepfather couldn't keep an eye on them every minute of the day.

Donar shut the curtains while I settled on the couch. Aidan grabbed an oil lamp and blew a thin flame at the wick, lighting it. Most of the time their fire went out after they stopped blowing, but I had learned they could keep a small blaze going if they concentrated hard enough.

"You need to stay here from now on," Aidan said, setting the lamp on the fireplace mantle. It cast a soft glow across the room and highlighted the left side of his face. He had sharp cheekbones that gave him a rough, but beautiful edge to his appearance.

My brows drew together. "Why? You covered my scent so they shouldn't be able to identify me."

"Not well enough." He shook his head. "If I'd had more time, perhaps, but I only covered it enough so they couldn't easily track us. Matrika will remember your scent, and the others will be able to pick it up at the park."

I ground my teeth. I'd never imagined attacking one particular dragon could cause this much trouble. "You can't expect me to abandon my friends. Who is going to protect them if I'm not living in the neighborhood anymore?"

"Has it occurred to you that their lives are in more danger with you there?" Aidan's gaze softened. "Until today, I've managed to cover your tracks, but your presence is now known among the dragons. The best way you can protect your friends is to avoid them as much as possible. A slayer's life is a lonely one, but that is the way it must be."

I closed my eyes. He'd been hinting at this for weeks, but I had ignored him. I'd never been a very social person, and yet I couldn't stand the thought of living by myself. Even a small circle of friends made life that much more bearable. How was I going to battle dragons on a regular basis, risking my life, and then come back here—to nothing? Conrad, Trish, Danae, and the others in the neighborhood were always there to patch me up and calm me down after a battle. Aidan would probably try to visit as often as he could, but sometimes a week passed between our meetings. He had a life that went beyond me.

"Why didn't you tell me about Matrika before?" I asked, getting up to pace the room.

He started to walk toward me and stopped halfway. This happened a lot when we were together. It was like Aidan's subconscious guided him to me, and he had to resist it constantly. Sometimes, I wondered what would happen if he ever stopped fighting that attraction. We'd kissed once, but he'd sworn it would never happen again.

Only under extreme circumstances—such as flying me across the city—did he even touch me. I hated that it had to be that way between us, but I also recognized it was necessary. The last thing I needed was to feel divided when the day came that I could return to my family. We could be allies, maybe even friends, but nothing more.

"I never thought you'd come across her," he replied, running a hand through his short spiky hair. "She usually doesn't go out alone, and she certainly doesn't have to hunt."

Donar's brows drew together. "How did you end up fighting her anyway?"

"She's been stealing human children recently. A man from a nearby neighborhood told me she's been targeting kids and asked for my help. So Conrad and I set up a lure to draw her to us instead."

"A lure?" Donar asked.

"Dead possum. We thought the scent would grab her attention," I explained.

Donar rubbed his chin. "That wasn't a bad idea. The pure dragons aren't as particular about their meat as we are, and if it's easy to obtain," he paused and scrunched his nose, "all the better."

Aidan's expression darkened. He'd been quiet for the last couple of minutes. "You said Matrika is targeting children? Taking them alive?"

"Yeah—except I don't know how long they'd last with her grabbing them."

He moved over to a cedar chest against the wall and drew out some bandages and ointment we kept stored there. His back was to me as he spoke, "It is said that she cannot produce viable eggs. She and her former mate tried for years with no success."

"So she's, uh, barren?" I asked.

"That is what we believe." He gestured at me. "Sit while I clean your wounds."

I glanced at my arm and chest. With everything that had happened, I'd forgotten about the gashes Matrika and Aidan had given me. They'd stopped bleeding before we'd even reached the house—another benefit of being a dragon slayer. It would take a day or two for them to heal, though.

"What does her being barren have to do with taking human children? It's not like she can make them grow up to be dragons." I didn't even see how she could attempt to properly take care of them.

Aidan kept his gaze on my wounds. He was making every effort to touch me as little as possible while he cleaned the punctures and gashes. "Perhaps she is jealous and wishes to make humans suffer as she does."

"My mother once told me a story about a dragon who kept human children in her den," Donar said, knitting his brows. "In this case, she'd had several children of her own, but they died in battle, and she could not have more. She began taking young humans and raising them to keep her company."

I gaped at him. "How could she have pulled that off? They have to be fed, clothed, bathed, and other stuff. She couldn't even touch them without burning them."

"I asked that same question." He shook his head, mystified. "This occurred long ago before we were banished to Kederrawien, but my mother said the dragon did not take them so young they could not do some things for themselves. I suppose she was also very careful. They lived to be adults and stayed with the to-riq for their entire lives."

"Do you think it's really true?" I asked.

Donar's expression turned thoughtful. "My mother heard it from her grandmother, who swore she saw the humans for herself. I do not know why she would lie about such a thing."

I wasn't sure if I should be relieved by that or more worried. The child who had been taken in Keith's neighborhood had been about six years old, and he'd told me while we had scouted the park that the other missing children were a similar age. That was young, but not so much the kids would be completely help-less. If the dragon gave them decent food to eat and protected them, it was possible they might survive—at least until I could track them down and get them back to their families. Now that I knew it was possible, I had to hold on to the belief that I could find the children alive.

"Do you have any idea how Matrika could grab the children without hurting them?" No matter how care-ful the dragon, she couldn't touch a human without burning them.

He shrugged. "We have used blankets in the past when we needed to pick up a human. Even if Matrika does not have one made of camrium cloth, she could still grasp the ends of a regular one with her claws, which aren't hot enough to burn through the material. She would just need to be very careful."

Sort of like a stork carrying a baby, except in this case it was a dragon doing the transporting. The visual made me shudder. The poor children had to have been terrified during that ride.

Aidan finished bandaging the worst of my wounds and stood. "We must return to the fortress soon, but I would not leave you without resources." He glanced in the direction of the kitchen. "Do you still have some of your food stores here?"

"Yeah, I do." It never hurt to stash supplies in more than one place. "It's enough to last me a few days."

He nodded. "Good. I will bring more as soon as I am able."

"Speaking of which." Donar rose to his feet. "Your sister was looking for you, Aidan. I believe she said it had something to do with your father."

Aidan nodded, then looked down at me. "You will be safe enough here, but do not leave until I come back."

Even without transportation, I couldn't make that promise. There was no way I could sit here alone and do nothing. I'd take a day to let my wounds heal, but after that, I'd be back out there hunting for those children. If I didn't do it, who would?

"Have fun at the fortress," I said.

"I doubt it," he replied.

4

AIDAN

Aidan and Donar landed in the field outside the clan fortress gate—a massive place built with dark-gray stone. The shape-shifter home was designed so no dragon could fly inside, and they had to be in human form to enter the keep. They passed a male and female guard, who stood alert at their posts. Being the pendragon's son, they recognized Aidan right away. He nodded at them and continued with Donar through a short tunnel cut through the wall, passing blazing torches as they went.

Upon entering the keep, dozens of small buildings appeared ahead of them. This was a market area during the afternoon where clan members could purchase or trade food and supplies. Now that night had fallen, most of the shopkeepers had shut down. Many of them would be preparing for the midnight meal, which was the largest of the day. Even the humans who lived here—now numbering more than one hundred—followed this practice. In its entirety, the fortress held approximately seven hundred and fifty occupants. About two hundred more resided beyond the walls in smaller dens scattered throughout their territory.

Their soft camrium boots made little sound as they walked down the cobblestone thoroughfare. At the end of the path, they could make out the dark-stoned castle ahead. It was Aidan's home where his family and some of the other high-ranking families dwelled, along with some of the human servants. Torches were lit at the entrance, welcoming those who wished to gather and socialize in the great hall. Aidan spotted his sister, Phoebe, standing on the steps speaking to their eldest brother, Zoran.

Donar stopped in the middle of the path. "And this is where I leave you."

"Coward."

His cousin glanced in Zoran's direction. "I'm in no mood to deal with *him* tonight."

Aidan didn't like his brother that well either, but he didn't get a choice in the matter.

"I will see you tomorrow then," Aidan said, clasping his cousin's arm in farewell before continuing toward the castle.

Phoebe caught sight of him first. "It's about time, brother. I have been looking for you."

Aidan took hold of his sister's upper arms and kissed her on the forehead. "What for?"

"Father wishes to see us."

Aidan glanced around, searching for his second oldest brother. "Where is Ruari?"

"Missing…much like you have been." Zoran scowled.

"Where were you?" Phoebe put her hands on her hips.

She was larger and taller than Bailey, with the well-honed muscles of a shifter warrior. Her long, black hair was pulled back with a tie, and several small braids—one of them containing strands of silver—framed her oval face. Many women in the clan envied Phoebe's high cheekbones and smooth olive skin. Most couldn't hope to compare to her beauty.

Aidan kept expecting to hear she'd finally selected a mate, but as of yet she'd rejected the majority of her suitors outright and paid little attention to the rest. At two-hundred and seventy-five years old, Phoebe still had much of her life ahead of her. He supposed he couldn't blame her for taking her time. Aidan was only sixty years younger than his sister, and he couldn't imagine tying himself to a mate yet. He knew of only one exception for Phoebe, but that was a long time ago, and that particular male was far out of her reach now.

"I was out patrolling," he answered.

She lifted her brows. "That's what you always say."

"Not all of us can rest on our tails the entire day, dear sister, doing nothing."

She shoved him in the chest, forcing him back a step. "I was training the next generation of female warriors. What did you accomplish?"

Aidan wasn't about to tell her how his day had really gone. "I can verify our northwest border has not been violated by another toriq."

Zoran grunted. "And what would you have done if they crossed, whelp? Shake your tail at them in a threatening manner?"

Aidan was sorely tempted to ask his brother how exactly that was done, but now was not the time to cross his brother—at least not yet. He had no doubt in his mind that once he began that fight, it would not end until one of them was dead. Zoran was as volatile and hot-natured as a dragon could possibly get.

"Actually, I scowled meaningfully at them," Aidan said, relaxing his posture into as much of a non-threatening position as he could muster. "You'd be surprised how quickly they flew away."

"You are a *fushka*." Zoran dismissed him and turned his attention to a point beyond Aidan's shoulder. "And there is the other idiot in our family now."

Ruari strode up the steps, appearing unrushed. "What is going on?"

"We must meet with father," Phoebe answered. "Let's go. He's been kept waiting long enough."

They entered the castle, passing through the great hall. It was still early enough in the evening that it wasn't too crowded yet, but a few shifters milled around chatting with each other. They continued past the large room and up several flights of stairs to the highest floor of the castle where the pendragon's suite was located.

Only one guard stood outside the large double doors today. Upon seeing Throm's children, he opened the chamber for them.

Zoran went inside first, ever quick to stand at their father's side. The rest of them followed behind. Aidan had hoped to find the pendragon in the sitting area next to the balcony, but instead he saw Throm lying on his bed. A red camrium blanket covered him, and his head was propped up by matching cushions. Aidan and his sister exchanged concerned glances. It was unlike the pendragon to allow himself many comforts. He usually slept on a stuffed camrium cloth mattress with no blankets or pillows.

"Come, children," Throm beckoned, his voice coming out weak and scratchy.

They gathered in a row next to the bed, with Zoran closest to the pendragon's head. Aidan's chest tightened upon seeing his father. Throm's normally tanned skin appeared pale, his hands frail, and his gray hair had thinned even more in the last few days. Their kind tended not to show their age until they reached somewhere around a thousand years old. Throm was just over eleven hundred. Few shape-shifters lived much longer than that, though pure dragons could reach double or more years.

"I've asked you here…" he paused to cough into his hand, "to tell you I am calling for the *Bitkal* ritual. It will take place in two weeks."

Phoebe gasped. "But father, it's too soon. You still have time."

Throm gazed up at her with a hint of regret in his yellow eyes. "I wish that were so, daughter, but I cannot risk waiting any longer."

It was one of the reasons their father didn't make many public appearances anymore. The pendragon didn't want anyone realizing how fast he was declining. Throm's own children were rarely allowed to see him except on his better days. This was only the third time Aidan had been allowed to visit while Throm was in bed.

"I agree with Phoebe. Two weeks seems a little too soon," Aidan said, catching his sister's grateful look for supporting her. To be honest, though, he wasn't ready to see his father die. The pendragon had his faults, but he'd been an excellent leader to their people and a pillar of strength for his children. Aidan couldn't imagine the world without him.

"Shut up, whelp, and respect our father's wishes," Zoran growled.

His inner dragon roared, though no one else heard it. The beast knew they were short on time before they'd have to stop playing submissive, but they had to tread carefully. Too much was at stake. Aidan's siblings had no idea of the dangers that lay ahead for their toriq, and they'd likely not believe him even if he told them.

The pendragon gave his eldest son a hard look. "In my presence, you will respect each other."

"I apologize, Father." Zoran bowed his head. It was an act, and everyone knew it, but it was enough to satisfy Throm.

"Now," the pendragon said, pushing himself into a semi-sitting position, "the elders' council and I will be deciding on the seven most eligible candidates to rule the Taugud after I die. Three of those positions are mine alone to choose. In the next few days, I will be giving each of you a task. If you perform it well, I will likely nominate you, but if you fail, I will not—even if that means choosing a candidate who is not my child."

"You can count on me, father." Zoran lifted his chin.

"Whatever you wish, it will be done," Ruari seconded.

Aidan and his sister murmured their own agreements, though neither of them was as quick to pander to Throm. They left the groveling to their elder brothers.

"Good, now go." The pendragon waved them off. "I must rest."

Hesitantly, they all filed out of the room. As soon as the guard shut the chamber doors, Zoran grabbed Aidan and shoved him against the wall. His head bounced off the stone, bringing stars to his vision. He was so stunned by the move he nearly forgot himself and fought back. It was all he could do to quiet his inner beast's growls and stand still. Gritting his teeth, he met his brother's gaze.

"Do not think for a moment you will be one of the three our father chooses." Zoran's yellow eyes were wild and filled with anger. "If I were you, I wouldn't even bother trying to complete the task he gives you—not if you wish to live past the Bitkal."

Aidan ground his jaw. His brother was merciless in a duel, and Aidan had no idea if he could win against Zoran in a fight. In the Bitkal, it was up to the fighters to decide whether to battle to the death or to allow the loser to submit. If the two of them fought, only one of them would come out alive.

"May Zorya be with you," Aidan said. For if it came to it, he'd kill Zoran before allowing himself to die. He had to survive the coming months at any cost.

5

BAILEY

I paced around the living room, debating what to do. Since waking up in Aidan's house—or lair as he usually referred to it—I'd been feeling restless. My days were usually filled with physical tasks that kept me busy. When I wasn't hunting dragons, I was often foraging for food and supplies. On the days I didn't go out, I helped build outhouses, worked on the neighborhood gardens, or collected water from a nearby creek after it rained. The only time we settled down at Earl's place was in the evenings when the dragons were active. Then we'd read by candlelight or tell stories to each other. I'd grown used to that and didn't know what to do in a house by myself.

First thing I'd done that morning was make some oatmeal for breakfast. The place was far enough outside of town that it had a propane tank with a line to the stove. After that, I'd spent two hours on target practice with the spare crossbow Aidan kept here. He actually maintained a full supply of weaponry in a storage room off the kitchen, not just for my training, but also as backups for himself. His cousin told me once that they didn't only have to worry about fighting pure dragons. There was danger from within their clan as well, though neither of the shifters talked about it much.

Stepping out onto the porch, I noted the sun high in the sky. The hot rays beat down relentlessly on the earth below, turning much of the vegetation a sickly brown. It had been a couple of weeks since the last storm came through. Assuming the dimensions colliding hadn't screwed up normal weather patterns too much, the temperature would be cooling soon, and more rain might come. I looked forward to that even as I dreaded the arrival of winter. The only good thing about that was the dragons would be hibernating during the coldest months.

But what about the missing children? Wounding Matrika last night might have slowed her down for a little while, but I doubted I'd stopped her. Not to mention the children she'd taken recently could still be alive. For all I knew, I was their only hope of ever getting back to their families.

I stared down the gravel road—the only way out of here. Even though I couldn't return to my neighborhood and friends right now, there was one place I could go and maybe get help locating the children. It was a nearby house safe from the dragon threat. I might not have my truck at the moment, but I still had two per-fectly good legs. A two-mile walk wouldn't kill me.

I went back into the house, grabbed my water can-teen—that magically refilled itself every hour—and a sword, then headed down the gravel drive toward Lindsey Street. Aidan's lair sat a little south of where the road ended, close to Lake Thunderbird, which was to the east. I couldn't see the water from his place, but I knew it was somewhere just beyond a thick canopy of trees and vegetation.

Filled with renewed purpose, the walk through the high heat didn't bother me as much as it might have. I headed west, passing farmhouses and ranches along the way until I reached the area where a sorceress lived. My mind was a little fuzzy on the exact placement of her house, but I was certain it had to be close. The damn woman had a nasty tendency to hide her home from me unless she wanted something.

"Verena!" I called out, spinning in a circle in the middle of the road. "Show yourself!"

No response—unless you counted a flock of doves flying off a nearby fence.

"I need to talk to you," I said, scowling at the end-less pastureland.

She still didn't reveal herself. This had to be some kind of test of my patience. The sorceress enjoyed play-ing games with me, and I wouldn't have put it past her to see how hard I'd try to reach her. Moving off to the side of the road, I sat down cross-legged and pulled out my canteen to drink some water. I could wait as long as it took for the sake of those children.

The minutes dragged by slowly. Since the dragon apocalypse, not many people came down this way, so there wasn't any traffic. A horse wandered into a near-by field, grazing on grass. I idly wondered if I should try catching the animal and riding it back to Aidan's place, but then what would I do with it? One thing I'd learned growing up on a ranch was that unless you wanted responsibility for an animal, you didn't mess with it. I'd had horses growing up and loved them, but if I took on the care of one now, I'd feel horrible if something happened to it. The animal seemed to be doing fine on its own. No point in messing that up.

Almost an hour—and a bucket of sweat later—the air glimmered around me. I squinted up the road. A house and barn were taking shape there, slowly coming into form. I stood up and started moving that way.

"It's about time," I said when Verena appeared in front of her driveway. She stood there wearing khaki shorts and a peach tank top.

"You chose to visit at an inconvenient time," she replied in her lilting Irish accent.

The sorceress was a slim woman with brown hair highlighted with strands of gray. She usually kept it in a braid down her back, but it flowed freely in the breeze now. Verena appeared to be around forty years old, but according to her, she'd been put under some kind of sleeping enchantment for a thousand years while the dragons were gone. She didn't wake up until the spell separating the dimensions started to weaken. That was two decades ago, so she'd been a young woman when she came out of stasis and into the modern world.

"You could have at least acknowledged me," I pointed out, trying not to sound too annoyed since I needed her help.

Verena shrugged. "If it was important, I knew you'd wait."

Danae stepped out of the house. The former combat medic had shoulder-length blond hair, toned muscles, and at 5'10" stood half a foot taller than me. As she walked across the lawn, I couldn't miss the strut in her steps. Danae was self-confident and unapologetic about it.

We'd become friends soon after she joined me and some other refugees in the Bizzell Library at the University of Oklahoma. That was where we'd lived until dragons burned down the place a little over a month ago in one of their rage-filled attacks. Those of us who weren't killed moved to a nearby neighborhood in Norman where one of my stepfather's friends, Earl, lived. That's where I'd been staying until yesterday.

Danae still lived there with our other friends, but she had begun coming to Verena's at least a couple of times a week. Just like I'd discovered I was a dragon slayer during the apocalypse, she had discovered she was a sorceress whose powers had been latent until recently. Someone had to train her in how to use her magic, especially since Danae had an affinity for healing. A rather handy skill now that hospitals were shut down. At the moment, Verena—who was raised in a family of sorcerers all those centuries ago—was the only one who could help her.

"Sorry, Bailey," Danae said, coming up to give me a hug. "Verena wanted to finish my lessons for the day before letting you visit."

I gave her a weak smile. "It's okay. I knew she'd let me in eventually."

Danae took a step back and looked me over, noting my wounds from the day before. "Conrad told me Aidan stopped you in the middle of a battle yesterday. What's going on?"

"Apparently, I attacked some sort of dragon princess," I said, scratching at a scab on my arm. I'd removed the bandages Aidan put on me as soon as the wounds started to close. "He says I can't kill her, despite the fact she's taking children, unless I want her entire clan after me. Even just attacking her has got them angry, and now they've got my scent."

Her expression hardened. "He told me about the children. Anything I can do?"

"Nothing yet. First, I've got to find out where the dragon is taking the children." I turned to Verena, addressing her since she'd proven good at finding people before. "Any chance you can help me with that?"

She waved a hand. "Bah! I won't have anything to do with it."

"What? Why?" Danae rounded on her. "These are children we're talking about."

Verena pursed her lips. "I'll do no more favors for the slayer until she repays me her debt."

"Then tell me what you want," I demanded. Every time I saw her, I asked about it only to be put off. I'd decided the woman enjoyed holding that favor over my head like an ax that could come down at any moment. God only knew what she wanted and what it would cost me.

"It's not time," she said, heading toward her house. "You'll be the first to know when it is."

I started to go after her. "But this can't wait..."

"Enough!" Verena put up a hand.

I hit an invisible wall, smacking my face into it. She huffed and walked away. Rubbing my abused nose, I watched her go into the house without so much as a backward glance. She seriously didn't care about anyone except for herself—unless she had something to gain by it. No wonder Aidan hated sorcerers so much and had reacted to Danae so badly when they first met. If the others he'd come across were anything like Verena, I couldn't blame him.

"Dammit, how am I supposed to find these kids without her?" I asked, exasperated.

"Come on," Danae said, taking my arm. "I'll give you a ride."

Left with no other choice, I didn't argue. The afternoon was waning, and dragons from Aidan's clan would be roaming the skies soon. Walking wouldn't be a good idea. They might not attack humans, but I still tried to avoid them as much as possible. They might notice that I was wearing some of their special fire-proof clothing and want to know where I got it.

We got in the white Ford Taurus that Danae used whenever she had to leave the neighborhood. The car wasn't hers, but the woman who owned it didn't like driving since D-day, so she loaned it out to whoever needed it.

"I don't suppose you could tell Conrad to bring my truck back to me," I said after telling her to head east.

She glanced over at me. "He was already planning on it, but they needed his help today finishing up the wall project."

Right. The brick perimeter wall we'd been building around our neighborhood, which consisted of three square blocks of houses. Everyone within it worked to-gether to gather food and supplies as well as protect each other from human gangs, random thugs, and dragons.

"How much did Conrad tell you about yesterday?" I asked.

Her hands tightened on the steering wheel. "Everything up until Aidan took you away. So how do you know that dragon might be stashing the kids in-stead of killing them?"

"For one, if they want to eat people, they would go for adults since we've got more meat on our bones. For two, Aidan and his cousin think the drag-on might have issues because she can't have her own babies. It's the only reason she'd take them alive like that."

Danae cursed. "That's just twisted. I don't even want to consider how she'd go about taking care of them—but it does mean there's a chance we can save them."

"Yeah, if we can find them and sneak past however many dragons might be guarding the nest. That's why I'm going to need all the help I can get to pull off a rescue." If Matrika was some kind of princess, I was willing to bet she lived in a large den with a lot of other dragons. By myself, I'd end up getting distracted in the battle and never reach the children.

"There might be someone who can help," Danae said, sounding hesitant, "but I'm going to tell you now I have my reservations about him. If it weren't for the kids, I wouldn't mention him at all."

I glanced over, noting her tight expression. "Who?"

She took a deep breath. "There's a sorcerer named Javier who has taken over most of downtown Norman. From what I can tell, he's rather powerful."

"Downtown?" I tried to visualize the place in my head and failed, which was enough to send my alarm bells ringing. How could I have forgotten something like that? Hell, I couldn't even remember what it looked like or how long it had been since I last passed through there—probably not since before D-day.

"Yeah, I couldn't picture it either until I started working on my powers with Verena," Danae said, sighing.

"Is this sorcerer...Javier, somehow blocking people from thinking about it?" I asked.

"Yeah." She nodded. "After I realized what he was doing, I went and stood at the edge of the zone he claimed for himself. People are walking around like there's no danger and dragons aren't a problem, but I think there's a lot more to it. Verena told me to stay away from there."

"You probably should," I agreed, "but I'm going to have to take the risk."

"I could go with you," she offered.

"No. If I don't make it out, you're the next best chance those kids have of getting saved."

Danae slowed as we reached the end of Lindsey Street, marked by a blank red sign with a wall of trees behind it. I indicated that she should go north up the gravel road to Aidan's lair.

"When will you see Javier?" she asked, parking next to the house.

"Tomorrow morning after Conrad brings me my truck. Make sure he comes early so I can go out while the dragons are still asleep." These days it was a real hassle getting around town once they were up and flying about since I got the urge to kill every single one of them I saw. It made focusing on hunting for food and supplies rather difficult.

Danae gave me a stern look. "I'll let him know, but you better find some way to get word back to me that you're okay, or I'll come looking for you."

"I will," I promised, giving her a quick hug before getting out of the car.

6

AIDAN

The pendragon's chamber was brighter and more welcoming than the prior evening. Aidan crossed the stone floor, moving past his father's empty bed, and headed toward the sitting area. Red curtains made of the finest woven camrium cloth had been pulled back, and the glass doors leading to the balcony were open, allowing the golden, late evening sun to shine within.

Just beyond the balustrade, he could view the tops of the dark gray fortress wall and the open field beyond where young dragons practiced their flying skills. He also caught the edge of the mountain range to the south. It was a land formation that came with them from *Kederrawien*—the dimension where Aidan was born. If he stepped outside, as he often did growing up, he could watch the inhabitants of the keep go about their day. The way people interacted and worked with each other had always fascinated him. It was the only time he could sit still in those early years of his life.

Throm stirred, turning his gaze toward Aidan. He sat on a black marble chair with a high back and wide arm rests that faced the open doors. There was nothing intricate about his seat or the other furniture. It was sturdy and fireproof, which was all that mattered.

The pendragon had been staring out at the world with a pensive expression on his face. He had the weight of the world on his shoulders and little time to make it lighter before his period on this plane of existence ended. Before long, Aidan's father would meet with *Zorya*—the dragon goddess—to fight at her side in the next world. His people believed they must live many lives with various challenges in each before they finally found eternal peace. To them, this was only the second stop in a very long journey for their *cryas*, or soul, as humans liked to call it.

"Father," Aidan said, coming to stand before Throm. He clasped his hands behind him and dipped his head in a show of submission.

The pendragon studied him for a moment. "I have a task for you."

Aidan lifted his head. "What is it?"

"You must negotiate a treaty with the Faegud clan and finalize it before the Bitkal."

Aidan sucked in a breath. "Sire, with all due respect, we have not been on good terms with them in nearly two hundred years. What makes you think I could change that now?"

"A spy has informed me their pendragon has passed to the next world." Throm gazed intently at Aidan. "I believe the successor may be more amenable."

Long ago, the Taugud and Faegud clans were great allies. Aidan remembered the time well, though he'd still been young. Then a new pendragon—Severne—took over. He did not care for old alliances and sought to expand his territory, including annexing areas belonging to his neighbors. When his army seized part of the Taugud land, a major battle was fought with many dying on both sides. The foolish pendragon not only attacked shifters, but the pure dragon clans as well. Within a few dozen years, Severne had less territory than before, and his people suffered badly for it.

Aidan had been sorry to lose such an alliance. The Faegud clan was unique from others due to their mixing with shape-shifters millennia ago. While much of that had been bred out over time, some of their members could still shift to human form if they chose. It made them far more amenable to work with than the pure dragons. Even those who couldn't shift tended to be more civilized and they did not attack humans without just cause.

"Have you heard anything else about them?" Aidan asked.

"Very little, though our spy should learn more soon." The pendragon worked his jaw. "It was not until we expanded our territory to the south that I risked sending her. I must rely on you to find out more."

Their last big push had been two weeks ago. His father had chosen to concentrate on gaining land in the countryside before turning their toriq's efforts to the urban areas. It had been easier to expand that way. The pure dragons were mostly concentrating on the cities and medium-sized towns for now where they could terrorize the humans.

This was a major task for the pendragon to ask of Aidan. Throm was depending on his youngest son to make an alliance with a clan who'd been their enemy for two centuries. There were those among the elders who had more experience and diplomatic skills.

Though Aidan felt honored to be given such a mission, he could not help asking the obvious question. "Are you certain I am the best one for the job?"

"Son," Throm sighed. "Of all my children you are the most observant and the best at adapting to your surroundings. Do not think I have not noticed the games you play with your brothers. They believe you are a fool, but I know better. You've made every effort to appear harmless to them because you are willing to do whatever it takes to survive. Neither Zoran nor Ruari have the patience or tact to work with the Faegud clan, but if I am to meet Zorya soon, I must know at least one of my children can handle such a difficult task."

Aidan's chest swelled. His father rarely gave compliments and even when he did, he kept them brief. Somehow, Throm had seen what Aidan's siblings had not—except, perhaps, for Phoebe. She had a knack for uncovering the truth no matter how well one cloaked it. Their toriq already had one fine female spy, but his sister would make an excellent second should she ever desire the position.

"I will not fail you, Father," Aidan vowed.

"See that you do not." Throm gave him a steely-eyed look. "And take Falcon with you. Your journey there will not be without some risk, and it is good to have at least one strong warrior at your side when dealing with another clan."

"As you wish," Aidan said, bowing slightly.

Throm nodded. "May Zorya be with you, Son."

"And you as well, Father." Aidan exited the pendragon's chamber.

His steps were light as he made his way down the corridor. Not only because his sire entrusted him with such an important task, but also because it supported Aidan's own cause. The Faegud clan's territory covered much of northern Texas—if he recalled the map Bailey showed him correctly. It would bring him one step closer to finding a way to take her home after she finished helping Aidan with his plans. Whether he wanted to let her go or not, he had to keep his promise. His honor depended on it.

Aidan searched the great hall for Kayla. He'd rescued her during a missile attack on the fortress several months ago, and she'd been loyal to him ever since. Though he insisted she owed him nothing, she kept a close eye on his brothers for him and reported anything suspicious. They would never guess the sixteen-year-old girl was watching their every action. Kayla, too, would make an excellent spy for their toriq once she became old enough.

The human girl had crossed over from Earth to Kederrawien two years ago, before their dimensions merged, and had been with them ever since. He'd offered to take her home to her family after they returned, but she refused to leave. Many humans chose to stay, though they were free to go at anytime. Most said they felt more comfortable and safe within the fortress after spending so much time there. Aidan suspected they were afraid of what they might find if they went home. According to Bailey, the world had changed a great deal in recent months and not for the better.

He found Kayla at one of the stone trestle tables, kneading dough for the midnight meal that would come in a few hours. She wore a beige camrium tunic and brown pants. Her long red hair was currently pulled into a ponytail, though a few strands hung around her face. Since she first started working with him, she'd put on a little weight and filled out her small figure. Aidan was glad to see her looking healthier now. The missile attack had burned her badly, and even with a healer's help, recovering took much of her strength.

As if she could sense him, she glanced over in his direction. Aidan nodded at her, then turned around and walked away. He headed for a little-used chamber down the corridor where they used to keep cleaning supplies before relocating them to another room closer to the kitchen. Five minutes later, Kayla slipped inside.

"Do you have any news for me?" Aidan asked.

She nodded. "I figured out what tasks your father gave Zoran and Phoebe."

After the last time he'd met with the pendragon, Aidan had asked Kayla to see if she could discover which tasks Throm gave his brothers and sister. The only thing he knew for certain was that he was the last to receive his task. He'd heard the summons each time one of his siblings was called to see the pendragon. They wouldn't announce their individual missions publicly, considering they wouldn't want their efforts sabotaged and end up looking bad to their father, which left Aidan to figure it out himself—or, rather, with a little help.

"Tell me," he said.

"Phoebe has to preside over the next Judgments Day and prove she can rule fairly." Kayla cocked her head. "That isn't too hard, is it?"

"Actually, it is. She must study each case ahead of time, review all the evidence, and speak with any witnesses. Some crimes are more complex and difficult to judge than others."

She frowned. "But I thought they do all that during the hearing."

"What you see and hear on Judgments Day is only for the benefit of the people so that they may know all the same information. The one who presides will ensure there is a clear case before allowing the accused to be tried publicly," Aidan explained. He might never have had to perform the duty, but his father had asked him to look into cases before if there were a greater number than usual. Throm only made the job seem easy.

"Okay, well, Zoran's task still sounds harder. He's got to kill the pendragon's oldest son from the Shadowan clan—without them knowing he did it."

Aidan shifted on his feet. "That will be difficult. Blayze rarely travels alone, and he's a fierce fighter. Zoran will have to kill him and anyone with him if he doesn't want witnesses."

"Wow, that's crazy." She knitted her brows. "And I thought my father was tough. He was always like, 'don't sneak out of the house again, Kayla' and 'stop talking to that boy, young lady' and other stuff. It drove me crazy, but I know now it was to protect me, not to put me in danger. You've got it way worse."

"Where is your father?" Aidan still didn't know much about the girl, though he tried to ask some pointed questions when the opportunity presented itself—such as now.

Kayla's gaze dipped to the floor, and she replied in a low voice, "He and my mom died in a car accident about a year before I crossed dimensions."

Aidan wanted to lay a comforting hand on the girl's shoulder, but he didn't want to risk burning her. His touch was far too hot. It would only take a few seconds before her skin would start to redden, and in a couple of minutes, it could leave permanent damage.

He waited until she lifted her head to reply. "I'm sorry to hear that. Who took care of you after they were gone?"

She shrugged. "I got stuck in foster homes. It sucked."

Aidan wasn't certain what that meant, but he guessed she'd been placed with people who weren't her family. With shape-shifters, it often happened since they were constantly at war, and children lost their parents. The toriq did its best to see after the orphans, though. They did not struggle to survive, and they were not mistreated.

He decided it was time to change the subject and give her something to take her mind off of her past. "How would you like to go meet Bailey tomorrow?"

Kayla's eyes widened, and her voice came out in a hushed whisper. "The dragon slayer? Really?"

Aidan had told the girl a few things about Bailey. He wasn't certain why he opened up to her, but in a way he found Kayla to be a kindred spirit. She was every bit as curious as he was at that age, and he had suspected she'd had a rough time during her childhood like he did, which was now proven true.

"For my task, I must go negotiate a peace treaty with a southern clan. These things usually take time, but I'm leaving tomorrow and will be gone for a couple of days." Aidan went on to explain the latest events with Bailey and her current location. "I'll need you to bring some food and supplies to my lair tomorrow."

Kayla grinned widely. "I can totally do that."

"You're certain you can obtain transportation?" he asked. His private lair was only a five-minute flight from the fortress, if one went the direct route—which he never did to be sure no one followed him. Aidan didn't know how long it took on the ground. He didn't want Kayla walking alone that far.

"No problem." She waved a hand. "We humans have a few cars and trucks stashed away to use when we're out looking for supplies. There's always at least one around to take."

He nodded. "Good. Now you must be careful while you're out. You won't be leaving the clan's territory, and this area is remote, but there are groups of humans who roam around. They can be dangerous."

"I got it," she said, giving him an impatient look. "I go out more than you realize."

That disturbed him, but he could do little to stop her. Humans had their freedom, after all. If the adults among her people let her leave the fortress whenever she wanted, then she could do so without needing a shifter's permission.

"Very well, then I will give you the directions."

7

AIDAN

Aidan peered around the corner, checking the great hall. It was crowded for the midnight meal, but he managed to catch sight of his father, Ruari, and Phoebe at the high table. They sat eating and chatting with each other. He did not see Zoran anywhere. It was unlike Aidan's eldest brother to miss a meal, especially on the rare occasion the pendragon made it downstairs. He needed to find Zoran and ensure he was currently occupied.

Ducking back down the corridor, Aidan headed to the second floor of the castle where both his brothers had rooms, as well as several other important members of the clan. He stopped on the last step when he overheard voices nearby.

"I'm only going to tell you this once," Zoran said, a growl in his voice. "Tell the elders you have no wish to participate in the Bitkal."

"Or you'll do what?" The second voice came from Nanoq—the Captain of the Guard.

Aidan held his breath and took the last step. He inched his way down the corridor until he reached a corner, peeking around it. Down the hall, his eldest brother had a death grip on Nanoq's neck where he held him against the wall. The Captain of the Guard didn't show any signs of fear. His fists were bunched, and he appeared ready to strike Aidan's brother.

Zoran leaned closer to Nanoq's face. "Anyone who attempts to take the pendragon seat from me will regret it."

"Murder is a crime, you know," the captain said with full conviction. No one had higher standards or principles than him, which was likely why Zoran felt threatened by him. Nanoq not only led the guards but also conducted most of the criminal investigations for the toriq.

Aidan's brother loosened his grip a fraction. "I don't believe I spoke of murder."

"No, but you implied it."

"Just stay out of my way." Zoran slapped the stones next to the captain forcefully.

Nanoq didn't flinch. "One day, that temper of yours is going to be your destruction, and I hope I'm around to see it."

"That's rather unlikely." Zoran gave him a final glare and stalked off toward his room down the corridor.

Aidan pulled back out of sight. Both males lived in this section of the castle, which didn't bode well.

They'd be in direct competition with each other in the coming weeks. A lot could happen in that period of time, especially with Zoran determined to secure his position and remove anyone in his way. Aidan wasn't certain if he should be thankful or not that he wasn't his brother's only target.

Nanoq came around the corner, stumbling to a halt when he found Aidan standing there. He was large in his human form, though not quite as muscular as Zoran. The shifter drew little attention from his looks, being considered plain at best, but he had the kind of appearance that led people to trust him. His red camrium uniform—the standard for the fortress guard—was always immaculate, and he kept his hair short and well-groomed.

When Aidan had been young, it was Nanoq who looked out for him. The captain had grown up with Zoran, their being only two years apart, and he'd been well aware of the mean streak running through the pendragon's eldest son. More than once, Nanoq had rescued Aidan from a beating he'd done nothing to deserve. They didn't speak often these days, but a bond still remained between them.

"Did you hear all of that?" Nanoq asked, lifting a brow.

Aidan nodded. "Most of it."

"If your brother wins the Bitkal, our toriq will be in trouble," he said, shaking his head.

"Then let us hope he doesn't."

Nanoq's expression became determined. "If not me, then I'd rather it be you."

A noise came from down the corridor. Aidan clasped the captain's arm and gave him a meaningful look. "Take care, friend."

Nanoq returned the gesture. "And you do the same."

Backing away, Aidan hurried downstairs. He'd lost precious time tracking his brother's whereabouts and speaking with the captain. For what he needed to do next, he had to get it done before the midnight meal ended.

When he reached the main floor, he headed to the other end of the castle. A row of classrooms for young dragons was on the far side. Aidan passed them and turned left, entering another corridor. Several of the head servants had chambers here. He continued beyond them to the clan library at the far end. The main entrance for it was outside the castle, but for Aidan's purposes, he needed to use the backdoor. Once he reached it, he pulled out a skeleton key no one knew he possessed and slid open the lock.

Aidan took one final backward glance, relieved to see no one behind him, and entered. The overwhelming scent of musty tombs assailed him right away. His toriq's history was recorded here on special fire-resistant parchment, along with various fictional tales their people had written and human texts they'd copied during their previous time on Earth. Aidan passed rows and rows of shelves crowding the rear of the library as he made his way toward the front.

"Uncle Kade," he called out.

Shuffling footsteps came from the right. Aidan turned and spotted his uncle ambling down an aisle overflowing with books haphazardly placed on the shelves and floor. His father's younger brother still had a full head of long black hair he left hanging in waves to his shoulders. There were a few lines creasing his forehead, but otherwise, he didn't appear much older than fifty in human years. In reality, he was closer to nine-hundred.

"You shouldn't be here," Kade said, his yellow eyes flashing with annoyance.

"Everyone is at midnight meal. They're too busy to worry about me," Aidan assured him.

His uncle stopped at the edge of the aisle. They were the same height and of similar build, though Kade had a few extra pounds of softness from not getting enough exercise. That happened when one was considered an outcast among their toriq and consigned to a life in the library and adjacent living quarters. On the other hand, his very status kept Kade alive and living in the fortress when the rest of his siblings—excluding Throm—either died or they were banished. Aidan never had the chance to meet his aunts and other uncles. He'd always wondered what they must have been like, and how much of a role his father had played in their downfalls. It wasn't something anyone dared discuss.

"I told you not to come here again until *he* is dead."

Aidan shifted on his feet. "My father has called for the Bitkal ceremony. It will take place in less than two weeks."

Kade frowned. "That is rather sudden."

"He wishes to ensure his heir is named before he dies."

A myriad of emotions crossed his uncle's eyes. "So his reign will finally end soon."

Aidan loved his father, but he could also understand Kade's point of view. He had been an outcast for most of his life thanks to his elder brother. Throm had known about Kade's visions of the far future with predictions no one could understand, and used it against him. The pendragon had his younger brother restricted to the library ever since the last Bitkal almost five centuries ago. Aside from one designated servant, no one was supposed to speak to Kade. Aidan could be severely punished if anyone found out he was talking to his uncle.

"My father's death won't free you," Aidan pointed out.

His shoulders slumped a little. "No, at least not yet."

"The pendragon is sending me to negotiate a treaty with the Faegud clan."

"He..." Kade froze, and his eyes glazed over. "*Former allies, turned enemies, shall become friends once more.*"

Aidan took an involuntary step back. He had heard that line from his uncle before, but it was back when he was a boy. In those days, he'd snuck into the library frequently to see his uncle. He had been caught once, but Aidan had been young enough back then that his punishment was light. His visits became infrequent after that, though. His father and siblings had begun to watch him much closer.

"Uncle," he said, grabbing Kade and shaking him from his trance.

The older man's eyes slowly cleared and focused on Aidan. "This is the beginning."

"Are you certain?"

Kade nodded. "I felt it was getting close. I told you as much the last time we saw each other."

That had been six months ago, shortly before they returned to Earth. "Is there anything else we should watch for?"

"If only I could find that book." His uncle looked about them, his gaze turning a little wild. "Everything I ever predicted is in there."

During his youth, Kade went through frequent blackout periods where he had visions of the future. He wrote each of them down, but once he committed the details to parchment, he promptly forgot them. The only thing he could recall afterward was that he had seen visions. When the blackouts slowed to only one or two a year and he no longer recorded or remembered them, he only had the final bound book for guidance. It went missing a century ago. That was during another blackout period, so Kade had no idea if he had been the one to hide the tome or if someone else did. He'd been searching for it ever since.

"I'm certain you'll find the book when the time is right," Aidan said, hoping to calm his uncle.

Kade was quiet for a moment and then his eyes lit up. "Did you find the dragon slayer?"

His uncle had believed Bailey would be the one they needed. He'd pointed her out to Aidan back when they could see into the human dimension, but not enter. Kade had specifically told him to target her, though his uncle couldn't explain why. Aidan followed his guidance because he remembered seeing something in the missing tome relating to a dragon slayer and how she'd be the one to help save his toriq. That had been shocking enough to stand out in his mind, but for some reason, he could not recall how it would happen. For now, all he could do was keep Bailey busy until they figured it out.

"Yes, she has completed the rite of passage, and she is becoming stronger every day," Aidan said, proud of her even as he worried. It wasn't going quite as smoothly as expected. He wasn't supposed to like her so much or develop feelings for her.

"Has she learned to control her instincts?" his uncle asked.

"Only when Donar and I are in human form," Aidan sighed. "It will take more time to overcome her need to kill when she sees us as dragons."

"Keep working with her. She must learn control if she is to help us." Kade patted him on the arm.

Aidan didn't need to be told. The burden of it sat heavily with him every day. "I promised her once she is done helping us that I will take her home. Her family has land far to the south of here."

"You shouldn't have made a promise you may not be able to keep," his uncle scolded.

Aidan took a step closer to him. "She will survive this, won't she? You've never said otherwise."

"That I don't know. Without the book…" Kade's voice wandered off.

"I will return her to her family," Aidan vowed.

His uncle closed his eyes. A full minute passed before he opened them. "You must negotiate this treaty first. Without that, you won't stand a chance of fulfilling your promise to her."

"So there is a chance?"

Kade lifted a shoulder. "There is always a chance. Now go. The midnight meal is nearly over."

Aidan nodded to his uncle and hurried from the library.

8

BAILEY

I was just finishing my breakfast of crackers and jam when the sound of wheels crunching on gravel outside drew my attention. It had to be Conrad, but I still made myself peek through the curtains first. These days, I couldn't take anything for granted.

Blinking against the early morning light, I caught sight of my familiar black, four-door Chevy Silverado. Conrad was guiding it toward the house. He didn't get many opportunities to drive my truck, so it was a little strange seeing him behind the wheel. I left the window and went to grab the few things I needed to take with me. There was no time to waste if I wanted to see the sorcerer and get back before the dragons started roaming.

"Hey, man," I said, giving Conrad a fist bump as I met him outside. "Thanks for bringing my truck."

He handed me my keys. "You're lucky Earl ain't with me."

"What does he want?" I asked. The older man, who was a friend of my stepfather's, felt an obligation to watch over me, but I didn't make the job easy for him.

"You know how he is." Conrad shrugged. "He worries about you."

"You can tell him I'm fine. Just got places to be." I gestured for him to move away from the driver's side door.

Conrad didn't budge. "Goin' to see Javier?"

Damn Danae for telling him about that. "Maybe."

He stuck his hands in the pockets of his khaki pants. Somehow, they were always free of wrinkles despite being hand-washed. He had a trick for that, but he refused to tell anyone.

"I'm goin' with you," he said, his tone brooking no argument.

I smiled. "Of course you are. I've got to give you a ride back to town, silly."

He narrowed his eyes. "You know that's not what I mean."

"Get in the truck. We'll talk about it on the way."

Conrad didn't move, other than to cross his arms. "Bailey, I ain't playin' with you. If you're gonna see a sorcerer powerful enough to make people forget downtown Norman exists, then I'm goin'."

"And if this guy attacks us, what do you plan to do? Use your crossbow against him?" I asked. Why couldn't anyone understand I didn't exclude them from things to be rude, but to protect them? I already put Conrad in enough danger when we hunted dragons without adding this to the list.

"I might." He set his jaw in a stubborn line. "What do you plan to do? If you can't resist Verena's spells, how do you think you're gonna resist Javier? He could do anything he wants to you, and all your badassness won't be able to stop him."

He had a point, though I hated to admit it. "Fine, you got me there, but there's still no point in both of us putting ourselves at risk."

"Yeah, there is—for the same reason you always let me come with you when you hunt dragons. Because I got your back, and I'm your good luck charm." He polished his fingernails on his shirt and gave me a cocky look. "You're still alive, aren't you?"

My lips twitched. "You're ridiculous."

"Girl, you know it's true."

We were wasting time arguing. When Conrad had his mind set on something, there was no changing it. I would hate that quality about him if I didn't appreciate his help so much.

"Fine." I worked my way around him and jerked the driver's side door open. "You can come, but don't blame me if you're missing fingers or toes afterward. Or worse, every time someone says 'dragon,' you hop up and down like a bunny." Actually, I liked that last one. Maybe I should test Javier's skills by asking him to do that.

Unaware of my evil thoughts, Conrad got around the truck and settled onto the passenger seat. "By the way, your sword is in the back. Why did Aidan give it to me, anyway?"

"Wasn't it obvious?" I started the engine. "He didn't want me stabbing him with it while we were flying through the air."

"Oh, right. That would have been bad—for your pet dragon," he said, heavy sarcasm in his voice.

I didn't bother responding. Conrad and Aidan were going to have to work out their differences without my help. I wasn't getting in between them. Instead, I flipped on the radio to see if Hank had any updates for the day. His voice immediately filled the cab of my truck.

"...road block on Lindsey Street, just past southeast 12th Avenue. They've already ambushed one unlucky traveler, so I suggest you go around. Alameda Street has also been shut down with multiple obstacles to keep you from getting through. When I went by to talk to them this morning, they said that unless people want to get shot, they had better stay away. I won't speculate why they've taken such extreme measures, but it might be best to avoid that area for a while," Hank said, speaking in the friendly yet informative voice all professional radio announcers used when reporting news.

"Damn," Conrad cursed. "We're gonna have to go the long way around."

I sighed. "It won't be the first time."

"Do you feel that?" I asked, clutching the wheel and fighting the urge to turn the truck around.

We were heading east on Main Street toward downtown after going the long way around because of the road blocks and other difficulties along the way. One would think that without traffic laws to obey, traveling would be faster instead of slower.

"Yeah," Conrad said through gritted teeth. "It's all I can do not to leap out of here right now."

"I'm gonna park. It's probably safer to go the rest of the way on foot." I pulled into a small parking area for a glass repair shop.

Seeing the place, I wished it was open so I could get the back window for my truck fixed. A couple of months ago, it got shot out when Conrad and I were ambushed by the same people who were blocking Lindsey Street now.

Though we'd managed to get away, the truck had taken some damage. We'd put a clear plastic sheet over the opening, but the constant billowing sound it made drove me crazy. Not to mention it wasn't easy to see through. The windshield was only in slightly better condition with just a couple of holes in it that we'd patched with duct tape. With so many abandoned vehicles around town, I could have grabbed something else, but this was *my* truck. I'd had it before everything in the world went to hell in a handbasket, and as long as it kept running, I planned to keep driving it.

Of course, that was only one of the many things that made life more difficult these days. The list grew longer all the time. More than once I'd woken up in the spare bedroom at Earl's, hoping it had all been a dream. I'd lie there for a few minutes and plan my day like it was a normal one. Go shopping, drink coffee at Starbucks, pay my cell phone bill—average, everyday things that were no longer possible. Then I'd force myself to get up and either forage for food or hunt dragons. God, how my life had changed.

"Before I left this morning, Danae told me a trick for resistin' the magic barrier," Conrad said after we got out of the truck.

"What's that?" I asked, resisting the urge to scratch my skin. The longer we stood there, the harder it became not to run the other way.

"You have to imagine you're somewhere else and concentrate on that place real hard. It's supposed to trick the spell," he explained.

"Okay." Together, we turned and faced northeast—the direction Main Street took into downtown Norman. At this juncture, there were mostly small shops and offices ahead. "What place should we think about?"

"The beach?"

Conrad shook his head. "Nah. Ain't neither one of us gonna believe we're at the beach enough for it to work."

He was probably right. Without the scent of an ocean breeze, I didn't think I could make myself believe it. We needed a place that smelled close to the same. "How about the university campus? It's not far, and we've walked through that thousands of times."

"Yeah, that'll work. Now just picture the South Oval the way it looks the first week of classes with all those groups trying to get you to join them and givin' away stuff."

I could remember that well enough. "Got it."

"Now imagine walking through it."

We began moving forward. Our footsteps sounded on pavement, but I pictured the green grass of the oval and didn't let myself see my real surroundings except to avoid walking into a street pole or something. We chatted about the various organizations and stuff they gave away to lure you to their booths. Flyers, pamphlets, food, drinks, and even first-aid kits.

"Really wishin' I'd saved all those Band-Aids and shit they gave me now," Conrad mused. "Never would have guessed they'd come in handy someday."

"I know, right?" I glanced over at him and smiled. For a moment, our world was normal and we were students again. I didn't think about the fact I'd graduated two days before D-day or that I should have been home with my family right now, helping run our ranch.

"Stop!" A woman ordered, breaking our concentration.

We stumbled to a halt. I gazed around and discovered we'd made it all the way to the railroad tracks. Just beyond them at a street corner was the Sooner Theatre. The Spanish Gothic-style building had been around since the late 1920s where it first showed movies and had since been repurposed to feature plays and concerts for the community. Trish had dragged me there a couple of years ago because a friend of hers was performing in a production. It didn't appear any different on the outside, so maybe no one had messed with it since the dragons arrived.

I turned my attention to the woman aiming a pistol at us and the man beside her who held a shotgun. Both of them appeared to be in their late twenties or early thirties. They had hard expressions on their faces and looked like they meant business. I took a step in front of Conrad. If the couple started shooting, it was better for me to take the bullets. I had a much better chance of surviving.

"We're here to see Javier," I said, choosing to meet the woman's gaze. Something told me she was the leader between the two.

She adjusted her gun. "How did you get this far?"

"We clicked our heels three times and recited a special incantation."

The man with the shotgun ducked his head and coughed. I didn't miss the slight grin on his face before he hid it. At least one of them had a sense of humor.

"The sorcerer doesn't see anyone who isn't invited," the woman said, lifting her weapon a little higher, so it was aimed at my head. "You need to leave."

If she was using weapons, she had to be human. Maybe I could appeal to the softer side of her—if there was one. "There's a dragon taking small children from their homes. I'm trying to stop it, but I need some help from Javier to locate the kids. That's all I want."

"Wait." She lowered the pistol a few degrees and squinted at me. "Are you the dragon slayer?"

Great. She'd heard of me. "Yeah."

A man wearing a sharp suit came walking toward us from up the street. He had short, dark hair that he'd slicked back, and tan skin. I estimated him to be in his mid-thirties, though he appeared to take such good care of himself he might have been a little older. The structure of his features told me he was likely of Hispanic heritage.

"It's okay, cariño. I will speak with her." He gestured at me. "Come."

Conrad and I followed the sorcerer down the street. We walked for about a block, passing a few humans along the way who gave us curious glances, before Javier stopped in front of a place that had been a restaurant before D-day. The ground floor, anyway. I never did figure out what they did with the upper level, though some downtown building owners rented out the second story as apartments. Others used them for storage.

"You, stay here," Javier ordered Conrad, pointing at the sidewalk by the door.

He shook his head. "I don't think so, man. Where Bailey goes, I go."

The sorcerer lifted a dark brow. "Even into dragon fire?"

Conrad just glared.

"It's okay," I said, putting a hand on his arm. "I'll be right inside."

He kept his gaze on Javier. "I don't like it."

"Your pet is cute," the sorcerer said, angling his head. "But you should consider putting him on a leash."

Conrad started to leap forward, but I managed to hold him back. "This isn't helping. We're here for a good reason, and I don't want you messing this up."

His angry gaze shot to me. "That guy needs to get his ass kicked."

"Is that more important than saving the children?" I asked.

Conrad deflated a little. "No, but I still don't like it."

"I promise I won't be in there long." When his gaze shot back to Javier, I gripped his arms harder. "Just wait here and don't do anything while I'm gone—I mean it."

He worked his jaw. "Alright, but if you ain't back in thirty minutes, I'm gonna come in and shoot his ass."

"You could try." The sorcerer smiled.

That sounded rather confident. Maybe that was why we still had our weapons. If I didn't need Javier's cooperation, I might have tested a theory or two.

"Let's go," I said, shooting Conrad a final warning glance.

We headed inside. The interior was dim, despite the row of windows in the front, but I didn't see another person around. We passed by about a dozen small, empty tables and continued toward the back where the right half had booths and the left side had a long bar with rows of liquor bottles stocked behind it. Javier gestured for me to sit on one of the stools while he went around and made himself a drink.

I drummed my fingernails on the wooden bar, feeling a little awkward being alone with a powerful sorcerer. He gave off mixed vibes. His smile was friendly enough, but the way he carried himself said he knew he was powerful.

"So what made you choose downtown as a place to take over?" I asked.

He gave me an amused look. "I like the history of it."

"How so?"

Oklahoma had only officially been a state for a little over a hundred years. White settlers weren't even allowed to move into the territory until the first land run in the late eighteen hundreds. Prior to that, it had been mostly American Indians living here, though there had been survey teams and army forts, as well as the occasional "sooner" who snuck inside. It wasn't until April 22nd, 1889, that hopeful people waited at the Kansas border until noon when starting signals—often pistols shot into the air—signaled they could enter the territory. Those who managed to stake a claim first got a hundred and sixty acres and all they had to do was live on it and make improvements to get the title. It was probably one of the most dangerous and competitive races to ever take place, all due to the promise of free land. If it had happened a little over a hundred years later, reality TV would have been all over it.

"This was one of the first towns to be founded," Javier said, pausing to take a sip of his drink. "Do you know they were already building Norman's downtown the morning after the land run? Smart businessmen planned it all ahead of time and even began lobbying to have the state's first university built here. I like the entrepreneurial spirit of that."

It was then I began to see the similarity. This was one of the first places in the world to be flooded with dragons and in a way it had been like a land run for them. Each clan had sought to claim territory, regardless of who was already here. Were the sorcerers doing the same thing?

"Tell me something." I narrowed my gaze at him. "Were you on Earth all along or did you cross over with the dragons?"

He knew his way around magic a little too well to have just come into his powers like Danae. On the other hand, he seemed to understand the human world too well for a new arrival. Verena had been under a sleep spell while magic was dormant on Earth, but I didn't know of any other sorcerers with similar circumstances.

Javier stared at me for so long I almost thought he wouldn't answer. "I suppose you could say both. When I was twenty years old, I was attending the University of Oklahoma. Then I accidentally crossed over into Kederrawien, and I was trapped in that dimension until a few months ago. When I returned here, I used my knowledge of both worlds to get what I wanted."

"I'm surprised you're telling me this." For some reason, I'd expected a powerful sorcerer to be a little less forthcoming. Maybe I'd watched too much television before D-day.

"Why not?" Javier shrugged. "Ever since I heard about you, I've been planning a meeting. It is my belief that we can help each other."

My brows drew together. "How?"

"You wish to rescue the children—which I fully support, by the way. I need something to continue keeping this place safe from the dragons." He leaned forward. "It is better to work together than apart, no?"

"How do you plan to help me?" I asked.

"I will tell you the location of the children," he said, waving his hand as if it was really that simple.

"Great!" I slapped my hand on the bar. "Tell me."

"Not so fast. You must do something for me first." He finished off his drink.

I wished I could say I was shocked. "How do I know you'll even keep your end of the deal or that you can?"

Javier described the exact location of Aidan's private lair. "Does that convince you?"

"It tells me that you probably can do it, but not that you will." I already owed one sorcerer. If I was going to owe this one as well, I wanted to be sure it was worth my while.

He sighed. "How can I convince you without giving you exactly what you want?"

I ground my jaw. "You do realize there are children being held by dragons *right now* and every moment they are with them only increases the danger they're in that much more? Does it not matter to you at all that they could get hurt or die because you didn't help me before it was too late?"

"It's not a bunch of children." He closed his eyes. "The female dragon has taken exactly four of them so far. She's still licking the wounds you gave her so it will likely be at least a few days before she goes out again searching for more. As for the young ones, she's keeping them somewhere safe and providing for their basic needs. I do not foresee them dying anytime soon."

"You can see them?" I asked, incredulous.

Something in his features softened. "Yes. Three boys and one girl—all between the ages of five and seven."

"Please tell me where they are," I said, giving him my best pleading expression. "All I want to do is save them."

He opened his mouth and then shut it, his expression hardening. "There are two hundred humans living under my care here. I protect them, give them shelter and food, and provide them with work. If my efforts are to continue, I need your help. Two hundred—including almost thirty children—outweighs the four you seek."

"And you don't trust me to pay you back after I rescue those four." I glared hard at him.

He gave me a wan smile. "I do not know you well enough to grant you my trust."

"Well, that makes two of us." I sighed. "What is it you need so badly it can't wait?"

He reached under the bar and pulled out a black ceramic container the size of a coffee can, complete with a lid. "Fill this with dragon scales. It can be mostly green, but I'll need at least a few red."

"You're joking, right?" This wasn't the favor I'd been expecting.

"No," he replied, shoving the container closer to me. "No one here knows the secret of how I keep the dragons away from my territory, except you now. The spell requires their scales and a replenishment of them every five to six months. My supply is almost depleted."

I glanced at the container. "Do you really have to have red ones?"

"If I don't, the magic won't work on them. They can have any other land they want, except these few square blocks I claim for myself. I do not believe that is too much to ask."

I picked up the can and opened it. The container seemed normal, but I had to ask. "Is this the exact amount or does this thing hold more than it appears."

Javier gave me an unrepentant smile. "It may hold a little more than you might think."

"How much more?" I demanded.

"Perhaps triple." He frowned at the container. "Or something close to that. It should not take too many dragons to get what you need if you shave enough off of each one. I prefer the scales on the belly, by the way. They are the softest and work the best for my spell."

"Fine, I will try to get enough, but if I don't fill it in a week, you're giving me the location of the children and taking whatever I manage to get." I had to put a limit in there somewhere, or this could take months.

"Agreed."

I narrowed my eyes. "You'll let me know if there's any change with the kids, too."

"Absolutely," he said.

Though it felt like I was making a deal with the devil, I shook the hand he held out to me. "Then I'll see you again soon."

9

KAYLA

Kayla walked down the corridor, keeping her gaze straight forward as she passed a few other servants along the way. Nothing to see here, folks—just a teenage girl carrying a heavy sack over her shoulder, but nothing suspicious. If it happened to be stuffed with food items taken from the kitchen when no one was looking, who cared? What was a few apples here, a loaf of bread there, and some dried venison from the cold storage? Certainly not something to get worked up over. Even if someone had questioned Kayla, she'd had a plan. She would have just said she was packing a lunch for some of the warriors going out on a scouting mission. It wouldn't have been the first time she'd helped out with something like that.

Stepping outside, Kayla headed toward the armory. It was a square stone building next to the castle where the dragons kept a large supply of swords, daggers, and range weapons. She couldn't go in there, but just behind it, there was a small structure that led to the underground tunnels. All the humans who went beyond the fortress wall used that route to leave. It was safer, and it took them straight to where they stashed their fleet of vehicles.

As Kayla got closer, she took a surreptitious glance around to be sure no one was paying attention. When she turned her gaze back again, she walked right into Ruari—her face smashing against his chest. Kayla was so stunned that she let go of her precious sack. It hit the ground, and a few pears rolled out.

"Oh…oh, my God. I'm so…so sorry," she stuttered, then knelt down to gather her things.

"You should watch where you're going," Ruari said. He crouched down beside her, grabbed a stray pear, and held it up to her face. "What are you doing with this?"

This was like the worst possible thing that could happen. She was facing Aidan's brother—someone who she knew had to be very dangerous. Kayla had spied on Ruari enough to know he hung out with some of the scariest shifters in the clan—males and females none of the humans would go near despite the fact they were supposed to be safe inside the fortress. Some people just gave off a vibe that said, "keep away at all costs!"

Kayla's heart raced. What if Ruari decided to turn into a dragon and eat her? Or worse, burn her alive slowly? A thousand thoughts raced through her mind as she lifted her gaze to meet his. Spying and running secret missions for Aidan was fun, but she'd never gotten caught before. How could she have missed him standing there? *Stupid, Kayla, so stupid.*

"Please, don't kill me," she said, her lips trembling.

He frowned at her. "Why would I kill you over a pear?"

She swallowed and dredged up some of the courage she usually had. "Well, you're kind of scary, you know."

"Really?" He chuckled. "I scare you?"

Kayla jerked her head up and down.

"Well, I'll give you a little tip." Ruari put the pear back in her sack, not even bothering to see what else was inside. "Young girls don't taste as good as you'd think, so you're safe from me."

She just stared at him. Was he serious? Ruari held her gaze for a moment and then he let out a full-bellied laugh. It went on for several endless moments before he finally got control of himself. The whole time, Kayla watched him with absolute mortification. Either Ruari had an actual sense of humor or he was crazy. She couldn't decide which.

"I'm sorry I ran into you," she said again.

He stood and gestured for her to get up. Kayla rose to her feet on shaky legs, clutching her bag tightly. It was all she could do not to run screaming back to the castle. Ruari was a big, scary shifter and something about his bald head just made him look that much meaner.

"Don't tell anyone, but I can be clumsy sometimes, too." He winked at her.

Kayla hesitated, unsure how to reply. "Really?"

Ruari leaned closer and spoke in a whisper. "The trick is to make your clumsiness look like you meant to do it or that it's someone else's fault. Better to let people think you're an ass than a fool."

"Okay...I'll remember that," she said, faking a smile.

He sighed and drew back a step. "I can see you're still scared of me. Ah, well. I'll let you continue on with your business, just try not to run into anyone else. Not everyone is as nice as me."

To this, Kayla did laugh. She still didn't trust the man any farther than she could throw him—which was not at all—but at least he didn't mean *her* harm. Ruari must save his cruel streak for his brother and other shifters.

"Take care, young lady." He grinned broadly at her, and then he was gone.

Kayla took a few deep breaths, waited for her heart to slow, and then headed for the entrance to the tunnels. She had a mission to complete. Bailey depended on her to get these supplies to her, and she would not let the slayer down. Kayla pulled the door open, squinting into the darkness. The structure wasn't much bigger than an outhouse with only a set of stairs leading down. She usually didn't come here without other people, but she didn't have a choice this time.

Stretching up on her toes, Kayla grabbed a torch from its sconce and lit it with a lighter she'd picked up a few weeks ago. Shadows danced on the walls and the stairs just ahead of her. She headed down, praying there were no spiders or snakes lurking below. Jeb, a twelve-year-old human boy who had lived at the fortress his whole life, was always telling Kayla about the creepy, crawly things he saw down here. She hadn't seen anything other than a couple of rats, but that didn't mean there weren't other things skittering around the stone supports and arches. Not to mention the random, narrow passages feeding off the main corridor that no one ever seemed to use. Anything could be prowling down one of those.

So many possibilities ran through her mind that Kayla all but ran down the tunnel. Other than one sharp curve, it was pretty much a straight path. She held the torch in front of her, hoping it would ward off anything that might try attacking her.

A thin ray of sunlight appeared up ahead. Kayla had reached the end of the tunnel where it opened at the edge of the woods, about half a mile from the fortress. After dousing the torch and setting it in a sconce on the wall, she climbed the steps toward the opening. There was normally a pair of heavy double doors blocking the entrance—sort of like what a storm cellar would have—but someone had left them open. After she climbed out, she braced her feet and shoved each door closed, having to use all her strength to do it. There were plenty of bushes and trees around so no one would ever find the entryway if they didn't know what to look for, but she figured it was better to be safe than sorry.

A soft flapping sound filtered down to her from the sky. She glanced up and found one of the dragons on morning guard duty hovered overhead, watching her. Kayla smiled and waved until it flew away. Most of the shape-shifters might not talk to her, but they all recognized her. She'd been told it was because of her bright red hair.

Kayla left the woods and hurried across a small clearing, making her way up to a nearby gas station. It hadn't been open for business since the dimensions collided, and people looted everything inside, but it had a big parking area that was a perfect place for leaving cars and trucks. With all the dragons flying around the area, no one messed with their vehicles.

There was a truck and a car waiting there—both older models. Kayla chose the white car since she didn't need to haul anything other than one sack of food. She reached under the dashboard and rubbed a couple of wires together. They didn't have keys, but one of the older men in their community had showed everyone how to get the vehicles started easily. He made it his job to keep them running and full of fuel. Kayla was glad for that since she wouldn't have had the first clue what to do.

She pulled the car onto Highway 9 and headed west like Aidan had instructed. At every intersection she passed, she checked the road signs. When she reached the one for 84th Street, she turned right. There wasn't anyone else driving around. It was kind of strange being out in the world without other people and traveling away from the protection of the shape-shifter fortress.

Aidan promised she wouldn't come anywhere close to green dragon territory, but she was still a little nervous. Kayla didn't know how to protect herself, except to run and hide from danger.

As she slowly drove north, she thought back to the last time she'd been on Earth. School had just let out, and she'd been walking to her foster parent's house when the next thing she knew, she was in another world. The air was dry, the land rugged with a sort of reddish-orange dirt, and the only plants were scrub brushes and half-dead trees. Kayla had been fourteen years old and terrified out of her mind. Then she had spotted a green dragon in the sky, roaring loudly. It had frightened her so badly she raced to a nearby set of boulders and hid between them.

For almost a full day, she didn't move from there. She kept ducking her head into her knees, hoping that things would go back to normal soon, but when she lifted her gaze again, everything was the same. Kayla had been convinced she'd die of either thirst or hunger. When a man came walking up to her sometime the next day, she'd thought about running. His eyes were a really scary yellow with black slits for pupils, but somehow, she also saw kindness in them. He felt like someone she could trust. Maybe she'd been a little delusional by that point, but her instincts later proved true. He spoke calmly to her for half an hour until she agreed to go with him. It wasn't like Kayla had much of a choice, considering she had nowhere else to go, and she was so thirsty. He took her to the shape-shifter fortress where she'd lived ever since. She now knew that man to be Nanoq—the Captain of the Guard.

Kayla spotted the turn for Lindsey Street and slowed the car to pull onto it. From there, she knew she didn't have much farther to go. She drove until the road ended at a big red sign, then she turned right onto a gravel drive. It led through a field and on toward a big, white house at the end. Aidan had chosen a nice place for his secret lair away from home. Seeing it reminded Kayla of the house where she and her parents used to live. That felt like a long time ago now and such a totally different life that someone else must have lived it.

She parked the car and got out. Kayla had expected the slayer to come out as soon as she pulled up, but everything was quiet. This had to be the right place. She'd been very careful to memorize Aidan's directions exactly as he gave them.

Grabbing the sack of food from the back seat, Kayla headed toward the house. There was a big white porch in the front that was also like her parent's home before they died. Theirs had a swing hanging from the roof that she used to sit on during the summer as a little girl, but this one had a couple of wicker chairs and a small table instead.

Kayla knocked on the door. She waited a couple of minutes, but no one answered. Aidan had said Bailey would be here because he'd left her with no truck or car to leave in. The only thing Kayla could guess was that the slayer may have gone for a walk. Exercise was probably a good idea when you had to fight dragons.

She tried the knob and found the door unlocked. Without cops around anymore, she supposed there wasn't much point in locking a place if you weren't home. Anyone wanting in would just break a window, and then you'd be stuck trying to find a way to replace it. After a moment of hesitation, she opened the door and stepped inside. The downstairs had a big open space for the living room on the right and a dining room and kitchen to the left. A staircase was directly in the middle. Everything looked cozy and clean.

Kayla carried the sack of food to the dining table and opened it, spreading all the contents out so Bailey could sort them the way she wanted when she returned. After that, she didn't have much left to do so she wandered through the rest of the house. She found only one locked door at the rear of the kitchen, but no matter how much she tried she couldn't get it open. Whatever was in there, Aidan must not have wanted anyone getting into it. Upstairs, she found a sword sitting on top of a dresser. It had a wicked looking blade with jagged edges. Kayla couldn't imagine what it would be like to fight with something like that.

Picking it up, she tested the weight. It was surprisingly light. She glanced around, half expecting someone to show up and tell her to put it down. Humans weren't allowed to handle weapons in the fortress, and her parents had certainly never let her play with them. If she was ever going to get the opportunity, it was now.

Kayla headed downstairs and went outside where she'd have more room. Then she slashed it left and right, loving the way it cut through the air. She could totally kill something with a blade like this and maybe even scare Ruari a little. She danced about, pretending there were enemies in front of her who needed to die. It was the most amazing feeling just to let go and have fun for a change. It had been years since she'd done anything that was just for herself.

Practicing with the sword was so entertaining that she didn't hear the vehicle pulling up until it almost reached the house. Kayla had made her way around to the other side of the place so whoever had come wouldn't have seen her yet. She flattened herself against the wall and then peeked around the corner. It was a black truck. There was no telling who that could be, but she didn't really want to find out. She ducked back out of sight and leaned against the wall, trying to think what to do. Kayla had a sword, but she didn't think she could really use it against someone.

A door slammed shut, and a set of footsteps headed in her direction, stopping about ten feet away. An angry female voice spoke, "I know you're hiding back there. Don't make me come get you or you won't like what happens."

"Bailey?" Kayla asked, praying she guessed right.

A pause. "How do you know my name?"

Kayla swallowed, still unable to face the scary-sounding woman. "Aidan sent me."

"Come out."

"You aren't going to kill me, are you?" She hadn't considered how frightened she'd be of the dragon slayer. Bailey was probably a foot taller than her and full of muscles. She could probably just look at Kayla and give her a heart attack.

There was a loud sigh. "I don't kill humans if I can help it."

Kayla frowned. "How do you know I'm not a shape-shifter?"

"For one?" Amusement laced Bailey's tone now. "They wouldn't hide from me. For two, you don't smell like a shape-shifter. You smell like a human."

"You can smell me?" Forgetting her fear, Kayla stepped out of hiding. She was shocked when she got her first glimpse of the slayer. Bailey was smaller than her, like ridiculously tiny. How was it even possible that such an itty bitty woman could take down a dragon? Now Kayla felt like a complete idiot for how she'd imagined Bailey to be before.

"Yes, I can smell you at this distance, but only because you were leaking so much fear," the slayer answered, running her gaze up and down Kayla. "Aren't you a little young for Aidan to be sending out? And why did he send you?"

Kayla put her hands on her hips. "I'm sixteen. That's not too young, and anyway, I do all kinds of favors for Aidan. He asked me to bring you food because he thought you didn't have a ride."

Bailey's expression hardened. "However old you are, you clearly don't know how to handle a sword." She stepped forward, holding out her hand. "Give that to me."

Kayla gave it to her. "I don't get how you could possibly fight dragons. They scare the shit out of me, and I've been living with them for two years."

Bailey frowned. "Have any of them hurt you?"

"No." Kayla shook her head. "It's just that even in their human bodies they all look big and tough, plus they're always getting into fights with each other. I try to stay out of their way."

"Except Aidan," Bailey said, not sounding all that pleased about it.

"He's different. He saved my life once when there was a missile attack on the fortress, and I was badly hurt. I feel like I owe him, though he says I don't," Kayla explained.

"Huh." Bailey seemed to mull that one over for a moment. "Well, let's get you inside. The dragons are going to be flying around soon, and it's best we're not seen together. Eventually, shifters are going to figure out who I am, and I don't want them tying you to me."

"Okay." Kayla followed Bailey into the house. "So, really, how do you kill dragons?"

The slayer turned around once she got halfway into the living room. Kayla had to admit she moved with grace and confidence, and there was a subtle strength about her. Of course, it helped that she was wearing the black camrium clothes that warriors wore. It made her look badass, but the tight garments also made her look even smaller.

A smile played at Bailey's lips. "Well, I take this sharp, pointy thing here." She indicated the sword.

"And I stab it into the dragon's heart. It takes them a few seconds to figure out they're dead, but then they fall over and stop breathing. Works every time."

"Very funny." Kayla rolled her eyes. "What about their fire? No human can get close to it without burning to death."

"It doesn't affect me." Bailey shrugged.

"Seriously? Like you can just stand there while they blow flames at you and not get burned at all?" Kayla couldn't even imagine it.

"Pretty much."

"Well, that explains a few things," Kayla said, looking back on the few times Aidan had spoken about Bailey. There'd been something in his voice that she'd been trying to identify, but now she thought she had it figured out. He could touch the slayer without hurting her.

"What do you mean?" Bailey asked.

"He cares about you. I didn't think much of it since shape-shifters can't even touch humans without burning them, but if you're immune…has he touched you? Like kissed you or something?"

Bailey's cheeks turned red, and she cleared her throat. "That is none of your business."

"Oh, my God. He has, hasn't he?" Kayla loved nothing more than discovering secrets and this was huge, not that she'd ever tell anyone. She was loyal to Aidan and would never betray him.

"Just one kiss before we both realized it was a bad idea," Bailey admitted, then looked away. "He's kept his distance ever since."

Kayla could detect a note of sadness in the slayer's voice. Bailey was trying to hide it, but when a person felt something deeply enough, they could never cover it up all the way. She decided to give the woman a little something to make her feel better.

"You know, ever since he came to Earth, he hasn't touched another woman. I mean, he wasn't going around before sleeping with a bunch of them or anything, but he wasn't a monk, either. It has to say something that he's not interested in anyone else." Kayla hoped she could find a man like that someday who wanted no one else except her—after she got a little older.

Bailey looked up. "Thanks, but that doesn't matter. In case you haven't noticed, Aidan and I are technically on opposing sides. We can't even be friends openly, much less anything else."

Kayla chewed her lip. She had grown up reading about fairy tales and impossible romances, but looking at it now, she realized what Bailey said was true. If Aidan's brothers ever found out he was meeting with a dragon slayer and maybe even had feelings for her? He'd either end up dead, locked in the dungeon, or branded as an outcast. Kayla didn't like any of those possibilities.

Her shoulders slumped. "Yeah, I see what you mean. I'm sorry."

"Don't be." Bailey came up and patted her shoulder. Her hands were warm, but not hot. "Aidan and I are well aware of the circumstances, and we accept them."

Kayla nodded. "I just want him to be happy. You have no idea how bad it is for him right now with his family."

Bailey's brows drew together. "How bad?"

"Do you have a few minutes?" Kayla asked.

"We better sit down."

They settled on the couch, and Kayla told Bailey everything she knew. Aidan probably wouldn't like it, but he had to trust the slayer with his life, or he wouldn't be working with her. Bailey deserved to know what she was getting herself into, and Kayla was happy to have someone to talk to after so many years of being alone. There weren't any other girls her age at the fortress and the older women just ordered her around.

It was liberating being out here. She was going to enjoy every moment until it was time to get back for midday meal preparations. After all, they'd notice if she didn't get her famous sweet buns in the oven on time. Bailey listened intently, letting her talk without interrupting her once. Kayla found herself thinking she'd have to find excuses to come back again.

10

AIDAN

The chasm came into view up ahead. Aidan had only come this far south once since crossing over to Earth, and that had been months ago while most of the dragons were still in Kederrawien. He'd been able to explore the countryside freely and get a better lay of the land than what he'd been able to view from the other dimension.

Aidan found the chasm to be every bit as massive as he remembered it. The ground had separated to leave a wide crack in the terrain that extended for hundreds of miles from east to west. It went down so deep Aidan couldn't make out what might be at the bottom. Perhaps someday humans would be able to engineer a bridge to cross, but not until civilization regained a foothold. He had no idea how long that would take.

Aidan and Falcon flew over the chasm, entering neutral territory. No toriq claimed this section of land, and any dragon could enter it without fear of reprisal.

They continued south until they reached what the humans called the "Red River," which marked the beginning of Faegud territory. Aidan and Falcon landed on the other side close to the bank. This was as far as they dared go if they wanted the other toriq to hear them out. Aidan folded his wings and searched the area, but he did not see any other dragons nearby. They'd be along soon enough. Every clan patrolled their domain frequently if they hoped to hold it.

Falcon let out a puff of steam through his nostrils and spoke telepathically to Aidan. *Did your father tell you who leads the Faegud now?*

No, Aidan answered. *He only said that their former leader died recently.*

The Faegud have many fierce warriors, Falcon said, wisdom shining in his eyes. *I've fought with them and against them. I'd certainly rather have them as an ally than an enemy—if I had a choice.*

Falcon was over five hundred years old and in the prime of his life. They'd dueled once a couple of months ago, and it had been the most difficult battle Aidan had ever fought. He'd won against the older shifter, but barely. Falcon worked to be among the best warriors of the clan because his people needed strong fighters, but he was wise enough to wish for peace over war. The older male had a good deal of experience that would be useful in their current endeavor.

It was too bad Falcon was not eligible to become pendragon. Aidan would have gladly supported the shifter over his own brothers, but he came from a lesser background, which worked to his disadvantage. There were only a handful of highborn families in the toriq with eligible shifters. The rest stood somewhere below them. Much of it had to do with the numbers of warriors each provided, as well as their past and current contributions to the overall welfare of the clan. Falcon was an anomaly—the only warrior in his family while most of the rest were lazy drunkards or outcasts who had been banished for one crime or another. He worked every day to rise above the stigma that followed him.

Let us hope this new leader is more amenable than the last, Aidan said.

Agreed.

They waited patiently for a few more minutes before the figure of a dragon appeared in the sky to the west, following a path along the river bank. Its coloring was different than that of the pure dragon clans in Oklahoma. Rather than being green, the Faegud's scales tended to run between beige and burnt orange. It was partly from mixing with shape-shifters, but also because clans in different regions developed distinctive coloring and traits unique to them—much like humans.

As the dragon got closer, Aidan recognized this particular male's markings. He had a beige underbelly, burnt-orange top scales and spikes jutting from his tail. Pure dragons didn't have spikes, only those with sufficient shifter blood. Aidan moved forward to greet his old childhood friend, but his welcome was met in a different way than expected. Lorcan flew straight for him, talons outstretched. Aidan lashed out with his teeth and clamped onto one of his legs, yanking the dragon to the ground. They rolled across the hard-packed earth, nipping and clawing each other.

It lasted for several minutes before Lorcan chuckled telepathically and called the battle off. *Enough, friend, I see you have not grown weak since our last meeting. I'd worried.*

I'd had the same concern about you, Aidan replied. *You were getting a little soft the last time we met. Too many females sniffing after you and keeping you in your den.*

A rumble came from Lorcan's chest. *I've never been soft anywhere it counts.*

So says the dragon without a scar on him. This came from Falcon, who strode up to them. Scars were a dragon's pride but not easy to obtain and survive. They came from being severely wounded in the same place several times so that the body no longer knitted back together cleanly. It was dangerous when it happened because the recovery took longer, and the risk of getting an untreatable infection rose.

Perhaps I am just a better fighter, Lorcan pointed out, smugness in his tone.

Falcon snorted. *Or perhaps you only fight one enemy at a time to preserve your worthless hide.*

He has you there, friend, Aidan flashed his teeth in a dragon smile.

Lorcan dipped his head in acknowledgment. *Tell me what brings you two here.*

We wish to negotiate a new alliance between our toriqan. We've heard Severne is dead, and you have a new pendragon who may be more amenable to peace. Is this true? Aidan asked.

The male dragon cocked his head. *Where did you hear that?*

Aidan exchanged a glance with Falcon. They could hardly reveal that their best spy—a female shifter with the rare ability to change the color of her scales and body type—had gained the information through duplicity. The fact that she could blend in anywhere made her an important asset to the Taugud. When they first discovered her gift as a young girl, the pendragon immediately ordered it to be kept secret, and she began training for espionage right away. That was less than a century ago. Only about a dozen members of their toriq knew about her abilities, including her immediate family.

Let us just say we have our ways," Aidan said.

Lorcan was quiet for a moment, then let out a huff of breath. *Fair enough. You are right that we elected a new pendragon just two weeks ago.*

Who is it? Falcon asked.

My mother—Hildegard of the Faegud.

Aidan hid his surprise. *That is excellent news.*

Indeed. Lorcan dipped his chin.

It wasn't often a female wrested power over a toriq, but he supposed if anyone could do it, Hildegard would be the one. When Aidan and Lorcan were not much beyond their first dragon shift, she'd swat them with a stick every time they passed by her to "toughen their hides." Throm was never bothered by the welts covering Aidan when he returned home. According to him, it was a sign of Hildegard's love that she beat on Aidan as well. It helped him to learn pain management—an important quality for a future warrior.

How did she take over? Aidan inquired.

Either Severne had died, or he'd been challenged in one form or another. If a dragon wished to take over leadership when the position was currently occupied, they had to prove the current pendragon incompetent and gain a majority vote with the elders. That was tricky if the current leader had many supporters who might sway sentiment. There was one other option—fight for it.

She challenged Severne to a death duel. He wasn't half the warrior he thought and didn't last ten minutes before she cut him to pieces. If the victor wasn't my mother, I might have been embarrassed to watch my uncle beaten so badly.

Aidan cocked his head. *Do you think she'll agree to peace negotiations?*

Will you be representing the Taugud clan? Lorcan asked, surprise in his orange eyes.

It is a task my father has set before me. Aidan refrained from explaining more. The Faegud might be less amenable to a treaty if they knew the current pendragon wouldn't be around much longer, and the next in line had not been selected yet. It would be a gamble for them.

Lorcan swished his tail. *You do realize that even if my mother agrees to meet with you, negotiating a treaty will not be easy. There are protocols to follow and elders you must impress. We've been under poor leadership for too long. Tensions remain high, and everyone is more than a little distrustful at the moment.*

Aidan was afraid of that, but he had little choice. He could not fail his father and would do whatever it took to make this treaty happen. The only thing he regretted was that he could not be more open and honest with his friend about the circumstances.

I understand, he said.

Lorcan unfurled his wings. *I will inform my mother of your request. You and Falcon may wait here until I return. Our guards will not bother you, but do not tread any farther into our territory until you are invited.*

How long must we wait?

The dragon lifted a shoulder in what passed for a shrug. *It is difficult to say. My mother is quite busy these days and will need time to consider it, but I will do my best to return tomorrow.*

Aidan had expected no less. There was a reason his father gave him until the Bitkal to conduct the negotiations. Every step would require time and patience.

You have my gratitude, friend. Aidan bowed his head. *We will await you here.*

11

BAILEY

Collecting dragon scales was my new top priority, but first, I had to stop by Earl's place to check in with him and my friends. Talking to Kayla the previous evening had reminded me of how important it was to stay in touch with those closest to me—even if I couldn't be around them much anymore. The teenage girl's loneliness had shown through during those hours we chatted and emphasized how easy it was to get caught up in the dragon world, losing part of yourself in the process. Though she had a few friends, none of them were close to her age. She moved about the world mostly unseen by it. I wished I could do something for her, but I had enough on my plate already.

After forming a strategy for the coming days and preparing my weapons, I'd left Aidan's lair a couple of hours before noon. That would give me just enough time to check in with everyone without the risk of drawing any dragons to the neighborhood.

I turned off Lindsey Street and headed up Berry Road toward Earl's neighborhood. Many of the houses in the area had been abandoned after all the disasters that struck, including earthquakes and a tornado that crossed the path I now drove. I passed a few homes that were totally demolished and a few more that were on the verge of collapse. Nothing had been repaired, but some of the power lines that had fallen were shoved out of the street. These days, the only reason anyone performed a public service was for their own benefit. In a lot of ways, Norman was like a ghost town now. It used to be all I wanted was to avoid people and crowds, but now I missed seeing the flow of life around me—even if I wasn't a direct part of it.

Justin and another young guy stood guard at the blockade to Earl's neighborhood. As soon as they saw me, they started rolling the fifty-five-gallon steel drums aside so I could drive through. The rest of the entryway was blocked by the stone wall they'd erected recently. Sometime soon, they planned to design a better gate system, but everything had to be taken one step at a time.

There were always two guards on duty—day and night. They protected against looters, but also provided an early warning against any approaching dragons. The neighborhood had several underground hideouts interspersed throughout, including one by the gate, where people could take cover. For reasons even Aidan couldn't explain, dragon flames couldn't burn dirt. You had to have at least six inches of it over your head for it to fully block the fire, though, or you'd still get torched. Over the last few months, we'd learned many things the hard way.

As I pulled up, Justin gestured at me. I stopped and rolled down my window, praying this wasn't going to be another one of his speeches about safety. He meant well, but he had major control issues. I'd been kind of glad not to see him for a few days.

"I heard the dragon doesn't want you living here anymore," Justin said, resting a hand on my truck. "Conrad told me something about how even that weird creature thinks you're too dangerous for us to be around."

He couldn't be bothered to say Aidan's name—the jackass.

I gritted my teeth and counted to five. "I'm killing dragons to protect people—like you. Do you seriously have a problem with that?"

"Well, that's not exactly my problem." Justin worked his jaw, silent for a moment. "I'm just…annoyed, I guess. Here I am—a trained soldier—and I can't defend my own damn neighborhood. You're nothing but a little college girl, but you get the ability to fight dragons like no one else can. It's…frustrating."

I gave him a surprised look—that admission was rather unexpected. "You're jealous?"

I'd had a suspicion that was his problem, but I never thought he'd admit it.

"Trish and I had a long talk about you last night," he said, referring to his girlfriend, who was also one of my best friends from college. "She said I've been a sexist pig and a few other things I won't get into. Let's just say I owe you an apology. You didn't ask to be what you are, but you've handled it better than most people would have under the circumstances."

I pinched my leg, certain I must be dreaming. It hurt, disproving that theory. "Uh, thanks."

"Just do me a favor and don't stay too long. The dragons will be coming out in an hour or so." He pointed up at the clear, blue sky where the sun steadily climbed overhead.

"I'll be quick," I promised.

Justin glanced down the street, his gaze focusing on a house with blue siding where he and Trish now lived. His fists clenched and unclenched several times before he turned his attention back to me. "But before you go, you might talk to Trish for a few minutes. She has something she needs to tell you."

That piqued my curiosity. How much had I missed after being gone a few days?

"Yeah, sure," I agreed.

He slapped the side of my truck, and I drove about halfway down the street before pulling into Earl's driveway. His red brick home wasn't as big as some of the other houses on the block, but he took good care of the lawn, and he had a nice sized basement underneath for storing survival gear. Aside from my one-month stay here, no one else had lived with him since his wife passed years ago. He was a bit cantankerous and tended to scare most people off.

I got out of the truck and headed toward Earl where he sat on his porch in a rickety lawn chair. His back was stooped a little, and he had a bit of a paunch in his belly, despite being limited to rations for the last few months, but he still moved around fairly well for a sixty-five-year-old. It was his rugged face with the faded shrapnel scar on his left cheek and the gray beard that made him look his age. He snubbed out the cigarette he was smoking with his boot and narrowed his gaze on me. I braced myself for what would likely be a long lecture.

"You get that damn dragon taking kids yet?" he asked, his voice coming out gruff.

I shrugged a shoulder. "Working on it."

"That's what I heard." He stared at me with clear blue eyes. "You do whatever it takes to get that thing, but you make sure to check in with me every so often. That's all I ask."

"I will."

"And you're gonna have to call your momma soon. You know how she gets if she don't hear from you." He spit on the sidewalk. "I don't wanna be the one explainin' why you're too busy to talk to her."

Earl had a satellite phone and a generator to charge it. Despite all the natural disasters, nothing had affected the satellites overhead, so those phones still worked. The trick was having one that was already operable before D-day and knowing the number to anyone else who owned one. Luckily my stepfather had one as well, partially because our ranch didn't get good cell phone reception and partially because he was a survivalist like Earl.

"I'll call her…soon." It was just that I didn't know what to say every time we talked. There was never anything good to tell my mom, and I hated lying to her about what I was up to.

At least Earl had kept the secret about me slaying dragons from my parents so far. The last thing they needed was one more thing to worry about. It was all they could do to protect the ranch and keep my brothers from getting themselves killed.

"I'll hold you to that," Earl replied, leaning back in his chair.

I left him and headed toward Trish's place two doors down. It really concerned me that Justin had asked me to talk to her. He wouldn't do that unless something was seriously wrong with her. Was she sick or depressed? We'd stocked up on as many kinds of medicine as we could, but we didn't have them all and Danae's healer abilities had limits. Diseases were still beyond her magic.

Please don't let anything be wrong with Trish, I prayed.

I knocked on the door and shifted on my feet as I waited. A few moments later, footsteps came from the inside, heading my way. The deadbolt slid with a click and Trish opened the door. Her curly red hair was a tangled mess, her eyes were swollen, and her t-shirt had stains on it like she'd been out working in the garden recently. Wordlessly, I pulled her into a hug. Her soft form squished against mine and she broke into tears.

"Did…did he tell you?" she asked, her voice coming out muffled from my shoulder.

"No," I said softly. "Justin just said I should come see you."

She took in several stuttering breaths, shaking against me. "Oh, God, Bailey. I'm in so much trouble."

"Shhh. It can't be that bad." I patted her shoulder.

"You don't understand," she wailed, pulling back to look at me. "It's worse than you can possibly imagine."

I examined her from head to toe, not seeing any sign of illness or injury. "Well, you've got all your working parts, Justin is still your boyfriend, and as long as I leave soon, you should be safe here. What could be so bad?"

Trish opened her mouth, closed it, and then opened it again. "I'm pregnant."

"What?" I took a step back to look at her closer. She'd put on a little weight recently, but not that much. I'd just assumed it was from stress eating. Everyone had their own way of dealing with the dramatic changes in the world, and she took consolation in food. I didn't judge. Heck, I even gave her some of my rations because it made her happy.

"I found out last night. Danae brought it up after she caught me puking for the third time. She sent Justin out to get a pregnancy test." Trish paused and seemed to calm a bit. "Would you believe there are still plenty of those in the stores even though almost everything else is gone?"

"Well, uh, I guess it wouldn't be a priority for the looters, but I thought you still had plenty of birth control and condoms." This was really the last thing I'd expected to hear. She'd told me a while back Justin was obsessed with preventing pregnancy for obvious reasons, and he had stocked up on everything he could. At the very least, they were going to get married first and wait until things weren't quite so dangerous.

"We did. We were so careful." She led me into the living room, and we sat on the couch. "But I guess this was one of those one percent cases or whatever."

My mind raced. I wanted to be supportive of her, but this was definitely not a good time for pregnancy. She couldn't bring a baby into the world now when the future was so uncertain, and there wouldn't be a hospital for her to give birth in. How was I going to help her when I couldn't even live here anymore? A thousand thoughts raced through my mind, but I couldn't think of anything appropriate to say. Was this why Justin had suddenly become friendlier? Even he didn't want to do anything to upset Trish further now that she was so vulnerable.

"What are you going to do?" I asked.

She shrugged. "Have the baby, I guess. Even if there was a way to get an abortion, I don't think I could do it and Justin is Catholic. He'd never agree to that."

No, he wouldn't, but I suspected he was about to redefine the meaning of over-protective. Trish was going to have her work cut out for her handling both this pregnancy and him.

"Do you have any idea how far along you are?"

She nodded. "I worked it out with Danae, and we think I'm two months."

"Wow, so you got pregnant back when we still lived in the library." That seemed like ages ago, rather than about five weeks.

"Yeah," she said, sighing. "Who knows where we'll be by the time this baby is born or if we can find an experienced midwife or doctor to help me...and now you're hardly around anymore."

Danae's combat medic training would have given her some basic skills on how to deliver a baby, but Trish would definitely need someone with more experience to monitor the pregnancy and handle any potential complications. I couldn't even consider the idea that she might die in childbirth the way many women had before medical advancement reduced the risk. There had to be at least a few people still around town who could help. It was only a matter of finding them, which I was certain Justin would make a priority. In this case, his being overprotective might be a good thing.

I grabbed Trish's hand and squeezed it. "I'm sorry I won't be around as much, but if you need anything—*anything at all*—just let me know."

"Thanks, Bailey." She managed a weak smile. "You have no idea how much I needed to hear that."

"Good." It relieved me to see her mood brighten a little. The last thing I wanted was to leave when she was still upset.

"So, um, you're staying at that house by the lake now? The one that Aidan uses?" she asked.

"Yeah."

She swallowed. "Maybe I can visit sometime."

"Maybe," I said, then glanced at the clock on the wall. It was almost noon. "But I have to go now."

"But you just got here," she argued.

I stood, grimacing with regret. "I'm sorry, but I can't risk staying any longer."

"When will you be back?" she asked, angling her pale face up at me.

"Hopefully in a few days."

Trish narrowed her eyes. "Promise?"

In the movies, people who made promises almost never kept them. I wasn't making that mistake. "I'll do my best."

She leaped up and gave me a hug. "I'm going to hold you to that."

I left her house and stepped outside. Two driveways down, Conrad leaned against my truck with his arms crossed. I made my way over to him.

"You're not going with me," I said.

"Yes, I am. Someone's gotta have your back."

That was the excuse he always gave. It had become almost a habit to go through this argument every time I went out hunting. "Fine, but if you rub it in my face that you're better with the crossbow, I'm ditching you."

"Damn, girl, you're no fun." He hopped in the truck, waiting until I started the engine and pulled out of the drive before grinning at me. "But I am better than you."

12

BAILEY

"Think they're goin' to be roaming around here?" Conrad asked.

We were driving around the west side of I-35 where the Thamaran clan of dragons hunted. According to Aidan, their territory took up the western half of Oklahoma with the interstate being the border. I didn't want to risk getting into it with the Shadowan yet, so I was targeting the other clan for now. I'd get back to Matrika and her fellow dragons soon enough.

A series of gunshots sounded in the distance, followed by the furious roar of a dragon. I glanced over at Conrad. "Think that's our cue?"

"Oh, yeah." He nodded, his eyes lighting up. "Let's get there before the dragon kills whoever is shooting at it."

I hit the gas, speeding up. "You're becoming such an adrenaline junky."

"It's all your fault."

More gunfire rang out and I followed the direction of the sound. We arrived at the intersection of 36th and Main Street. On the northeast corner where the local mall was located, a group of bikers were pulling on a red dragon with hooks and ropes they'd somehow gotten into him.

"Oh, shit," Conrad said. "That's not Aidan is it?"

I leaned forward, trying to get a good look at the creature while also trying to control my slayer instincts. My blood pressure was already beginning to rise. "No, the coloring isn't quite the same and Aidan is out of town right now on a mission for his father."

"How in the hell did they manage to trap a dragon like that?" Conrad asked.

"No idea." My foot pressed down on the gas pedal. The closer I got to the battle, the more my instincts took over and all I could think about was attacking the dragon.

"Bailey," Conrad said, speaking my name slowly. "Aidan's gonna be pissed if you help those bikers kill one of his people."

I slammed on my breaks about a hundred feet from the bikers, set the gearshift into park, and reached for my sword. "Can't...help it."

The primitive part of my mind had taken over. Conrad grabbed my arm, but I shrugged him off and got out of the truck. I raced across the pavement toward the struggling red dragon. Half a dozen bikers gathered around the beast, holding it with their ropes and shooting at it. The hook was stuck in its upper and lower jaws, keeping its mouth shut, but it loosened a little more with each toss of the creature's head. Any moment, that dragon was going to get free.

"Get back!" I yelled.

Two of the men glanced at me, but none of them stopped what they were doing. They needed to get the hell out of the way before they got hurt. I ran up to the three guys holding the rope extending from the dragon's mouth and switched my sword to my non-dominant hand to free the other. I took hold of the nearest man and tossed him twenty feet. He landed with a thud, knocking his head into the ground. The adrenaline coursing through my veins fueled my need to move the humans and attack the dragon. I grabbed the next guy, tossing him toward his buddy.

Just as I reached for the third man's shoulder, the dragon reared up, and the hook came loose from its mouth. It roared a stream of flames at us. Everything went red and orange, blinding me. The man who I'd been grasping disintegrated beneath my fingertips. I was too late. If I'd had just a few more seconds, I could have gotten him out of the way.

The flames extinguished, and I pulled my sword up, slashing at the dragon's chest. Its yellow eyes registered shock, and it backed away a few steps. It was then that I caught sight of the three men who'd held the second rope. They were running away. The other hook still hung from the dragon's hind quarter, pierced deeply into its hip.

I leaped forward and slashed at the beast again, catching it across the chest again. The creature let out a yelp of pain. Something in my mind registered this was not a pure dragon and that he was not my enemy. That thought gave me a brief moment of clarity. I seriously doubted this dragon had instigated the fight, or the men would have been dead before I arrived. They only got their hooks into him because they'd caught him off guard, and he hadn't wanted to kill the humans. There was no other way they could have possibly captured him.

"Go!" I screamed at it. "I can't control myself much longer."

The sword shook in my hand with the need to attack and kill him. Understanding flashed in the dragon's eyes. For a second, I could see the man inside and his desperate need for survival. He unfurled his wings. In his weakened condition, it took several tries for him to get off the ground. As my slayer instincts took over once more and I leaped forward with my blade, he finally found the strength and lifted into the air. My sword missed him by mere inches.

I watched him fly away. A part of me wished I'd finished him off since he had killed one human, but the other part was relieved I hadn't. He'd only been defending himself. After he was out of sight, I turned around. The two bikers I'd tossed were sitting up, gripping their heads. The other three were standing next to them and glaring at me.

"What the fuck?" a forty-something man wearing a black t-shirt, jeans, and boots asked. His head was bare, but he had a thick, brown goatee and his arms were covered in tattoos. "You just got our friend killed."

"No, you did that," I said, walking up to him. "What were you thinking attacking a dragon? You're lucky the rest of you are still alive."

One of the guys on the ground stared up at me. A touch of blood stained his short, blond hair where his head had hit the pavement. There was a mixture of pain and anger in his eyes. "One of them took my son last night. We're gonna kill every damn dragon we find until I get my kid back."

"Which you fucked up by getting in our way," the man with the goatee said to me with a growl.

Not another child, I thought, a chill running through me.

If only I'd been able to kill Matrika the other day, the boy would still be with his father. I gave the biker on the ground a sympathetic look. "I'm sorry to hear about your son, but that wasn't the dragon who took him. It's a green one taking children, not red."

"What the hell difference does it make?" Goatee guy took a menacing step toward me.

I stood my ground. He'd seen what I could do, otherwise he would have attacked me already. All he was doing now was posturing because his buddies were watching.

"The red ones can shift into humans, and they're sympathetic to us. The green ones are pure dragons. They're the ones you need to be worried about."

"That's the biggest bullshit story I've ever heard," he said, spitting on the ground. "There ain't no dragons turnin' into humans."

"She's telling the truth," Conrad said, walking up. I silently willed him back to the truck, but he didn't get the message.

One of the other bikers frowned. "How'd you survive the flames?"

"Yeah," another guy seconded. "That dragon burned Charlie like he was nothin', but she ain't even got so much as a sunburn. I seen some crazy shit lately, but that takes the cake."

There was no point in lying to them. "I'm a dragon slayer."

Several of them laughed, and the goatee guy pointed at me. "You? You've got to be kiddin' me."

"I survived the flames didn't I?" I lifted a brow. "How else would you explain it?"

He shifted on his feet. "I ain't figured that part out yet."

Conrad touched my arm. "Bailey, let's go. We've got dragons to hunt if we're goin' to save those kids."

The man with the missing son struggled to his feet. "What's he talking about?"

"Your son isn't the first one to be taken—there's more. I'm trying to find them," I said.

"They could be anywhere." He swung his arm out for emphasis. "How you gonna find them?"

"Let's just say I've got sources in town who can help me. I will find the kids," I swore.

Goatee guy barked at him, "Don't be gettin' your hopes up, Larry. She's just a little girl. Ain't no way she's gonna get your kid or anyone else's free from dragons. Not even with her friend there."

Conrad glanced at me, amusement in his brown eyes. "I love how they always underestimate you."

"Easy for you to say." I sighed. It was starting to get old.

Larry looked at the goatee guy. "Boss, you missed it, but that little girl tossed me and Bruce twenty feet through the air like it was nothin'. Then she got two good strikes on that dragon before she scared him off. If she ain't a dragon slayer, then I don't know what the fuck she is."

The "boss" shifted on his feet, still undecided. Conrad was right that we didn't have time for this. I took hold of Larry's arm. "Look, I'm sorry about throwing you and busting your head, but I promise I'll do everything I can to get your son back. Please don't attack any more dragons in the meantime. It's only going to get you and more of your friends killed."

He stared at me for a full minute before nodding. "How will I know if you find my kid?"

I mulled that over and then a simple solution came to me. "Listen to the radio. I'll get Hank to spread the word once I've got the children."

"Alright," he agreed, though I could still hear a note of skepticism in his voice.

I glanced at the "boss man" and found he hadn't softened a bit. "Keep these guys safe, will you?

"That ain't none of your concern." He crossed his arms.

Except that it was, whether either of us liked it or not.

13

RUARI

The hook bit into Ruari's hip with a vengeance, digging into the bone farther every time he jostled it. Blood filled his mouth from puncture wounds by the second hook, the human bullets made his belly ache where they'd embedded into his scales and skin, and the cuts the slayer had made across his chest stung with every beat of his wings. He didn't have the same pain tolerance as his brothers. His father, the pendragon, had bemoaned Ruari's weakness more than once—to his shame.

He flew for as long as he could before his suffering became too great. The Taugud territory was just up ahead. Ruari spotted a place to land—a house in the middle of a neighborhood with a large backyard and a cove of trees at the far end. It wasn't perfect, but it would have to do. His body couldn't begin to heal, or even stop bleeding, if he didn't rest for a few minutes.

Ruari flared his wings and slowed his descent as best he could. It wasn't enough. He crashed into the ground like a fledgling who'd just taken his first flight and rolled twice before coming to a stop. His right wing crumpled beneath him. It was all he could do to keep from growling as pain shot through every part of his body. Those crazy humans had attacked him for no reason. He had been minding his own business on a mission to complete his father's task, which was to locate Shadowan and Thamaran lairs. While surveying a large human building and flying low to reduce his chances of being seen, the men had leaped out from underneath an awning and threw hooks into him.

There had been no time to fly away. He was such a *fushka* for not scenting the humans beforehand and redirecting his flight path. His father was always saying he did not have the mindset of a warrior, and today he would have been proven right, but Ruari was determined to change the pendragon's mind. He could travel through enemy territory without getting caught. The humans were just so small and unintimidating that he had never paid much attention to them before.

He would *not* make that mistake again.

Twisting his head around, he inspected the hook. It was buried deep within his hip, going through the bone. If he blew fire on it, the flames would only melt the section of metal that protruded out of him. The remaining half inside would still be there. The only way to be certain he disintegrated the whole hook and ridded himself of the bullets littering his belly was to shift to human form. No foreign objects would survive that process. It was risky changing so close to Shadowan lands, though. He'd stopped right along the border. If they caught him alone and vulnerable, he would surely be dead, and his father would likely say good riddance.

Ruari listened carefully for anyone nearby—human or dragon. Other than the chirping of birds and the sound of a dog barking in the distance, he heard nothing else. He sniffed the air next, inhaling a myriad of scents—flowers, various types of small animals, cat urine, and hint of rain coming soon. Ruari found no immediate threats to worry about.

He took a deep breath and let his inner fire consume him. The process was not without pain, but unlike his wounds, it passed quickly. In less than a minute, he stood naked in his human form. His skin was covered with open wounds and blood. He could have pulled his camrium clothing from shiggara, but he did not wish to soil them.

That thought triggered a memory. Was it his imagination or had the slayer been wearing camrium warrior clothing? He had been in so much pain and struggling so hard to get free that the memory of her was unclear. She had certainly been wearing black, and she had black hair. He might have mistaken her for a shifter if not for her scent. Ruari remembered that well enough—as any dragon would—and it had been distinctly human. If she did have camrium clothing, someone had given it to her, but why? Who in his toriq would wish to help a slayer? He

SUSAN ILLENE

did not have time to investigate it now with his father's task still unfinished, but he would be on the lookout for her potential ally. There were so many things he could do with that information.

Limping toward a tree, Ruari sat and leaned against it. All the bugs nearby scurried away, scared off by his dragon heat. There was only one insect that would dare bite a shifter, but it had not been seen since they'd crossed over to Earth. He was rather glad of that, considering it had dangerous venom that could make its victim very ill. Hopefully, that particular bug would stay gone.

Ruari closed his eyes, desiring a little rest before he flew the rest of the way home. Today had proven disastrous, and it would set him back a couple of days while he recovered, but he'd return to his father's task as soon as he was able. He could not allow himself to fail. Above all, he wanted to be pendragon—to rule over the toriq and see the respect in his people's eyes. Zoran and Phoebe already had their regard. Even Aidan, who had always been considered the weakest son, was gaining favor. All his younger brother had to do was perform a few minor feats in recent months and opinion changed as swiftly as a breeze.

Ruari ground his jaw. No matter what he did, it never seemed to be enough. He caught the suspicious looks they all gave him. Every bad thing that happened, they blamed him for it. He was never given a chance to defend himself—to prove he wasn't as bad as they thought. Sure, he was no saint, and he would

134

take advantage of another's weaknesses, but that was the way of the dragons. It was just his wretched luck that terrible things happened around him. Such as today and how those humans attacked him without provocation. Sometimes he wondered if a sorcerer had cursed him.

As much as he hated to admit it, the dragon slayer may have saved his life today. If not for her pulling those humans away, they may have found a way to do him grave injury. They would have continued shooting their little projectiles into his body until they broke past his thick skin and scales to his internal organs. Or worse yet, they might have decided to use a more effective weapon. The men had already figured out his belly was his most vulnerable area, and once they saw his blood pouring from the first wound they created there, they'd begun targeting his stomach. He'd been at their mercy and thought he might die.

He rubbed at his stomach, thankful that the bullets were gone now and he'd stopped bleeding. His skin was even beginning to knit back together. Ruari felt along his cheeks and jaw next, noting the raw punctures there from where the hook had gone in and come back out. With his face such a mess, he would have to avoid being seen by anyone when he returned to the fortress. It would likely take the rest of the day for his skin to smooth back over and another day before his internal injuries healed enough to risk leaving again. Never mind his hip, which had swollen considerably in the last few minutes while he sat. Bones healed the slowest of all and that hook had done severe damage despite being human made. Thicker metals such as that could resist dragon heat for much longer than the thinner ones, which melted quicker.

Curse, Zorya.

Ruari had to find two sizeable pure dragon dens, identify the number residing in each, and report them to his father within ten days. With this setback, how would he manage it? One would think it would be an easy task, but their kind had a way of naturally obscuring their homes. They had a sort of magic that cloaked any place they established as a den, confining their scent and sounds to a very close range. An outsider more or less had to stumble upon it to find it—unless they already knew where the den was located, which was his job.

Ruari looked up at the sky and estimated an hour had passed. The rest of his wounds had stopped bleeding, and the skin had knit back together enough it should not reopen. On the inside, he still had a great deal of healing to do, but he didn't have time to wait for that.

He tentatively climbed to his feet, testing his body. Ruari winced at the pain in his hip, hardly able to put weight on it. Few places on him didn't hurt, but that one was by far the worst. His father would have told him he was a weakling for letting his wounds affect him so much. That made one more reason he had to excel at the pendragon's task if he wanted to be chosen for the Bitkal. Under no circumstances could he give the excuse he'd been attacked and wounded by humans. His whole toriq would laugh at him.

After doing a thorough survey of the area around him, he changed into his dragon form. The strain of shifting twice in a short time weakened him further, but at least his wounds were not as bad as when he first landed. Ruari pushed off the ground, favoring his hip as he did so, and lifted into the air. Not wanting to be caught off guard again, he regularly checked his surroundings by sight, scent, and sound. His former battle instructor had pushed that point over and over when he was young. He'd finally learned his lesson.

Up ahead, he caught sight of two red dragons flying next to each other through the sky. The roving guards took note of him as they passed and let out a greeting roar. Ruari usually didn't bother with such pleasantries—he was the pendragon's son after all—but he was so relieved to be nearing the fortress that he made a greeting call back. Then he continued on his way, doing his best to show no sign that he had been injured. If anyone noticed, they'd question him about it, and he couldn't risk that. All it would take was a glimpse of his wounds to see the damage had not been done by a dragon.

He caught sight of the fortress ahead. Ruari was tempted to head toward the tunnel entrance, but there were too many guards roaming around who had already spotted him. Dragons didn't use the underground passages except during sieges or for clandestine purposes. They'd take note if he made use of them now.

Anticipating his landing would disturb his hip, he was careful to slow his descent, but not so much that it would draw suspicion. At the last moment, he flared his wings. His feet touched the ground with a soft thud. The landing was not without discomfort, but the pain was not so great he couldn't bear it.

He began shifting into human form, his body taking longer than usual to finish. Ruari was forced to feel each and every cell altering as his skin and bones reshaped themselves. He was grateful the flames surrounded him and hid the agony that would have shown on his face. By the time it was over, he was panting heavily. Dear Zorya, that had been one of the worst shifts he had ever experienced. This was why he avoided fighting in battles as much as possible.

Ruari pretended to study his surroundings while he waited to catch his breath. To his relief, not a soul appeared to be paying any attention to him. A group of young warriors trained farther afield, but they faced the opposite direction. The guards in the sky had roamed toward the woods and didn't look his way, either. Even the males on the fortress walls kept their gazes beyond him.

When Ruari's pain finally subsided to a more tolerable level, he made his way past the gate and inside the keep, ducking his head down as much as possible. It was a good thing his tunic had a high collar to help hide the healing wounds on his jaw. If not for that, he'd have had some difficulty concealing them. The main thoroughfare was crowded with people he could not avoid. While clansmen might move out of Zoran's way without hesitation, they did not do so for Ruari. He was forced to weave his way through the throng, getting bumped and jostled with almost every step. A woman hit him directly in the hip and he had to bite his tongue to keep from crying out. Why couldn't the fools just watch where they were going?

Honestly, the first thing he'd do once he became pendragon was send a third of these people to live outside the walls like some of the other members of their toriq already did. He swore their numbers seemed to grow by the day, especially the humans. Why did his father keep giving them sanctuary anyway? A few dozen was fine since they made good servants, but any more than that was a nuisance.

Ember appeared ahead of him on the path. The woman had trained as a warrior and still dressed herself as such, but it was her feminine wiles that she used as her best weapons. She was a temptress who had managed to seduce and hold his attention for a while before he'd realized she carried an evil streak unlike anything he'd ever seen. Sexual relations with her were exciting, but the experience left one wondering if they might find a dagger in the heart before the end of it.

The female shifter had soft, black hair that she kept cut to just above her shoulders, so it framed her delicate face. Her skin was a darker olive than most others in the clan, but common within her family. She was also shorter than most, only reaching his chin. If there wasn't a glint of malevolence in her yellow eyes, one might be inspired to protect her. Ruari had thought she would prove useful at one time, but he'd soon learned that nothing good came from being near her.

When their gazes met, he considered turning the other way. She had already seen him, though, and he could not let her think he feared her. Ember made her way toward him, studying every inch of him with such sensuality he hardened against his will. Ruari took a few more steps toward her, and false concern touched her gaze.

She closed the distance and took hold of his arms. "You've been injured!"

"Not here," he hissed. Damn the woman. She hadn't spoken loudly, but one couldn't be too careful. He never said anything in public that he didn't want overheard.

Ruari took the hand gripping him and pulled her down a narrow alley. Gritting his teeth against the pain of his injuries, he rushed past several small residences—all of them carrying a human scent—until they reached a small garden. Few knew about this place other than the residents, and he did not worry about them overmuch. As that young girl, Kayla, proved the other day, they were too scared of Ruari to cross him. It was the closest place he and Ember were going to find for privacy without going to their homes.

He turned on her. "I told you weeks ago that we are finished."

"But you're injured." She lifted a hand and grazed his cheek. "How can I not worry for you?"

Ruari was surprised she did not ask how his face got marked. He needed to finish this conversation quickly before she did get around to it. Ember had a way of drawing information out of him if he gave her the chance.

"Don't," he bit out, pushing her away.

"You are concerned about the Bitkal coming up. I understand," she said, bleeding sympathy into her voice.

For Zorya's sake, could she not take a hint? "Stay out of my business."

Ember composed her features. "I can help you. Just tell me what task your father gave you and I will make certain it is done."

"No." Ruari shook his head. "I don't want any more of your help." The price was far too high, even for him.

She had already gone behind his back and drugged Donar a couple of months ago with an herb Ruari had obtained because she said her brother needed it while he recovered from an injury. Instead, she used it on his cousin, impairing Donar enough that he fell from the fortress walls while he was working on them. It was a small miracle he had survived.

All he'd said to Ember was that it would be better if his cousin was not in the running for candidacy, but he hadn't told her to murder him. After Ruari had discovered what she had done, he ended his relationship with her. Weakening a competitor was one thing, attempting to kill them another.

Her gaze hardened. "You won't become pendragon without me, you know."

Ruari wasn't fooled in the least. She wanted him to owe her, and she would do anything to make that happen. Her family was so far beneath most of the others in the toriq that it would take strong allies for her to rise higher.

"Enough. I do not want your help," he growled.

"But…"

He grabbed her by the shoulders and shoved her against the nearest stone wall. "Do not do anything. Do you understand?"

Ember bit her lip, then nodded. "Yes."

Ruari let her go and walked away, hoping that was the end of it.

14

AIDAN

Aidan and Falcon sloshed through the river, rinsing themselves off after finishing their dinner. They'd captured a deer after they woke for the day and ate it together. There weren't many occasions that required them to stay in dragon form for long periods and shifters rarely chose to live that way. Their warrior training included a few field exercises where they couldn't do anything as humans, and it sometimes happened during protracted battles. That was about it, though, other than the annual clan hunt just before the first snow. Needless to say, he and Falcon had made a bit of a mess of themselves.

They dipped and rolled in the water, doing the best they could to clean between their scales. Once finished, they moved onto the bank to dry in the sun. There wouldn't be many warm days left. Aidan could almost feel it in the air, and some of the leaves on the trees were beginning to change color. He didn't much care for autumn, but mostly because it meant the cold would soon come.

The shape of a dragon appeared in the gray sky. Falcon and Aidan monitored its approach, judging its flight path. The Faegud clan had sent patrols regularly to check on them from the air. With each sighting, they hoped it was Lorcan returning instead. It did not sit well with them to remain in the open for so long without proper shelter and a storm approached from the west. It would likely reach them within an hour.

A minute later, Aidan identified the shape and coloring of the beast, confirming Lorcan was heading toward them. He skimmed the trees and came in low, landing a dozen paces away. Aidan attempted to judge his old friend's mood, but the dragon gave away nothing. He stomped toward them, his orange eyes somber.

Loran directed his attention to Aidan. *The pendragon has accepted your request. Our toriq will need time to prepare for the treaty process and associated activities, but I've convinced her to begin the negotiations sooner than she first proposed. You may return here in three days with two other members of your clan and I will escort you to our jakhal.*

Aidan was surprised the Faegud pendragon would invite them to their seat of power. It was rare outsiders were allowed near a jakhal. In all his life, the only time he could remember a delegation being allowed inside their fortress was when the Straegud, a clan of shapeshifters from the east, sent several members of their toriq to revive relations with the Taugud. That had been when Aidan was thirty years old—almost two centuries ago. Something had happened to the Straegud since then, and they had not been heard from in almost two decades. The few scouts his toriq had sent were unable to locate them.

Please tell your pendragon that we thank her for her consideration. Aidan dipped his head. *We will look forward to the opportunity to visit and rebuild peace with your toriq.*

Lorcan bowed his head in return. *Rest well in the meantime, friend. There will be little time for sleep once negotiations begin.*

May Zorya be with you, Aidan said.

And you as well.

Aidan and Falcon left, taking flight into the sky and heading north. He waited a few minutes before opening communications. *What does he mean there will be little rest?*

Falcon let out a mental chuckle. *You've never attended treaty negotiations between toriqan before, have you?*

No. What should I expect? Throm had given him minimal guidance on the matter, likely testing his ability to handle such a difficult task without the pendragon's help.

Ceremonies, contests of strength and prowess, and bountiful feasts. It is custom for the host of the event to include a variety of festivities before negotiations begin. To do otherwise would mean they expect the talks to fail. Falcon glanced over at him. *You will be exhausted afterward, but it will be great fun for your inner beast.*

You do realize you'll be joining me for this as well, don't you? Aidan pointed out.

The older dragon flapped his wings hard, surging ahead. *I wouldn't miss it for all the clan's gold and jewels.*

The thunderstorm slowed their travels midway to the fortress, but Aidan and Falcon managed to return home a couple of hours before the midnight meal. It was full dark outside, and thick clouds concealed the moon's light. They landed near the gates where torches burned, breaking through the darkness.

Did you see the crowd near the standing stones? Falcon asked.

He referred to the clan's mystical stones around the other side of the fortress, just beyond the walls. There were seventeen dark gray blocks in all, set in a wide circle. Their power was most often used by the healer to repair grievous injuries. With so many clansmen there now, something dire must have happened.

Aidan looked at the two gate guards who stood in human form, holding spears in their right hands. They would have to know something. *What has happened?*

"Our captain was found with his throat cut in the east bathhouse," the one on the left answered, speaking aloud with a pained expression on his face. He could have communicated telepathically in human form, but it took more concentration. "Nanoq was found near death and immediately taken to the healing stones."

The image of the captain being attacked in such a brutal way twisted Aidan's gut. He could only pray to Zorya that Nanoq survived the assault. The shifter was a good man who Aidan had always respected—most of the toriq did. He did not want to think his last memory of the captain would be that night Zoran assaulted and threatened Nanoq upstairs. That was not the way to remember such a fine warrior. But could it have been Aidan's eldest brother who did it?

Do you have any idea who attacked him? Falcon asked.

The guard shook his head. "No one saw anything."

Aidan and Falcon exchanged glances and took off in flight, heading around the fortress to where the standing stones were located. They landed in the open field nearby and shifted into their human forms before joining the crowd of onlookers. The pendragon was already there. Throm's face was red and steam puffed from his nostrils as he paced near the stones.

The clan healer, a wizened old man, came out and pulled the pendragon aside. They did not speak aloud, but by the expressions on their faces, they were communicating by telepathic means. This went on for several minutes before they turned to face the crowd.

The healer cleared his throat, and everyone quieted to listen to him speak. "Nanoq did not survive. I am afraid his throat was cut too deeply, and I could not heal him in time before he bled out."

Aidan's chest tightened. Dragons died all the time in battle, but not like this. Not while sitting in their bath, surrounded by the protection of the fortress walls and their clansmen. The very thought of a coward sneaking in to take the honorable shifter's life when he was most vulnerable made Aidan sick.

Murmurs ran through the crowd around him and one woman screamed—Nanoq's mother. Her mate pulled her close, anguish reflecting in his eyes as well. The healer did not allow anyone inside the circle of stones while he worked, so the captain's parents had been required to wait outside the same as everyone else. They'd lost those final precious moments with their son.

The mother pushed away her mate and marched toward the pendragon. "I demand justice!" she said, tears streaking down her cheeks as she shook her fist. "Whoever did this must be punished!"

Throm took her by the shoulders. "I vow the killer will be found."

Nanoq's father nodded at the pendragon. "We expect no less."

The captain's parents met with the healer next, no doubt to discuss the burial ceremony. According to toriq custom, it would have to take place within the next twenty-four hours. The family would decide whether it was private or if guests were allowed attend, but first, the healer would clean and wrap the body. He took great pride in ensuring the families would not have to perform that burden themselves. For all that shifters were fierce, they took death very hard.

Throm ran his gaze across the assembled crowd until it caught on Phoebe. He beckoned her forward, waiting until she stood in front of him. "Your new task is to find the killer before the Bitkal. Do not fail me."

"I will not," she said fiercely and bowed her head.

Aidan's sister would have a little over one week to manage it, but from past experience, he knew if the killer wasn't found by then, it was unlikely it would ever happen. It was rare for new evidence to turn up after that. For Nanoq's sake, Aidan hoped she succeeded. He wanted the bastard who did this captured and executed.

Phoebe turned toward the crowd and spoke, her voice loud and authoritative, "I want to speak to everyone who has been in or near the east bathhouse tonight, and anyone who saw the Captain of the Guard today. Meet me in the great hall in one hour." She marched through the crowd, heading straight for Aidan and Falcon. "You two, come with me."

Since she didn't stop, they hurried after her as she stormed toward the fortress gates.

Aidan quickly came alongside his sister. "What is it you need?"

"You and Falcon just returned from your trip, correct?" she asked.

"Yes," he confirmed.

She stopped and turned around. "Then at this time you two are the only ones I can rule out as suspects. I need you to help me identify the scents in the bathhouse and search for any evidence."

Aidan lifted a brow. "You do realize a hundred or more people may have been in there today, don't you?"

The only reason Nanoq had been caught alone was that, as the Captain of the Guard, he had a one hour block of time in the bath house in the evenings. It was a privilege of his position, which everyone knew about. Dragons loved baths, but few had the luxury of washing alone. They had always used communal baths to save on water resources.

"Which is why I need your help." Phoebe glanced over at the standing stones. "Three sets of eyes are better than one, and I'll be damned if anyone thinks our family had anything to do with Nanoq's death, so I'm going to make certain I find the actual killer."

Aidan gave her a confused look. "Why would they suspect us?"

"Ruari was seen in the keep earlier this evening, acting suspicious. Someone saw him slip away with Ember—who is linked to countless crimes, though there isn't enough evidence to try her yet. No one has any idea where Zoran has been since this afternoon. You and I are the only ones with solid alibis." She sighed. "Everyone knows this is a time when potential candidates for the Bitkal are most likely to turn up dead—usually killed by their competition."

Aidan found it rather interesting that Phoebe had been keeping watch over their brother. Did she have spies on Ruari as well?

"I overheard Zoran and Nanoq speaking in private the other day," Aidan admitted. "Our eldest brother was taunting the captain and telling him that he should not try to become pendragon."

Phoebe let out a frustrated noise. "Oh, that's just great."

Falcon spoke up, "Though I do not trust Zoran, I'm not certain slitting a man's throat in the bathhouse is his style. He seems more likely to challenge a person openly instead."

"Perhaps," Aidan snorted. "But I'd like to know where Ember has been since her meeting with Ruari."

"I'll look into it," Phoebe said. Her eyes rounded as she saw something behind Aidan and Falcon. "Look!"

They turned and caught sight of Zoran in his dragon form, landing nearby with a large sack hanging from his mouth. He dropped it and shifted to human form. As soon as the flames died down, Zoran grabbed the sack and headed in their direction. There was a look of complete smugness in his expression. Aidan noted the crowd near the standing stones watching his arrival as well.

Zoran stopped about a dozen paces away and gazed around to make certain he held everyone's attention. Then he opened the bag and pulled a green dragon head from it. Aidan had no doubt whose body the head belonged to or which clan.

"This," Zoran called out, twisting the head around with its still-open red eyes for everyone to see, "is the head of Blayze—eldest son of the Shadowan pendragon."

Phoebe stiffened. "Well, that rules out Zoran as a suspect."

"And he has completed our father's task," Aidan added grimly.

15

AIDAN

Aidan hefted a heavy set of chains up, letting Bailey get a good look at them. "Do you trust me?"

"With those?" She eyed him warily. "What are you going to do with them?"

"You see that large tree over there?" Aidan nodded across the field at the largest one nearby.

She glanced that way. "Yeah."

"I'm going to chain you to it so you can't get free while I'm in my dragon form."

Aidan was resorting to rather drastic measures, but he didn't have much of a choice. The way Bailey had reacted to seeing him as a dragon last time proved they needed to work harder on her gaining control. His visit with his uncle in the library had also confirmed it.

He purposely woke up earlier than usual today—before noon and the rest of the toriq arose—just for this reason. It was the only time Aidan could spare.

At most, he had two hours before he had to return to the fortress and resume helping his sister with her investigation.

They hadn't found any evidence at the bathhouse—there were too many scents to narrow down a suspect—but Phoebe had gotten a few potential clues after questioning the witnesses last night. She wanted his assistance following up on them today. It wasn't really his job, but the death of the Captain of the Guard was serious. Nanoq had been a good man, and he had not deserved to die that way. Aidan wanted the killer caught as much as anyone.

"Okay," Bailey said, expelling a breath. "Let's do it."

Aidan raised a quizzical brow. "Truly? I'd expected more resistance from you."

"I'll do whatever it takes if it helps me get control and…I trust you." She met his gaze and he could see the truth of her words in her eyes. "Right now, I'm too dangerous, and I don't want to risk hurting you or anyone else."

He'd half thought she'd punch him in the face for suggesting chains and tell him to go hell—which he still needed to ask what that meant. Instead, she appeared more desperate than him to do this. Aidan glanced back at the house and gestured for Donar to join them. He'd thought it best to talk to Bailey in private before bringing his cousin into it.

"What's *he* going to be doing?" Bailey asked, giving Aidan an accusing glare. She didn't care for Donar all that much, nor he for her. Perhaps someday they would work out their differences, but Aidan doubted it would be today.

"Donar will help talk you through the process while I'm in dragon form. He will also act as a safeguard on the minor chance you manage to break free." Aidan didn't think it would happen, and they'd locked all the weapons away already, but it was better to be safe than sorry.

Bailey cast Donar a skeptical look, then turned to Aidan. "Why can't you talk to me instead?"

"When he is in dragon form, you don't hesitate to attack, but I've noted some hesitation when you're around me. I want to build on that before trying it again with my cousin," Aidan said.

"And she's more likely to break those chains if it's me," Donar added with a hint of annoyance. "For once, I'd like to come out of this unscathed."

For their last two attempts with Bailey, she had managed to injure Donar with whatever objects she'd found on the ground. Aidan had learned to clear away all nearby sticks and rocks, but she could always become more creative. He studied the ground now to be certain nothing could be converted into an effective weapon. There wasn't anything except dirt and grass.

Bailey gave Donar an apologetic look. "I'm sorry, if that means anything."

His cousin stiffened. "Learn to control yourself and that will mean more."

"Sit against the tree," Aidan ordered Bailey, not wanting to waste any more precious time with talk.

She did as instructed, staring straight ahead as he began wrapping the chains around her chest and stomach. He trusted his cousin with his life, but he could not stand the idea of Donar being the one to bind Bailey. Aidan had asked her to do this, and he'd ensure the chains were tight without restricting her ability to breathe. It was the least he could do. No other dragon slayer would ever allow a shape-shifter such liberties or care to learn control.

"How do you feel," he asked, going around for the third loop.

Bailey flexed her hands where they rested near her thighs. "Fine."

Aidan studied her face. She wasn't quite meeting his eyes, as if something was bothering her. "Are you certain?"

"The chains are fine, but there's something else." Guilt flooded her features. "This is probably not the best time to tell you, but...uh, I attacked a red dragon yesterday."

"What?" Donar stomped forward.

Aidan closed his eyes. This was why Bailey had been so cooperative today. "Did you kill him...or her?"

"No," she said, shaking her head. "I wounded him a couple of times, but somehow I managed to get control of myself long enough to tell him to go, and he flew off."

He was relieved she'd managed such a feat without anyone there to help. Aidan hadn't thought she was at a stage where she could gain control—even for a few seconds—while facing an unknown dragon. That gave him some degree of hope.

"Did you confront him here?" he asked. It had suddenly dawned on him that his lair may have been compromised, though he had not caught Ruari's scent anywhere.

"No." A fresh look of guilt washed over her face. "I was out hunting pure dragons in town."

Aidan took the chain and wrapped it around her a final time—a little tighter than before—and locked it into place. "After I told you it was too dangerous right now?"

"I was in Thamaran territory. I figured that would be okay and I sure as heck didn't expect to see one of your guys that far out," she defended.

"Thamaran territory?" Aidan glanced at his cousin. "Any idea why one of our people would be there?"

Donar rubbed his chin. "None. Zoran's task was with the Shadowan, and Phoebe has been busy inside the fortress. I haven't heard of any scouting parties going that way, which leaves..."

"Ruari," Aidan finished. He redirected his attention to Bailey. "Did he have silver tips on his scales?"

She mulled it over for a moment. "Yeah, he did."

"Whatever task father set before Ruari, it must have something to do with the Thamaran." Then something else occurred to him. "When did this take place?"

Bailey frowned. "Mid-afternoon, I think. When I came across him, there was a group of human men who'd caught him with hooks and ropes. They were shooting at him too, so he was already wounded when

I arrived. I found out later they thought he was one of the dragons taking children, and they had set up a trap to catch him."

Donar laughed heartily. "I wish I'd been there to see that."

"What happened after you arrived?" Aidan asked.

"Well, I started tossing the men out of the way because he had a hook in his mouth. I figured it could loosen at any time with the way he was struggling, and then he could have burned the humans to death. Well, the hook did come out, and he burned one man to death before I cut him with my sword."

Aidan bowed his head. This was not good at all. "He must have figured out you were a dragon slayer then."

"Between my outfit and lack of burning to death in his flames…" Bailey sighed. "Yeah, he had to have known or figured it out later."

"How badly injured was he?"

Bailey's brows drew together. "He ripped a hook out of his jaws, so I imagine that was pretty bad. There was another one stuck in his hip that was still in him when he flew away. I slashed him a couple of times in the chest, and his belly was bleeding where the human guys shot him. It was all he could do to get up in the air before I lost control."

"He has a low tolerance for pain," Aidan said, shaking his head. "With those sorts of injuries, I am surprised he got away at all."

Donar glared at Aidan. "This plan of yours is getting more dangerous by the second."

"There is no turning back," Aidan reminded him. "And he will never tell anyone what happened because of the shame it would bring him."

"Fine, then let's get this started." Donar gestured at Bailey. "I don't want to be away from the fortress any longer than necessary if Ruari knows someone is helping a dragon slayer."

"Calm yourself, cousin, or you will be of no use here." If Donar didn't compose himself, Bailey would only feed off of his mood once they started.

"Of course, you are right." His cousin took a few deep breaths and relaxed his shoulders. "I'm good now."

Aidan walked halfway down the field to shift into his dragon form. The first step was to get Bailey used to seeing him at a distance since she seemed to have more control that way. Then he'd come closer as time passed. He prayed to Zorya that the control she had managed with Ruari would be even greater with him.

As he shifted, the scents in the air became stronger. Aidan could identify which animals had crossed the field in the past few days, and he caught the faint scent of Kayla from when she'd recently visited. Bailey had told him when he arrived today that the visit went well. She'd had a rather pleased expression on her face when she said it, which worried him. What had that human girl told the slayer? He would have to remember to ask Kayla when he found the spare time.

For now, Aidan had to ignore those things and focus on Bailey. Even across the field, he could see her brown eyes watching him. She didn't move, which was a good sign. Her legs were splayed out in front of her, and her forearms rested against her sides. He'd purposely left some of her lower half free so he could better gauge her mood. The more she kicked and struggled, the greater the indication she'd lost control.

When she didn't twitch, he took several slow paces forward. Bailey stiffened a degree, but nothing more. He overheard Donar speaking to her.

"Breathe, relax," his cousin said in a soothing tone.

"I'm trying," she replied through gritted teeth, then closed her eyes.

"No, open them," Donar ordered. "You've got to be able to do this while seeing the dragon."

Aidan did his best to appear harmless, but it wasn't easy while wearing the beast's skin. His inner dragon wanted to run to her. Not to attack, but to assure her he would not harm her. The beast did not understand why she could not accept his true form. Some of the hurt he felt affected Aidan, though he tried not to let it get to him.

He took a few more steps forward. Bailey's knees jerked, and he stopped. She was breathing hard now and a solitary tear ran down her cheek. The beast wanted to go lick it away.

"It's getting harder," she said, straining and looking away.

"Think of Aidan as a man," Donar suggested. "Remember the way he looks when he's not a dragon.

Shape-shifters are people too, with hopes and dreams just like humans."

Bailey expelled a breath and turned her gaze back to Aidan, studying him. She stared into his eyes as if she could truly see past the beast to the heart of him. He began to lumber forward again, encouraged with each step when she didn't change expressions. There was a softness in her gaze that made him wonder what she thought about to keep herself calm. He would have paid dearly to find out.

Aidan didn't stop until his nose almost came level with her legs. She lifted a hand with wonder—just barely able to touch his face—that reminded him of the first time they'd been this close prior to her becoming a dragon slayer. It had been in this very field, though without her chained. It was only after her rite of passage that her full instincts had taken over and she couldn't control herself anymore.

A smile stretched across Donar's lips. "She has done it."

I believe your instruction helped, cousin. I thank you for that.

Donar gave him a short nod, then his gaze shot to the sky and he cursed. "Shifitt, we've got incoming."

Aidan swung his body around. Just above the tree line, a red dragon with a silver underbelly approached—Phoebe. How in Zorya's name had his sister found them? And what was she doing out here anyway when they weren't due to meet for almost two hours?

Bailey began to thrash, kicking her foot into Aidan's jaw. The glancing pain jolted him into action.

He leaped forward and put himself between the slayer and his sister. Somehow, he had to protect the women from each other, or this could end very badly.

Keep Bailey as still as you can, Aidan ordered Donar. *I'll handle Phoebe.*

"I'll try, but I think she's going to rip these chains off," his cousin said, leaning down to grip the slayer's shoulders.

"Let me go, you filthy fucking dragon," she screamed, her eyes wild.

She had lost any semblance of the calm woman who'd been sitting there moments before. It pained Aidan to see her like that. Though he knew she didn't mean those words, it still bothered him to hear her say them.

What is the meaning of this? Phoebe demanded, landing half a dozen paces away. She stalked forward, her yellow eyes zooming in on Bailey. *Why is that girl chained and what is wrong with her?*

Aidan sidestepped to hide the slayer from her view. *You must leave—now!*

I will not. Phoebe tilted her head around, trying to get a better view.

This is not your business. Go now and I'll explain later, Aidan said. Bailey was screaming obscenities behind him, and Donar was cursing as he tried to keep her still.

Why is she wearing warrior clothes? Phoebe sniffed. *She is not one of us.*

A loud snap sounded as one of the links in the chains broke.

Look out! Donar yelled.

Aidan twisted around in time to see Bailey punch his cousin in the face, sending him flying several paces away. The slayer's gaze turned to Phoebe next, and she charged. Aidan leaped toward her, tackling the slayer to the ground with his bulky form.

Bailey pounded into his chest. "Dammit, let me go!"

He noted her blows were not nearly as painful as they could have been. Despite everything, Bailey was holding back. Her instincts might will her to attack and kill dragons, but she was somehow fighting that need when it came to him. Each strike felt lighter than the last until she finally grabbed his forearms and clutched them like a lifeline.

"Aidan," she said, voice desperate. "I can't..."

Calm yourself, little one. You are safe.

It was the beast who spoke to her telepathically and nuzzled Bailey's neck. He'd taken over the moment he saw her anguish. Aidan was nothing more than a passenger watching the dragon attempt to pacify the slayer. The beast recognized how hard she fought to get control of herself and wanted to help.

Bailey blinked up at him. "Did you just speak into my head?"

There are many secrets in this world you've yet to learn, it replied, surprising Aidan. He hadn't known such a thing was possible, though he'd always known his inner dragon had wisdom far beyond what it revealed. It was said a shape-shifter's inner beast had a direct connection with Zorya herself. This was just the first time it had ever taken over and revealed itself to anyone else. Such a thing was rare, even among shifter mates.

"It's the dragon talking, isn't it?" Bailey said, awed. Her fingers came up to graze the side of his head, and the dragon made a rumbling sound similar to that of a cat's purr.

It is me, little one, it replied. *I am here—always.*

Aidan was beginning to get jealous of his own beast. The dragon was the one who found a way to reach Bailey, and she seemed to respond to it far better than him. Internally, he told it to give him control again. The beast was reluctant and nuzzled Bailey's neck one last time before retreating.

Dear Zorya, Phoebe said, stomping closer. *She's not burning, and it appears your beast is talking to her. What is going on?*

Bailey twisted underneath him and screamed at his sister. "You!"

She attempted to scramble out from underneath Aidan. He had no choice except to put all of his weight on top of her. The slayer was small and slippery with sweat from the heat of his body, making it that much more difficult to keep her down.

Stop, he ordered Phoebe. *Bailey has gained some measure of control, but she does not know you. If you insist on staying here, you must shift to human form.*

His sister gave him a furious look. *You've got a lot of explaining to do, brother.*

To Aidan's relief, she let the flames consume her and began to shift. He waited until she was finished before doing the same. Bailey quieted underneath him. After finishing the process, he looked down at her, checking for any signs she might still attack.

The slayer glanced at Phoebe for a long moment and then at Aidan. There was a stricken expression on her face. "Who is she?"

He cocked his head. "Does it matter?"

"Is she…is she your girlfriend or something?"

Phoebe let out an ironic laugh. "Oh, this is even more complicated than I thought. Aidan, you've really gotten yourself into a mess this time."

He stood and helped Bailey to her feet. "It is not what you think."

"Then what is it?" Phoebe asked, lifting a brow.

"She did not know she was a slayer until we arrived here. I have been training her to fight the pure dragons and helping her gain control so she won't attack us," he explained, knowing that would not be nearly enough to satisfy his sister.

"Oh, right, of course," she said sarcastically. "Because that was obviously the thing to do. Brother, we do not work with dragon slayers!"

Donar came to stand next to Aidan. "It is not as bad as it seems. Bailey is getting rather good at slaying and helping clear the way for our toriq to take over this region. She also has a connection with the local humans that we lack and will need if we are to have peace."

"If you believe that, you are as crazy as my brother." Phoebe shook her head. "The clan is going to banish you both when they find out."

Aidan crossed his arms. "You are not going to tell them."

"I don't know what I'm going to do. If anyone finds out I knew and didn't say anything, I could be punished right along with you." She paced in front of them, muttering expletives under her breath in the dragon language. At least she'd had the sense to speak English in front of Bailey—that had to be a good sign.

"I've kept many secrets for you. Such as that dragon from the Faegud clan who you were…" Aidan began.

Phoebe spun around and pointed a finger at him. "Don't you dare say another word!"

He smiled smugly. When relations between their clan and the Faegud broke off all those years ago, Phoebe had continued seeing one of their members in secret. It wasn't until the Faegud lost the section of territory where their borders met that she was forced to end the relationship. He suspected it was part of the reason she had never seriously courted another male since then. She could very well still be pining for him, and it would also explain why she monitored Aidan's task so closely.

"Very well, but I only point out I'm not the first to see the so-called enemy in secret. If you would give Bailey a chance, you would see having her on our side is to our advantage."

Phoebe gave Aidan a rueful look. "You do realize the irony of this when I'm in charge of the next Judgments Day? I should be the one punishing you for this crime."

"And?" He shrugged. "You've got more important matters to attend. Such as a murder investigation."

"A murder?" Bailey interrupted.

"One of our members was killed last night. I'm helping my sister find out who did it," Aidan explained, glancing down at her.

"Speaking of which," Phoebe said, keeping her eyes on him and avoiding looking at the slayer. "I found the garrote used to kill Nanoq. It was in a gutter near the bathhouse with his blood still on it. The reason I came to find you was I wanted you to take a look at it and see if you had any idea who it might have belonged to."

"A garrote?" Donar frowned. "What a strange choice of weapon."

Aidan agreed. It was something a human might use, but shifters usually preferred swords and daggers. Aidan couldn't imagine any of the humans murdering the Captain of the Guard—he was always quick to protect them—which made the case even stranger. It had to have been a shifter, but who? He still didn't rule out Ruari as a suspect, but if his brother had been injured as much as Bailey had described, it was doubtful he would have been up for killing anyone until he recovered. That would take at least a couple of days, not hours.

"I'll take a look at it," Aidan said, then gestured at Bailey. "But my continued assistance depends upon you keeping the secret about her."

Phoebe stepped closer and studied the slayer. "How many dragons have you killed?"

"Eight," Bailey answered, lifting her chin.

That was two more than Aidan knew about. She'd said she had been hunting them when she ran into Ruari. He could only guess that she found two of the pure dragons after that and took her aggression out on them. Aidan didn't like the idea of her fighting on her own now without him, but the fact she could spoke to her increasing skills. She would need to continue training on new weapons, especially the crossbow since she needed something with range. But before long, he expected she would become a formidable warrior any dragon would fear.

Phoebe's brows drew together. "When was your first kill?"

Bailey glanced at Aidan, then back at his sister. "About five weeks ago."

"The first was Mirrikh," Aidan added.

Phoebe's expression registered surprise. "If she could take him down...yes, she might be useful after all." She directed her attention to Aidan. "But we must be careful that our toriq does not find out. Maybe someday when the right time comes, but not now."

"Agreed."

"And you." She pointed her finger at Bailey. "Hurt my brother and I will kill you."

The slayer narrowed her eyes. "In case you missed it, I have no intention of hurting him—no matter what."

"Good. Keep it that way."

Aidan had allowed this conversation to go on long enough. "Phoebe, why don't you return to the fortress? I'll finish up here and meet you in an hour."

It would give him time to question the slayer further about the attack on his brother.

Phoebe ran her gaze across Aidan, Donar, and Bailey. "Fine, but do not take too long. We have more important things to do."

His sister stalked away, smart enough to shift out of sight of the slayer.

16

AIDAN

Aidan found his sister in the pendragon's office, sitting at Throm's massive stone desk. Phoebe appeared like a child studying her lessons behind it as she stared at piles of notes with a frustrated expression on her face. While she had been doing that, Aidan had taken the murder weapon—now washed clean—to each of the five weapons makers they had in the fortress to see if any of them recognized the work. None of them knew its origins. The garrote had not been protected by the second dragon fire, and its material wasn't even suited for it. Without the alloy being at least fifty percent zaphiriam, the slim metal string could not hold up to the hardening process.

"The answer is here somewhere," Phoebe said, brows drawing together. "I am just not seeing it."

Aidan settled in a seat across from her and set the garrote on the desk. "Unfortunately, the murderer killed the man who usually does these investigations."

Nanoq hadn't only been an excellent Captain of the Guard, but also quite good at solving crimes. Few of them went unsolved under his watch, and he had always given Throm a roster of wrongdoers for Judgments Day. He would have made a fine pendragon if he had been given the chance to compete. Regardless, the clan would feel the loss of him for a long time to come. The regular guard was still deciding who to elect to take Nanoq's place. Throm had given them a week to settle it among themselves.

"I still don't understand why they used this," Phoebe said, picking up the garrote. "What did you learn?"

Aidan gave her the details of what he'd discovered, or rather not discovered, finishing with a shrug. "It must have come from outside the fortress."

Phoebe scowled. "That is going to be almost impossible to trace."

"What about the witnesses? Did you learn anything useful from them?" Aidan had sat through a few of the questionings yesterday evening, but he'd also had to meet with his father and prepare for the treaty negotiations with the Faegud.

Phoebe set the garrote down and picked up several pieces of parchment. "As you know, it was Nanoq's private time at the bathhouse, so no one else was there. Only two people entered when his time was up—one of them being a human servant who had come to do a cleaning. The other one, a male shifter, found him first and called for help. Every other witness worked or shopped near there, but they all said they didn't see anyone else enter."

"Do they know how long Nanoq lay there before he was found?" Aidan asked.

His sister nodded. "The healer believes it must have been between thirty to forty minutes. Even for a shifter, it's a miracle he survived that long."

"The captain was tough, but I'm surprised the killer didn't finish him off." That had been bothering him. Why stop at cutting his neck part way if you mean for the person to die?

"I have my suspicions about that." Phoebe sat back in her seat. "I wasn't allowed to see his body before the burial ceremony, but the healer informed me Nanoq did fight back. His knuckles were red, and the cut in his neck was ragged like he'd jerked around a lot. Maybe he injured his attacker and scared them off."

"Why didn't they let you examine the body?" She might have been able to get a scent off of it.

Phoebe's lips thinned. "Our father decreed that no one should see the captain's corpse because Nanoq was too honorable to be remembered like that."

It was too late to do anything about it now. The burial ceremony had been last night with most of the Taugud in attendance. Nanoq's body had been fully shrouded in black, and he'd been placed in the fortress cemetery. While pure dragons disintegrated to dust within forty-eight hours, shifters returned to human form—if they weren't in that state already—and decomposed the same as any normal person or animal would upon death.

"Let me see the list of who was near the bath house." Aidan reached out his hand.

His sister gave him several sheets of parchment, and he began skimming her report. She listed each name, their activities an hour before and after the attack, and anything they saw. Most of the people were low-born or human and had absolutely no reason to kill Nanoq.

"Do you think Ruari could have done it? Somehow gotten in and out without anyone seeing him?" Phoebe asked, worrying her lower lip. "I don't think he'd be above doing such a thing, though I hope he didn't."

Aidan paused his perusal. "As much as I hate to admit this, I don't think our brother was in any shape to be murdering that night."

"What do you mean?" she asked.

He set the parchment down. "A group of humans over in Thamaran territory attacked Ruari earlier that day. They shot many of their bullets into his belly."

"How could you possibly know that?" She gave him an incredulous look. "Our brother hasn't mentioned it to anyone, and I doubt he ever would, considering the embarrassment it would cause him."

If it wasn't pertinent to her investigation, he might not have told her, but she needed to know why Ruari was likely innocent. "Bailey told me. The humans had tethered him with hooks and ropes when she arrived. Her initial instincts forced her to push the humans out of the way and attack our brother, but she managed to gain control long enough to let him escape. She said he was badly wounded when he flew off."

Phoebe's jaw dropped. "How bad?"

"I think Bailey only struck him twice with her sword, but she said the hooks did some damage to his hip and mouth and the bullets struck his belly. She saw a lot of blood on him, but if he could manage to return home that afternoon when our witnesses placed him in the market, then the wounds couldn't have been too grave."

She let out an exasperated breath. "This is why you shouldn't have gotten involved with the slayer. If Ruari ever finds out you're working with the one who attacked him, you could be executed for it."

"I'm aware."

It was one of the reasons Aidan was careful about when he met Bailey and for how long. The less time they spent together, the lower the chance they might get caught. If she wasn't so important to his plans— ones that no one other than Kade and Donar knew about—he might have had to abandon her. Of course, his inner dragon might have had something to say about that. He growled every time Aidan even thought about it—not that cutting ties with Bailey would be much easier for him. He'd grown to care for the slayer more than he liked to admit.

"Brother." Phoebe stood and leaned her hands on the desk, giving him a heavy look. "I don't warn you of the danger to give you a hard time. I do so because I care for you, and I do not want to lose you. Before you were born, all I had was Zoran and Ruari. Both of them could be quite cruel until I grew strong enough to fight back and even then they never took me very seriously. Then you came. You were so different than them—bright, compassionate, and full of curiosity."

She paused and took a shuddering breath. "Please don't do anything that would result in me being left behind alone with them."

Aidan was surprised to hear his sister's heartfelt plea. With shifters, they rarely allowed their emotions to show outwardly. It was considered a sign of weakness. The only exception was when they truly trusted someone enough to give them that sort of power.

"I love you too, sister." He reached out and cupped her cheek. "But I assure you I do nothing that is not for the greater good of the clan. One day, you will understand why the slayer is so important to me."

She squeezed his hand before lowering it. "And your dragon? It is almost unheard of for the beast to communicate with a human, much less a slayer."

"Almost?" Aidan lifted a brow. "I didn't know it was possible at all outside of mates."

"When I was younger and hiding from our older brothers, I used to spend hours reading scrolls from the archives. I found a few mentions of it happening, but those instances occurred before we were banished to Kederrawien."

"Could you find those scrolls now?" There could be all manner of helpful information in them. Aidan had perused a few of the ancient texts before, but there were thousands stored in the oldest corner of the library. He'd lacked the patience to go through them all.

She shook her head. "That was nearly two and half centuries ago. I can't begin to remember which shelf they were even on now."

"I know you're busy now, but if you find some spare time, please look. Anything that might help me with Bailey could be useful." Aidan would also have to find a chance to sneak back there again sometime soon to speak with his uncle. Kade would want to know about the latest developments, and perhaps he could find some information to help as well.

Phoebe lifted her chin. "You're going to owe me for that kind of favor. I find dust a lot more irritating now than I did in my youth—not to mention attempting to read scrawled, faded print."

"Anything you need," he promised.

"Then help me figure out where this garrote came from before you return to the Faegud tomorrow," she said.

Aidan smiled. He had already formed a plan before coming to her office.

"Just a moment." He walked to the door and opened it, beckoning Kayla inside. While he couldn't give away all his secrets to Phoebe, he trusted her with this one as well.

The teenage girl came in, keeping her head ducked low. She always did that with shifters except for Aidan and Donar. Her slight form appeared so subservient and inconsequential that she almost blended with the stone walls.

"Phoebe, meet Kayla. This is one of the human servants who lives in the fortress," Aidan said, gesturing at the girl.

His sister's brows furrowed. "Why have you brought her here?"

"Kayla, look at me," he ordered, waiting until the teenager lifted her head. "You are aware of the murder of the Captain of the Guard, yes?"

"Y-y-yes," she answered. It was the oddest thing, but if she wasn't comfortable with someone it could reduce her to stuttering. He couldn't figure out how she could be so brave except when around strangers.

"You are safe." Aidan put a hand on her shoulder where her tunic protected her skin. "My sister would never harm you. We just need you to answer a few questions to help with the investigation."

Kayla swallowed. "Yeah, okay."

"Were you anywhere near the bathhouse two days ago?" Aidan asked.

She jerked her chin. "About…an hour or so before the captain was killed."

Aidan had noticed Kayla was not on Phoebe's list. Either no one noticed her there, or it was too long prior to the murder to consider. "Did you see anything strange or out of place?"

Kayla shot him a worried look. "Um."

"You're scaring the poor girl to death," Phoebe said. She smiled at the teenager and softened her voice. "It is okay. I promise that nothing you say here will get you into trouble."

"Trust my sister as you would me."

"Alright." Kayla straightened, some of her confidence returning. "After I followed Ruari back to his room in the fortress where I'm fairly certain he stayed the rest of the night, I came back out and walked around the market. About two hours before the murder, I caught Ember walking down the main thoroughfare. Then she turned and headed toward the east end of the keep. She kept looking back so I couldn't get too close and then she disappeared. It wasn't too far from the bath house. I waited around for a while, but she never showed back up."

Aidan turned to Phoebe. "Ember isn't on the list, is she?"

"No." His sister frowned.

Kayla gasped. "Wait. What if she had a way of getting out of there without anyone seeing her?"

"What do you mean?" Aidan and Phoebe had walked the whole area. There were no back alleys or places to hide. At least, not without help from the shopkeepers who were unlikely to assist anyone that would kill the captain.

"You know that tunnel underneath the keep?" Kayla waited until they nodded. "Well, there are small passageways down there that I've never figured out where they go. Maybe one of them comes up near the bathhouse."

Phoebe's eyes widened, and she looked at Aidan. "Where have you been hiding this girl and why am I just noticing her? She's brilliant."

"I know." He crossed his arms. "And you better consider yourself lucky I'm pointing her out to you now."

His sister paced the room, her energy renewed. "I've got to check those tunnels and Father will know

more about them. If we can somehow tie Ember to the
murder this way, we will have it solved. There's just the
matter of the garrote that I still can't figure out. Where
could she have gotten one from that was strong enough
to cut a shifter's neck?"

Kayla spoke up. "There is a place in the city where
she could have gotten it."

"What place?" Aidan asked.

The teenager's gaze dipped down. "Um, well, I
haven't been there, but I've heard about it. There's a
sorcerer who has claimed downtown Norman for himself. He's really picky about who can get near the area,
and he has a protection spell blocking anyone—including dragons—who he wants to keep out. A couple of
people here tried to get in and check it out, but something made them turn back. They barely remembered
they'd even gone there."

"You should take the garrote to one of our sorcerers and see if it has been spelled," Aidan suggested.

Phoebe glanced over at the murder weapon on the
desk. "I'll do that."

"Do you guys have any more questions for me?"
Kayla glanced between them both. "I don't want to
stay here too long, or people might figure out I'm
helping."

Aidan's sister cast him an accusing look. "You use
that young girl as a spy, don't you?"

"I volunteered after he saved my life," Kayla said,
defending him.

Aidan shrugged. "It was Donar's idea."

Phoebe sighed and shook her head. "I should have known he was involved in this as well."

"So can I go?" Kayla asked.

"Yes." Phoebe waved a hand.

The teenager escaped out the door without a backward glance.

"I must take my leave as well," Aidan said after the door closed. "There is much to do before I depart for my trip tomorrow."

Phoebe's shoulders slumped. Their father's task weighed just as heavily on her as the one Throm had given Aidan, perhaps more so. She had to find the murderer of one of the toriq's most popular shifters, or she would lose all respect. He, on the other hand, had cultivated an image of not being all that responsible. They wouldn't think much if Aidan failed. It had been to prevent his brothers from seeing him as a threat, but he could not keep up that charade much longer.

His sister came over and embraced him. "Thank you, Aidan. I'm not certain I could have gotten this far without you. Our brothers would hold it against me if they knew how much you've helped with my task."

He stepped away and gave her a serious look. "The mark of a wise leader is not in how much they can do on their own, but whether or not they know when to ask for help. I'd follow you anywhere, sister."

"I appreciate that." She bowed her head.

17

BAILEY

An eight-foot long green tail swung toward me. Before I could leap out of the way, it struck my thighs and sent me feet over head into the air. I crashed into the asphalt on my butt, sending zings of pain through my tailbone. Damn, that hurt. Aidan had taught me to watch out for tails, but this dragon fought scrappier than any other one I'd encountered. The beast would have made a great cage fighter, if dragons were into that sort of thing.

The creature didn't waste any time coming at me again. It lumbered across the parking lot, limping on its right front leg where I'd stabbed its toes a couple of minutes ago. At this point, I wasn't picky about where I injured him as long as it slowed the damn beast down.

I leaped to my feet and raised my sword. *Come on, you little bastard, get ready to taste my blade.*

It let out a bellow of fire that enveloped me like a steamy cloud. I couldn't see a damn thing except orange and red, but I had noted the beast's trajectory. Aiming my sword to swing at about hip height, I struck out. The blade connected with solid flesh. When the flames died down a second later, I found my sword stuck sideways in the dragon's open mouth. It chomped down, but the zaphiriam blade was too strong to break. I jerked back and forth on my weapon, slicing through the beast's cheeks. It growled and spat the sword out. I felt like someone who'd just won a tug of war contest with their dog—except this was a much more gruesome version of the game, and there was a dragon involved instead.

The beast tried to back away, blood pouring from its mouth, but I was on it in an instant. I sliced and stabbed as fast as my body could move until my opponent was too weak to fight any longer. The slayer part of me wanted to draw the creature's death out, but the human in me found that idea repulsive. Working with Aidan to improve my control was paying off. With each successive battle I fought, I enhanced my ability to focus and not let my rage take over. The killing instinct was definitely still there, but it didn't rule me quite as much as before.

I kicked the beast onto its side and brought the sword down, sinking the blade through tough flesh and into its heart. The dragon's body twitched a few times before expelling its final breath. I pulled the sword back out, wiped it against the grass to get the worst of the blood off, and sheathed it.

Conrad ran up, holding the container the sorcerer had given me. He also had a zaphiriam knife so he could help me shave the scales off.

"Damn, girl. That fight was some crazy shit," he said, grinning at me. "I was sitting there watching and wishing there was a bookie nearby cuz I was about to put my money on the dragon. He almost had you there for a second."

I gave him a deadpan look. "Your concern and support are very touching."

He bumped his shoulder into mine. "Just calling it like I see it."

Despite the gravity of what we were doing, I appreciated that Conrad kept some levity. This job would be so much more difficult without it. There were times when I feared fighting fire-breathing beasts every day would eventually take too much of a toll, and I would lose part of myself in the process. So far, I had managed to keep the slayer side of me separate from the compassionate woman who wanted to help people. Conrad was a big help with that.

"Next time, you can fight the dragon," I said, holding out my sword.

"Nah, that's your gig." He pressed a finger to the flat of the blade and pushed it away. "I'll stick with the crossbow—which you suck at."

He was never going to let that go. "Thanks for the reminder."

We kneeled down and worked fast to get as many scales as we could. The dragon had roared several times during the battle, and it was only a matter of time before one of its clan members showed up. I wanted to be long gone before that happened.

"So what was she like?" Conrad asked, dumping a handful of scales into the container.

"Who?" I asked.

He scowled at me. "Aidan's sister."

Oh, right. I'd just been telling him about my meeting with her when we ran into the latest dragon. He'd gotten most of the story, but not all of it.

"She looks badass and a little scary, but I get the feeling she's pretty cool with the people she likes." I sighed. "I'm not sure I'll ever fit in that category."

Conrad made a clucking sound with his tongue. "Wish I could have been there to meet her."

"Trust me. It's better you weren't there. When she figured out what I was, and that Aidan had been working with me, things got pretty intense."

Conrad dumped another handful of scales into the seemingly bottomless container. He was faster than me at peeling them off, which had all sorts of frightening implications. I made a mental note to keep paring knives away from him.

"You should let me stay with you," he said, his tone turning serious. "It's all work and no play back at the neighborhood. Folks there are driving me crazy. It's all 'Winter is coming' like this is an episode of Game of Thrones or some shit. Oklahoma don't get that damn cold. I'll be surprised if we have more than three days of snow on the ground."

"Sorry." I shook my head. "Aidan specifically told me you could visit but not stay. He was very adamant about that."

"That jackass," Conrad cursed.

"He's just trying to be…" I paused when the hairs on the back of my neck rose.

I looked up and found a man in jeans and a plaid shirt standing across the street staring at us. He looked like he was probably in his fifties with long black hair, leathery skin, and dark eyes that pierced right into me—even from two hundred feet away. I was fairly certain he was Native American, though I couldn't be certain at our current distance.

"You see that guy?" I asked.

Conrad followed my line of sight. "Yeah. Is he just standing there watching us?"

"Looks like it."

He frowned. "Should we do anything? Talk to him or something?"

"I don't know. He's kind of creeping me out."

Occasionally, we had observers when I was fighting dragons, but something about this felt different. Maybe it was the way the man stood there with no expression on his face—like he'd made it his mission to weigh and judge me, but for what? I didn't think the Olympics would be holding an event for dragon slaying anytime soon.

"Maybe us shaving these scales is what attracted his attention," Conrad suggested, dumping a few more into the container. "Don't see folks doing this very often—or at all."

It was a good thing the beast's heat lowered considerably after it died, or Conrad wouldn't have been able to help. I was working as fast as I could, but not fast enough. The container appeared to only be about a quarter full. I estimated it would take at least ten dragons to get all we needed.

"I don't think it's the scales that have interested the guy. He's staring right at me. Maybe I should talk to him and see what he wants," I said, standing and wiping my hands. We'd just about shaved all the easy to remove scales off anyway and needed to do a final cleanup.

"You sure he ain't planning to kill you or something?" Conrad asked.

I gave him an incredulous look. "After he just watched me slay a dragon?"

"Maybe he's a shifter," he suggested.

"No." I shook my head. "His eyes are dark. Shapeshifters have yellow eyes."

"It's your call." He grabbed the container holding the scales. "I'll go get the lighter fluid and torch this place."

"Good idea."

Conrad headed for my truck. The dragon body wouldn't burn, but we'd come up with a new method of hiding our scents from any others who might come across the scene. A little lighter fluid and some flames wiped out any other odors. Of course, we could only do that when I killed the dragon on pavement since starting a fire on grass would create new problems.

The beast's flames might extinguish the moment they stopped blowing them, but human-made fire still followed normal rules—except that it didn't burn me, either.

I started walking toward the street with the full intent to confront the man. He lifted a brow, then turned his gaze upward to the sky. I followed the direction he looked and caught sight of a dragon heading our way. Dammit, talking to him would have to wait. I pulled out my sword from its scabbard and glanced one last time at the man. He nodded curtly, as if he'd just given me his permission. This was just getting weirder and weirder by the second.

Turning around, I was relieved to find Conrad had caught sight of the dragon and had taken cover behind a nearby dumpster. It wouldn't protect him from fire, but as long as the creature didn't see him, it was unlikely to attack in that direction. Plus, I would be keeping the beast busy.

I came to stand next to the dead carcass, knowing that would be all the incentive the creature needed to focus its attention on me. It let out a strangled cry and dove downward toward the parking lot where I stood. I gripped my sword, watching the dragon's descent and planning my opening strike. The more I fought them, the more I learned their attack strategies and could anticipate their moves. This one flew low, but it didn't slow enough to land. Predicting how it would attack, I didn't move.

Keep coming, keep coming, I silently willed it.

The red rage in its eyes grew as it closed the gap between us. The flames came next, engulfing me. At the last moment, I dropped to my knees, counted to two, and thrust my sword upward. It struck against ribs, grinding against them. Dammit, I should have counted to three—too late for that now. Gripping the blade handle tightly, I let the tip drag along the dragon's torso and cut into its scales as it continued its flight over me. Outstretched claws from its hind feet skimmed my head, pulling at my hair. I winced as it yanked a few strands out and cut scratches into my scalp. Then the shadow of the beast passed.

I swung around, still in a crouched position, and used my free hand to brush my loosened hair from my face. It had grown just past my shoulders in the last few months—a good hair stylist was hard to find these days, and I had no idea what became of mine—so I usually kept it in a short ponytail or braid when battling dragons.

The beast twisted about midair and landed twenty feet across the parking lot, positioning itself to charge me. From the corner of my eye, I caught the strange man still watching me from across the street. He hadn't budged an inch or bothered to take cover. Did he have no sense of self-preservation?

I refocused my attention on the dragon, whose belly dripped blood onto the ground. Allowing my slayer instincts to drive me, I sprinted toward it. The beast pivoted and sent its tail flying. I leaped upward and tucked in my knees, getting about five feet of air beneath me. The tail arced high and came within an inch of my boots. After it passed, I landed with a jarring thud. Ignoring the pain in my knees, I ran up the creature's back. It bucked like a bronco at a rodeo. I fell and clutched its shoulders to keep from sliding off, then I straddled the enraged beast, hugging its body with my thighs. Who knew helping my stepfather break horses would come in handy for fighting dragons?

Though it wasn't easy to attack from that position, I'd recently discovered the spaces between a dragon's ribs were farther apart near its shoulders. I aimed for the spot I'd found once before and stuck down with the sword tip. The blade sunk straight through the flesh and into the body.

The dragon made a gurgling sound as I twisted and worked my way toward its heart. I could only guess I hit one of its lungs. The beast pushed up with its hind legs, attempting to buck me off again. I tucked the tips of my boots under the curve of its belly and held on tightly to my sword. Wrenching the hilt, I cut back and forth, searching for the heart. It was somewhere close, dammit. When the dragon jerked and groaned underneath me, I knew I'd grazed the organ.

I pushed the hilt forward, forcing the tip in the direction I guessed the heart to be. The beast slumped flat on the ground and expelled a croaking breath. I was certain I had gotten it, but I waited a full minute to be sure it was dead before removing my blade and climbing off. Some of the smart ones faked their deaths to lull me into a false sense of security. I'd nearly lost my leg the first time that happened a few weeks ago. If Aidan hadn't been there to push me out of the way, I would have been in trouble. I kind of missed him not being around to help anymore.

Conrad raced up to me, holding the gas can. "You're gonna be sore after that ride!"

"No kidding," I said, sighing.

My body was much stronger than before I'd become a slayer, but fighting battles every day without a break still took its toll. These last two dragons had worn me out even more than most, and I just wanted to be finished.

He reached out toward my head, pulling a few locks of hair away. "Duck lower next time."

"I was as low as I could get without lying flat," I defended. It was always easier to judge a person's fighting tactics while watching from the sidelines.

"Yeah, yeah. Excuses." His gaze ran past my shoulder, and he frowned. "That guy is gone."

"What?" I spun on my heels. "He was still there halfway through the battle."

"Guess he'd seen enough."

Well, that was weird. Maybe I'd given him enough entertainment for one day. "Let's get the scales off this one and get out of here. I want to leave before any more dragons show up."

We kneeled down and got to work.

18

AIDAN

"Is that it?" Donar asked, referring to the river up ahead as he flew on Aidan's right.

"Yes," he replied.

Donar had not been this far south yet, but he'd been anticipating the trip ever since Aidan had asked him to come along. He knew there would be competitions, which fueled his enthusiasm. They had always avoided contests of strength and prowess at the fortress so as to avoid drawing notice from Aidan's brothers. Even when they did battle in duels, they usually held back. This was a chance for his cousin to let loose and give the competitions all he had.

"Lorcan and two other dragons are waiting for us on the ground," Falcon said, having the sharpest vision of them all. He flew on the left, dipping and rising to coast with the wind.

In essence, Falcon and Donar were there to act as advisors and guards for Aidan—not that the three of them had any chance of making it out alive if things didn't go well. They would be severely outnumbered among the Faegud, but they didn't believe it would be an issue anyway. Dragon honor dictated that emissaries to treaty negotiations could not be harmed beyond the usual activities required of such processes. The only reason it was even a consideration was because the last Faegud pendragon had not been one to follow such long-standing traditions.

Aidan led the way, soaring down low as they approached the river. Lorcan and his two clan members watched them from the opposite bank. They did not move until Aidan landed and approached them on foot. Despite the jovialness of their last meeting, there was tension in the air this time. One never knew how a treaty negotiation would go, and the first day set the tone for the rest—however long that might be.

It is good to see you again, Lorcan acknowledged, dipping his head. *I trust the weather was favorable for your journey?*

This was the most formal Aidan had ever seen his friend. *Indeed, Zorya favors us this day.*

Lorcan turned to Donar. *You have grown large over the years. It is clear you take after our side, cousin.*

Aidan would have said the use of "cousin" was stretching it a bit. Lorcan and Donar shared a great-great-grandfather who had died over fifteen hundred years ago. It had been because of that alliance that their two clans had maintained good relations for as long as they did, but Aidan considered it ancient history after all that time.

I believe it is my mother's cooking that has helped me the most, Donar replied.

Lorcan laughed, unable to hold the formality any longer. *Ah, I'm glad to hear she is well and still watching after you.*

Nagging would be more like it. Donar let out a puff of steam.

Then you shall have a break from her for the next few days. Lorcan turned to address Aidan. *Shall we journey to the jakhal?*

Of course. Aidan bowed his head.

The Faegud dragons led the way. It was a sign of respect that they allowed Aidan and his two escorts to follow them from behind where they were most vulnerable. They flew south for more than an hour, passing over human towns with no signs of life, before reaching a valley. On one side, there were half a dozen houses with people walking around. Aidan was surprised to see humans within the Faegud jakhal. This was the first he'd heard of any pure dragon clan—or mostly pure dragon—welcoming people among them.

Our last pendragon captured them as slaves, Lorcan explained, noting Aidan's confusion. *When my mother took over a few weeks ago, she offered them the choice to stay and be treated fairly or to go. We lost most of them right away, but some have returned in recent days as they discovered the difficulties of life outside. Here, they are fed and protected. Out there, they must fend for themselves, which they found more difficult than expected.*

It is the same with us, Aidan acknowledged, though he left out the part that they'd never made their humans slaves. They were always free to come and go as long as they obeyed clan law and labored for their food and shelter.

My mother believes if we are to survive and flourish in this world, then we must find a way to live with the humans— not against them, Lorcan continued. *I agree with her.*

Then you are both wise, Falcon said, entering their open conversation.

Their group landed in an open area near the center where the pendragon and half a dozen others waited. Formations of rocks formed all around them in intricate designs, denoting the Faegud clan's worship of the dragon goddess, Zorya. Each formation had a meaning. Some were for protection, some for strength, and a few were for fertility. Aidan's clan had a few smaller ones at the rear of the keep near the gardens, but the Faegud had designed theirs on a much grander scale.

Just beyond the rock formations, there were numerous gaping holes in the ground—more than wide enough for the dragons to enter. Aidan recalled from his youth that the Faegud chose to build their homes beneath the earth in a vast network of tunnels. That made it much more difficult for the enemy to attack them. While dirt was one of the only things that would not burn in dragon flames, it could be heated enough to seal the tunnel walls so they would not crumble or leak moisture. It was not a bad way to live, if you liked your home cramped and perpetually dark.

Lorcan led the way, marching them up to the pendragon. Aidan could sense countless eyes on him. Not just from those assembled around the rock formations, but also across the valley. His party was likely the first outsiders to visit the Faegud in a very long time.

Mother, may I present Aidan of Taugud, son of Throm, Lorcan said. After giving a brief bow, he stepped to the side with his two companions doing the same.

It is a pleasure to see you once again. Aidan dipped his head.

Hildegard stomped forward, blowing a breath of steam from her snout. She had the same burnt-orange coloring as her son, but her scales were tinged with black at the tips. The pendragon appeared every bit as large as Aidan remembered and just as intimidating. He held his ground as she moved into his space and sniffed at him. It was not something shifters did with each other, but pure dragons were very keen on scenting those around them.

You are not the weak, little whelp I remember, she said, circling around to his tail. Even that got a sniff before she moved on. Aidan had not suffered this sort of inspection in so long that it was all he could do not to thwack her with his tail spikes for offending him. She knew very well he would not enjoy it and only did so to test him.

Hildegard returned to the front to face him. *I would have preferred your father present himself to us instead,*

197

but you will do. Far better than those annoying brothers of yours. I would have sent them wingless into the chasm rather than speak to them.

That was a comforting thought.

It is generous of you to welcome my brethren and me into your home. I thank you. Aidan bowed his head again.

Your manners have improved as well. She narrowed her orange eyes. *Tell me, what is it you hope to accomplish with this treaty?*

Aidan had spoken at length with his father about what he should and shouldn't say to the Faegud. Which concessions he could allow and which he could not. Throm had done much more to prepare him this time than his last trip, but there were always variables that could not be anticipated. Aidan could only hope he handled himself well on his first diplomatic mission. This was his last chance to do something for his father, and he did not wish to let him down.

He met the pendragon's gaze. *I hope to create an alliance that will promote peace between our clans, mutual defense from our enemies, and open trade.*

Hildegard was quiet for a long moment, and it seemed as if everyone held their breath. *I wish the same with one addition. Many in our clan have lost the ability to shift to human form—to our detriment now that we have returned to Earth. It is my hope that we may come to an agreement that allows for matings between our toriqan. Ones that will produce strong offspring and give fresh blood to both our clans.*

Aidan stiffened. He and his father had foreseen many things, but not this. The Faegud had made it clear for centuries they detested the human form and wanted little to do with it, except in rare cases where a task could not be completed as a dragon. He had never dreamed they would ask for matings.

Aidan could hardly run back to the pendragon now to ask for guidance, and it would be up to him to decide how to handle it. This was the only the first day, though. All he needed to do was acknowledge her point and leave the negotiations for later.

Your wishes will be taken into consideration, he said, keeping his tone neutral.

Excellent, the pendragon purred. *Then it is time for us to feast. Our humans have prepared an excellent meal worthy of you and your clansmen. I am certain you will enjoy it.*

Aidan braced himself. As he recalled, Hildegard's idea of a good meal involved a freshly killed animal that must be eaten in its entirety. There was not much preparation involved with that, so he hoped that she had allowed the humans to put a little more effort into it.

As the pendragon led the way through the stone formations and toward the open field near the houses, Lorcan moved closer to him. *Do not worry. She has been fixated on human methods of doing things since we returned. The food will be cooked.*

Aidan wished that made him feel better, but he had no idea what Hildegard's idea of "cooked" meant. He supposed he would have to find out the hard way and hope his belly survived the ordeal.

19

Conrad and I sat parked under a tree, waiting to see if any solitary dragons showed up. Two days before, we had noticed one circling this part of northwest Norman, which consisted of a mixture of businesses and homes. We'd decided to check it out next time we went hunting. With fuel being in short supply, this was the way to go if we wanted our prey to come to us.

It had been an hour since we settled in the back of the truck, and as of yet there was no sign of the dragon, but it was still early afternoon. It could show up at any time. The weather had cooled to the low 80s, so at least we weren't sweating while we waited. It was the boredom and need to get this over with that got to us more than anything. I estimated I only needed to kill two or three more dragons to finish filling the container Javier gave me. My body was exhausted from fighting day after day, minor injuries that weren't healing fast enough plagued me, and I just wanted to be done. Whatever energy I had left needed to go into rescuing the children.

"Hey, I'm going to go make use of the bushes," Conrad said, grabbing a package of tissues and jumping from the back of the truck.

We were parked next to a small woodsy area that gave us cover from anything flying overhead, and a place to use the bathroom—for lack of a less graphic term—during the stakeout. Nothing was worse than being stuck in a place where you couldn't get a little privacy. We might be friends, but we had our limits on how much we shared.

"Not going to take a magazine?" I asked.

"Oh, right." Conrad opened the passenger door to the truck and pulled an old Playboy out. He waved it at me. "Don't know what I'd do without you."

"Get drafted into helping Norma with her gardens, most likely."

He shuddered. "I *do not* do farming."

"But that straw hat she makes you wear looks so cute on you," I teased.

Conrad scowled at me. "It's not funny."

"Oh, yes, it is."

After a moment of hesitation where I was certain he would argue further, Conrad stomped off into the woods. Ah well, he must have had to go badly. I'd just have to wait until he came back to harass him some more.

I leaned back to scan the skies. A minute later, movement drew my attention. I sat up and gripped my sword. A lone dragon swooped downward in a way I recognized as their intent to land somewhere. I followed its trajectory to a three-story office building down the street. That was strange. Most of the time, I could tell if a large structure was being used as a den, but nothing about that one stood out. Most of the windows were still intact, and none of the walls had holes in them.

I leaped out of the truck and edged closer to the woods to hiss at Conrad. "Hey, a dragon is coming in to land on that office building. I'm gonna go take it out."

"What?" The bushes where he crouched behind rustled. "Bailey, wait…"

The creature touched down on the roof and disappeared. There was nothing Conrad could do to help me at this point, so I ran. All my senses focused on reaching the beast and attacking it. My instincts were trying to take over again. I forced myself to think and strategize as I moved up the street. Yes, I needed its scales, but I did not have to let the rage take over.

Reaching the building, I jerked the entrance door open and ripped it partway off its hinges. There was no time to bother trying to pick the lock. I scanned the dim interior, finding myself in a lobby. Nobody had raided the place or disturbed it yet. With a dragon lair on the roof, that probably discouraged human visitors. I spotted an emergency stairwell over to the right and raced toward the door. After opening it, I allowed myself a few seconds to memorize the layout before heading inside. The door shut behind me with a soft click, wrapping me in complete darkness. I raced up the stairs, going round and round until I hit the top floor.

My breath slowed as my fingers sought out and found the door handle. In my other hand, I gripped my sword. There was a rustling sound coming from the other side. The dragon was moving about, doing something. I was almost certain it hadn't noticed my arrival.

Pressing the latch, I pulled the door open a crack and peeked through it. My eyes rounded. There was a giant nest in the middle of the floor, built from a bunch of tree branches—some of them a little scorched. The dragon lay on top, its back to me, with two eggs peeking from underneath it. The beast had burned a hole in the far side of the roof just big enough for it to fly inside, but the ceiling over the nest was still intact—most likely to provide some shelter from the elements. This was the first time I'd seen a setup like this, but I didn't run into too many nests, so it was hard to make a comparison.

I took in every inch of the open floor, using precious seconds to plan my strategy. The nest took up half the space. A scent that was something like rot and decay assailed my nose, drawing my attention to the far side. The dragon had stockpiled food there. A heap of dead animals were stacked on top of each other, some half-eaten. Bile rose up my throat. I dragged my gaze away and spotted a second exposed stairwell that led to the roof. If I had to make a quick exit for some reason, that's where I would do it. On the run up the street, I had spotted a ladder on the side of the building I could use to get down.

The dragon made a rumbling noise that sounded suspiciously like a snore. Good, maybe it had fallen asleep. Still, it had the advantage where it lay in its nest. Fighting from the lower position was never a good thing, and especially not if you fought a parent protecting their unborn children. I'd have to try drawing it away from there if I had any chance of winning. This wasn't going to be the same as the last time I ran into a situation like this. I was a full slayer now. I had over a dozen kills under my belt, and no humans nearby to protect.

Inching my way inside, I raced for the open area beyond the nest and near the other stairwell. The dragon spun around, spotting me in an instant with angry red eyes. Guess she wasn't sleeping very heavily. The beast roared and flapped its wings, but it didn't blow any flames. I had guessed it wouldn't. The creature wouldn't want to risk destroying its home and the eggs it protected.

Racing around the other side of the room, I lifted my sword. "Come on, big girl. Leave your nest and come to me."

The dragon narrowed its eyes and took a single step, placing its foot at the edge. It wavered there. To leave or not to leave, I could almost hear it asking itself that question.

"I don't care about your eggs. You're the one I'm after," I told it. Not that I expected the beast to be reassured by that, but I had to do something to draw it out.

A few seconds passed, and it crawled halfway out of the nest. That was a start. Every part of me wanted to leap forward and attack, but I forced myself to be patient. Let the beast come to me where we could level the playing field. Actually, I'd have the advantage since I could move around a lot easier than the eight-foot-tall dragon could in the open room. The roof wasn't very far above its head.

It finally crawled out of the nest, though it didn't go more than half a dozen feet beyond that. Unable to wait any longer, I went on the attack. I lifted my sword and sent it arcing down on the beast's head. The dragon sidestepped at the last moment, so the tip only grazed its neck. I swung the blade back around, thrusting straight at the creature this time. My sword struck in its shoulder, the point finding a space between scales to dig deep. The beast roared and spun around, its massive body on a collision course with my much smaller one.

I backpedaled until the edge of the tail came around and then made a short hop, landing on my feet right after it passed. As soon as its head came close, I swung my blade into its nose. The sight of blood dripping from its snout sent my heart pumping. Now was the time to finish this. I hacked into the dragon's face, striking it repeatedly in the cheeks, eyes, and anywhere else I could hit. It made screeching noises and attempted to swipe at me, but its arms were too short to reach. The beast took a step back and then another. I gave no quarter, following it.

A roar sounded from somewhere above. I cast a quick glance up at the opening and cursed. A second green dragon had arrived, and it looked pissed. Crap. I had to finish the first one off quick, or I was in trouble. The beast in front of me answered the roar of its mate. I shoved my sword straight down its throat, cutting off the sound. I twisted and pushed the blade until it came out the back of its neck.

Before I could finish pulling the sword all the way out, the dragon swung its head with enough force to send me flying through the air. I landed with a thud and rolled a few feet, losing grip on my blade handle. It took a brief second to realize the beast had managed to toss me onto the roof. I pushed onto my hands and knees, coming eye to eye with the second green dragon.

Oh, shit.

Where was my sword? Where was my damn sword? I didn't dare take my eyes off the hulking creature as my right hand scraped across the roof until it came into contact with the blade. Oh, thank God. I got hold of the handle and pulled it up just as the beast's jaws opened wide. With steam billowing from its mouth, it struck. I dove sideways and its razor-sharp teeth latched onto my left shoulder. A scream tore through me.

I thrust the blade into its chest, but the tip stuck in the dragon's ribs. The beast wouldn't let me go. Its

needle-like teeth ripped through my skin and muscles, bringing tears to my eyes. It hurt so badly I almost couldn't think. With my good arm, I kept digging
the blade deeper, attempting to cut a way through the
bones. The dragon growled and shook its head. My
body swung around like a rag doll as I got slammed
against the roof again and again.

The sword came loose. This was too close quarters
for me to get a good angle. In a brief moment of clarity, I let go of the hilt, letting it clatter to the ground
and reached for a small knife I had sheathed at my hip.
I yanked it out and stabbed the dragon in the eye. It
roared, letting go of my shoulder. The pain intensified
as my blood began running freely and my vision swam
like I was seeing everything underwater, but I had to
find a way to survive. I could not die this way. While the
dragon pawed at its face, I grabbed my sword again and
began inching backward. A bit of space—that was all I
needed. I kept blinking until my vision cleared enough
to make out more than rough shapes.

A moment later, the beast got the knife out of its
eye and charged forward, intent on running me over.
I waited a heartbeat to lift my blade, thrusting upward into the middle of its vulnerable underside. The
dragon stopped, its face hovering over me and dripping drops of blood onto my cheeks. The heat of them
seared my skin.

We stared at each other—beast to slayer—and I
had no mercy to give. I twisted the sword and waited
for the beast's body to jerk as I found its heart. Using

the last vestiges of my strength, I yanked the blade and cut through the organ. The dragon heaved, and I scrambled to get out from underneath him just before he fell flat on the rooftop.

It took several moments to catch my breath. I was in so much pain, and my vision was becoming blurry again. A big part of me wanted to pass out right there and sleep for the next decade, but an insistent voice kept calling my name.

"Bailey!"

I frowned and searched around, not seeing any human shapes.

"Bailey!" Conrad yelled. This time, his voice came out louder, and I figured out he was shouting at me from somewhere far below.

Muttering a string of curses, I crawled to the edge of the rooftop. "What?"

Even from this distance, I could see his eyes round in horror. "Behind you!"

I scrambled around. The first dragon I'd fought had made its way to the roof. Pieces of its flesh hung from where I'd hacked away at its face, but that didn't stop it from stalking toward me. As soon as our gazes met, it charged. I rose to my feet and began to run, but the beast was faster. It collided into me, sending me flying off the roof. The air zoomed past me, and I kicked my arms and legs as if that would somehow slow my descent.

I hit the ground with the force of a freight train, and everything went dark. There was no telling how much time had passed, but it couldn't have been long because when I came to, I still lay on the grassy patch where I'd landed, attempting to draw in a breath. The thin blades were cool beneath my fingertips. My head felt like it had been split open and I couldn't see anything. I was also fairly certain my right leg was broken. It was numb and sitting at an odd angle from the left one.

Another minute passed before I managed to get a full breath, and my hearing returned at the same time. I listened, expecting the dragon to come finish me off. Instead, the sounds of fighting came from nearby, maybe twenty feet or so? Surely Conrad hadn't decided to take the beast on himself? I attempted to rise, and a fresh wave of pain washed over me. My stomach lurched and bile burned my throat.

"Thank God, Bailey, you're alive," Conrad said, the sounds of his footsteps hurrying toward me.

"What?" I barely managed to gurgle out. I'd bitten my tongue during my fall and blood filled my mouth.

"Don't talk." He put a hand on my semi-good shoulder. "That strange guy we saw the other day is taking care of the dragon, so you don't have to worry about it."

I wished I could see Conrad—and watch the strange man fight. I should have known he was a dragon slayer. There had been something about him, and that confidence he'd shown even when one of the beasts approached.

"Oh, man," Conrad said, his voice filled with awe. "He just took that dragon's head clean off."

A moment later a thick, deep voice spoke, "We must get her to a healer."

"Danae," I choked out.

"Yeah, we know someone," Conrad answered the man.

"Get her truck and bring it here. I will handle her."

"Uh..." Conrad hesitated.

My mind was growing foggy. It was all I could to hang on and listen to what they said.

"Go!" the man ordered, clearly used to being obeyed.

The next thing I knew, my body was being lifted and cradled in strong arms. Though he took care to avoid the worst of my injuries, a fresh wave of pain still ran through me. He didn't move, giving me time to adjust. After a moment, I caught the fresh scent of him. There was a bit of spiciness in it, but mostly it just smelled comforting.

"Hold on, girl. You'll be okay soon enough."

Something in his voice eased me. I let the blackness take over and passed out.

20

BAILEY

The grind of an old generator starting up woke me. I opened my eyes and took in my surroundings, relieved to find them familiar. There was the full-size bed I lay on with a blue quilt covering me. Off to my right, there was an antique dresser with a lamp on top of it, and to the left, there was a single window. Someone had pulled the curtain closed so that only a crack of sunlight filtered into the room. Conrad sat on a wooden chair in the corner. He had fallen asleep with his dark arms hugged around himself, and his head leaning against the wall.

I couldn't recall how I got here, but the pain running through numerous parts of my body triggered a few memories. There was the fight with the two dragons, and the fall from the office building roof. How had I survived that? Then there was the strange man—the one I'd seen once before. He'd finished that last dragon off and then picked me up in his arms. That was all I could remember, though. Everything beyond that was a blank.

I took stock of my injuries and the soreness I still felt. My head was surprisingly fine, considering I was rather certain I'd busted it up pretty good during the fight and when I fell. On the other hand, my shoulder, ribs, and leg only felt marginally better than before. They'd hardly healed at all.

How much time had passed since the battle? At least a few hours, considering someone had stripped off my camrium warrior outfit and put me in a tank and shorts. They'd also cleaned me up and splinted my leg. It better have been a woman who did the job, or a man was going to be dying soon—right after I could walk again and find my sword.

Taking one of the spare pillows next to me, I used my good arm to throw it at Conrad and croaked at him. "Hey!"

He leaped to his feet and looked around with a wild-eyed gaze before his eyes settled on me. "Oh, hey girl. It's about time you woke up. I was beginning to think you were gonna sleep until next week."

"How long was I out?" I asked.

He checked his watch. "About eighteen hours. It's almost ten in the morning now."

I should have known it was morning, or Earl wouldn't have started up the generator. "Who patched me up?"

"Danae and Trish. They kicked the rest of us out until they were done." Conrad came and sat on the corner of the bed. "How you feelin'?"

"Like I got my butt kicked by dragons and thrown off a roof."

He shook his head. "Ain't it sad that you aren't exaggeratin'? If it was still possible to get a life insurance policy, you'd straight up be out of luck."

"No kidding." I pulled myself up to a sitting position, wincing as a shot of pain went up my shoulder and another down my leg. "Alright, tell me everything that happened after I fell."

Guilt flooded his features. "That was my fault. If I hadn't been calling your name, you wouldn't have come close to the edge and that dragon wouldn't have knocked you off. I've been feeling like shit about that."

It wasn't entirely his fault. I knew that other dragon wasn't dead and should have been watching for it. I'd just been too injured to think straight. Of course, it never hurt to give the guy a hard time for a bit before telling him that. "Do I get to smack you for it once I'm healed?"

Conrad's shoulders slumped. "Twice if you want."

Damn. He really was feeling bad. "Don't worry about it. You couldn't have known I hadn't finished the other one off yet."

"Then why did you come to the edge?" he asked.

"I'd wounded it pretty badly and left it on the floor below while I fought the other one. It was nowhere to be seen so…" I paused and sighed. "Anyway, I was already in a lot of pain and out of my mind. This past week has worn me out."

"No, shit. You should get a medal or something. I kept wondering how you were finding the energy to keep fightin' so much." He gave me a concerned look. "Even you gotta rest sometime, Bailey."

I dropped my gaze and fiddled with a loose thread on the quilt. "Every day I'm not out hunting is one more those kids have to suffer with that dragon. Even now, all I'm thinking about is that because I got hurt we lost the scales for two of them and I'll have to make up for that. By the time I can fight again…"

I swallowed, unable to finish. Because I hadn't been paying close enough attention, I'd messed up. Those kids were depending on me, even if they didn't know it, and I had to save them. No matter what it took and no matter the toll on my body.

Conrad gave me a reproachful look. "You ain't no good to them if you're dead—or me, for that matter. If you leave me with these crazy people," he paused and swept his arm out, "I'm gonna seriously be pissed."

He had a point, even if I didn't want to admit it. "Well, I'm fine so it's all good."

"Your f—," he stopped and cleared his throat. "That dragon slayer guy said you've got to rest for a few days before you can fight again. He told us you had too many injuries, and it will take longer than usual to heal even with Danae's help."

I frowned and felt the back of my head. The spot where I was sure my skull had been cracked only had a drying scab over it now. "Did she fix this?"

"Yeah. You were bleeding too much, and we worried if she didn't take care of that first you might die. She was exhausted afterward, though, so she couldn't do much else last night." He glanced at my shoulder and my leg. "Trish was the one who bandaged and splinted you."

I sighed, imagining how freaked out my best friend must have been seeing me like that. It probably wasn't good for her pregnancy, either. Then another thought occurred to me. "I shouldn't be here. What if the dragons figure it out and attack?"

The last thing I wanted was for everyone in the neighborhood to die because of me.

"Don't worry about that. Wayne's got it covered until you're back on your feet," he said, patting my good leg.

"Wayne?"

"Oh, that's your...rescuer. He's the one who killed that other dragon and helped me get you back here." An odd expression came over his face. "I told him the problem, and he promised to keep an eye out for the next couple of days."

"Did he happen to say where he came from?" I asked.

Conrad shrugged. "You should probably talk to Earl about that. He spent a lot more time talking to Wayne than I did."

There was something very weird about all this. Like Conrad was holding something back, and I couldn't figure out why. Sure, it was kind of strange for this Wayne guy to suddenly show up, but why act all funny about it?

"Oh, by the way," Conrad said, perking up as he changed the subject. "I did go back and get those scales, so you don't have to worry about that. I'm thinking we only need one more dragon, and you'll be done."

A weight lifted from my chest, though my ribs would have said otherwise. Damn, the longer I was awake, the more they hurt. I must have cracked or broken at least half of them the way the pain radiated out through most of my chest.

"You went back there by yourself?"

Conrad nodded. "The dragons who lived there were dead, and Justin came with me as backup. He was itchin' to get out, and he knew it was for a good cause. The guy ain't half bad when he's not barking orders at everyone."

"You should have seen him before the dragons came. He was even nice back then," I said, remembering the good old days. It seemed like ages ago now.

A knock sounded at the door.

"Come in," I said.

Trish poked her head inside, gave me a once-over and entered. Danae followed on her heels, checking me out as well. The two women came to hover over me like clucking hens. I was sorely tempted to pull the blanket over my head and pretend I couldn't see the monsters. Conrad had the good sense to scurry back to his corner where they might not pay as much attention to him.

"I brought you some soup," Trish said, holding up a bowl.

"Put it on the dresser," Danae ordered. "She can eat after I'm done with her."

"You've come to torture me, haven't you?" I asked, giving her a terrified look. "I swear I don't know anything."

This was the way with us—always trying to keep the mood light.

Danae wagged a finger at me. "That's the problem. If you'd known better, you wouldn't have gotten into a fight with two dragons, and you wouldn't be falling off of three-story roofs. From what I understand, the only reason you're not dead is because you're...well, what you are."

"You try killing dragons every day and see how easy you find it," I defended, though we both knew Danae was only giving me a hard time because she worried about me.

Trish cleared her throat. "I, uh, cleaned up your clothes, but the shoulder strap was torn so you might ask Aidan if there's a way to repair it. Any of the thread I use will just get burned."

I gave her a grateful look—both for taking care of my stuff and changing the subject. "Thanks. I've got a spare set back at his lair, so I'll just have to hope I don't get into a battle between here and there. It sucks fighting naked."

That had happened once, and no matter the danger involved, it was still awkward. Donar and Aidan had been there to get the full unobstructed view of me before taking over the fight so I could get away. That incident had occurred before I was a full slayer when I'd accidentally run into a different dragon nest with eggs. Considering what happened the day before, there seemed to be a pattern forming. I was going to have to be more careful and start avoiding nests altogether.

"Okay," Danae said, looking me up and down. "You've got a few choices. I can either heal your shoulder, your ribs, or your leg. It's up to you. Verena says my powers will get stronger with time, but for now, I can't heal more than one injury a day. Apparently, even being able to do that much this early into my training is supposedly impressive."

I mulled it over. "Do my leg. That way at least I won't need help getting to the outhouse."

"I figured that's what you'd say." She gestured at Trish. "Give me some space."

Not knowing what to expect since I was unconscious the last time she worked on me, I braced myself. Danae leaned down, putting her hands over my right leg. A sort of warmth infused into my muscles. She knitted her brows, and my skin began to tingle, then she stopped.

"What?" I asked.

"That was just me examining you—sort of like an X-ray." She beckoned at Conrad. "I need you to hold her down. Her leg is broken in two places, and it's going to hurt while I set it."

Oh, damn. I took a pillow and stuffed it over my face. This was something I had experienced before when I broke an arm as a kid, and I had hoped to never go through that again. Conrad put a hand on my good shoulder and another on my hip. Though sound was muffled, I overheard Danae tell Trish something to do with my leg.

A minute later, I felt the pull as they reset my bone. Everything had been semi-numb until that point as long as I didn't move, but it was like they lit me on fire when they began to work. I tried really hard not to scream into my pillow and didn't do a very good job of it. Maybe five minutes passed, maybe an hour, but eventually they stopped.

Danae then went to work with her magic again, speeding up the healing process. That wasn't nearly as bad. I could almost feel my bones knitting back together. By the time she finished, there was almost no pain.

Conrad pulled the pillow off my head. "Alright, you weakling. She's done."

"Thanks, Danae," I rasped, wanting her to know I appreciated her efforts even if I didn't find them particularly pleasant.

"You're welcome, but I still want you to stay off of that leg until tomorrow," Danae said, her tone stern. "For the healing to take full effect, it needs time, and you can't put too much weight on it."

"Then someone is going to have to help me to the outhouse." I'd held out as long as I could, hoping I could take care of that issue myself.

"I'll help," Trish offered.

"Are you sure?" I glanced down at her tummy. It hadn't gotten any bigger, but I couldn't help picturing a baby inside there.

She rolled her eyes. "I'm pregnant—not broken."

I glanced at Danae for confirmation since I wasn't an expert at these things. She nodded.

"Alright," I agreed.

Trish kept a tight grip on me as we made our way through the house and out the back door. Since the semi-apocalypse, water was down and plumbing no longer worked. We'd been reduced to doing things the old-fashioned way. Earl built his outhouse months ago, and I'd gotten used to using it, though I dreamed of being able to flush a toilet again someday.

Hopping along to the far corner of the backyard with Trish taking some of my weight, I managed to make it there without falling flat on my face. She guided me inside but left me alone to take care of business. I finished as quickly as I could, though it took longer since every little movement hurt. Trish was ready for me when I came back out, and she even had some moistened wipes so I could clean my hands. By the time we returned, Danae and Conrad were gone.

"Where did they go?" I asked, confused.

Earl came up behind us. "I asked them to step out. We need to talk."

That didn't sound good. He had an unreadable expression on his face, but I got the sense he was about to tell me something I didn't want to hear.

"I'll check in with you later," Trish said after helping me settle back into the bed and bringing my bowl of soup to me from the dresser.

Something in her eyes told me she knew what this was about, but she didn't give away any clues. She just squeezed my hand once and left. Earl shut the door behind her and came to sit next to me on the bed.

"You should eat a little first," he said, gesturing at my soup.

"Okay." This wasn't weird or anything.

If I wasn't suddenly feeling hungry, thanks to my slayer metabolism kicking in, I might have argued. Instead, I quickly ate the whole bowl of soup, finishing it in a few minutes.

Earl took the dish away and set it back on the dresser. "Do you have any idea who the man is who brought you here yesterday evenin'?"

I shook my head. "No, should I?"

Earl pulled a pack of cigarettes out of his pocket, stared at them, and put them back. He had hoarded a ton of them, but even he knew they would eventually run out, especially if he smoked them too fast. "There's no easy way to tell you this, Bailey, but that man is your father."

My jaw dropped. "What? How can you possibly know that? How can he know?"

"Your mother already told him she was pregnant before he left," Earl paused, scratching at his beard.

223

"Well, it was more like he accidentally crossed over to the dragon dimension, so he didn't get much of a choice in the matter. When he finally came back to Oklahoma a few months ago, he ended up in Tulsa. It wasn't until about a week ago that he heard about a dragon slayer bein' here—a young woman with a description that could fit his kid."

It took me a full minute to process that. "And he knew the slayer gene was inherited."

"He did."

"That still doesn't necessarily make him my father. Aidan says there are hundreds of slayers out there— maybe a thousand or more across the world. How can he be sure I'm his daughter?" I asked.

I didn't know why the thought scared me, but maybe it was because I hadn't been expecting it. For all this time, I'd hated my father for leaving me before I was born. The thought that he might not have had a choice would mean that I'd blamed him for something out of his control.

Earl gave me a meaningful look. "You think I didn't ask those same questions? He was adamant that he could see your mother in your face and some of him too, which you do share his eyes and nose, along with that mark on your arm."

There was no point in telling him that it was just a slayer mark and didn't mean anything. "So that's all it took to convince you?"

"Of course, not." Earl appeared offended. "I called your mother and made him talk to her."

I stiffened. "You didn't."

"What else was I supposed to do?" He threw up his hands. "That was the only way to be sure the man wasn't lyin' to us."

"Did the subject of slaying dragons come up?" Admittedly, that worried me more than anything.

He nodded. "There wasn't much way around it. He refused to lie to your mother about that, though I told him you hadn't wanted to worry her."

I rubbed my face. "So he is my father?"

"No doubt about it—and you owe your mother a call. She knows you've been injured and she wants to hear for herself that you're alright." There was a note of apology in his voice. I was rather certain his talk with her was only marginally better than mine was going to be.

"So where is Wayne now and why isn't he telling me all this?" I asked.

Earl shook his head. "He's out there, watchin' for dragons, but I don't think he's ready to talk to you just yet. It's kinda awkward when a man meets his daughter for the first time after twenty-two years. Gotta come at its own pace."

"He just saved my life, Earl. It's a little late for being shy," I said.

"That's different." He gave me a pointed look. "If he let you die, he'd never get a chance to talk to you."

I leaned back against the headboard, feeling suddenly tired. "Think he'll come tomorrow?"

Earl's lips thinned. "Wayne said something about as soon as you're feelin' better again he's gotta be headin' back up to Tulsa. Ain't no one defendin' the folks up there against dragons right now, and we've got you down here. His words, not mine."

"He's not ready to face me yet," I interpreted.

"No, but he will be—in time."

"Okay," I said, not really understanding. It kind of hurt. My father had talked to Earl and my friends but not me. Did he not consider how that would make me feel?

"Just a minute." Earl stepped out of the room, returning with the sat phone a moment later. "It's time to call your mother."

"Now?"

He nodded. "Look at it this way. You can always cut the call short by telling her how injured and tired you are."

"Have you met my mother?" I asked wryly.

He started dialing and handed the phone over once he was finished. "Good luck."

"Bastard," I muttered.

My mom answered on the first ring. "Bailey?"

"Yeah, it's me."

"Do you have any idea how worried I've been about you? And I have to find out from your long-lost father that you're a dragon slayer?" She made a sound of frustration. "I don't even know where to begin!"

I was fairly certain she'd figure it out. "I'm sorry, Mom."

"You better be sorry! Grady has worked himself into a fit and he's trying to figure out a way to come get you so we can put a stop to this. You're gonna get yourself killed!"

As she continued her rant from there, I slumped in the bed. That was going to be a long conversation. I loved my mother, but she could yell for longer than anyone I knew. Hopefully, this didn't affect her heart. I'd have to figure out a way to pacify her once she stopped long enough to take a breath. Too bad I couldn't bribe her with ice cream the way I used to do.

21

AIDAN

No one ever truly appreciates their home until they are away from it. Aidan decided he'd never been more grateful to be born a Taugud than now. This morning he, Falcon, and Donar had been woken by several Faegud dragons and told they'd be participating in a tournament—one that was designed to test the speed, strength, and battle prowess of a warrior. The toriq would not begin negotiations with the Taugud until they proved their worthiness.

For the first activity, they conducted a race. It required Aidan and his companions, along with thirty-seven others, to fly up to the Red River. Once there, they were to pick up one of the blue stones waiting for them and return to the Jakhal. There were no other rules, so knocking out one's opponents, taking more than one blue stone, or any other manner of devious behavior was allowed.

For Aidan, he might have been smaller than most of the other dragons, but he was also lean and fast. Only one Faegud ever got close enough to attack him—in the early part of the race—and he found himself with a torn wing for his troubles. Aidan picked up speed after that and never looked back. As it turned out, there was a dragon ahead of him who must have broken away from the pack early, but that was the only one who'd bested him.

Falcon was attacked several times, being slower and farther behind. He beat off his opponents, picked up one of the few remaining blue stones, and managed to come in twelfth in the race. Donar had never been a particularly fast flyer. When they were growing up, he almost always came in last or very near it. By the time he reached the Red River, all the blue stones were gone except a single one that four dragons were fighting over. What Donar lacked in speed, he made up for in strength and fierceness. He wormed his way into that fight, grabbed the blue stone, and made it a good distance away before the others realized it had been taken. Aidan was rather certain Donar flew faster than he'd ever managed before in his life, barely making it back before the others closed in on him.

After the race, they were given a light meal and told to prepare for the next event—tunnel digging. This was considered an important event to the Faegud. Aidan understood that, considering their living quarters, but he didn't much care for doing it as a sport.

Shape-shifters never dug unless they were burying the body of a loved one.

For that second event, they gathered at a field approximately a ten-minute flight from the jakhal. The forty participants were each given a section of land and a direction which to dig so that there would be no crossing over each other. Aidan and his companions were told to make their tunnels go as far as possible in the two hours they were given. Whoever dug the longest one would win, but all participants would have theirs measured and ranked. He, Falcon, and Donar had given each other meaningful looks at this news. There was no way they could compete against dragons that used tunnels as a way of life, but they had to do their best if they did not want their toriq to appear weak.

Aidan had formulated a strategy for his digging before the contest began. Two hours was a long time to be doing any physical activity and to begin fast would only wear him out too soon. He'd pawed at the ground and tested the soil, waiting for the pendragon's roar to begin. It wasn't soft, and he suspected there had been no rain there in weeks.

When it was time to begin, he started slowly and methodically. Aidan wanted his opening to be just the right size for him to fit, but not so large it would create more work for him. He also sealed the walls with flames as he went so that no dirt could come down on him. During the event, there were several cave-ins from dragons rushing too much and forgetting to seal their tunnels. Each had to be dug out and disqualified from participating further.

An hour into his digging, Aidan's claws were already chipping and breaking. It was painful to keep going, especially once his feet started bleeding. Still, he did not give up and continued at a steady pace until the pendragon roared once more, ending the event.

Donar did surprisingly well, but as a stone builder he performed quite a lot of lifting and shaping of earth materials that gave him an advantage. He came in ninth out of the forty contestants who started. Falcon ranked eighteenth. With the regular strength and agility training he performed on a daily basis, he had been able to put it to good use. Aidan came in twenty-seventh out of the thirty-five who finished, but it didn't bother him much. This was not his sort of event and at least he made it to the end.

They had just returned to the jakhal for a one-hour break, and a chance to clean up before the final event of the evening. It took everything Aidan had not to limp as he made his way to the small creek that ran at the far end of the valley. He was sore, filthy, and tired. There was dirt packed in his scales that would take weeks to dig out if it weren't for his ability to shift to human form and wash it away—not that he'd have the opportunity before he went home. When Lorcan had warned him the treaty activities would be exhausting, his old friend had not been exaggerating.

Aidan glanced over at Falcon, whose head hung lower than usual. He, too, felt the strain of the day's events. The older dragon had several bite marks on his body from the race, and he had lost most of his claws from digging the tunnels.

What do you believe they'll have us do next? Aidan asked.

Falcon didn't answer right away, appearing to consider it. *Something to do with testing our battle skills, I'm certain. It is the one thing we have not done yet—directly, anyway.*

Perhaps they'll have us impale ourselves to see who can stand it the longest before begging to be freed, Donar suggested, then shook his head to rid himself of some loose grains of dirt. *I would not put it past them.*

Falcon gave him a censorious look. *Do not be flippant. These events may be tiring and difficult, but we must be proud we've done as well as we have thus far. Do you not think they chose their best clan members to compete against us, and that these are activities they likely perform on a regular basis? They don't expect us to win, but they do expect us to give our best effort. Remember, you are representing the Taugud, and no task should ever be too big or small for your toriq.*

You are right, of course. Donar dropped his head. It was no doubt the strenuous activities and difficult time they had sleeping in the stifling tunnels causing him to behave more irritably than usual.

There is only one event left for the day, Aidan said as they reached the creek. *Whatever it is, we will give it all that we have and hope we represent ourselves with good form.*

Well said, Falcon acknowledged.

They drank their fill at the creek and rinsed their faces and feet. There was no point in doing a full wash since the next event would likely get them filthy all over again. Aidan planned to have a much more thorough bathing later that night. He might be a dragon, but he appreciated cleanliness as much as any human might.

On their way back to the staging area for the competitions, Lorcan met with them. He held a long red ribbon in his mouth. The dragon dropped it at Aidan's feet. *This is for you.*

What for? he asked, confused. Dragons might appreciate jewels and gold, but they weren't much for ribbons or other odd human finery.

Do you see that female over there? Lorcan pointed his snout across the field where a lone dragon stood. She was roundly shaped with pleasant enough eyes and scales the color of an orange sunset, but she was no warrior. There was minimal muscle on her, and her posture was a little too submissive for Aidan's liking. He preferred strong females with good backbones on them.

I see her. Though Aidan didn't like where this was heading.

Her name is Felienne. She wishes to give the ribbon to you for luck in the next event, Lorcan explained.

Aidan let out a snort. *I do not need luck, and I am not interested.*

My friend, it would be wise to take the ribbon. Lorcan gave him a plaintive look. *Felienne comes from a rich family with a considerable horde of treasure and two of her brothers are great warriors. It is an honor that she has chosen to show an interest in you. Many a male has attempted to gain her attention and failed.*

Aidan swished his tail in annoyance. *But she is not a warrior herself?*

Well, no. Her family never wanted that for her.

Of course not. Dragons might respect strength, but many males liked their females soft and biddable, which was likely the way Felienne's family raised her.

Do you suppose her interest has anything to do with my being a pendragon's son and a shape-shifter? Aidan asked, though he already suspected the answer.

A flash of guilt reflected in Lorcan's eyes. *Those elements may have factored into it.*

Even if I did show an interest, we could not mate and live at the Taugud fortress. It is not designed for those who cannot shift to human form, Aidan said. This was a ridiculous conversation, and one he didn't appreciate having during his brief break between events. He would have preferred to rest for the little time he had left.

Lorcan blinked. *She is aware of that. Felienne is not looking for a permanent mating, but rather one of a temporary nature. She only wishes for you to give her a child. It would be raised among our clan, though you could visit whenever you wished.*

Aidan blanched. He'd heard of such arrangements happening, but not in recent memory. Was the Faegud pendragon really so desperate to gain more shifters in her toriq that she would ask her females to make such advancements? This did not bode well for the upcoming negotiations. Most males in his clan preferred to raise their offspring, not leave them like Lorcan suggested. In Aidan's case, any children he had would be eligible for pendragon once they became old enough. It would be an easy entry to gaining power in his clan if the Faegud played it right.

I think not, he said firmly.

Lorcan let out a heavy sigh. *I will tell her this is not the right time for such a gift, but that you thank her for it.*

Fair enough. Aidan would have preferred to deny Felienne outright, but he had to remember he was here in a diplomatic capacity and could not risk offending anyone.

What is the next event? Falcon asked.

I suppose you could describe it as a brawl of sorts. Lorcan pawed at the ground. His claws were clean since he had not participated in any events and instead stood on the sidelines judging them. *We will divide the participants into two teams, and you will battle each other for half an hour. Whichever side has the most members still standing wins.*

Falcon flashed his sharp teeth in the dragon version of a smile. *Excellent. I look forward to it.*

Aidan was actually interested as well. Their clan did something similar every year on the pendragon's birthday, except they used three teams and it lasted for an hour. Their method required a bit more strategy so it wasn't all fighting, but also making temporary alliances to finish one of the teams off quicker.

If you'll go that way. Lorcan raised his paw to gesture across the field. *The humans will mark you with paint to denote your team.*

Aidan, Falcon, and Donar made their way in that direction. Most of the Faegud had turned out to watch the final event, and several of them were already betting on how many would still be standing at the end. They kept their communications open, filling Aidan's head with countless conversations. It was beginning to give him a headache. Shape-shifters tended to be more private when speaking telepathically unless they were engaged in battle. Of course, in human form they had the ability to speak aloud, rendering the point moot.

Do you think they'll put us on the same team? Donar asked.

Aidan guided them to the end of the line of dragons waiting to be painted. *I have no idea.*

It would be better if they did not, Falcon said, taking up the rear of their group. *This way at least one of us will be on the winning side.*

Donar made a grunting sound. *If we were all on the same side, then we'd surely win.*

Never assume anything. It is as much up to our teammates as us to fight well, Falcon replied.

They moved to the head of the line, and a human man painted a white circle around Aidan's head, laying it on thick over his scales. When Donar came up, he got a bright yellow one. He scowled, but said nothing. Falcon got a white circle.

Best of luck, cousin, Aidan said, meaning it. No matter which team won or lost, it was important they all remained standing at the end.

Donar bowed his head and then left to join his team. Each group had a section where they were being directed to gather. Aidan and Falcon headed toward their team on the opposite side of the field. The terrain the Faegud had chosen for the brawl was mostly flat and had little vegetation. It didn't leave much for strategy. This was going to be an ugly fight and the only rule was not to kill your opponent. Aidan suspected he would be more than a little tired and sore once they finally got to the negotiations part of this visit.

Lorcan came to stand in the middle of the field between the two teams. He looked to the designated leader for each, waiting until they acknowledged their side was ready. Aidan joined the others in a loud roar, his heart beginning to race with excitement. He might be tired from the previous events, but his dragon was not.

Do you wish to take over for this, Aidan asked his inner beast. He'd never made such an offer before. Either he kept complete control, or they worked together. It wasn't until the other day with Bailey that he realized he could let go of his control.

With pleasure. The beast purred in his head.

This was going to be more than a little interesting. Aidan took a deep breath and then concentrated on receding to the back of his mind. It wasn't easy, but he knew where to go now that he'd been there before.

After a minute, the dragon came to the forefront, and Aidan became a spectator. He could no longer control his movements or even his breathing. It was more than a little unsettling.

Beast, as the dragon referred to himself, shook his body and tail. He lifted each paw and sniffed around, getting a feel for the physical form that he usually stayed trapped inside. Ah, it was a good feeling not having to lurk anymore—now he was in control! It was only too bad he could not just fly away and do whatever he wanted, no matter how tempting. Aidan had entrusted him to help win this brawl, and he would prove more than equal to the task.

Lorcan let out a roar, signaling that they could attack. Beast let out a gleeful snarl. Those dragons with the yellow circles painted on them would not stand a chance against him. He was a mighty beast. For too many years he had been forced to hold back, but no more. He would give these backward dragons a real fight.

As each of the teams leaped into the air, beginning the assault with aerial combat, he rose with them. Beast enjoyed testing his wings and making them go faster. He eyed the opponent directly ahead of him, a dragon with no sign of shifter blood in him. He had short forelegs, rather than long forearms, which put him at a disadvantage despite his bulky body. Beast did not concern himself with his opponent's size. That would only make him slower and less quick to react.

He clashed with the other dragon midair and tore into him with his teeth and what remained of his poor, damaged talons—which was Aidan's fault, the fushka. There was no mercy in his attack. Beast tore through scales, ripped chunks out of his opponent, and tossed him down to the ground once he was finished. He found another dragon with the yellow circle painted on her neck. She was a female warrior with a well-honed form and a vicious gaze. She'd just finished her first opponent, and her eyes were filled with bloodlust for more.

Beast went after her, flying as fast as he could. He caught hold of her shoulders and folded his wings so that she had to take all of his weight. She screeched, having to work twice as hard to stay aloft. Beast clamped his jaws around her throat and kicked at her. The talons on his hind feet were in better condition and did much damage to the female dragon, tearing into her belly and ripping off her scales. She struggled against him, but he had cut off her ability to breathe, and she weakened by the second.

When she began to tumble, he opened his wings enough to slow their descent. They struck the ground with his sharp incisors still in her neck. She pressed against Beast's chest, but her attempts were weak. He waited until she passed out before letting go. The female dragon would survive, but she would wake up later with a headache and a sore throat.

Pounding footsteps came from behind him. Aidan, lurking in the far recesses of his mind, urged him to turn. Beast spun around just in time to raise his forearm and block the blow from a Faegud dragon with shifter blood in him. With his right hand, Beast punched his opponent in the jaw and sent him reeling backward to the ground. Then he leaped on top of him and tore into his soft belly, growling as he did so. A hot, metallic tang splashed into his mouth. Ah, the heady taste of enemy blood. Aidan did not appreciate it the way he should. In fact, Aidan took many things for granted that Beast did not.

After a few moments of chomping, he remembered that he must stop. This was not a real enemy, and Beast could not kill him. He left the dragon lying there, breathing heavily and flailing his little arms. What a weak creature. Even when Aidan was in control, he never gave into his pain and fought until the end.

Beast sought out and attacked several more dragons, tearing into them with the same relish as the others. One managed to get a swipe at his belly, but except for that, they took all the damage. He was hardly winded when the roar sounded, ending the battle. Beast searched around, finding only eight dragons left standing. Six of them were from his team, including Falcon. His gaze sought out Donar and spotted the bloody dragon wavering on his feet. He had barely survived the battle. Beast would have to ask Aidan to let him work with Donar's beast sometime. There would be much to be gained by that.

Lorcan beckoned those who still stood. Beast padded his way toward the dragon, stepping over a few moaning bodies. There were far too many who fell so easily. He was embarrassed for his kind, especially for those with pure blood who did not have to compete with a human soul. They had no excuse not to be as vicious as they wanted in this brawl.

It is time to return control, Aidan said.

Beast stopped when he reached Lorcan. *I think not. You will give me the rest of tonight in reward for me fighting this battle and winning.*

That is not what we agreed.

Lorcan is saying there will be another feast. I wish to taste my meal for once, instead of only receiving the dull sensations you share. You will give me this, Beast demanded. He was not asking for much. There was nothing significant to-night that required Aidan to be in control. He would gladly recede to his normal place once it was time to sleep.

Fine. Aidan made a sighing sound in his mind. *But don't do or say anything that will cause trouble or embarrass me.*

Hah! If you will recall, I am usually the voice of reason between us, Beast said.

Aidan let out a snort. *That is a matter of perspective, my friend.*

22

AIDAN

The Faegud pendragon led them to a secluded area about a twenty-minute flight from the jakhal. Aidan was still sore from yesterday's activities—particularly from Beast's brutal takeover and his overeating at the feast afterward. Donar and Falcon had noticed his odd behavior, to which the dragon told them to mind their own business, but thankfully no one else caught the difference. Aidan was grateful when he woke up as himself again. The more he flew, the more his muscles loosened and he became in sync with his body.

He gazed at the small clearing they flew toward and noted a small tunnel opening in the ground. It was barely wide enough for a dragon to fit through and much narrower than what he'd seen at the jakhal.

Aidan addressed Lorcan, *Why are we here?*

My mother is concerned about spies. There are those who still prefer the former pendragon's ways and resist hers. We have executed several dragons so far who we caught attempting to ally with our neighboring toriq—the Ghastanan. She does not want to risk any others interfering or revealing what is discussed today, Lorcan explained, his tone grim. *I will remain out here guarding the entrance while you negotiate with my mother and the elders.*

Aidan did not like the sound of that. It appeared the Faegud clan had as much instability and internal strife as the Taugud, perhaps more. He could only hope their efforts were not wasted. This agreement would be important to his toriq's future, but only if it had a chance of succeeding.

Do not worry. This is normal for a treaty negotiation, Falcon privately explained.

To negotiate away from the jakhal? Aidan asked, skeptical. Then again, he had not been alive when his toriq negotiated the last treaty with a dragon clan not consisting fully of shifters. Perhaps he was being paranoid.

Yes, Falcon said.

You all may change now, Hildegard announced. She led the way by allowing the flames to consume her, and the elders followed her example a moment later.

Aidan, Falcon, and Donar gave each other surprised looks. This was more than a little unexpected. They'd anticipated remaining in dragon form for their entire stay with the Faegud, but after a moment of hesitation, they shifted as well.

It was such a natural act for them that it took less than a minute for them to appear in human form. Hildegard and the others remained consumed by the flames for far longer before finally emerging in their new bodies. It was painful to spend that amount of time shifting. Only the youngest dragons in their to-riq underwent such a slow process, but Aidan had to remember the Faegud were different. The human side of them lurked much deeper and required a lot more concentration to bring out. He was surprised all of the elders—five in attendance—could do it. He had been under the impression the remaining shifters of their toriq were few and far between. These males and fe-males, though, showed their age and had to be at least a thousand years old, perhaps more. They likely came from a time when their people had stronger traces of human characteristics in their blood.

Hildegard finished shifting first and stood before them. She had long, dark-brown hair that went to her waist, smooth skin that was lightly tanned, and features reflecting a middle-aged woman. The build of her hu-man body was similar to Phoebe's, with a larger bone structure and toned muscles. Her eyes had remained the same orange color as when she wore her dragon shape. She wore a fine red tunic and black pants.

As Aidan recalled, their clan still had a few fami-lies capable of producing the second flames that could fire-proof camrium cloth and certain other items such as stone or zaphiriam. There were only a small number of materials that could endure the process, but it was a skill no toriq would want to go to waste.

The elders emerged from the fire last, each with pained expressions on their faces. Their tunics ranged in colors from dark blue to brown to green, but they all wore black pants. Black was the most common color for shifter garments because of the special plant—*sude camria*—from which they used to manufacture their fire-proof cloth.

Lorcan stayed in his dragon form, taking a position to stand guard. Hildegard beckoned everyone else, and they followed her down the tunnel entrance. It went at a steady decline for about two dozen paces before flattening. Just after that, it curved to the right and eventually led to an open cavern with large flat stones for seats. The female pendragon settled at the far end, with the elders taking positions on either side of her. Aidan, Falcon, and Donar sat on the remaining boulders with their backs to the entrance. Tension thickened the air as they waited for the pendragon to speak.

"Today we have the opportunity to renew ties between the Faegud and Taugud," she began in a clear, strong voice. "And it is a long time coming."

Lorcan's mother went on to state the goals of their meeting, and her hope that they could come to a mutually satisfying agreement that would benefit both toriqan. Only Hildegard and Aidan would be allowed to speak openly, though they could privately confer with their advisors during the negotiations. After she finished laying out the guiding principles, she looked at Aidan.

"Perhaps we should speak of trade first?"

He nodded. "That would be acceptable."

Hildegard folded her hands in her lap. "Now that we have returned to Earth, our remaining needs are few. The food is plentiful, and there are many materials lying about for the taking. We truly only lack in one area—gray stone and the ability to shape it. Those with the talent to breathe the second fire have maintained the skill to create clothing, but it has been too long since we have wished to build structures above ground. You have quarries for gray stone and masons who could help train our people in how to carve and shield it, do you not?"

Aidan glanced at his cousin. Hildegard knew very well that Donar's family came from a long line of masons who could work gray stone. "We do. Our artisans are kept quite busy, but arrangements could be made for them to visit for a short period to train your people. We could also supply you with enough gray stone to build a few small structures."

"That would do for a start, and three months with two of your masons should be sufficient for an instruction period," the pendragon said.

None of us can spare that kind of time, Donar spoke telepathically to Aidan.

I am aware, as I am certain Hildegard is as well.

His cousin blinked. *Of course. I suppose I could possibly spare one month, and there is another mason's son who could do the same. That would be enough for them to learn all the requisite skills. Any progress after that would have to come from their practicing on their own.*

Very well. I will take that under advisement, Aidan replied, then returned his attention to the Faegud pendragon.

"Our masons are quite busy with projects for our toriq," he said, keeping his tone neutral. "We have two, including my cousin, who could each spare two weeks to train your people."

Hildegard's lips thinned. "That would hardly give them time to learn all they need to know. I would agree to six weeks, but nothing less."

Aidan mulled that over, using his own experience at carving stone as a basis. "Four weeks to start. Your people will then practice on their own—which is necessary to increase their skills—and our masons will return after six months to help them refine their techniques for a period of two weeks. That should be more than sufficient."

Donar jerked his gaze to Aidan, frowning at him, but he kept quiet.

"Agreed," Hildegard said, then narrowed her gaze. "But I require that the masons and gray stone supply come within two weeks. We wish to have at least one shelter built before winter arrives where humans and shifters can come together for meals."

Aidan considered it. "Two weeks should be enough time to prepare both."

One of the elders produced a sheet of parchment and penned the terms onto it. At the end of the negotiations, he and the pendragon would review the document, and if satisfied, they would sign it.

"For the Taugud, we do not require anything material from you. As you mentioned, food and supplies are plentiful enough now that we are on Earth. Our current needs run more toward a requirement for security and reinforcements in battle. I have a request I would ask of you in return for the supply of stone and the use of our masons."

Hildegard narrowed her gaze. "What is it you want?"

"The Taugud have gained all the land we want to the south. In fact, we have expanded our territory to cover much of what the humans would refer to as southeastern Oklahoma. The difficulty will be in holding the land and acquiring the city in the middle of the state. Large sections of it are currently being held by the Shadowan and Thamaran."

The pendragon was quiet for a moment. "Which territories do these toriqan currently hold?"

"The Shadowan have the northeast part of Oklahoma, as well as sections of what is called Kansas and Arkansas. The Thamaran have the entire west half of the state and something the humans refer to as the panhandles for Texas and Oklahoma." Bailey had pointed at these places on a map for Aidan to see. He understood where they were located, but he could not quite grasp why they called them panhandles. She gave up explaining it to him after they argued about it for more than ten minutes. In his mind, the state of Oklahoma appeared more like a pot that was melting at the bottom and Texas did not look like any cooking implement he had ever seen.

A large, colorful sheet of parchment appeared in Hildegard's hands that she must have pulled from shiggara. Aidan was surprised to discover she kept a map in her mystical pouch. The pendragon stood and held it flat against the wall where they could both look at it. He found it depicted much of the region where their toriqan lived, and it was perfect for their discussion.

"Show me," she said.

Aidan pointed at the panhandles and outlined the rest of the territories for his clan and the pure dragons. Hildegard had added the chasm to the map as well with a inky black line, indicating where it ran almost parallel to the Red River with an approximate half-hour flight between them.

She pointed at Oklahoma City. "This is a large human population center. You want to hold all of it?"

"Eventually, yes, though we recognize it will take time and many battles to accomplish," he replied.

Aidan's father believed getting the humans on their side would be beneficial to their toriq. Not only for security reasons, but also because the advanced technology they used could prove useful. The first way to do that was to force the pure dragons out of the city, as this would show the humans that shape-shifters could be allies. Gaining mutual respect and trust would have to be taken in small steps after that, though Bailey's participation would help speed up the process. First, though, Aidan would have to prove she was not a threat to his toriq. He was still waiting for an opportunity to present itself on that delicate matter.

"Why?" Hildegard asked, knitting her brows. "The Thamaran and Shadowan are not going to give up that territory easily. Many of the pure dragons still seek revenge on humans, and others have plans to enslave them after their numbers are sufficiently dwindled—not that I agree with their ideas, mind you."

Aidan met her gaze. "We are aware of that, but we are thinking ahead, like you. Human allies could make all the difference to our future."

Hildegard's gaze turned guarded. She appeared to be mulling something over and possibly speaking privately with the elders. Aidan waited several minutes before the pendragon spoke again.

"Do you see this city here?" she asked, pointing at the map.

He eyed the word above her finger and remembered the name from Bailey mentioning it before. "Dallas."

"Yes. We have plans to take this city in the spring from a neighboring toriq. If you agree to assist us with that, we will help with your plans after winter as well."

"You do realize our toriq is much smaller than yours, and we cannot provide an equal number of warriors?" The Taugud had a little over two-hundred if the castle guards were counted as well as the shifters who lived outside the fortress, but the Faegud must have closer to seven or eight hundred.

Hildegard nodded. "That may be, but in the early spring when the weather is cold as often as it is warm, you will have the advantage. Most of our warriors are pure dragons that will be hampered by cooler temperatures—the same as our enemies. The more shifters we have fighting, the greater our chances of success even if the numbers are not in our favor."

Aidan could see the value in that. "Very well, but in return, the Taugud will require you agree to come to our aid any time we need warrior support."

Thankfully for Aidan, this was a subject he and his father had discussed at length. He knew exactly what assurances he must gain from the Faegud. It was too late in the year to coordinate any large-scale battles together, especially with preparations for winter keeping dragons busy, but his toriq could handle any smaller skirmishes that came up in the meantime anyway.

Hildegard turned to face him, her lips thinning. "You ask too much. We can hardly agree to protect your clan indefinitely and whenever you ask. There must be limits."

"If you want a steady supply of our gray stone, as well as assistance from our masons, then you must give something in return. This is the only thing we want from you."

She made a disgruntled noise. "What if we agree to provide warrior support up to three times a year?"

"No." Aidan shook his head. "It must be unlimited."

Steam flared out of Hildegard's nostrils. "Absolutely not!"

"Then I suppose we are done here." Aidan spun on his heels and gestured at Donar and Falcon to follow him.

They made it partway down the tunnel before the pendragon shouted, "Wait!"

He stopped and turned around. "Yes?"

"We would be willing to assist in the defense of your territory for as long as our treaty holds, but it would come with a condition."

Aidan came back down the tunnel with his companions trailing behind. "What is it?"

"We want at least twenty of our dragons to breed with twenty of yours over winter." Hildegard glanced at the elders as if confirming something with them. "Of course, that would only be the beginning. In all, we require an entire new generation of offspring born with shifter blood numbering at least fifty in the next ten years."

He stiffened. Fifty? Surely the Faegud did not think they could alter the makeup of their clan at such a fast pace. It was all Aidan could do to keep his expression impassive. "That is a lot to ask. We are lucky to have that many children of our own in such a time. You are more or less asking to take an entire generation of our toriq from us, though we are already much smaller than you."

Her eyes gleamed knowingly. "One of the reasons neither of our people produce many offspring is because we lack fresh blood. Surely you have heard a male and female from different toriqan are more successful at reproducing than those from the same."

He looked to Falcon. *Is this true?*

I have heard as much, he said, dipping his chin. *Our toriq gave up the practice of breeding with other clans before your father was born, but the shifters to the west—the Craegud—began intermixing with the pure dragons about a century and a half ago. Their clan has nearly doubled since then with almost eighteen hundred members.*

Aidan considered Falcon's words. Though he detested the idea of asking his people to mate with another clan, they did need something to help them. Each generation seemed smaller than the last, and that could not be allowed to continue.

"There are two problems I foresee with this," Aidan began. "One is that shifters love their children deeply, and few would be willing to part with their offspring—even if they were allowed visitation. The other is that we cannot force our people to mate. They must be willing to do so of their own free will and on their own terms."

Hildegard gave him a patient smile. "Let us sit."

They returned to their stone seats before she continued. "We have neutral territory between the chasm and Red River, do we not?"

"Yes," Aidan agreed.

"Perhaps we could encourage those among our toriqan who are unmated and of the appropriate age to meet there. They may work it out among themselves to do whatever is most comfortable—whether it is to permanently mate or have something temporary. All of my clan's females, though, would have to raise their children here. That is not negotiable."

Aidan ground his jaw. "I would propose we give the couples the option to live in the neutral territory where a sizable den can be built for those who wish to reside there. Both of our toriqan can send a contingent of warriors to protect it. Once the children are grown, they can choose where they wish to ultimately settle."

Hildegard glanced between the elders before returning her attention to Aidan. "We would be willing to allow that, but only if the interbreeding continues indefinitely with no time limit, and you must participate as well."

"No," Aidan said. It came out before he even had a chance to think about it.

The pendragon's brows furrowed. "I was under the impression you are not mated."

Aidan took a deep breath, attempting to calm his inner beast. Neither of them liked the idea of mating with an unknown female, but he could not risk offending Hildegard.

Cousin, Donar said telepathically. *Do not let your feelings for the slayer ruin this treaty for us. We need the warriors the Faegud can provide.*

Aidan jerked his gaze to his cousin. Donar had seen the problem before he did, and the ramifications of it. It was true. He and his inner dragon wanted Bailey and no one else. It was affecting Aidan's ability to make the wisest decision for his clan, rather than for himself. Still, he'd lost interest in other females since meeting the slayer. He did not know how he could even bring himself to join with one.

"I do not have a mate, but I regret to say I am not ready to take one yet."

Hildegard frowned. "Your father believes you are mature and responsible enough to negotiate a treaty with another toriq. Surely impregnating one female cannot be that difficult a job. We are not asking you to take responsibility for the child, and we'll waive any claim it might have to the pendragon seat, should he or she become eligible for candidacy."

Her second point had been a concern, but alleviating it did not make him feel better. There was no way he could explain to the Faegud that he had a preference for a dragon slayer—that would certainly not go over well. "Does it need to be me or would any of my siblings do?"

Hildegard pursed her lips. "One of them would be a suitable substitute, but what if they decline the offer as well?"

It would be a deep insult if neither Aidan nor his siblings were willing to mate with the Faegud. He could only hold out hope that Phoebe would choose to mate with the male she was courting before, assuming that dragon was still available. He prayed to Zorya that was so.

"If none of my siblings are interested, then I will join with one of your females," he promised.

His inner beast roared in outrage, but Aidan ignored it. If this was what it took to protect his clan's future, then he would make that sacrifice. It wasn't only about defense, but also increasing their population with a strong, new generation. He had to set aside his personal preferences no matter how much it twisted his gut and made him want to walk away right then.

A slow smile spread across Hildegard's face. "Excellent. Now that the big issues are out of the way, we can discuss the finer points of the treaty."

Aidan let out a breath. This was going to take a while.

23

BAILEY

We pulled up to Aidan's house, and I breathed a sigh of relief to finally be back. I'd been annoyed with him for making me stay here at first, but it didn't take long before I appreciated the solitude. It was now a sort of refuge where I could relax without anyone bothering me. A few days of staying at Earl's again had reminded me how I wasn't much of a people person. Sure, I enjoyed saving them. I just didn't want to have to actually talk to them beyond saying, "Go hide, I'll take care of this."

Danae set the gearshift to park. She was the one doing the driving since she'd only healed my ribs that morning and my left shoulder was still on the mend. The bites and tears from the dragon's teeth had closed up, but the bones, muscles, and ligaments inside still needed time. My shoulder had been ripped apart and then smashed after I fell three stories. Danae had said when she looked at it through her healer's vision that it was beyond her abilities to repair. A clean break was one thing, but she didn't even know where to start with the mess she found in there. I'd have to let my body do all the work. At least that morning it had started to take the form of a shoulder again instead of looking like misshapen Playdough. There was still a lot of bruising, though, and it looked like this time I would be left with some scars. I didn't look forward to explaining that to Aidan.

"Are you sure you don't want to stay at Earl's another day or two?" Danae asked, frowning at me.

I nodded. "With my father gone, I think it's for the best."

She blew out a breath, stirring several strands of her blond hair. "How are you doing with that? I can't believe he didn't even say goodbye to you."

In fact, Wayne had let Earl know early this morning that he was leaving. My father said I would be back in fighting shape soon enough, and it was up to me to take care of my own city. There'd been no goodbye—not even a note. For not really knowing the man, that had hurt more than I expected.

"I guess he's gotta do what he's gotta do." I shrugged with my good shoulder.

She gave me a weak smile. "At least he saved your life. That has to count for something, right?"

"That's what I keep telling myself." I opened the door and got out of the truck.

Trish and Conrad pulled up in the other car. They'd followed behind so that Danae would have a ride home, and because I suspected they wanted to make sure I would be okay here. I was amazed Justin had let his pregnant girlfriend out of the neighborhood, but she had put her foot down and said something about cutting pieces of him off if he tried to stop her. Trish would only be out for the morning when dragons were sleeping, and we used the radio to find out where any ambush points were to avoid them. Hank was seriously cutting into the road bandits' enterprise.

Conrad came up and gave me a half-hug, avoiding my bad shoulder. "I'll be back tomorrow to check on you. Don't be goin' and killin' any dragons without me."

"It isn't going to happen today," I said, taking a step back. "But I can't promise what will happen tomorrow."

Trish glared at me. "Bailey, you need at least a couple more days to rest."

"And the kids? Can they really wait?" I asked. This was the sticking point, and the one no one could argue no matter how much they tried. Maybe if I had been able to get my father to help, that would have been different, but I'd lost that chance.

"Still…just take it easy today, okay?" Trish pleaded, and then lifted a bag. "I fixed some stew you can heat up later."

She was becoming rather good at making meals that could last a couple of days even without refrigeration—as long as you kept the food in a cool place. Trish was also working on mastering the art of baking bread from scratch, but getting all the right ingredients to practice with wasn't easy. One of these days, I would have to introduce her to Kayla—who had mentioned she did a lot of baking at the fortress.

"Thanks," I said, reaching out for the bag.

"I'll take it inside." Conrad grabbed it before I could. He already held the bag with my other belongings, including my sword and clothes. Before I could argue, he headed toward the house. Conrad had been determined not to let me do anything strenuous until I recovered. I tried not to be annoyed about it since he meant well.

"Are you sure you're going to be okay?" Trish asked, shifting from foot to foot. "We could stay with you for the night or something if you want."

I sighed. I loved that they cared, but they were driving me crazy. "I'm not an invalid—I'll be fine."

Trish didn't look convinced. "What about your mom? You seemed pretty upset after you talked to her again this morning."

Oh, I was more than upset after round two with Mom, but it wasn't something I was ready to talk about. I suspected my mother's biggest problem was that my stepfather still couldn't find a way to get up here, which set her off even worse than last time. It didn't help that I wouldn't swear not to fight dragons anymore.

My mother had started into me as soon as I answered the phone, crying and yelling at me for an hour like she'd just discovered I sold drugs for a living—except worse. Mom had used the same tone as when I was sixteen, and she caught me and a friend in the barn drinking one night. I'd had to shovel horse manure for a week after that. Since it was usually my older step-brother, Sean, who did the job, I suspected him of ratting me out. This time, I knew it was my father who told her, but she didn't bring Wayne up this time. I still didn't know what exactly he said to her when they had talked.

Listening to her had drained me in ways even my last dragon battle couldn't even manage. Fighting fire-breathing beasts wasn't personal. Hearing my mother's grief and worry because she'd discovered her only daughter was slaying dragons took a huge emotional toll. Mom had a heart condition and limited medicine to manage it since the apocalypse. The last thing I wanted was to risk her health. If something happened to my mother because of me, I'd never forgive myself.

"I just need to be alone," I said, feeling about as defeated as I could get. First, I nearly got myself killed in my last battle, then I met a father who didn't want to talk to me, and to top it off, I'd nearly given my mother a heart attack. The best thing I could do was stay away from everyone for a bit until I pulled myself together.

Trish and Danae gave each other meaningful looks. They appeared like they were about to say something else when Conrad returned from the house. He gazed around at all of us, then grabbed each of the women by their arms.

"Time to go. Bailey needs to rest, and she ain't gonna do that with you two mother hens hoverin' over her," he said, giving me a nod.

I returned his gesture with a grateful smile. Conrad and I had spent enough time together now that he understood me in ways no one else did. For a nineteen-year-old guy, he was surprisingly intuitive.

"See you tomorrow." I gave them a wave with my good arm and headed for the house.

By the time I shut the front door and leaned against it, their car engine had started. Thank God they were leaving. I waited until the sound of tires crunching on gravel faded, then headed for the couch. Going upstairs to bed was beyond my capabilities at the moment. I settled down, careful of my shoulder, and dozed off within a few minutes.

It was hours later when a sound outside woke me. I jerked upright, wincing as pain shot through my shoulder, and listened carefully. Something was moving around out there. It could have been a dog or a deer, but my instincts told me otherwise. I got up and moved toward the dining room. Conrad had left my sword and the bag with my belongings in there where I could find them easily.

I pulled the blade from its sheath. Footsteps sounded on the porch outside and moved toward the door. I knew it couldn't be Aidan. He wouldn't have skulked around like this or wasted any time coming inside. This was someone who was being cautious with their approach.

The doorknob jiggled. Stepping carefully, I positioned myself a few feet from the entrance, so I could attack whoever came in before they had a chance to put up a defense. It creaked open. I probably could have put some WD-40 on the hinges, but I liked the early warning the noise provided.

I lifted the sword, ready to strike the intruder, but then a head of black hair with a silver streak poked through the opening. Phoebe's gaze met mine, and she lifted a brow. "Bailey?"

I lowered the blade a fraction. "Yeah. What are you doing here?"

She pushed the door wider and only took one step inside, smart enough not to come any closer while I remained in an attack position. "I just want to talk."

"About what?" I asked. Phoebe hadn't seemed all that pleased about her brother and I working together. I wasn't letting my guard down just yet, especially with him out of town.

"Aidan told you about the murder case I'm working on. Something came up, and I thought you might be able to help..." she paused, her gaze narrowing on my shoulder. I was only wearing a tank top, so she couldn't miss the damage. "What happened?"

I thought about not telling her, but she'd probably figure it out anyway. "Got in a fight with two dragons at once."

"Aren't you a little new to slaying to be taking on two?" She inched closer, still studying my shoulder. "How bad was it? This looks like it's at least a couple of days old."

Aidan had said Phoebe was a warrior. She'd probably been in enough battles to know how to identify injuries and how long they took to heal. Supposedly, my recovery time was similar to the shape-shifters. The more injuries we got, though, the longer it took them to heal because our enhanced immune systems were working on multiple fronts.

I lowered my sword another fraction since her concern seemed genuine enough. "It was a few days ago. There was only one dragon at first, but a second showed up. Things got a little tricky from there."

"I'm impressed your shoulder is the only thing you injured then. It takes most dragon slayers a year or two before they can take on two by themselves." She cocked her head. "Maybe Aidan is right that you really are good."

The compliment would have felt nice if I deserved it. I didn't dare tell her about my father, but I could at least admit the battle didn't happen that easy. Otherwise, she might get the idea I was ready to be thrown into fights with multiple opponents right now.

"Actually, I broke a few other bones. My shoulder is just the only thing that hasn't finished healing yet," I admitted.

"Ah, well, that makes more sense. I don't suppose you could put that down?" Phoebe gestured at my blade.

"You haven't earned my trust yet."

She put her hands up. "I'm not armed."

I snorted. "Like you couldn't pull something out of shiggara in a second if you wanted."

"Very well, keep the sword, but maybe we should sit down." She nodded toward the living room. "You don't look like you should be on your feet right now."

She had a point. My arm was already starting to shake from holding the sword up for a few minutes. I really did need another good night of rest to get my strength back. If not for my brief nap, I might have appeared worse.

"Okay, you take that chair, and I'll take the one across from it." I pointed at the dining room table. That seemed like a good neutral spot for the conversation she had in mind, and we would have a large piece of furniture between us. It was a small thing, but it made me feel better.

"Alright," she agreed.

We settled across from each other with me keeping my sword in my lap. Phoebe reclined back in her chair and propped her feet on top of the oak table. At first, I was surprised to see her relax that much in front of me, but then I realized the position served two purposes. It showed she had no intention of harming me, and she didn't think I could harm her. That last part grated, but she was Aidan's sister, so I'd try to get along with her.

"What is it you want to know?" I asked. Might as well help her if it would get my mind off of my current problems.

"I believe I've figured out who killed our Captain of the Guard, but the tricky part is proving it. The killer used a garrote, which is not a weapon we make at the fortress, yet this one managed to cut through the victim's neck."

"And a human-made one would have melted," I surmised.

The only reason shifters could get away with sitting on regular furniture for long was because of the camrium clothes they wore. With direct contact, they'd eventually start to singe it. But with the garrote going into the body, that was even worse. The coolest part of shifters was the outside layer of their skin.

Phoebe nodded. "Maybe it wouldn't have melted at first, but by the time they finished the job, it should have at least begun to melt."

I mulled that over. "If a sorcerer spelled it, could that work?"

"Yes, it could," she answered, seeming pleased with my question. "I've had it examined by some of our sorcerers, but they couldn't have done it. They are watched too closely."

I leaned forward in my seat. "You have sorcerers at the fortress?"

"Aidan didn't tell you?"

"No. I got the impression he hated them and thought they weren't to be trusted." He'd reacted very badly when he first met Danae.

"They're not," she said, folding her hands in her lap. "But ours have been with us for many generations, and they're not allowed to roam freely."

"You keep them as slaves?" That seemed a little harsh.

She scowled. "If you knew what they were really capable of, you wouldn't want them out on their own, either. They are masters of manipulation, and most of them don't care for anyone except themselves."

That didn't describe Danae, but it could fit a couple of other sorcerers I knew. I considered Verena and whether she might have had anything to do with the garrote. As far as I could tell, she didn't like associating with much of anyone and certainly wouldn't help a dragon—even to murder another one. That left Javier. He was enterprising and more than a little shady. I'd only met him once, but he could have been the one to provide the garrote.

"There's a sorcerer downtown," I said, and went on to tell her what I knew about him.

"Wait." She held a hand up. "You said he's got a following of people there?"

"Yeah." I knitted my brows. The tone of her voice had me worried.

She dropped her feet to the floor. "Shifitt. That's the last thing we need right now."

"I don't suppose you could explain the problem?"

"There are some breeds of sorcerers who derive their power from their followers. The more they have, the stronger they get. Most prefer to be alone, though, so if this one is amassing a lot of humans to work for him…"

"He's doing it for the power," I finished. That was just great. I'd made a deal with the devil, and I couldn't even think of a way around it. He was my key to finding the missing children.

Phoebe eyed me closely. "Have you met him?"

"Once." I shifted in my seat. "Almost a week ago. It wasn't easy getting to him since he's got protection spells all around his base of operations."

"But he let you in?" she asked.

"Yeah."

She gave me a dark look. "Why did you go to him?"

"The children," I said, sighing. "I had to see him because of them."

"What children?"

I explained about the kids Matrika was taking from their families.

Phoebe's eyes softened. "It will not be easy getting them back."

"Exactly. That's why I had to ask for his help." I rubbed my face. "This sort of thing is way beyond my skill set, but I have to do something—it's not like anyone else can."

She worked her jaw. "What does Javier want in return for his help?"

"Dragon scales. A lot of them."

Phoebe cursed. "To keep us out of his domain."

"Not you." I shook my head. "I'll give him the green scales because the people following him deserve protection even if he doesn't. There are children in there, too. He's not getting any red ones, though."

I'd come to that decision days ago when I'd last seen Aidan. During our brief wrestling match when I wanted to attack Phoebe, I'd knocked some of his scales from him, but I didn't collect them. Javier could take the green ones and be happy with what he got.

"What, precisely, is he giving you in return?" Phoebe asked.

"The location of the children."

She was quiet for a moment. "When are you going to see him again?"

"Tomorrow." I'd try to kill one more dragon in the afternoon to finish filling the canister, but if I couldn't do it, I'd still go. I'd told him I'd be back in one week regardless.

"You are taking me with you," she said.

"What?" I sputtered. "Why?"

"Because I want to question him about the garrote." She paused. "And you're my way in."

24

I drove through Norman toward Shadowan territory. My companions and I didn't have time to go all the way over to the west side of town where the Thamaran dragons roamed. At least, not if we wanted to get to downtown before dark when things got really dangerous, so we were taking our chances with the Shadowans. Aidan wasn't here to stop me, anyway.

"Was it truly necessary to bring him?" Phoebe asked, jerking her gaze toward the backseat where Conrad prepared his crossbow.

"Yes," I said, gripping the wheel.

She'd asked that question a few times since we all met at Aidan's lair this afternoon. We'd even gotten delayed leaving because of it. Phoebe had insisted on coming with me to hunt the last dragon I needed to fill the scale canister. Partly because she wanted to help kill one of her enemies and partly because she said I was still in no shape to fight alone. I figured she only cared what happened to me because I was her way in to see Javier. It wouldn't be useful if I got killed. No way did I believe her excuse that her brother would be mad if she didn't watch out for me. She couldn't possibly care about that.

"But he's human. They are fragile and die easily."

Conrad raised his crossbow and pointed it at her head. "Want to test how fragile *you* are?"

Phoebe blew a light breath of flames that streamed just above the crossbow and stopped just short of his nose. "Try me."

He dropped the crossbow. "Do you perform at birthday parties? I know this chick who has a little girl with a birthday coming up…"

"Conrad," I interrupted. "Stop trying to piss off the dragon. If my truck gets burned, it's going to be *me* killing you."

He muttered a few expletives and dropped the crossbow.

Phoebe settled into her seat, then bounced a little on it. "I can see why you humans like these vehicles so much. I've always wanted to ride in one."

"If only we could fire-proof them," I said.

She frowned. "Yes, that is a problem."

I bumped my way over the railroad tracks, which we all knew marked the beginning of Shadowan territory. Silence filled the passenger compartment as we began searching the sky for any flying green dragons. It was about four in the afternoon, which was when they usually began hunting, but not so early they'd be roaming in packs. Mostly, the loners tended to come out at this time of day.

"There," I said, spotting one off to the right.

Phoebe leaned toward the window. "Oh, yes. That one will do."

At least having Aidan's sister with us would guarantee I didn't attack a dragon that might cause me more trouble like with Matrika. This beast would cross paths with us in just a couple of minutes if we stayed on this block. I searched for a place to park and found a bank with a sheltered drive-through area. Anything that would give the vehicle a little cover and reduce the chances of it getting caught in the crossfire worked for me. I parked underneath, and everyone got out.

"How about I set up over there?" Conrad asked, pointing at a set of bushes.

Phoebe's brows furrowed. "What does he mean?"

"The dragons don't always come if we try yelling at them, especially since they know there's a slayer running around town hunting them now. Shooting at them first gets them angry enough they'll come down to retaliate—even if they know it's me." Usually, anyway, but I didn't have time for a full account of how things worked.

"I could shift and attack first," Phoebe suggested.

I shook my head. "There's no time, and I don't want to risk you having all the fun without me."

"Fine." She put her hands on her hips. "Then what shall we do while he's shooting at it? Stand here like *fushkan*?"

"Fushkan?"

She knitted her brows. "Fushka means something like idiot or fool, and fushkan is the plural for it."

"Oh, okay." I'd have to remember that one. "Yes, we should stand like fushkan, except do it over there." I pointed across the street to a large parking lot in front of a grocery store. Conrad and I always tried to keep our positions separate when possible so I could buy him time to get out of the way and hide.

"Very well." She didn't sound happy, but I was glad she was at least cooperating.

We hurried across the street and stopped next to a couple of half-burned cars. It was as good a place as any for a staging area. I preferred to plan my attacks out a little better than this, but we were trying to make this a quick kill.

A moment later we heard the zing of a bolt, followed by the roar of the dragon. Two more zipped through the air before the beast came over the trees. Phoebe whistled, calling it toward us. To my surprise, the dragon turned and came straight for our position.

I raised my sword. "Come on, you little bastard."

It was soaring about twenty feet above the parking lot and dropping steadily, but I didn't think it planned to land. The dragon had positioned itself for a fiery drive-by.

"You take the right wing, and I'll take the left," Phoebe whispered, standing next to me.

I didn't have to ask what she meant. "Got it."

The green dragon soared lower and blew out a massive breath of flames. Just before the fire reached us, we dropped to our knees. I counted to three and thrust my sword upward at an angle, slicing through the creature's right wing as it flew over my head. The dragon screeched and went crashing into the pavement. Phoebe and I turned to watch it tumble along before rolling to a stop.

We raced after it. She grabbed one of its torn wings and flipped it over onto its back. I put a foot on its chest and aimed my sword downward, stabbing it in the heart. This was almost too easy. Even when Aidan had been with me on my early slayings, he had me do all the work. The only time he had stepped in was when another dragon showed up. I understood why he preferred to observe, but I didn't mind Phoebe's help this time. I hadn't been sure how well I would battle with my shoulder not quite healed. It was still too sore and stiff to use much.

"Good work," Phoebe said, a hint of surprise in her gaze. "You showed no hesitation, and your instincts and timing were good. My brother has trained you well."

I hid my surprise at her compliment. "Thank you."

It suddenly occurred to me that she may have wanted in on this fight just to see how I handled myself. Aidan once told me dragons enjoyed testing each other's fighting skills, and he may have mentioned once that Phoebe trained young female shifters who hoped to become warriors someday. Maybe it was natural she was curious.

Conrad ran up to us, carrying the canister. "Man, I wish I could have recorded that and put it on YouTube. It would have gotten a million hits, easy."

"Maybe someday we'll get the internet back," I said, though I lost hope by the day of that ever happening. Civilization had eroded so much it didn't seem possible anymore.

"What's YouTube?" Phoebe asked.

"Uhhh." I glanced at Conrad, who shrugged. "I'll explain that later. Let's just collect the scales and get out of here."

I parked at the glass shop again. That overwhelming feeling of needing to turn back didn't hit Conrad and me this time. Javier had promised he would rework the barrier spell to make exceptions for us, and he'd kept his promise. Oddly, Phoebe didn't seem too bothered by it either, despite the fact the magic should have affected her. She frowned a little and scrunched her brows, but other than that I could hardly tell she noticed it.

"Don't you feel the spell?" I asked.

Phoebe's lips thinned. "A little, yes, but I'm resistant to sorcerer magic. It doesn't affect me as much as other dragons."

Conrad leaned forward in his seat. "Really? How did that happen?"

"I don't know." She gave him a dark look until he put some distance between them again. "It's always been that way."

We got out of the truck and began heading down Main Street. The same male and female guards stopped us at around the same spot as before. They narrowed their gazes on Phoebe.

"She is not an authorized guest," the woman said.

I held up the scale canister. "If your boss wants what we have for him, he'll make an exception."

The female nodded at the guy next to her. "Go tell Javier the slayer and two of her friends are here."

Phoebe crossed her arms and proceeded to have a staring contest with the remaining female guard. If I wasn't so impatient to get the visit with the sorcerer over with, I might have found it funny. Posturing was never my thing. I fought when I needed to, but I didn't feel a need to rank in any hierarchy. That was the kind of thing social people did, not loners like me.

The male guard returned a few minutes later and gestured at us. "Follow me."

He led us to a building on the south side of the street this time. We went inside and found ourselves surrounded by rows of shelves stocked with food, house-hold items, sanitary products, and other useful items. Everything was packed in tightly with no space left to spare. I could only imagine Javier had sent his people out to gather it all before the stores were cleared out. Heck, maybe that's why they'd emptied so fast. The bastard had plenty of time to plan, considering everyone in Kederrawien knew they'd be crossing over to Earth years before it even happened.

"Like what you see?" Javier asked, strutting down the main aisle where we walked.

I frowned. "This isn't even all of it, is it?"

"Not even close, mi querida. Perhaps…" He tapped on his chin. "Ten percent."

Well, that was a comforting thought. Once our own supplies ran low, we might have no choice except to come to the sorcerer. He certainly had enough buildings in downtown to store the goods and dole them out as he chose. God only knew what he might ask for in return, though.

Conrad crossed his arms. "You know there are people starving out there while you hoard all this in here."

"They can come to me and either swear their allegiance or offer to trade," Javier said, his tone remaining friendly. "I am not inaccessible to the humans if they are truly in need."

Phoebe took a menacing step forward. "Of course not. You want the power they can offer."

"Ah, if it is not the pendragon's only daughter. How gracious of you to honor me with your presence." Javier smiled. He was putting on the charm, but I caught a whiff of fear in him. The sorcerer had not expected me to bring a shifter along.

"I'm not honoring you," Phoebe said through gritted teeth. It was a small miracle steam didn't come puffing out of her nostrils. "I have questions for you."

He lifted a brow, and then turned his attention to me. "Did you bring the canister filled to the top as I requested?"

I held it up. "Yep, though it only has green scales."

Javier scowled. "I asked for both..."

"If you want the other ones, I brought a whole, live red dragon so you can collect them yourself." I gestured at Phoebe.

She let out a low growl.

"Green will do," Javier said, taking a step back. "Perhaps we should talk in my office."

"Good idea," I agreed.

We walked all the way to the back of the place, which was surprisingly far, until we reached a set of narrow switchback stairs next to the rear exit. The sorcerer led us up to the second floor and down a short hall to an office at the end. Going inside was like walking into an old-fashioned study with cherry wood furniture, wall to wall shelves, a massive desk, and a sitting area off to the right. No window, though. The only lighting came from two oil lamps set at each end of the room.

Javier gestured at us to take a seat. "Would you like anything to drink?"

"No," Conrad and I said quickly.

Phoebe just stood there and crossed her arms, refusing to sit with the rest of us. She might be in human form, but with her black camrium warrior garb and wild, yellow eyes, you wouldn't mistake her for a normal person. I could feel the heat emanating off of her from where she positioned herself a few feet away. It was like her temper had turned her into a furnace.

Javier let the silence drag on for a minute before addressing me, "May I see the canister?"

"After you answer her questions," I said, gesturing at Aidan's sister.

"Very well." Javier leaned forward in his chair and looked up at Phoebe. "What is it you want to know, daughter of Throm?"

Phoebe leveled her gaze on him and spoke in a flat voice. "Have you sold a garrote that could have been used to kill a shifter recently?"

The sorcerer didn't blink. "I do not discuss my client's transactions with anyone else."

"Brave words, sorcerer." She took several steps toward Javier and leaned down until their faces were only a foot apart. "I could kill you where you sit, and nothing could stop me."

He lifted a hand, sending blue sparks toward Phoebe. She flinched but showed no other signs his magic had affected her. Conrad and I exchanged confused looks. What the hell had he just tried to do to her?

"Nice try," she said in a cold voice. "But I'm no easy target."

Javier's gaze hardened. He snapped his fingers, and a dozen sharp spikes appeared floating in the middle of the room. With a wave of his hand, he sent them flying at Phoebe. She straightened and let every one of them bounce off of her. Even the ones that struck her face and throat only left the tiniest of scratches. That explained what she meant by resistant to magic—she only took the tiniest hit from the spells. I wondered if that meant she could see through Verena's concealment spells on her house. That could be useful in the future.

"I'm growing weary of your stall tactics, sorcerer. Tell me what I want to know…" She reached out and put a hand around his neck. "Or I will kill you."

I leaped up. "Wait. He still has to tell me where the children are."

"Oh, he will," she said, keeping her gaze on him.

The scent of scorched skin began to permeate the air.

Javier held still, his lips pressed tightly together for another minute before his shoulders slumped. I got the impression he'd tried to fight off the heat coming from Phoebe's fingertips and failed.

"I'll tell you," he croaked.

She removed her hand, revealing the angry, red marks on his throat, but stayed close to him. "Who purchased the garrote?"

"A female shifter." He paused to cough and loosen his shirt collar. "She didn't give her name, but I gathered it from her aura. It was Ember."

A slow smile spread across Phoebe's face. "That's what I thought. When did she purchase it, and what did you trade for it?"

"Eight days ago. She offered information in exchange," he replied.

It occurred to me that I'd missed Ember by a day when I'd come to visit Javier. If I had been here one day earlier, I might have run into her. What kind of shifter murdered someone else in their clan for no good reason? Phoebe had told me the victim was well-liked and respected.

Phoebe narrowed her eyes. "What information?"

He hesitated. "Information about your clan. She… she told me about your father and the upcoming Bitkal."

Was that how Javier got his information? Not necessarily through magic but by trading it for material goods? Could he have been dealing with the pure dragons as well? I had so many questions, but I wouldn't trust his answers even if he offered them freely.

"What else did she tell you?" Phoebe asked.

He shook his head. "Nothing."

Her nostrils flared. "Liar! I can smell the stench of mistruth on you."

"She said…" Javier worked his jaw. "She said that your eldest brother Zoran would become the next pendragon."

Phoebe's eyes sparked. "The Bitkal has not been held yet. How could she know that?"

The sorcerer shook his head. "I asked that as well, but she refused to say."

Aidan's sister stared hard at him for a minute, judging him. "Are you certain of that?"

"Yes," he said, sounding strained.

Phoebe asked him a few more pointed questions, but she didn't learn anything useful. Once she was done, she nodded toward me. "Now give her the address."

"I would check the container first." Javier's expression and tone were firm. His pride had been hurt enough for one day, and he wasn't giving in to any more bullying from Phoebe.

"Here." I handed it over.

The sorcerer took hold of it and lifted the lid. After a moment of eyeing it closely, he shocked me by dumping the scales onto the coffee table between us. They piled up in glittering flecks of green, some spilling over the sides onto the floor. It took a while before he shook the last of them free. Conrad and I shifted in our seats, getting our first good look at exactly how much we'd gathered. I estimated it to be enough to fill half a dozen milk jugs—gallon sized.

"Holy shit," Conrad swore under his breath.

Phoebe lifted a brow at me. "You've been busy."

Javier sorted through the pile the way a ginseng buyer would check roots. Did he think I would put some fake plastic ones in there or something? I was beginning to feel a little offended by the time he stopped and looked up.

"This is of sufficient quality—though I'd prefer if next time you took a little more care when prying them off the dragon bodies." He picked up one of the scales that had chips in it from one of the knives we used. "This is hardly usable."

I glared at him. "Every minute I sit there prying those off is another minute the dead dragon's buddies might show up. It's dangerous. Have you ever tried getting them yourself?"

"No." He tossed the scale over his shoulder. "But the other dragon slayers I've worked with have done a better job."

"Oh, and where are the others?" I asked.

He didn't answer.

I wished I could say it was a comfort to know I wasn't the only one of my kind to work with him, but it only annoyed me more that he had manipulated other slayers as well. Could my father be included among Javier's previous clients? Was that why he rushed out of town so quickly? Maybe it wasn't just me, and there was more to it than I knew.

"Give her the address," Phoebe said, staring down at him. "I'm ready to leave this place."

Javier sighed and got up. He headed over to his desk where he took out a paper and pen, jotting something down. After he finished, he held the paper out to me. "Here."

I moved toward him, taking it. "The airport?"

"Most of the hangars there are being used as dragon dens. I don't know which one has the children, though. My sources only go so far."

"Seriously, man?" Conrad stared at him in disgust. "You made us do all that work and you can't even give us full intel?"

Javier shrugged. "That is all I have."

"We'll figure it out," Phoebe promised, giving me a confident look. "Let's get out of here."

"Just one warning," the sorcerer said as we reached the door. "There are dozens of dragons living there with new arrivals coming in regularly. You might want to bring help."

Phoebe gave Javier a haughty look. "Don't worry your pretty little head, sorcerer. We'll be just fine."

I was beginning to like Aidan's sister.

25

AIDAN

idan stood before the assembled dragons at the center of the jakhal. They had concluded the last of the negotiations during the afternoon, eaten a celebratory feast for the midday meal, and now all he had to do was say farewell. He couldn't get out of there fast enough to return home. Aidan stepped toward the pendragon and blew a puff of steam in her face.

She smiled in pleasure and returned the gesture. *Be well during your travels, son of Throm.*

He bowed his head. *May your toriq always be blessed with strength and cunning.*

Lorcan came to his side. *I will escort you and your brethren to the border.*

Aidan had expected no less. With a final nod for the pendragon, they lifted into the air. He and Lorcan took the lead while Falcon, Donar, and three escorts flew behind them. It was early evening now, and the

289

sun had begun its descent in the sky. Aidan estimated
that if there were no delays, they would make it home
an hour or so after it set. It occurred to him that he was
in a hurry because he was anxious to check on Bailey.
The slayer wouldn't have sat still at his lair for such a
long length of time, and she'd likely gone out to fight
more dragons. Her skills had improved considerably
over the last weeks, but she still had much to learn. He
could only hope she had not gotten herself into trouble
during his absence. Aidan had been feeling this itch
since shortly after he left, telling him he needed to
check on her. It had been all he could do to ignore it
and focus on his activities with the Faegud.

You did better than I expected with the negotiations,
Lorcan said, breaking the silence through private com-
munication with Aidan.

Your mother makes an excellent pendragon, he replied.
It was the truth. Hildegard might be tough, but she was
just what the toriq needed to regain their former glory.

She does, Lorcan agreed, staring straight ahead at
the horizon. *But she did not expect you to be such a natural
diplomat—neither did I.*

Aidan did not feel like a diplomat. He'd hated every
moment of the treaty negotiations, and the idea of the
clan's future being on his shoulders. Last night, after
he returned to his guest quarters, he'd told Falcon as
much. The older dragon had said, "the day that major
decisions don't trouble you is the day you are no longer
fit to do the job." Excellent advice, though it did little
to console Aidan. Would his father be pleased or upset

by the signed treaty he was bringing back with him? He would find out soon enough.

I do what I must for my toriq, Aidan eventually replied.

A quizzical expression came over Lorcan's eyes. *Will you truly mate with one of our females if your siblings do not?*

Aidan barely managed to keep his expression neutral. *Yes.*

It takes one far less observant than I to see you would rather not. Perhaps your sister will save you from making that sacrifice, Lorcan suggested.

I do not suppose you know who her lover was all those years ago, Aidan asked. Lorcan was one of the few who also knew about Phoebe's liaisons with a Faegud dragon. Often, he had arranged the meetings so that they could see each other without anyone knowing.

Lorcan filled Aidan's mind with ironic laughter. *She never told you the identity of her lover?*

No, he growled. It still annoyed him that his sister could not trust him with such a thing when he already knew the rest.

Ask her again and perhaps she'll tell you now that there is peace between our toriqan.

I plan on it, Aidan replied.

They approached the Red River. The two males grew silent until they reached it.

Lorcan gave him a parting look. *I will see you again soon, friend.*

I'll look forward to it, Aidan said.

He watched the Faegud dragons break off and turn around. Falcon and Donar caught up to him, and they picked up speed. All of them were tired and ready to return to the fortress as soon as possible.

Remind me to never go with you to negotiate a treaty again, Donar grumbled. *The food was terrible. It will take me a week to get the bird feathers out of my teeth.*

There are brushes for that, Aidan pointed out. Even in their dragon forms, shifters had enough dexterity in the fingers to use implements to clean their teeth. The pure dragons, though, had other tricks they used since their forelegs were too short and they lacked coordination in their paws.

Donar glared. *You know what I mean.*

Do you ever stop complaining? Falcon asked.

Aidan snorted. *He gets this way when he is tired or bored.*

And what puts him in a good mood? the older dragon asked, curious.

When he is eating his mother's cooking, when he is fighting in battle, and when he's had a romping night with...

Enough! Donar interrupted. *I did not complain that much this trip.*

Aidan and Falcon exchanged glances, but decided to let it go. They sped up their flight a little more, almost turning it into a race. Their speed was so great, in fact, that they arrived at the fortress in less than two hours—far better time than on the way down to see the Faegud.

After landing, Aidan asked the gate guards for his father's current whereabouts. They informed him the pendragon was in his office. That was a good sign. If

Throm was up and about, he must have been having a good day. More than anything, Aidan wanted his father to live for as long as possible. He didn't like to think about how life would become once the pendragon was gone—regardless of who replaced him.

Aidan parted ways with Falcon and Donar after entering the keep and headed straight for the castle. The main thoroughfare was crowded, slowing him down. He had to weave his way around numerous shifters and humans. It was all he could do not to growl at them, impatient to give his father the good news so that he could go check on Bailey after that.

The scent of meat cooking over an open fire pit reached his nose. Aidan might have only been gone for four days, but he had missed the familiar smells of the keep. It wasn't enough to deter him from his mission, though. He could wait until midnight meal to fill his belly and rid himself of the horrible taste of Faegud cooking.

Finally reaching the castle, he hurried through the great hall and down the corridors until he reached Throm's office. The door stood open, as if the pendragon expected him. His father looked up as Aidan entered.

"Come in," Throm said, his eyes lighting up. "And shut the door behind you."

Aidan closed it and moved to stand in front of his father's desk. Though he wanted to tell him the news right then, he had to wait for the pendragon to ask. It was the way of things and always had been. When he was a child, he would rush to say things without so much as a greeting, and he would be punished for it every time with a sound thwacking to the head. It had taken until his sixteenth year before he learned his lesson.

"I trust you had a safe journey, and the Faegud treated you well?" Throm asked.

Aidan nodded. "They did."

The pendragon held out his hand. "You may give me the treaty."

"Father?" Aidan gave him a confused look. He hadn't even had the opportunity to say he'd succeeded in securing one.

"Son, if you had failed the guilt would be in your eyes—never mind the excuses you would have no doubt contrived for me." Throm gestured with his fingers. "Now give me the treaty."

Aidan pulled it from shiggara and handed it to the pendragon. Perhaps it was a silly thing, but he had looked forward to announcing the news. He should have known it would be all business with his father.

Long minutes ticked by as the pendragon read over the long document, unfurling it as he went. The entire time, Aidan thought about every stipulation and agreement, worrying over what faults his father might find. He had done the best he could and fought for every advantage he could possibly gain, but he had never even read a treaty document before. His father had refused to let him peruse them, saying it was best to see how Aidan did without relying on precedent. The only thing the pendragon had done was give him the details of what he could or could not give as concessions. It was barely enough to get him started.

Throm grunted. "They asked for interbreeding?"

"Yes." Aidan held his hands behind his back. "Hildegard insisted there could be no treaty without it."

The pendragon narrowed his eyes. "And you went ahead with the negotiations anyway?"

"You did not tell me it was something that could not be included...and to send word to ask you would have been seen as a sign of weakness," Aidan said, standing behind his decision even if it meant losing his father's regard.

Throm looked over that section of the document again, his expression unreadable. Aidan mentally prepared himself to be exiled from the toriq at any moment. His father had said that was a possibility if he failed on this task.

"Did Hildegard attempt to demand a certain amount of the children stay with her clan?" Throm asked.

"She did."

The pendragon rubbed at his chin. "Yet the treaty says that every child has the right to choose their allegiance when they come of age."

"They do," Aidan said, a glimmer of hope rising that perhaps his father was not too disappointed.

"You have also outlined a neutral territory between the clans and designated it as a place for where couples may live if they cannot or will not live within either jakhal." He gazed closer at the document.

"I am surprised you thought this far ahead, though I shouldn't be."

Aidan slowly let out the breath he'd been holding and replied, "Hildegard would have kept most of the offspring from our alliance if she had gotten her way. I pointed out that her clan is far larger than ours, and we need shape-shifter children as much as she does."

"That female always was a greedy one, but I am pleased to hear she is the new Faegud leader. Hildegard has always honored her promises—unlike Severne. This treaty will keep her in line with all that you have put into it. I see that you have even ensured they must come to our defense, but we are not required to come to theirs with the exception of one battle planned for the spring. That is most impressive to get such a concession."

Aidan bowed his head, grateful he had fought for that point. "I am pleased to hear it, father."

"Will you be the one to mate with one of their clan?" Throm asked, perusing back up the scroll. "That part is not clear. It only says one of my children must do so."

"I thought to give Zoran, Phoebe, and Ruari that option first," Aidan answered.

Throm grimaced. "I'm not surprised Hildegard forced that concession out of you, but I hope it is one of your siblings instead. This clan needs you here, son. Whether you succeed me or not, I know you will look out for our people."

Aidan refrained from checking his ears to be certain they operated properly. "Thank you, father. I am pleased you think so."

"Give me time to read the rest of this over. I am certain it is all in working order, but I may have more questions for you on the morrow." Throm rose up from his seat and came around the desk, pulling a surprised Aidan into a tight embrace. "You have done very well. Now go enjoy what is left of the evening and give an old dragon some peace."

Aidan's chest was tight as he left the office. He believed his father was proud of him, but for Throm to show his feelings so easily, it must have meant he had little time remaining. There were those who said an elder dragon always knew when his death approached. It left Aidan with a cold feeling inside. Was his father's seemingly renewed energy a last gasp before he left them for good? He certainly hoped not.

26

On the way back from seeing Javier, a roadblock appeared up ahead. If I had been listening to the radio while driving, I might have known it was there ahead of time, but I didn't want Phoebe finding out about Hank. He was our only source of news, and I had no idea how she, Aidan, or their clan would react if they discovered humans had a network for communicating news to each other. Unless a good reason came up to tell the shifters, there was no reason to reveal the radio station to them.

The road bandits had parked a line of cars across Lindsey Street with armed men and women standing guard behind them. I probably should have turned around and gone some other way, but I was tired, and my shoulder was beginning to ache. Pain made me grouchy. Danae and Trish had been right that I should have given myself another day, but it had been worth going out. I had the location of the missing children, and Phoebe had confirmed her murder suspect.

"Bailey, what are you doing?" Conrad asked as I kept driving forward. I hadn't dropped him off at Earl's since he'd used one of the neighborhood cars to meet me at Aidan's house earlier.

"I'm going to talk to these guys," I said, tightening my hands on the wheel. "It's getting old going around them every damn time they feel like harassing people who drive down this street. If they want to have a conversation, I'm going to give them one."

From the rear view mirror, I caught sight of a semi truck moving to block the street behind us—so predictable. The road bandits never changed their tactics. To make matters worse, they had long since figured out dragons were no longer attacking humans on this side of town where the shifters roamed, so they could rob people any time of day they wanted.

"What's this about?" Phoebe asked, narrowing her gaze on the road block ahead.

Of course, she wouldn't know. She usually got to fly over all the problems the rest of us faced on the ground. I continued inching my truck forward as I explained the issue. "These guys like to rob people of their cars and anything they've got with them. At least once or twice a week they block the road, and if you don't see it in time to turn around, they trap you."

"Do they kill their victims as well?" she asked, a puff of steam coming out of her nostrils.

I shrugged. "Only if you fight them."

"We're in my territory now. We will have this conversation with them."

Conrad let out a martyred sigh from the backseat. "Great. This is what happens when you get two tough women in the same vehicle. They get all macho and shit."

"Quit being a baby," I admonished. "This could be fun."

I stopped the truck about thirty feet in front of the road block, shut the engine off, and pulled the keys from the ignition. Grabbing a pair of sunglasses, I handed them to Phoebe and instructed her to put them on. It would be dark soon, but I didn't want the thieves getting a good look at her eyes if I could help it.

Several men and women headed toward us with their rifles trained in our direction. They were a little on the grungy side, but they looked like they knew their way around weapons—which I could confirm from a previous experience with them.

A burly guy with a long beard called out, "Get out of the truck, nice and slowly, with your hands up. Don't try anything funny and don't try to be a hero—it'll get you dead."

"He should move to Hollywood and get himself an agent," I mumbled, pulling my door open. I paused to glance over at Phoebe and Conrad. "Just follow my lead."

We got out of the truck and walked toward the armed road bandits.

"Is this really necessary?" I asked, keeping my hands high.

A woman with oily-blond hair who appeared to be in her mid-twenties glared at me and then at Phoebe. "What kind of crazy clothes are ya'll wearin'? It ain't Halloween for a few more weeks."

"Would you believe me if I told you they're bullet-proof?" I asked, keeping my voice light and calm.

The woman laughed. "We got us a few crazies."

"Gimme the keys to the truck," the burly man demanded, reaching out a hand.

"I'm afraid I can't do that," I said, giving him a tight-lipped smile. "It's kind of hard to track down dragons and kill them if I have to walk everywhere."

He frowned. "You can't be the…"

"That's the slayer!" said a young guy standing behind the cars. He lowered his pistol and started walking up to me. "She looks just like the radio guy said she would."

The blond woman rolled her eyes at him. "That's just whimsy talk. There ain't no damn dragon slayer—ain't no such thing."

"Actually, there is." This came from an older woman with curly gray hair. "I caught a glimpse of her a few weeks back, and she's real."

The younger woman gave her a skeptical look. "Are you sure?"

"Yep." She nodded. "Same girl, same truck."

"But she's too little," the blond argued.

I listened to them with amusement, waiting for them to work it out amongst themselves.

The older woman muttered an expletive under her breath. "It don't change the truth and that young man there—" She pointed at Conrad. "He was with her, too."

"Are you really the dragon slayer?" the burly man asked, gazing at me closely as if it would be written somewhere on my forehead.

I nodded. "Yes."

He glanced down to my sheathed sword. "How many you killed?"

"I think seventeen or eighteen now." I wasn't sure if I should count the one my father finished off. "It's getting harder to keep track."

He rubbed at his beard. "Well, if you're killin' them, I reckon we gotta let you go. We already lost a few friends and family to those damn dragons, and we want to see the rest of them gone. Think you can do that?"

"I'm working on it," I said.

Phoebe started to say something, but I shook my head at her. No way did I want to try explaining the intricacies of dragon politics to these people. At least, not until we got the green dragons out of Norman, and the shape-shifters could fully take over.

"Alright, listen up!" The man turned around and addressed his crew. "This lady here and her friends are not to be bothered. If you see 'em comin', you let 'em pass. Got that?"

The men and women mumbled their agreements.

He turned back to me. "Go on, then. We'll make room for you to pass."

"Thank you." I gestured at Phoebe and Conrad, and we headed back for the truck.

Once we were inside, Conrad blew out a breath. "I didn't think that was really going to work."

"Something must be done about them," Phoebe said as I started up the truck. "They can't be allowed to keep robbing people."

I agreed, but we had bigger problems at the moment than some road bandits. If I tried stopping all the criminal activity that had risen up since D-day, I'd never actually get to kill dragons. For now, I just needed people to leave me alone so I could do what I was born to do. Someone else would have to take up the job of policing the human population of the city.

The bandits pushed one of the cars out of the way, opening the road block enough for my truck to pass. The old man gave me a salute, and I waved back. They might not be the good guys, but I needed to at least act civil with them if I wanted to move about freely. It had gotten old in the last few months trying to avoid their ambush points. The dents on my truck and my broken windows were proof enough of that.

We continued on our way toward Aidan's house. Verena's place didn't appear around the area I thought it should be located, and Phoebe didn't note it. Of course, the country house looked pretty harmless if you didn't know who lived there. Even if she did see it, she might not have a reason to ask about it.

The sun had set by the time we got back. I tensed when my headlights flashed on Aidan, who stood in the middle of the field with his arms crossed and a dark expression on his face. How long had he been waiting there?

"Shifitt," Phoebe said under her breath. "He is back already."

Conrad leaned forward, poking his head between our seats. "Man, he don't look happy."

"He'll get over it." I drove past Aidan to park the truck.

When I went to open the door, he was already there. "Where have you been?"

"Running errands," I said, getting out to stand in front of him.

He narrowed his eyes. "What errands?"

Phoebe came around to join us. "We just went to see that sorcerer your little spy told us about, brother. Nothing to worry your thick brows about."

"You what?" He glared at her.

She shrugged. "He had information we needed."

"I'm beginning to like her," Conrad said, standing over by the back of the truck where he could keep a healthy distance from Aidan.

The shape-shifter glanced at him and then at me. "What is he doing here?"

"It's a long story, and if we could go inside, we'll tell you all about it." I grabbed his arm, and he reluctantly followed along with me. "So how did the peace treaty thing work out?"

"It is done," he said, speaking through gritted teeth.

I smiled at him. "Good. I knew you could do it."

He worked his jaw. "Thank you."

We entered the house and everyone took a seat in the living room. I let Phoebe tell her side of the story first, revealing the news about the killer and why I'd had to come with her. He listened to her finish without interrupting once.

"So not only is Ember a murderer, but she has also betrayed our clan," Phoebe said, shaking her head in anger.

"We will deal with her as soon as we return to the fortress," Aidan reassured his sister, then turned his attention to me. "And you made a deal with the sorcerer as well?"

I lifted my chin. "The dragons needed to be killed anyway. It wasn't that big of a deal to collect the scales if it meant I could get the location of the children."

"And you got it?" he asked. There was something deadly quiet about his tone.

"Yes."

His gaze ran over to my shoulder. "Was it worth risking your life?"

I unconsciously rubbed my arm. "What are you talking about? It's just a flesh wound."

"You walked stiffly when we came into the house, you've hardly moved that arm, and the skin is permanently scarred. I suspect you were hurt days ago, and that a dragon must have sunk his teeth into you for it not to heal completely." He shot a look at his sister. "How bad was she hurt?"

Phoebe spread her hands in innocence. "I have no idea. I didn't see her until yesterday, and all I know about is her shoulder."

"Tell me, Bailey," Aidan commanded.

"I'm fine." Good grief, he was acting more protective than usual.

Aidan leaned forward and grabbed my left arm, lifting halfway up until I cried out. He hadn't moved it in a direction that would have hurt if I hadn't injured it. He let go, but kept his gaze hard on me. "You have a friend who can heal injuries. I suspect if she did not help you with this one, it is either because it was beyond her abilities, or she was too busy healing other parts of you."

Conrad cleared his throat. "Actually, it was both."

I gave him an incredulous look, which he ignored.

Aidan directed his gaze on the younger man. "Tell me"

"Her shoulder was bitten and crushed by dragon teeth. Danae couldn't do anything for that. She just healed Bailey's cracked skull, broken leg, and busted ribs—which was from falling off a three-story building. I don't even know how she survived all that."

"You traitor," I bit out.

Conrad shrugged a shoulder. "You don't want to listen to anybody else, but I figure you might listen to him. I told you not to push yourself so hard."

"She was already tired when this occurred?" Aidan asked.

"Yep. I tried talking her into taking a break, but she just wanted to get those scales."

I leaped to my feet. "To save the children!"

"Come with me," Aidan said, taking hold of my right hand.

He dragged me upstairs to the bedroom he used when he stayed at the house. Shutting the door, he spun me around and trapped me against the wall with his arms braced on both sides. For a minute, we stayed like that—close, but not quite touching. The heat from his body warmed my skin, and his breaths tickled my cheeks. I had no idea what to say or do. He'd averted his face, hiding any clue of his thoughts from me.

Finally, he met my gaze. "Don't put yourself in danger like that again."

"It's sort of my job—which you trained me to do."

He lifted a hesitant hand and cupped my cheek. "Why is it that no matter how hard I try, I cannot help caring about you?"

I put my hand over his. "Sometimes I want to ask you the same question."

Aidan searched my face. For what, I didn't know. "If something were to happen to you, I'm not certain what I would do—but it would not be good. Please do not put yourself in unnecessary danger."

I swallowed. It wasn't often he let me see this side of himself. "I wouldn't have if children weren't involved."

"Next time, wait for me." He pulled me into a hug, careful of my shoulder. "If I know I can't stop you, I will always fight by your side."

I rested my cheek against his chest and closed my eyes, breathing in the musky scent of him. The only time I ever felt totally relaxed and safe was when I was with Aidan. It seemed like the more we fought our attraction, the stronger it got.

"We're going to scout the dragon den tomorrow," I said, opening my eyes and gazing up at him. Aidan was about eight inches taller than me, making it a bit of a stretch.

His lips quirked. "I'll come with you."

"It's easier if Conrad stays here tonight so we can go first thing. Phoebe was already planning to come earlier than you guys usually get up. If you come with her in the morning, we can hopefully get there before any of the Shadowan are awake," I said.

Aidan scowled. "I don't like that boy here."

"You know he's just a friend, right?" I asked, wanting to get that point cleared up once and for all. Conrad wouldn't be so defensive all the time if Aidan didn't make him that way.

"He is with you all the time," he argued.

I lifted a brow. "Kind of like Donar is with you all the time? Conrad watches my back, he makes me laugh sometimes, and he's there to pick me up when I fall—literally, sometimes. That is it. There is nothing between us except friendship, and there never will be anything more."

Aidan was quiet for a moment. "With males and females, such relationships can change."

He was going to force me to say something I really didn't want to admit, not even to myself, but maybe it was time to fully clear the air. We'd been dancing around this topic ever since we first kissed, and I could see that he didn't know for sure where he stood with me. Maybe we couldn't be together, but at least we could be open about our feelings.

"Aidan." I took a deep breath. "As long as you're in my life, I don't think I can ever look at another man the way I do you. That's just…that's just the way it is whether I like it or not. Please don't worry about Conrad because he is not you, and that's all there is to it."

Aidan expelled a breath. "It should not relieve me as much as it does to hear that."

I grabbed hold of his camrium vest. "So can Conrad stay the night then?"

He worked his jaw. "Yes, but in a different room."

"You're impossible." I shook my head. Not that I planned on sharing a room with Conrad when there were several available in the house, but it still seemed ridiculous that he had to make that a condition.

"Perhaps I am," he admitted.

Footsteps sounded on the stairs, and we broke apart.

"I guess you should go catch that murderer," I said.

He nodded. "My sister and I will return in the morning."

Our gazes lingered on each other a moment longer, and then he opened the door and walked out.

27

AIDAN

Aidan and Phoebe flew toward the fortress, sailing through the clear night air. From above, they couldn't miss the numerous torches lighting the keep and castle. He'd always thought this was the best time to fly. Dragons were most alert when the moon rose, and their senses became more acute.

She's not as bad as I thought she'd be, Phoebe said, breaking into Aidan's thoughts.

He glanced over at his sister. *You mean Bailey?*

Yes, who else would I be talking about?

I am surprised you asked for her help. The last thing he'd expected was to find his sister and the dragon slayer together when he returned. Rather, he'd come to his empty lair and worried something had happened to Bailey. She wasn't one to stay out late into the evening. If they had not returned minutes after he arrived, he would have gone searching for her. His beast had been in such a panic it only made Aidan's concern worse.

It was not as if he spent every day with the slayer, but for some reason being so far from her this time bothered him more than normal. He had felt on edge the entire trip. Aidan had told himself he simply wanted the comfort of home, but he'd lied to himself. His beast had somehow sensed something was wrong with Bailey. Considering the extent of her injuries, she could have died, and he had not been there. That bothered him on a deep, primal level that he could not deny. Just because she had grown strong did not mean she never needed help. Even Aidan had strong warriors to assist him including Donar, Falcon, and his sister. Bailey had Conrad—a weak, little human. The young man may try his best to watch over the slayer, but he was no match for a dragon.

Phoebe broke into Aidan's thoughts. *I put it off, but I couldn't figure out a way to locate the sorcerer on my own. He is well shielded—even to me. It was not until Bailey led me straight to him that I could see past the guise he's put up to protect his domain.*

What did you make of him? Aidan didn't like the idea of his sister anywhere near an unknown sorcerer, but he might have done the same in her position. He only wished he could have gone with them.

Javier is ambitious and greedy, but it is too early to tell if he will become a problem for us. If he does not expand beyond the land he claims now, it would not be such a bad thing. I only worry he might want more—they usually do.

That is what concerns me as well, Aidan said.

He nudged his sister with his wingtip, and they descended to the open area in front of the fortress gates.

Upon landing, they immediately shifted to their human forms. Aidan wanted to deal with Ember as quickly as possible so that he would not miss the midnight meal. He'd been thinking about it ever since returning that evening.

They stopped in front of the gates and Phoebe addressed the guard on the right. "Is Ember within the keep?"

"She has not left the fortress today," he replied. There was curiosity in the guard's gaze, but he did not dare ask why she wanted to know.

"Do you have any idea where she is?" Aidan asked. The current guards would have just begun their shift when night fell. It was possible they may have seen Ember around the keep before that.

The guard on the left answered, "I saw her in the great hall for first meal but not since then."

The other shifter only shook his head. They thanked the guards for their assistance and headed into the keep.

"We'll check her home first," Aidan said.

Phoebe stopped and turned to face him. "Her family could be there as well. This might get ugly—whether she's with them or not."

That much was true. Ember's family did not have any notable warriors, but they were known to fight dirty. It was one of the reasons their status within the toriq remained so low.

Aidan eyed the guard headquarters back near the gate. "We will get assistance."

They managed to find four males who didn't have any other pressing duties and instructed them to come along. As they made their way through the main thoroughfare, they ran into Ruari. Their older brother eyed them with suspicion.

"What are you two doing?" he asked.

Aidan leveled his gaze on him, unwilling to play their usual game. "Where is Ember?"

"How should I know?" Ruari gave him an offended look. "I do not talk to her anymore."

Phoebe stepped closer to her elder brother, her expression accusing. "We know you talked to her the day the head guard was murdered. Do not act innocent with us."

Ruari worked his jaw. "I had nothing to do with that."

"Then tell us where your *think* Ember might be," Aidan said.

Comprehension dawned in his brother's eyes. "You suspect she killed Nanoq."

Phoebe growled. "Will you tell us or not?"

"I may know where she is at this time of night. There is a little-known tavern you two would never find on your own." Ruari turned on his feet. "Follow me."

Aidan took hold of his brother's shoulder and swung him around. "Just tell us the location. You are not going with us."

A determined expression came over Ruari's eyes. "Oh, I am going. Ember has caused me enough trouble, and I will not have my brother and sister believing

I had anything to do with Nanoq's death. If that means I must help you, then I will do it."

Aidan stepped back, surprised. He hadn't expected this sort of reaction out of Ruari. When he glanced at Phoebe, she showed the same astonishment. Their elder brother was always up to something, but perhaps he truly didn't have any part in this.

"Lead the way," Aidan said.

Ruari took them away from the main thoroughfare and wound through several narrow paths. The farther they went, the filthier the cobblestones became until it seemed only mud, piss, and dung remained beneath their feet. There were many animals kept within the fortress, including goats, chickens, and the occasional milk cow. The shifters who lived in this section of the keep did not clean up after their livestock as well as they should.

Aidan's nose twitched at the rancid stench. He was about ready to call it off, thinking his brother only wished to torture them, when Ruari stopped at a dead end. He nodded at a well-worn door that did not sit properly on its hinges. There was no sign to mark it. If not for the boisterous noise inside, one wouldn't have guessed it for a tavern. This was in the seedier section of the keep where Aidan rarely visited, and by the expression on Phoebe's face, she did not come here often, either.

"Are there any other ways inside?" Aidan asked.

His brother pointed to a second-story window that led onto the front overhang. From there, one could skip over nearby rooftops and lose any pursuers. All the structures were clustered close together and the paths too narrow in this neighborhood. If Ember escaped from that window, they'd surely lose her in moments to the darkness.

Phoebe came to the same conclusion and pointed at two of the guards. "Climb up there and don't let anyone out."

"And you two," Aidan addressed the remaining shifters. "Guard this entrance. If Ember comes out, you must stop her."

They nodded and took positions on either side of the tavern door. After assuring themselves there were no other methods of escape, Aidan and his siblings went inside. His eyes began to water as soon as he entered. The odors in the alleyway could not compare to the insufferable stench within the tavern. Numerous unwashed bodies, spilled alefire (of low quality), and food left to rot on the floor filled the air. It was also hot and rather crowded.

Ruari had to yell for Aidan and his sister to hear him. "She is over in the corner, sitting with two of her brothers drinking."

He turned his gaze that way and spotted Ember. Despite the nastiness of the place, she somehow managed to keep herself and her warrior garb clean. Her black hair was pulled back in a bun, and she just had a few loose strands in the front plastered to her face from sweat. Even a dragon could only handle so much heat. One could have almost baked bread just by putting the dough on a table in here. Their body temperatures ran so high it was never a good idea to have so many shift-ers in such a small space. Even in the great hall, the ceiling was three times as high as the tavern, and they restricted how many clansmen could be in there at any given time.

"Let's get her," Phoebe said, shoving her way through the crowd.

It took them several minutes, despite the distance not being that far away, but they eventually broke through the throng of patrons to the dark corner where Ember and her family sat. For a moment, she and her brothers continued to drink and shout at each other, unaware of the attention on them. Then Ember turned her head. Her eyes widened, and she leaped to her feet, reaching for a knife strapped to her belt.

Phoebe leaped forward and punched the female shifter in the face. Ember fell into her oldest brother's lap. As she gripped her broken nose, Phoebe yanked her up and tossed her to the floor. Several patrons stepped on Ember in their effort to get out of the way. Aidan's sister jumped on her back, and a pair of man-acles appeared in her hand. He could only guess she had anticipated this arrest ahead of time and put a set of bindings in shiggara for this purpose.

Phoebe began snapping the cuffs into place. A roar came from behind Aidan, and he braced himself as a male shifter charged into him. He and Ember's brother went down in a tangle, wrestling for the higher position. Aidan kneed the male in the stomach and crawled out from under him, then stomped on the shifter's face. Ember's brother—whose name escaped him—groaned. Aidan kicked him a few more times until he fell unconscious.

When he turned around, he found Ruari had taken care of the other brother. The shifter lay sprawled next to his chair with his face bloodied beyond recognition. Ruari might not be the greatest warrior, but he was strong and well trained. Aidan checked on Phoebe and found his sister had Ember on her feet, fully manacled.

"Unless you want this place shut down, get out of the way!" he shouted to the patrons.

Aidan received quite a few nasty looks, but the shifters moved to clear a path. Moments later they were outside and calling the two guards down from the rooftop. They moved steadily away from the seedier section of the keep and its foul stench. Every shifter who saw them stood agape as they watched their female prisoner led down the path. Ember's hair had come loose in her fight with Phoebe, and blood ran down her face. Still, one could not miss the rage in her eyes.

They hauled her straight to the dungeons, using an outside entrance on the east side of the castle. Ember struggled when she saw where they were taking her. Up to this point, they had not even told her why she was apprehended. She had to know the reason, though. If she had been innocent, she would have asked rather than fighting them the moment they showed up.

Aidan took the lead, taking a spare torch from the entrance to light the way. This was the oldest part of the fortress and went quite deep into the earth.

According to the history he'd learned as a child, his ancestors built their stone homes underground thousands of years ago where they could live until the castle was completed. It was the only way to stay safe from the pure dragons at that time. Thinking of the Faegud, he supposed his toriq was not that dissimilar. The only difference being his people had always chosen to live in shifter form, which was evident in the winding stairs being far too narrow for a dragon to traverse.

They were deep underground by the time they reached the main corridor. It branched off in multiple directions, almost like a maze, but some areas had been sealed with stone walls when they'd fallen into disrepair. There was no point in restoring them. Their people did not have so many criminals to need more than half a dozen prison cells. Even then, Aidan had never seen them all filled. Only two prisoners sat in them now.

Phoebe led Ember to the largest room first where most interrogations were done. Inside, there was only a stone table and two benches. One of the seats had metal hooks where the shackles could be connected. His sister shoved Ember onto that bench and locked her in place.

The angry shifter glared up at Phoebe. "Why have you brought me here?"

Aidan stood off to the side, careful not to lean on the grimy wall. "You are just now asking?"

"You know why you are here," Phoebe said, coming around the table to glare into Ember's face. "Do not play stupid with us."

The female shifter turned to Ruari and gave him a pleading expression. "You have to help me. Whatever they think I've done, it's not true!"

Aidan grunted. "If that was the case, you wouldn't have fought us when we came to see you in the tavern."

"My brother has a point," Ruari agreed. "It does make you appear rather guilty."

Ember shifted on her seat, rattling her shackles. "Then tell me my crime."

"You killed Nanoq," Phoebe said.

"It's not true!"

She was a horrible liar. Even when Ember tried pleading with Ruari, her body language and tone rang false. There wasn't an innocent bone in that female's body.

Phoebe braced her hands on the table. "Why did you kill Nanoq?"

"I didn't." Ember jutted her chin out. "I hardly even knew him."

Phoebe lifted a brow. "Really? I went through his office, which was oddly missing a lot of documents, but when I searched his quarters, I found notes he'd written about you. He'd had an open investigation regarding serious accidents befalling several of our clansmen after they ingested powerful herbs they didn't recall taking. He believed someone was slipping them into their drinks. On one parchment, in particular, he had circled your name several times. I can't imagine he never questioned you."

Aidan and Ruari exchanged surprised glances. Their sister hadn't told either of them about this development, but perhaps she had known it alone wouldn't be enough to convict Ember. Phoebe would have needed more to convince their toriq of her guilt. Crimes such as murder had to have overwhelming evidence or else the accuser could get themselves in a lot of trouble. Dragons were rather particular in that way.

"He questioned me once and searched my home... but he found nothing," Ember said defensively.

Phoebe straightened. "And yet his notes said you were seen near the apothecary around the time the herbs went missing."

That came as no surprise to Aidan. He had known Ruari took the herbs from the apothecary and given them to Ember soon after. Donar nearly died due to her drugging his cousin's drink during his mealtime, just before he went back to work on the fortress walls. The herbs didn't go into effect until he was at the top. He grew dizzy and fell off, sustaining serious injuries. Could Nanoq have figured these things out as well? If so, the Captain of the Guard had been keeping it quiet.

"It is just a coincidence," Ember said, jerking on her shackles.

Phoebe cocked her head. "Perhaps, but is it a coincidence as well that a sorcerer who goes by the name Javier told me he gave you a garrote that fits the description of Nanoq's murder weapon? Interesting also, that you supplied him with important information about our toriq in exchange. That alone is treason, for which the punishment is execution or banishment."

"She did what?" Ruari asked, his expression shocked. He turned an accusing look on Ember. "What were you thinking?"

She clamped her lips shut and averted her face. Phoebe continued presenting her evidence piece by piece, but the female shape-shifter refused to speak again or even look at them. This went on for an hour before the pendragon entered the room. Throm pulled Phoebe outside while the rest of them stayed in the room.

Ruari glanced over at him. "It is impressive what you and our sister can accomplish when you work together."

"You would do well to remember that," Aidan said, giving him a pointed look.

"Hah! I did not say you were that good." Ruari's lips spread into a mischievous grin.

Aidan decided to ignore his brother.

After more than fifteen minutes passed, Ember shot a pensive glance at the door. It was one thing to get questioned by Phoebe, but the pendragon could do things to her—or rather have things done to her—that no one else could. Aidan wondered if it would come to that, or if Throm would be satisfied with the information they had. It was more than enough to convict the female shifter, but they still had a lot of unanswered questions. The main one being what had motivated her.

Ruari was a fairly good liar, but even he had seemed genuinely shocked by her actions.

The pendragon came bursting through the door, his complexion red with rage. "Admit your crimes now, or I will resort to drastic measures."

Ember's eyes watered, and her chin wobbled, but she said nothing.

"I will not ask again," Throm said, straightening to his full, imposing height. He might have been weaker than he was a year ago, but he could still be quite intimidating.

The female shape-shifter looked away.

Throm poked his head out the door. "Call Xanath. Tell him to get here right away."

"Are you sure you want to do that, father?" Phoebe asked.

"Do you dare question me? I want the truth, and I want it now!" the pendragon shouted.

She dropped her gaze and took a step back. "Of course."

Ruari scooted toward the far corner of the room. Even Aidan was starting to feel nervous around the pendragon, and he was rather certain he'd done nothing wrong—that his father knew about, anyway. Throm had that kind of effect when he was in a bad mood.

A short while later, Xanath entered the room. The old sorcerer wore a long, black robe and his hair was gray and curly. He had been alive for slightly longer than Aidan, but he wouldn't last much longer. While sorcerers didn't live nearly as long as dragons, they could extend their life through magic to three times that of the average human. It was one of the few spells they were allowed to perform within the fortress without requiring permission first. Of course, it took most of their magic to slow their aging process, and it had to be regularly maintained. Most of those who lived in the outside world would not make that kind of sacrifice. On the other hand, sorcerers who lived with shape-shifters usually only performed minor spells, such as ones to protect warrior garments, leaving them enough magic to extend their lifespan.

"What is it you wish for, milord?" Xanath asked.

"I want to know every crime she's ever committed, and what her motivations are for attacking Nanoq. Get everything you can out of her," the pendragon commanded.

The sorcerer's face blanched. "Are you certain? I could extract some details without irreparable damage."

Ember whimpered. She knew what was coming, and still she didn't speak up.

"I want everything," Throm said curtly, then left the room.

Phoebe came to stand by Aidan. "This is going to take a while."

"I know."

She glanced at him. "Midnight meal is about to start. Maybe you should eat and come back. I doubt you'll miss much."

"No, I won't make you watch this alone." Their father had made them observe the process once before a few decades ago for another traitor who'd been giving information to the Shadowan clan about them. That shifter had fallen in love with one of their females, and he had been willing to do anything for her. He was long dead now.

Xanath moved over to Ember. She pulled on her shackles, attempting to scoot as far from him as she could. He only came closer with a grim line of determination forming on his lips. The sorcerer was rarely called upon to perform dark magic, and he didn't enjoy using it. If ever there was one of his race Aidan could say he liked, it would be Xanath. He had always been kind to everyone he met, unless commanded to do otherwise.

"I am sorry, my dear," he murmured.

Ember cried out as he put a hand to her head. She scrunched her eyes shut and pulled her knees to her chest, making herself as small as she could. Xanath pushed his fingers harder into her skull, and a soft glow emanated from his fingertips. Ember began to sob in earnest.

"Do not fight it," the sorcerer said, his voice a scratchy whisper. "It will only make it worse for you."

She trembled and shook her head. The minutes passed excruciatingly slow. Ruari began to pace back and forth across the room, taking the five steps it required to reach one end to the other. Aidan had thought his brother might leave when Xanath arrived, but he appeared determined to stay and find out what information Ember had to divulge. Was Ruari as guilty as the female shifter?

Ember began twitching hard and fell onto her side on the bench. This lasted for half an hour while the sorcerer whispered chants, thickening the air with his magic. Then the screams began—loud piercing wails that went on almost without end. That was the sign Xanath had breached the most intimate parts of her mind. He kept one hand on her head, and the other braced on the table. With every minute that passed, the fatigue on his face grew.

About the time Aidan was convinced they would all suffer permanent hearing loss, the screams broke off, and drool spilled from the corner of Ember's mouth where she lay sprawled across the bench. The expression in her eyes turned vacant. There was nothing left of her mind, and it was unlikely any part of it would ever return. If only she hadn't fought the sorcerer so hard, she might have kept some semblance of herself. What could make a person sacrifice themselves in such a way? Aidan couldn't begin to comprehend it.

Xanath looked at Ruari. "You feared you would be the cause of what she did."

Aidan's brother gave a short nod. "But I never wanted any of this."

"Not to worry. You may not be a complete innocent, but she had her own reasons for what she did that had nothing to do with you—at least not directly," the sorcerer replied.

"Then why?" Phoebe asked.

That was the question they all wanted to be answered.

Xanath clasped his hands together, and his sleeves fell to cover them. "It was for your other brother, Zoran. Ember was in love with him, but he wanted nothing to do with her. After he refused her many times, she asked if she ensured he became the next pendragon if he would reconsider." The sorcerer sighed. "He gave her the impression that he would."

"Did he know what she was doing?" Phoebe moved toward Xanath. "Did he order her to do these things?"

"Not precisely. He told her who he wanted out of his way, but he did not explicitly state how she should go about doing it."

Ruari stared at Ember dumfounded. "But she said she wanted to help me."

"She was spying on you for Zoran. Everything she said and did in your company—including the most intimate of acts—was for him. She cared nothing for you at all," Xanath said, shaking his head. "This woman was not of sound mind, and she was obsessed."

Phoebe rubbed her neck. "Well, I guess it's time to go talk to our father and tell him the news."

"There is more I must tell the pendragon," Xanath said, his shoulders stooping. "But it should be done in private. I will go with you."

Aidan and his siblings exchanged curious looks. What more could there be?

"Very well." Phoebe opened the door. As the sorcerer went through, she glanced at Aidan and Ruari.

"I'll have the guards move Ember to a cell. You two can try to catch the end of midnight meal if you want."

The four guards they had gathered earlier were still standing in the tunnel corridor, waiting for orders. Aidan was glad they had not let them go yet. He wanted no part of touching the drooling mess that Ember had become. She probably wouldn't live more than a few weeks, but others would have to care for her body until it died naturally. It was the way their toriq always handled such things, which thankfully did not occur often.

"Let me know how it goes," Aidan said.

Phoebe nodded. "I will."

As she left the room, Ruari came up beside Aidan. "What else do you think Xanath discovered?"

"I have no idea."

28

BAILEY

I parked the truck in the corner of the YMCA parking lot next to a row of trees, and everyone piled
out of the vehicle. At a quarter-mile away, it was as
close as we could safely get to watch the airport hangars where Javier said the children had been taken.

All the roads leading to the airport were surrounded by flat open fields with few trees and buildings to
break up the landscape. Even to get as close as we did,
we'd had to wait for a flying green dragon patrol to
pass as it headed to the south. Most of the beasts were
asleep at ten o'clock in the morning, but a major lair
like this had to have extra security. It left me on edge.

"Here," Conrad said, handing me a pair of binoculars. "I don't see any movement, but you can look for
yourself."

"Thanks." I peeked through the binoculars.

The Max Westheimer Airport only had two main
runways, which we couldn't see from our position, but

329

it used to get a decent amount of traffic before D-day. Dozens of hangars and administrative buildings dotted the area, some with gaping holes and scorch marks. I only spotted a few small planes and most of those were half-burnt shells, useless to humans. The beasts had taken over and made the place their home.

A light breeze kicked up from the west, and Aidan sniffed the air. "There are many dragons nesting in there."

One of the reasons we'd chosen to come from the east was because of the wind direction. The last thing we needed was for our scent to give us away, but the shape-shifters could use our position to their advantage. I just prayed that Oklahoma's wacky weather didn't do anything to mess that up, or we'd be in trouble.

"It is like a small jakhal," Phoebe said, also taking in the breeze. "I am thinking there must be seventy or eighty dragons in there."

Aidan grunted in agreement.

I scanned a few more buildings with the binoculars and caught a glimpse of a green dragon inside a hangar, sleeping with its head tucked into its tail like a cat. The beast didn't appear to have a care in the world—and why should it? Anger rose inside of me, and I clutched the binoculars harder. My feet itched to run toward the dragon and slay it right where it lay.

Aidan touched my arm. "Calm yourself. This is not the time."

"I know," I said, dropping the binoculars and handing them back to Conrad. It was safer if he did the observing. If I lost control of myself and went into attack mode, we'd wake the whole nest and end up dead in minutes. My sense of smell didn't rate up there with the shifters, but I could almost "feel" all the dragons near us. It was like an angry buzzing in my head. I hadn't considered being even this far from the nest could trigger my instincts, but it was good to know for future reference. If only I could figure out which building held the kids, and how many dragons I'd have to get past to reach them.

I glanced up at Aidan. "Any idea where Matrika would have stashed the kids in there?"

"Certainly closer to the middle," he said, frowning. "If she is treating them like her own young, she will want them well protected."

"Check it out!" Conrad hissed.

I jerked my gaze in the direction he pointed and caught sight of a green dragon coming out of a white hangar. It was barely recognizable at this distance, but the way it moved was familiar enough. Why would she come out this early?

Aidan stiffened and held out a hand. "Let me see those."

Conrad handed the binoculars over, avoiding my questioning look. He helped adjust the lenses for Aidan, whose lips thinned as he observed whatever activity I couldn't make out. A few seconds passed before I noticed a second green dragon walking across the pavement in front of the hangar.

"What's going on?" I asked, grabbing his arm. A part of me wanted to jerk the binoculars out of his hands.

"She is bringing the children out." Aidan hesitated. "There appear to be six of them."

"Give me those!" I demanded.

He shook his head. "No. You won't be able to control yourself."

"Dammit, Aidan. I have a right to check if they're okay." I gave him a frosty glare. "We wouldn't even know they were here if I hadn't risked my life to get the location."

"They appear to be fine. I do not see signs of obvious injuries on any of them," he said, keeping his tone calm and reassuring.

I shot a desperate look toward the airport, unable to spot their small figures—only the large dragons around them. The children were so close and yet so far away. It was almost like I could touch them. All I had to do was run over there, slay two dragons, and take the kids home.

Strong arms wrapped around me, lifting me off my feet. I hadn't even realized I'd begun to move, but as I took a look around, I realized I'd passed the trees we'd been using for cover. Aidan dragged me back to Phoebe and Conrad.

"Please," I begged. "They're right there."

"Which tells us where to find them when we come back with reinforcements." Aidan set me down on my feet, keeping a firm grip on me. "But that time has not yet come."

"We'll need the support of the clan to manage this," Phoebe said.

Conrad knitted his brows. "How you gonna do that if Bailey is involved?"

Aidan appeared to mull it over. "We'll attack first. While everyone is busy fighting, she can rescue the children."

"By herself?" Conrad asked.

"No," Phoebe said, glancing at me. "I will be with her. Everyone else will be too busy fighting to notice what we are doing, and I may even be able to convince my father the children need rescuing since it will improve relations with the humans."

Conrad frowned. "But won't they wonder why Bailey is with you?"

"I will say I must give the children to someone." Phoebe shrugged. "She will just need to cover her warrior garb and weapons so no one will suspect she is a slayer."

With Aidan keeping me facing away from the dragons, my head cleared enough to get the gist of their conversation. "Why would you help me?"

"I'm not helping you," Phoebe snorted. "I'm helping the children and ensuring you don't get distracted and kill any shifters."

I wanted to be offended, but she had a point. "My control is getting better."

She narrowed her gaze. "But not good enough."

"You must continue to practice over the next few days," Aidan said, loosening his hold on me. When I didn't move, he let go altogether, though he didn't step away. I was keeping my attention away from the dragons, which helped.

"She's taking the children back inside," Conrad said, giving us an update while looking through the binoculars. "Why would she have brought them out, anyway?"

"Matrika is treating them like she would her own young," Aidan answered.

Phoebe elaborated further, "Even young dragons need time outside to exercise and feel the sun. Mothers usually take their children out in the mornings when it is quiet, and they can play without getting in the way of the adults."

"How do the children look to you?" I asked Conrad.

His expression darkened. "They don't look hurt, but they mostly stood around so I couldn't tell for sure. One of the dragons just sort of prodded them with her nose to get them moving."

"Wouldn't that have burned them?" I asked.

Aidan shook his head. "Our noses are cooler as long as we aren't blowing steam from them. It shouldn't have harmed the children."

"Matrika may be talking to them, too," Phoebe said, staring toward the airport. "I did not scent any fear from the children, which should have been strong if they had been hurt at all."

"Talking? Like Aidan did with me in my head?" I asked.

She nodded. "If she thinks of them as hers, she might be able to do it."

I shuddered. "Wouldn't that freak the children out more?"

"I don't know." Phoebe frowned. "This isn't something I've seen for myself before."

"We have to get them out of there right away," I said to Aidan, giving him an imploring look. "They might not be hurt now, but it's only a matter of time."

His lips formed a grim line. "I promise we will, but we must gather the clan first."

"Aidan!" Phoebe hissed, a warning in her voice.

I cast a glance over my shoulder and my blood ran cold. A man walked toward us, coming from around the other side of the YMCA building. He had the same yellow eyes as the shifter keeping a tight hold on me. His stride was just as predatory, too.

"Well, well. This is the last thing I expected to find my brother and sister out doing. Consorting with a dragon slayer?" He honed in his gaze on me. "And it's the same little girl who attacked me not long ago."

"Ruari," Aidan said, speaking the name like a curse.

Oh, shit. This wasn't good.

29

AIDAN

He could almost see his future flashing before his eyes in that moment. Aidan had no doubt Ruari would use Bailey against him and Phoebe—maybe even see them executed. They had been so careful to ensure no one followed them, and yet his brother found them anyway. How had he managed it? Ruari was good at getting into other people's business but not this good.

"What are you doing here?" Aidan asked through clenched teeth.

"Father's task." Ruari stepped up next to Bailey's truck and leaned his back against it. His expression was one of a dragon who had just discovered a treasure chest full of jewels. "He assigned me to locate any large dens in the area. The Thamaran lair wasn't too difficult to locate—small as it is—but I've been searching for days to find where the Shadowan have been hiding themselves. If I hadn't caught your scent on the breeze,

I might still be searching. I suppose I should thank you for that."

So not only had Aidan and Phoebe given their brother a way to ruin their chances for becoming pendragon, but they had also helped Ruari finish his task. In a way, his brother had found a treasure chest filled with shiny, golden information he could use. Aidan's relief at locating the children's whereabouts and his anticipation of the impending battle they would fight to get the kids back was gone. He and his sister were now at Ruari's mercy and likely about to lose everything. The best Aidan could hope for was that Bailey did not go down with them.

Phoebe composed her features. "Ruari, this is not what you think. We are with the slayer for a very good reason."

"Oh really?" He gave her an amused look. "And what could possibly be worth getting charged for treason?"

"They have taken human children, and they're holding them in those buildings over there." She pointed toward the airport. "We have to get them back to their parents," she said, speaking calmly despite the nervous tension rising around them.

Ruari cocked his head. "Did the humans come to us for help? I am certain I didn't hear anything about this."

"No. I did," Bailey said, stepping away from Aidan.

"A dragon slayer seeking help from dragons?" Ruari asked, skeptical. "How is it you're even able to be around us without attacking? That kind of discipline could only have come with a good deal of help and exposure to us."

Bailey balled her fists. "Maybe I should remind you that if I hadn't been working on my control, you'd be dead right now."

Ruari rubbed at his chest, as if recalling the wounds she'd given him there. "True, but I still felt the sting of your blade."

"If you do something to get Aidan into trouble," Bailey said, a fierce expression on her face. "I swear I won't hold back the next time I see you. I will cut you into little pieces and string them around town for everyone to see."

Ruari straightened and closed the gap between them. Aidan started to intercede, but his brother shook his head, and Bailey waved him off. He glanced at his sister, whose face reflected fear. If it came down to it, could he kill Ruari to save them all? Aidan didn't want that sort of blood on his hands, but neither did he want to face the alternative.

"Perhaps you and I can make a deal, slayer." Ruari lifted his brows. "Something that could satisfy us all."

"What?" Bailey asked in a biting tone.

"I will tell no one about your friendship with Aidan and Phoebe. In fact, I'll even propose to my father that we attack this den as soon as possible so that you might rescue the children, but my brother and sister must give me something in return."

Bailey drew in a breath. "And that is…?"

"They will forfeit their claims to become pendragon."

"You've got to be kidding me!" Bailey gave him an enraged look.

He shrugged. "If I tell my father about what I've discovered today, my brother and sister may very well be executed by sunset tomorrow, and you will be hunted and slaughtered. I think this is a rather fair trade."

"I could kill you right now," Aidan growled, coming to Bailey's side. "And no one would ever know."

"You could try, but I promise that every dragon in that den over there will hear me scream," Ruari said. The threat in his gaze was proof he would do it.

Aidan stilled. "You're mad."

"You have always thought that about me anyway," Ruari sighed and glanced at their sister, including her in that statement. "I might as well bring us all down at once if that is the only option left to me. But of course, you could let me leave now—without delay—and join me at the fortress for first meal. We can speak to father together about our plans, and no one has to know anything about your relationship with the slayer."

Aidan bowed his head. Ruari had thought of everything and given him no choice. If Aidan wanted to save himself, Phoebe, Bailey, and the children, he had to agree to his brother's plans.

"Fine, I will forfeit candidacy, but I beg you not to ask that of Phoebe." He glanced at his sister. "She is only here because of me."

"Sorry, brother." Ruari shook his head. "My terms are non-negotiable."

"It's alright," Phoebe said, lifting her chin. "I will do as he asks as long as he keeps his end of the deal."

"Oh, I will. Having a tamed dragon slayer on our side could prove useful in the future." Ruari turned his gaze to Bailey. "Especially with a little more training."

Aidan jerked the slayer behind him. "You will stay away from her!"

"Ah, so protective." Ruari smiled. "I thought I sensed something more going on between you two. This relationship has been going on a lot longer than you wish me to think."

And Aidan had just played right into his brother's hands.

"Can I kill him?" Conrad asked, aiming a crossbow at Ruari's head. While they'd been talking to each other, the young man had been taking action by sneaking around the truck to grab his weapon. Aidan decided Conrad might have his uses after all.

"Another slayer?" Ruari asked, his expression appalled.

"Nope," Conrad answered. "But I got no problem getting my hands a little singed watching the slayer's back."

That much, no one could doubt, including Ruari who took a step back.

Aidan glared at his brother. "Perhaps you should get out of here before we decide the reward for killing you is greater than the risk of drawing the Shadowan to us."

Ruari worked his jaw, knowing he was outmatched. "Very well, see you at home then."

Aidan and Phoebe found their brother waiting for them outside the pendragon's office. He leaned against the wall with his arms crossed. Torchlight flickered across his self-satisfied expression and highlighted his shaved head. Of course, Ruari was pleased with himself, considering he had just knocked two of his siblings out of the running, and there was a possibility the pendragon would not choose Zoran either after what they'd learned from Ember. They still didn't know the full outcome of that, other than Throm, who had not been seen around the fortress since hearing whatever the sorcerer told him.

"Ready?" Ruari asked.

Aidan glanced at his sister, who gave a curt nod. "We are."

"I will tell him about the Shadowan den we found first before you two put him in a bad mood," Ruari said, then pushed the door open.

Throm sat at his desk, appearing as healthy as the day before. His bouts of illness came and went more frequently since they'd arrived on Earth, but Aidan found hope that this healthy period had lasted for almost two weeks now. No matter who became pendragon next—and he prayed it wasn't Ruari—it would take time for them to grow into the position.

The toriq couldn't afford inexperienced leadership at a time like this.

"Three of my children at once?" Throm lifted a brow. "To what do I owe this visit?"

Ruari moved in front of the desk, standing tall and proud before their father. "With Aidan and Phoebe's assistance, I have managed to locate the Shadowan den in the nearby human town. From what I could gather, it has at least eighty dragons nesting there."

Aidan was rather surprised to hear his brother admitting he had help, though there was no rule against it. Falcon and Donar had helped him, and he had worked with Phoebe on her murder case. It was just that Ruari usually tried to take all the credit for anything he did that might please the pendragon.

Throm frowned. "That is a large den to be this close to their jakhal."

Aidan had thought the same thing. Their jakhal was just to the north in what the humans called downtown Oklahoma City where there were many tall buildings for dragons to build their nests up higher. It was a prized area for them, and they'd fought the Thamaran heavily for it. In fact, the battle had been so great the tallest building was destroyed in the process.

"Perhaps it is because we are on their southeastern border, and they wish to remind us of their presence," Aidan suggested.

Throm nodded. "You may be right."

"Father, if I may," Phoebe said, drawing the pendragon's attention.

"Yes?"

"We have been hearing reports of human children in town being stolen by green dragons. Upon following up on this, we discovered Matrika to be the one taking them. Once we…" she paused to gesture at Aidan and Ruari, "looked at their den this morning we witnessed at least six children being led around outside."

Throm drew his brows together. "What made you look into the missing children?"

"Why would I not? If we are to rule this territory and live with the humans peacefully, we must have their trust and cooperation. Locating and returning their children would be a good first step to showing them we are not like the pure dragons." She took a deep breath. "Otherwise, they will have no reason to believe we are any different, and we will be forced to fight them as well."

The pendragon studied Phoebe. "You grow wiser with each passing year, Daughter."

Ruari cleared his throat. "I believe if we wish to save these human children before any more harm comes to them then we must attack soon."

Of course, he was attempting to take credit for the idea along with Phoebe. Aidan was sorely tempted to point out that Ruari had only just learned about the children, and it was unlikely he cared at all, but it would not serve any purpose. Their most important objective was to gain the pendragon's assent for the battle.

"It will take several days to plan and launch a proper offense. In the meantime, we have the Bitkal to conduct." Throm stood. "The elders and I have come to a decision on which candidates we will nominate."

"About that, father..." Aidan began.

"Come. The announcement will be made in the great hall. First meal is about to begin, and I would have as many witnesses as possible for it," he said, sweeping out of the office without a backward glance.

Ruari shot Aidan and Phoebe a warning look. In their heads, he sent them a private message—*Do not forget our deal!*

They rushed to catch up with Throm, who walked at a surprisingly brisk pace for a man with little time left to live. Aidan couldn't help thinking his father looked forward to this moment. He wanted to announce his chosen candidates for succession and discover who the elders had selected. Such an occasion only came around once every few centuries. In this case, it had been more than five hundred years. Not many in the toriq could recall the last one.

They entered the great hall, and the pendragon moved in front of the main fireplace. It was so massive that five men could stand inside and only need to crouch a little to fit—the mantle was even with Throm's forehead. The pendragon beckoned the elders to stand beside him while Aidan and his siblings moved closer to the tables.

This was the moment they had been waiting for, and yet Aidan dreaded hearing the announcement. If his father didn't select him, he would feel like he failed. If Throm did choose him, he would have to let his father down by declining. Phoebe stood stiffly next to him, likely thinking the same thing. As the pendragon began to speak, Aidan pulled himself from his thoughts to listen with both fear and anticipation of who he would choose.

"It is time to announce the participants for the Bitkal," Throm said, his voice booming through the great hall. "I will not delay your meal long by making a lengthy speech—we all know the significance of this moment. I will announce my three choices first, and after I have finished the elders will name theirs."

The room went silent. Everyone waited to hear who might be the next pendragon, knowing their future would soon be in the hands of one of those choices. Zoran stood in the corner of the room, his expression dark and stormy. Had the pendragon spoken to him already and what had he said? Aidan wished he could have been there.

"My first two choices are…" Throm paused, ratcheting up the tension. "My son, Aidan, and my daughter, Phoebe. Both have proven to me they are loyal and that they have the best interests of the toriq at heart. Either of them would make a fine pendragon."

Aidan felt fingers wrap around the back of his arm. Phoebe didn't look at him, but she clutched him like he was the only thing keeping her standing. He understood her anxiety. Ruari stared at them both with an expression that said if they did not decline their nominations, he would do it for them. Already, he inched his way closer to their father in a threatening manner.

"And my final selection…" the pendragon began.

Ruari paused and puffed out his chest, ready to hear his name.

"...is Nanoq," Throm finished. Then he gestured toward a man wearing a dark robe who entered from the far corridor. The male shifter moved to stand next to the pendragon and lowered his hood, revealing the face of the supposedly dead Captain of the Guard.

Shocked gasps filled the room and Aidan's jaw dropped. Nanoq was alive? He glanced at Phoebe, who appeared just as surprised. She'd solved a murder case for a man who wasn't really dead, but his attacker wouldn't be long for this world.

"I don't believe it," she muttered.

A trace of a smile crossed Nanoq's lips. "I do not die as easily as some might think."

"I realize you have many questions," Throm said, putting his hands up to gesture for silence. "When Nanoq was attacked, his wounds were grave. Enough that I chose to let our people think him dead so that we could investigate the crime with the would-be murderer believing they had succeeded. It reduced the chance they might flee before we caught them. I had hoped Nanoq would be able to name his attacker once he awoke from the healing process, but it took days for him to recover, and he had no memory of what occurred."

The pendragon gestured at Phoebe. "Then my daughter found the one who assaulted him—Ember—and we received the confession we needed. But we also learned more. Guards, bring my eldest son forward!"

Zoran looked around him, saw the guards coming, and began to run for the main doors. Falcon stood in his path. The shape-shifter thrust an arm out, catching Zoran around the neck as he went by him. Aidan's brother went heels up into the air and landed heavily on his back. The guards caught up to Zoran. Three piled on top of him to keep him down while the fourth produced a set of shackles to wrap around his wrists. After he was fully restrained, they hauled him to his feet.

Spitting mad and stumbling with each step, he was brought before the pendragon. "Father, I have done nothing wrong!"

Throm must not have told his son the details of Ember's arrest and subsequent questioning, though their father must have said something to put Zoran on guard.

"First, I find out you did not kill Blayze as you led us all to believe," the pendragon began, tone furious. "You took credit for it after a man—a male dragon slayer who you should have reported being in the area—had already killed Blayze and left his body and detached head for you to find!"

A male dragon slayer? Aidan glanced at Phoebe and found a guilty expression on her face. She leaned into him and whispered. "I'm sorry I didn't say anything, but father forbade me from telling anyone. Apparently, there was a strange male dragon slayer in town for a short while. He has since disappeared, but not before he killed the Shadowan pendragon's son. It was actually

Ember who witnessed the battle and reported it back to Zoran so he could collect the head. Our brother never got near Blayze while he was alive."

Aidan was so shocked he didn't know what to say. It was difficult enough wrapping his head around the idea that Zoran had cheated to such a degree on his task, but why hadn't Bailey mentioned another dragon slayer being in the area. Did she not see him? It was possible, but he would still ask her about it the next time he saw her.

"...but I also find out you have been plotting with the female who sought to kill the Captain of the Guard, and you did nothing to dissuade her plans," the furious pendragon continued. "I am ashamed to call you my son and from this day forward you will have no relation to me and mine. I sentence you to one year in the dungeon to be followed by banishment!"

Dear Zorya, Aidan could not believe what he was hearing. He had known Throm would be furious that his eldest son had been working with Ember, but it appeared Zoran claiming credit for Blayze's head had sealed his fate. The punishment was even more extreme than expected. Aidan could only think that because one of the pendragon's own children had acted in such an abhorrent manner, he felt he must make an example out of him.

"Father, please don't do this," Zoran said, falling to his knees. "I will do anything you want to make up for my actions, but I beg you not to banish me. This is my home and my life."

Throm did not look at him. "Guards, take him from my sight and see that he is placed in the darkest and dankest cell we have."

For the first time that Aidan could recall, Zoran cried. Tears streamed down his face as he begged and pleaded for their father to have mercy. For a brief moment, Aidan almost felt sorry for him, but then he remembered how his eldest brother used to lock him down in the dungeons for hours or even days at a time, simply for his own amusement. Zoran had never been a good person, and that would not change. Aidan turned away, not even caring to watch his brother dragged from the great hall.

Ruari caught his gaze. *You will decline when they call you forward.*

I will, Aidan said, resigned to do what he must.

He certainly did not want to join Zoran down in the dungeons and be stuck with his oldest brother down there for the next year—assuming Throm didn't order Aidan executed for consorting with a dragon slayer. With his father's current mood, that was a possibility.

In light of what has happened with Zoran and my not being chosen, I would not seek to break father's heart further by requiring Phoebe to decline her nomination as well. One of us must participate in the Bitkal and if it cannot be me, then I will allow it to be her.

Aidan worked his jaw. *That is very gracious of you.*

Ruari's gaze turned to Phoebe, and she stiffened. Aidan could only assume their brother was telling her the news. When she relaxed a fraction next to him, he was sure of it.

"We will now announce the other four candidates," an elder announced loudly, breaking through the rumble of discussions taking place after so many shocking revelations. Zoran's yelling from down the corridor had finally faded away.

The elder who spoke didn't appear to be old by human standards—perhaps fifty—but he was actually closer to eight hundred. He had shoulder-length black hair and a sturdy build. Aidan had studied under him when he was a child taking his lessons, and he remembered the old shifter as a stern taskmaster.

The elder began to call out the names, "We have chosen Sabryn, Elgar, Gvaram, and Donar."

Aidan wasn't surprised to hear Donar's name among the candidates. Though his cousin could be grouchy at times, he was also kind and helpful to everyone in the toriq. He had also begun to develop a reputation as a strong fighter, particularly after the most recent battles they'd fought since returning to Earth. Donar and Aidan may have done their best to hide their fighting skills before, but with the danger that surrounded them over the past few months some of their prowess had shown through despite their holding back.

The elders naming Sabryn didn't come as a shock, either. She was one of the strongest female warriors in the toriq and she fought in every battle. Sabryn was his cousin through Throm's sister, who'd passed long before Aidan was born. He wasn't particularly close to her since she ran in a different circle of friends, and she was three times older than him, but she had never given him a reason to dislike her. Aidan simply didn't know enough to say whether she would make a good leader. Outside of her battle prowess and her defeating Phoebe in a duel once, she had never made much of an impression on him.

As for Gvaram, he was the grandson of the last pendragon—before Throm—through his mother's side. When his family lost the seat and the power that came with it, they moved outside the fortress. Gvaram fought in all the battles and brought fresh meat he had hunted to the fortress once a fortnight as payment for taxes, but otherwise, he was not seen around often.

Elgar came from another high-born family who was in charge of mining the zaphiriam in the nearby mountains. He and Zoran had been best friends since childhood, and they shared a similar temperament. Both could fight well, but they did not get along with anyone except each other. It was one of the most likely reasons he had not been targeted. Aidan had no doubt Elgar would have purposely lost in the Bitkal rather than defeat Zoran—if it had come to that.

Throm beckoned all of the candidates forward. Aidan walked with his sister, lining up next to the others in front of the pendragon. One by one, they were asked to accept or decline their nominations. All of them accepted until it was Aidan's turn.

His throat swelled as he forced his mouth to open. He had to say the words no matter how much they pained him—for himself, Phoebe, and Bailey. Aidan had to give up what would likely be the only opportunity in his lifetime to become pendragon. That wasn't what bothered him, though, considering he had never sought power and did not really want it. What made him hesitate was the proud look in his father's eyes as he waited for his son to accept. It was almost too much to bear to take that from the pendragon after what had already occurred that day.

"I must respectfully decline," Aidan said, managing to make the words come out clear.

Throm's gaze turned furious, but he moved on and asked Phoebe next.

She stood tall and proud. "I accept."

The pendragon nodded, some of his anger diminishing. Aidan could only imagine what his father was thinking in that moment, but he must have known something prompted his son's response. He would never know the truth, though. Much like no one knew exactly how Throm came to be in power despite having three brothers and two sisters who had just as great a chance as him. By the time the last Bitkal came, most of his siblings were dead or disgraced.

"Fortune favor those who have accepted," the pendragon called out, his voice echoing across the room. Then he turned and began making his way out of the great hall.

As members of the clan came to congratulate those who'd accepted their nomination, Aidan followed his father. He did not want there to be bad blood between them during such a time. The pendragon would not live that much longer. Aidan could not bear the thought that Throm might hate him for what time they had left together.

"Father, wait," he said, racing to catch up.

Throm stopped and turned around in the middle of the corridor. His voice was cold as ice as he spoke, "You have disappointed me. Of all my children, I put my faith and trust in you being the one to take over upon my death. If I am certain of anything, it is that you have always put our toriq before yourself. I do not know what has prompted you to decline my nomination, but I cannot think it good."

"I did not mean to disappoint you," Aidan said, barely managing not to flinch under the pendragon's heavy stare.

"And yet you have." Throm turned around and began walking again. "I have nothing further to say to you—now or ever."

Aidan stood frozen in place. If his father said such a thing, he meant it. Though he would try, there would be little chance Aidan could ever gain the pendragon's forgiveness. He wanted to go throttle Ruari, but that would not change anything. All he could do was help his sister prepare for the Bitkal, which would come in just two short days.

30

BAILEY

I drew back the bow, praying that this time my arrow would find its target. A few weeks ago, Aidan had spent an afternoon training me on basic archery, but I hadn't had time to practice since then. I was full of restless energy today, thinking about our run-in with Ruari the day before, and I decided to work on my range weapon skills. Conrad could have his big, heavy crossbow. I wanted something that gave me a little more control and didn't feel as unwieldy. When you were short and small, bigger weapons didn't necessarily mean better.

Releasing the arrow, I watched it sail through the air and strike the tree. It stuck just inside the circle I'd painted. Finally! A weapon that might actually work for me. I sent a few more arrows at the tree and managed to get two in the bull's-eye. Something about the bow felt much more natural than some of the others I'd tried.

The sound of wings flapping through the air drew my attention across the field. Aidan was coming in to land, heading straight for me. A spike of adrenaline shot through my veins as I stared at his red dragon form. My slayer instincts called for me to attack him, but the human side of me watched his graceful body move closer in awe. For the first time, I even noticed a light smattering of silver on his belly. I had always been so caught up in rage before that I always missed it.

I set the bow down on the ground and straightened. Aidan landed about five feet from me, puffing steam from his nostrils. Our gazes met, and I knew what he was thinking—can she handle this? I walked forward and pressed my palm to the side of his face. A rumbling sound came from deep inside him. He tilted his head, pushing into my hand.

"It's okay. We're okay," I said, smiling at him.

Aidan rose up on his hind legs, and I took a step back. Sudden movements still triggered my slayer instincts, but I could push them down if I concentrated hard enough. With every deep breath I took, my heart rate slowed a little more.

Fire began racing up his body and out around him. It was even harder to watch him shift, but I stood still and ignored the itch in my skin that begged me to attack. Seconds passed as his body changed shapes, going from dragon to human form. It appeared painful, though Aidan assured me it wasn't that bad.

Once he was finished and the flames died down, I found his face was an emotionless mask. Whatever bonding moment we might have had before he shifted, it was gone now. His gaze didn't quite reach mine before he turned in the direction of the tree with my arrows stuck in it. Aidan raised a brow.

"How much have you been practicing?" he asked.

"Just this afternoon."

He was quiet a moment. "This is good, though we will continue to try other things as well."

"Like what?"

"There are many possibilities, and I am working on something new that might be better than anything currently available to us." Aidan finally looked at me. "I will let you know."

"So...about yesterday," I began.

His gaze hardened. "It is done. I do not wish to discuss it further right now."

Okay, that didn't sound good. I swallowed. "Sorry."

"Was there a male dragon slayer in town recently?" he asked, voice deadly soft.

I stiffened. This was one conversation I'd hoped we could avoid. "Uh, yeah."

"And you didn't tell me?"

"Well," I paused, not knowing what to say with him staring so hard at me. This wasn't the way Aidan usually behaved even when he was upset about something. "It's complicated."

He crossed his arms. "Did you talk to this dragon slayer?"

"No, but he…he saved my life." I stared at the ground. "The fight where I hurt my shoulder might have been a little worse than I let on."

"You didn't talk to him, but he saved your life. Am I really suppose to believe that?" he asked, his tone incredulous.

"Maybe I did and don't remember it." I sighed and met his furious gaze. "My skull was cracked open from the fall, so I barely remember him even showing up."

Aidan worked his jaw. "Did you meet him before then?"

"Conrad and I spotted him watching us once—that's it." I wasn't sure if I really owed Aidan an explanation, but I didn't want him worrying that I would ever betray him. We needed to have a certain level of honesty for our partnership to work.

"And the second time he saw you, he saved your life." Aidan shook his head. "Was he attracted to you? Where is he now?"

I almost smiled. His mood stemmed more from jealousy than worry I'd betray him to another slayer. "He was drawn to me because apparently he is my father. And he left town before I recovered enough to speak to him."

Aidan blinked. "Your father? Are you certain?"

I'd told him once that I never met my real dad. "Yeah, Earl didn't believe it either so he made the man call my mother. She confirmed he is my father."

Though I didn't tell Aidan about the radio, he did know about phones. It was the only way to explain how I got updates on my family with them living so far away.

"Then why did your father not speak with you before he left?" Aidan asked, now appearing upset for me.

"No idea." I shrugged, trying not to show the hurt I felt over that. "Earl thinks he doesn't know what to say to a grown up daughter he has just found." Then I went on to explain how my father had been trapped in the dragon dimension since before I was born.

Light dawned in Aidan's eyes. "Then he is the one."

"The one? Who?" I asked, confused.

"The one all dragons fear—The Shadow—because it is always in the shadows that he waits for us. He has grown powerful enough that he can cut off our heads with a single stroke of his blade, and he can track us better than any slayer who has come before him. When I first saw you, I thought there was a resemblance." Aidan studied me. "Now I know it's true, and you are his daughter."

A cold chill ran through me. "How have you seen him before and survived?"

"Several years ago, I came upon The Shadow fighting a dragon renowned for its ferociousness. It was a brutal and bloody fight. For a moment, I watched as your father tore into the dragon, but then my better sense prevailed, and I fled before he could turn on me next."

"Well, that's just great," I grumbled. "At least my father can spare time for dragons if not me." It was petty for me to be jealous of the beasts Wayne killed, but it seemed to me they got more of his attention. If he hadn't saved my life, I might not have thought he cared at all.

Aidan put a hand on my shoulder. "If the rumors hold true, your father is not a social person. He prefers to walk his path alone, living only for his next battle. Earl may be right that he does not know what to say to you, but at least he made the effort to find you."

I expelled a breath. "Yeah, I guess, but whose father leaves his daughter to handle a huge city of dragons by herself after watching her nearly die?"

He was quiet for a moment and then his gaze darkened. "Were you wearing shifter warrior garb when he found you?"

I nodded.

"Then he knows you are working with us." Aidan gave me a sympathetic look. "It is likely that he sees it as a betrayal to your heritage."

I stilled. The outfit I'd worn that day had never crossed my mind once as I wondered why my father would not talk to me. He'd been a slayer long enough to know there was only one way I could have gotten the camrium uniform. Finally figuring out the answer didn't make me feel any better.

"You're probably right." I rubbed my face. "He can't be happy about that."

Aidan gave me a weak smile. "If it helps, my father will no longer speak to me because I refused my nomination."

"That doesn't help." I gave him a disgruntled look. "Now I only feel worse because working together is causing a rift between us and our families."

He stared at me for a moment. "I have to believe that what we are doing is worth the sacrifice. No matter the cost to ourselves, we have a chance to make things better for my toriq and your people. Do not lessen the importance of our alliance."

"You're right." And he was. I didn't know my father before, and his refusal to speak to me now didn't change anything. As long as I could eventually reunite with the family who did care about me, I'd be okay.

Aidan's expression turned serious. "Speaking of which, the battle will commence in three days. You should make transportation arrangements for the children. Phoebe has informed my father she will be focusing on their rescue during the battle so no one will question you being there as long as you blend in as a human."

I would have to fight with normal clothes over my camrium uniform, but it would be worth it to avoid any more trouble for Aidan and his sister. "Alright, I can handle that."

"Good." He nodded. "Phoebe and I will return soon to discuss the final arrangements."

"You have to go already?" I had hoped he would stay and train with me for a while.

"There is much to do." Aidan took a step back. "Continue working on your control as much as you can. It is important that you can keep your focus on the children during the battle."

"I will," I said, having already considered the same thing.

"Take care, Bailey."

He shifted into his dragon form again, not bothering to move far from me. It was another test, but I had no trouble passing it this time. Seeing Aidan in his dragon form seemed to get easier every time I did it. He took off into the sky a moment later, leaving me alone in the field.

31

BAILEY

It was early afternoon, and the streets were mostly deserted as I drove through them on my way to Earl's. I hated to risk going there at this time of day, but I wanted to give him as much notice as possible about the impending rescue operation. We had to start planning how to transport the kids out of there and get them returned to their parents.

On that thought, I turned on the radio to listen to Hank's latest updates. He would be a part of my plan, assuming Earl could get in contact with him in time.

"Hey, folks. For those who missed the news earlier today, I've got an interesting development for you. A reliable source has told me that the U.S. military has consolidated its forces on the East Coast somewhere around the Virginia and North Carolina border. They have begun waging a war against the dragons in that area, and they've made some headway."

I glanced at the radio, shocked. That was the first good news I'd heard from Hank since last month when he announced a farmer was giving away all of his corn if people would just come out and pick it for him. Yeah, that wasn't something that should seem like a big deal, but when you don't have stores to purchase your food from anymore, it becomes one. Still, Hank's news today made me feel optimistic for the first time in a while. I'd written off the military, figuring they had disbanded sometime soon after they stopped dropping bombs on the dragons in Oklahoma. There had been no reports of their activity in nearby states, either, making everyone think they'd lost the fight. How had Hank managed to find this out?

"…according to my source, they've managed to establish a one-hundred-square-mile safe area between Virginia and North Carolina. Having said that—don't go packing your bags just yet. The perimeter is a hot zone and too dangerous to be crossed. The military is fighting daily battles against the dragons to keep them out. Countless people have already died trying to get close, and I don't want to see ya'll end up among the dead."

I listened to Hank continue his update while scanning the sky. I'd just passed the railroad tracks as I drove down Boyd Street, and I had entered Shadowan territory. There were a couple of dragons flying off to the north, but they were too far away to be a concern. Oklahoma University came up on my left. The grass was overgrown, many buildings had storm or fire damage, and the only living thing visible on the grounds was a dog roaming around. Every time I took this route, it hurt to see what had become of the campus. Had it really just been last spring that I'd been a student taking classes there?

After Boyd Street narrowed to two lanes, I turned my attention back to the road and caught sight of a blond woman ahead waving her arms. She stood on the sidewalk, a desperate look on her face. I considered not stopping, but the tears on her face seemed too genuine to ignore. She needed help and seemed to know exactly who my truck belonged to.

Pulling up alongside her, I rolled down my window. "Do you need help?"

"Yes!" She dashed up to me and clutched the door. "A dragon took my daughter, and I've been trying to find you. People say you can help."

Now that I could see her up close, I recognized her. This was the same woman who I had rescued when her house was hit by a tornado a few months ago. She had a cute little girl with her that we also pulled from the debris. Conrad had taken her and her daughter up to some relative's house not far from here. He still went back to visit them sometimes, but I never saw them again. It took me a moment to remember the woman's name, though Conrad had mentioned it a few times.

"You're Christine, right?" I asked.

Her eyes rounded. "How did you know?"

"I was with Conrad when we pulled you out of your house after the tornado."

"Oh!" She gasped. "That was you? And here I am asking for your help again."

I shook my head. "Don't worry about that. Now tell me what happened with your daughter."

She wiped a tear from her cheek. "Last night. I was asleep, and I didn't hear Lacy go outside. The dragon must have seen her in the backyard and taken her."

I gave her a look of sympathy, hating to ask the next question. "How can you be sure it was a dragon if you were asleep?"

In my experience, humans were just as bad if not worse since D-day, and they were just as likely to take the girl. I'd counted six kids yesterday and if Lacy was another then that made seven. How many children did the damn dragon need before it was satisfied?

"My aunt told me." Christine sucked in a breath. "She doesn't get around well, but she heard a noise and peeked out her bedroom window. The dragon was carrying Lacy away."

Damn—there was no denying that. My chest tightened as the little girl's face entered my mind with her pink cheeks and ringlets of blond hair. As I recalled, she couldn't have been more than five years old the last time I saw her. This was the first missing child I had actually met before, and it made the situation seem that much worse. Not that I hadn't been taking it seriously. It was just a little closer to home this time now that I knew one of the victims.

"I've already got a plan in the works to rescue all the missing kids," I said, thinking about how best to help the woman. "Why don't you come with me, and you can hear all about it."

"Do you really think you can save her?" Christine asked.

"I'll do my best." Nothing was guaranteed, but I'd rescue those kids or die trying.

Something about that thought struck me. When had I become the person who people came to for help? Just a few short months ago, I'd been the kind of girl who kept a low profile and avoided attention. The very thought of anyone seeking me out would have sent me running, but I didn't have much of a choice anymore. I had the ability to protect people and with that came a huge amount of responsibility.

Christine hesitated. "I, uh, don't know if I should go…"

"Unless you're a dragon, you're safe with me," I promised.

She gave me a weak smile and after another moment hopped into the truck. I checked the area to be sure we hadn't drawn any unwanted attention. This was a neighborhood with a lot of trees and a limited view of the sky, but I didn't spot any flying green objects. Hitting the gas, I continued on my way to Earl's neighborhood. We only had a few blocks left to go so it didn't take long to hit the perimeter they'd set up.

Miles—a former military guy in his mid-twenties—and an older man I didn't know well stood guard. They lowered their weapons as soon as they recognized my truck. I hadn't seen Miles around much since he joined some secret group in town that tested alternative ways to take down dragons. He had asked me to help out, but I didn't have the time, and I didn't want to encourage them. His group was still struggling to come up with something effective, which was tough when almost every resource they had could be burned in an instant.

The few ideas they'd attempted so far had gotten several of their members killed. There was no easy way to fight dragons unless you were fireproof, and the clever beasts learned any tactics humans came up with rather quickly. The only tried and true method I'd found that worked was to get up in their face and poke my sword into them until they died. Once again, fireproofing required. If I could have talked Aidan into some special gear for Miles and his group, it might have been different, but he refused. I suspected he worried they'd come after shifters as well.

Miles stepped in front of my window, and his gaze shot to Christine. "Who is that?"

"A woman whose daughter was just taken by the dragons."

His gaze softened a fraction. "I'm sorry to hear that."

Christine sniffled. I probably could have mentioned her daughter in an easier way, but Miles tended to put me on my guard. He was too stiff and completely lacked a sense of humor. Danae and I had pulled numerous pranks on him during the summer hoping to lighten him up, but nothing worked. I suspected he was born without the necessary facial muscles required to laugh or smile.

"She won't be here too long, don't worry. I just need to take her with me to talk to Earl."

Miles nodded. "No problem."

"How's it going?" I asked while we waited for the other guard to open the make-shift gate.

Miles glared at me. "It would be better if you joined my group and helped us out."

"Sorry, but missing kids take priority," I said, giving him an unapologetic look.

"Yeah, and how is that going?" He crossed his arms.

"I know where they are now. It's just a matter of getting to them."

"You know!" Christine grabbed my arm. "Why didn't you say that?"

"Yeah, and why haven't you rescued them already?" Miles narrowed his eyes.

I caught a glimpse of Earl standing in his yard down the street, watching us. The second guard had removed the barrier, opening the way for my truck. "I'm only explaining this once so if you want to know, you're gonna have to get someone to take over guard duty and join us."

Not bothering to wait for his reply, I hit the gas pedal and hurried down the street. Ten minutes later I had everyone gathered in Earl's living room, including Miles, Justin, Danae, Conrad, and Trish. As soon as they'd seen me enter the neighborhood, they'd figured something was up for me to come here in the middle of the afternoon. Christine might not have recognized me right away, but she was happy to see Conrad. They were now sitting next to each other on the couch, and he was doing his best to console her while appearing rather upset himself.

"Okay," I said, pacing in front of everyone. Moving around helped me focus, and it reduced the anxiety I felt at having so many people looking at me. "Some of you may have heard from Conrad that a bunch of dragons are living at the airport."

Earl nodded, but everyone else shook their heads. I'd told Conrad to keep the news to himself until I had more information, and he had apparently taken that order to heart.

"At my current count, there are seven children there," I said.

"And how many dragons?" Miles asked, looking at me with disdain. "Since you just left the kids there without rescuing them."

Danae punched him in the arm. "You are such an asshole. Let her talk."

Miles ground his teeth, but he kept his mouth shut.

I turned my attention to Earl. "We checked out the place during the morning when they were sleeping in their dens. There was no way to get a precise count, but with Aidan and his sister's help we were able to determine there are at least seventy or eighty."

"His sister?" Earl scrunched his nose. "Since when are you working with more of them?"

Christine held up a hand. "Wait, who is Aidan?"

"He's a shape-shifter dragon," Conrad explained. "Bailey has a truce with a few of them since they hate the pure dragons as much as we do."

"A what?" Christine asked.

Justin snorted. "I wouldn't have believed it either if I hadn't seen it for myself."

I addressed Christine, "Have you seen any red dragons flying around before?"

She nodded jerkily. "Twice. I've been wondering why there are two colors."

"The red ones are shape-shifters, which means they can look like humans or turn into dragons. They're sympathetic to us, and they even have humans living with them in their fortress." That was about the most abbreviated explanation I could give.

"They have a fortress?" She shot a look at Conrad. "How did I not know about this?"

"From what we heard, it came over with the dragons. Bailey and I ain't seen it, but it's supposed to be somewhere south of Lake Thunderbird. I'm not tryin' to get too close to that."

"Oh," Christine said, still appearing lost and confused. At least we'd managed to distract her from her grief over her daughter. "And they can look like humans?"

"Except for their creepy yellow eyes," Justin said, scowling. "That's how you know they're something else."

Aidan and his clan were going to have their work cut out for them if they ever wanted to win humans over. Half the people in Earl's neighborhood still questioned what they'd seen when they caught Aidan shifting forms. It was one thing to discover a mythical creature like a dragon exists—they're only a step away from dinosaurs. It was another to wrap your head around the idea of someone capable of being both a human and a dragon. The open-minded people accepted it fairly readily, but those with a tendency toward skepticism had a much more difficult time.

"Alright," Miles spoke up. "If there are eighty dragons surrounding those kids, how can any of us get to them without us all getting killed?"

I clasped my hands together. "That's what I came here to tell you guys. Aidan's clan is planning to attack the dragon den in three days. While they're battling it out, his sister and I will sneak in and grab the kids. All I need is for a few of you to wait nearby with transportation to get them away."

"I'm game for that," Conrad said.

Danae nodded. "I'll be there too in case any of the kids are injured and need my help."

I suspected she'd want to come regardless, but someone with healing skills would definitely be a bonus. "Good."

"I'm comin' too." Earl slapped his knees. "If we need to get away fast, ain't no one know these streets better than I do."

Justin cocked his head. "What will you do after you get the kids to us?"

I shrugged. "Make sure you get out of there safely."

"I'm going to get the maps," Danae said, getting up from her seat. "We need to plan a strategy."

"Is there something I should do?" Christine asked, gazing at me with fear in her eyes. I'd only wanted her here so she knew we had a plan, but I didn't actually expect her to do anything dangerous. A little busy work might not hurt her, though.

"Well, we need to find a way to contact the other children's parents." I glanced at Earl. "Can you get in touch with Hank?"

He scratched at his beard. "Yeah, I got a way, and you—" he gestured at Christine, "can help Hank figure out what to say. There are gonna be a lot of worried parents out there, and it couldn't hurt for you to lend your voice."

She nodded. "I can do that."

"Oh, and we need to get some snacks together for the kids," Trish spoke up. "I bet they're going to be hungry when we get them back here."

Everyone else started talking at once. I left them to their plans and headed for the kitchen. Trish's mention of food reminded me I hadn't eaten since that morning, and I couldn't handle being around that many people at once for much longer anyway.

32

AIDAN

Most of the toriq gathered on the field outside the fortress, observing the Bitkal. Aidan's cousin, Donar, had already won his first round against Gvaram. It had been a good fight, but Gvaram's warrior skills were not at the level of his grandfather—the pendragon who ruled before Throm—whose reputation had been legendary. Donar had conquered his opponent in less than five minutes with only one slice in his arm to show he had even been in a duel.

Phoebe and Sabryn were just taking the field. The two female shifters stood at about equal height—a couple of inches shorter than Aidan—and the women had similar builds. Sabryn had about ten more pounds in muscle on her, though. It likely came from the hours of exercise and practice she did each day, always working to prove herself against her male counterparts.

The females shifted into their dragon forms and after nodding to indicate they were ready, Throm let out a roar for them to begin. Each lifted into the air and flew straight for the other. They clashed in a flurry of wings, biting and clawing at each other. Phoebe chomped into her opponent's shoulder, and Sabryn bit her in the neck. For more than a minute, they were locked into that position, flapping their wings heavily as both refused to let go. Their angry growls filtered down to the ground. Each attempted to bite down harder but getting the right amount of leverage was more difficult in the air.

From behind Aidan, he overheard several males placing bets on who would win. The odds were almost even. Many hoped Phoebe would win, but most thought Sabryn had a better chance. It would all come down to who managed to get the fatal blow that would make the other shifter submit. Aidan believed his sister to be a fine warrior, but even he could not predict the outcome of this match.

A loud snap sounded, and a strangled cry came from Sabryn. Phoebe had bitten down hard enough to break her opponent's left shoulder. It wouldn't stop Sabryn from fighting, but the pain would slow the female warrior down. She had already lost her grip on Phoebe's neck, taking away that advantage. Sabryn used her good arm to lash out, raking her talons across Phoebe's face and slashing her left eye. Aidan winced, sympathetic to his sister's pain.

Phoebe snarled, then ducked her head low and rammed into Sabryn's injured shoulder. Unmercifully, she pushed the female warrior down toward the ground. Sabryn struggled against her opponent, managing to strike a few weak blows. But when her wings faltered, she had to grip Phoebe just to keep from plummeting to the earth. Everyone held their breath as the females lost altitude at an alarming speed. They hit the ground with a flurry of dust and loud grunts, tangled together.

Aidan clenched his fists, waiting to see if they would rise.

Relief assailed him as Phoebe lifted herself and braced her hands and feet on either side of her opponent. Sabryn lay on her back, howling in pain. Aidan's sister opened her jaws wide and struck at the female shifter's throat. Before she could get a proper grip, Sabryn bended her knees and dug her feet into Phoebe's lower belly, sending her flying off.

Aidan's sister's landed hard on her butt, and her wing snapped. She let out a strangled cry. Breaking a wing bone was a lot like busting one's toe. It wasn't significant enough to incapacitate you, but it hurt enough you needed a few moments to overcome the pain.

Sabryn rolled off her back and rose to her feet, holding her injured arm close to her. While Phoebe attempted to tuck in her wings so that she could get off the ground, the other female shifter charged her, moving swiftly despite her wounds. Sabryn dove on top of Aidan's sister and latched onto her neck. This time, she had the proper leverage to do real damage. The female warrior growled and bit down hard, showing she meant business. Aidan knew from experience it was impossible to get free from such a hold and if his sister did not surrender, Sabryn was within her rights to kill her opponent. He prayed to Zorya it did not come to that.

Phoebe struggled for a minute, resisting the inevitable for as long as she dared, but then she called out telepathically for all to hear. *I submit.*

Aidan sighed—relieved and yet disappointed. He had truly hoped his sister could take Sabryn and continue to the next round of the Bitkal. She had been the only hope among his siblings, and it would have been helpful to have such an ally as the toriq's leader.

Throm marched across the field with a scowl on his face. He shot a disappointed look at his daughter before moving on to congratulate Sabryn. While he did that, Aidan hurried toward his sister, who still struggled to rise off her broken wing. Phoebe was much heavier in dragon form, but he managed to lift her onto her feet. She let out a little moan, then shifted into human form. The expression in her eyes when the flames died down was not one he would ever forget—humiliation and shame. Phoebe hung her head low as he escorted her off of the field. She moved slower than normal, the effects of the damaged wing now reflecting in her back.

"He'll never forgive me for this," she said softly.

Aidan took her to the edge of the crowd where they could have a little more privacy. "Our father will forgive you before he does me. At least you participated in the Bitkal."

"We must be such a disappointment to him." She wiped away some of the blood running down from her injured eye.

He ignored the start of the next duel between Nanoq and Elgar. Aidan had full faith the Captain of the Guard win against Zoran's old friend. Elgar was a competent warrior, but he lacked strategy and finesse.

"Perhaps we can redeem ourselves tomorrow during the battle," Aidan said, hoping to take Phoebe's mind off of her lost duel. He had never seen her this upset.

"Maybe," she said, not sounding all that convinced.

Cheers rose up from the crowd. Aidan turned to find Nanoq had laid Elgar flat on the ground. The growling warrior struggled as the captain tore into his belly with his sharp talons. Still, Elgar did not yield. He began swinging side to side, attempting to knock Nanoq off of him. The captain lashed out and bashed Elgar in the head with a force that nearly snapped his neck. His eyes turned dazed as his body slackened.

With Elgar's throat now bared, Nanoq took advantage. He bit down hard with his teeth digging deep. Still, no cry of submission came. The crowd turned quiet. Nanoq had a death lock on Elgar that he couldn't possibly break. Aidan could no longer see if the dragon on the ground's eyes had sharpened since the last blow he took. A long minute passed where no one moved, including the two contestants.

Finally, Throm called out, "Finished. Nanoq is the winner!"

The captain let go of Elgar and backed away. Aidan finally got a full view of the dragon on the ground. Though his chest rose and fell with each breath, he lay still. Throm called for the healer, who came running a moment later. Others joined in to help carry Elgar off the field. The blow to his head must have been even harder than it appeared.

"Brain damage," Phoebe murmured.

"The healer will handle it."

She glanced at Aidan. "At least I don't have to worry about fighting Nanoq."

He wouldn't have minded a chance to duel the captain, but it was too late for that now. "Sabryn will fight him next."

She nodded. "Zorya be with her because that is going to be one battle she might not win."

"Agreed."

Aidan took his sister back to the fortress to tend her wounds. There would be a brief break to allow Nanoq to recover before the next duel so they wouldn't be missing anything. They reached the apothecary, and he ordered her to sit on a bench against the wall. There was a male shifter in attendance there, but Aidan preferred to take care of Phoebe himself.

"You don't need to fuss over me," she protested.

He moistened a cloth and dabbed it at her torn cheek. "You are my favorite sister, of course I must tend you."

She glared at him. "I'm your only sister."

"Even if there were more, you would be my favorite," he said, a teasing note in his voice.

Some of the tension eased from her shoulders. "Thanks. I don't know what I would do without you."

Aidan took a poultice the shifter handed him and began to rub it into Phoebe's wounds. "Spend time with Ruari, I suppose."

"Very funny. The very thought of it is going to give me nightmares tonight."

He decided to change the subject. "I haven't told you this yet, but one of the stipulations in the treaty I negotiated with the Faegud requires matings between our toriqan."

Phoebe froze. "What? Why didn't you tell me this sooner?"

"If you have not noticed, we have been rather busy lately." More than once, Aidan had tried to find the right time to broach the subject, but it seemed to never come.

"Did father request you put that in the treaty?" she asked, frowning.

He shook his head. "Hildegard demanded it."

"Sweet, Zorya." Phoebe's expression was unreadable.

"One of father's children must mate with one of the Faegud. Hildegard required that as part of the treaty as well," he said, nervous of his sister's reaction so far. Aidan couldn't begin to judge her mood. All he knew was that with Zoran out of the running that left only him, Phoebe, and Ruari. The odds of their brother going along with mating a Faegud dragon were slim.

Phoebe averted her gaze. "I had not expected this."

"I am hoping you might be interested in making the sacrifice."

She rose to her feet. "I'm going to need to think about this."

Before Aidan could reply, she hurried out of the room. He stared after her, wondering at her reaction. Should he consider that a good sign? At least she had not outright denied the possibility of reuniting with her lover—whoever that might be.

With nothing left to do, he returned to the Bitkal. Aidan had just reached the spectators when they roared with excitement and chanted Nanoq's name. He must have taken longer in the apothecary than he thought. The next duel had already finished.

He weaved his way through the crowd to reach the front and found Nanoq stepping away from Sabryn. Both dragons were covered in blood. There was a deep gash across the captain's face and another one across his chest. Sabryn's shoulder looked worse than after she had fought Phoebe, and her throat had puncture wounds in it.

Aidan sought out Donar, who would fight Nanoq next after another break. His cousin stood near the center of the crowd with his arms crossed and a pensive expression on his face. Though he would be fresher, and only had one minor wound from his previous fight, Nanoq was going to be the toughest opponent Donar ever faced. The captain had little mercy in a duel, though at least he didn't kill to finish it. If Zoran had participated, there likely would have been at least one dead shifter before the end of the Bitkal.

"Nanoq has the favor of the people," Donar said as Aidan came to stand beside him.

"Do not worry about that."

His cousin snorted. "Easy for you to say. Ruari saved you the trouble of fighting."

In a way, Aidan was relieved that he didn't have to compete in the Bitkal. It bothered him to disappoint his father, but he had no desire to carry the weight of leadership on his shoulders. Aidan worked best behind the scenes with no one watching. He was just glad that the two final contenders were shifters he could respect and support. No matter how this next duel went, the toriq would be in good hands after Throm passed on to the next world. Still, Aidan would prefer Donar to win since he would turn a blind eye to certain activities such as his relationship with the slayer. Nanoq would not be so forgiving.

"You're a fine warrior. Just remember your training and you will do well," Aidan said, patting his cousin on the shoulder.

Donar nodded. "I believe I can do this."

"That is the spirit."

Aidan watched as his cousin paced around, getting his heart rate up. It probably wouldn't help him during the fight, but at least it helped Donar release some of his nervous energy. A half hour later, the pendragon called the contestants forward.

"Zorya be with you, cousin." Aidan gave him a solemn nod.

Donar hurried to his position on the field and shifted into his dragon form. Nanoq was still in his since it would have expended too much energy to change between duels. The captain had the poor luck of having to fight all his opponents one after another, but with only six contestants to start it was bound to happen to one of them. The Bitkal was not meant to be easy. Toriq law dictated that it must begin and end during the same afternoon.

After ensuring both males were ready, the pendragon roared for the battle to begin. Both dragons leaped into the air, though Donar stayed hovering over his position. He waited for Nanoq to come to him. The captain did not hesitate to fly the extra distance, gaining extra speed as he did so. At the last moment, Donar brought in his wings and let himself fall for several lengths before flaring them again. Nanoq flew right over him.

Aidan's cousin quickly spun about and zoomed toward Nanoq, who was forced to make a wider turn because of his speed. Donar struck from below, latching onto the captain's right wing and dragging him downward. Nanoq beat his other wing in an attempt to fight the pull, but he only slowed it down.

As soon as Donar's toes touched the ground, he jerked the captain's wing, slinging the dragon's body into the dirt with a hard thud. It was an impressive feat of strength. Nanoq's wing was badly torn, and it took him a few moments to recover. By the time he rose to his feet, Donar was on top of the captain's back and biting into the nape of his neck. Aidan's cousin caught enough flesh between his teeth to get a good hold and then began clawing into Nanoq's back. Red scales went flying. Donar dug hard enough that if he kept it up, he would soon create a tunnel through the captain.

Nanoq bucked and roared, but he could not shake Donar loose. He started to run next, picking up speed fast. Then he came to a grinding halt, digging his talons in the dirt. Donar lost his grip and went flying off.

Aidan took a step forward when he saw his cousin land in a heap of wings and upturned feet about a dozen paces away. Donar was such a large dragon that when he ended up on his back, it took a lot of effort to roll over. He was never going to recover in time.

It was all Aidan could do to stay put and watch as Nanoq leaped on top of his cousin and went for his throat. Donar tucked in his head to protect his neck and thrust his talons out, clawing at the captain's snout and splitting it open. They nipped and slashed at each other, their angry growls growing louder with each moment that passed. Despite his cousin's weaker position, he wasn't going down without a fight. Aidan was proud to see Donar battling so well against an older, more experienced warrior. Now that he no longer had to hold back, he proved himself more than competent.

Their fierce grappling continued for several minutes until Nanoq managed to lock his jaws around Donar's throat. The younger shifter raked his talons along the captain's ribs, but to no avail. He could not break free. His struggles weakened with each passing moment that he could not draw breath. Then his legs fell to his sides.

I yield! Donar called out telepathically.

Nanoq withdrew. *Well fought.*

As each of the shifters changed back to their human forms, the pendragon moved to the center of the field. He waited for the captain to join him before officially announcing the winner. Nanoq was covered in blood and wounds, but he stood tall and proud next to the pendragon. Aidan was genuinely pleased for him. He only worried about how the captain would rule the toriq once he took over. It was well known that Nanoq managed the fortress guard with strict rules and tough punishments for any infractions. Of course, it was also said that he never acted rashly and that he took good care of those under him. Life could be good under his rule, assuming one did not get into any trouble.

The pendragon lifted the captain's hand and shouted in a clear and booming voice, "To my successor—Nanoq of Taugud!"

Aidan wasn't certain how his father really felt about the outcome. Throm embraced Nanoq and told him he was proud that such a fine warrior would be the next to lead the toriq. His jovialness seemed genuine enough, and the pendragon had given Nanoq one of his three nominations. Did the pendragon plan for this outcome? Aidan couldn't make sense of it and doubted his father would ever tell him.

"Tomorrow evening our toriq will face our greatest battle yet," Throm said, stepping closer to the crowd. "There is a large Shadowan den too close to our territory. We will force them back and show them we will not tolerate such an encroachment. Now that I have a successor, I will be joining the fine warriors of the Taugud in one last battle!"

Cheers rose up among the spectators, but Aidan did not join them. His father may "appear" to be fine at the moment, but Aidan knew it must take every bit of Throm's strength to appear so. If he fought in the battle tomorrow evening, it would be his last. The pendragon would no doubt require Nanoq to stay back at the fortress so that he could take over the position right away. Aidan was not ready for his father to die, not this soon. He would have to stay close to Throm and do all he could to protect him.

33

One-hundred and twenty shifters flew in a V formation over the human town of Norman, skirting the southern edge. It was the largest force of Taugud warriors they'd amassed since returning to Earth and it was a fearsome sight to behold. Nothing moved on the ground below. This was the time of the dragons, and if people had not hidden in their homes yet, they did now.

Aidan hoped shifters could overcome the human's fear of them someday. Even those who lived in the area where his toriq had taken over did not understand that red dragons would not attack unless provoked. He did not like to see them cower in fear from them when it was not necessary. Perhaps after today they would see that the shifters meant them no harm, and that they could live peacefully together in the same territory.

Aidan, Donar, and Falcon currently flew just behind the lead dragons. Throm was behind them, vortex surfacing along the slipstream created by the others ahead of him. The plan was to travel west until they reached the interstate, head north, and then double back to attack the Shadowan den from the other side. It was to their advantage that their enemy be forced to face the setting sun while the Taugud had their backs to it.

As they headed north, Aidan continually scanned the area for green dragons. When two appeared on the ground, feeding off of an animal they'd killed, several warriors from the rear of the V formation broke off to take them down. The success of their attack relied on the Shadowan not knowing of their approach until it was too late to form a proper defense.

The shopping center west of the airport came into view. As they made their turn east, dozens of dragons began pouring out of the larger structures. Aidan had suspected the Shadowan used the market buildings, along with the airport hangars, but when they did their reconnaissance, they could not get close enough to be certain. He was forced to re-estimate the den's population to something closer to one hundred. His people still had the advantage, but not as much as they'd thought. He hoped Bailey and his sister, who waited somewhere east of the airport, took full advantage of the distraction to get the children. There would be no better time than once the full battle began.

Aidan and the other warriors soared downward, heading on a collision course with the Shadowan coming to meet them. Loud roars filled the air as the pure dragons called to their brethren for assistance. The Taugud reformed into a battle line.

Let us show them that we are not weak, and we will not accept their presence among us! the pendragon shouted to their collective.

The shifters returned his call for action with snarls and roars.

Aidan chose his target, a green dragon with a long scar across its face and only half of a tail. It was a sign that this one was a warrior with heavy battle experience. Throm flew just behind Aidan, but he surged forward, seeking out the same foe. His father might be determined to die in battle, but not if his son could help it. Aidan used his lither, faster body to pick up speed and take the green dragon first.

That one is mine! Throm yelled into his head.

You may punish me later, father.

The pendragon growled at him and broke away.

Aidan collided mid-air with the Shadowan warrior, talons outstretched. He slashed at his opponent's face, digging deep. The older dragon nipped at Aidan's arms and ripped off a few scales. It felt much like having chunks of one's hair pulled out—painful, but not debilitating. Aidan growled and punched the warrior in the face, catching him on the side of his large snout. Blood sprayed as his opponent opened his jaws wide to let out a roar of pain.

It was exactly what Aidan had hoped the dragon would do.

He gripped the warrior's head, holding him still, and bit down on his snout. This needed to be done carefully, or others would notice what he was doing. Aidan could not afford for the Taugud or Shadowan to figure out he could use this particular battle strategy. Only Donar knew he was even capable of it. He called for his second flame, the one that hardened Zaphiriam and fire-proofed camrium cloth, and sent a stream of it down his enemy's nostrils. The dragon wheezed and began raking his talons down Aidan's chest, slicing across his scales. He ignored the pain. It was best to kill the dragon quickly and move onto the next.

The warrior began to choke as his throat and lungs were hardened, and his wings slackened. Aidan continued holding him, bearing all their weight and even flying them higher into the air where few others fought. After a few more moments, his struggles became nothing more than weak pawing gestures. The green dragon could no longer draw a breath, and his red eyes drifted shut. Aidan dug his teeth deeper into the warrior's snout and ripped it off, spitting it away. That should be enough to conceal the method of death. He let his enemy go, watching as the green dragon plummeted to the earth hundreds of feet below. Its body landed on the airport runway, misshapen and grotesque.

Aidan searched for his father and found him engaged with another warrior. Throm's jaws were locked on his opponent's shoulder, while the green dragon clawed at him. His father was viciously tearing into his enemy, ripping through scales and skin. He reached the warrior's throat and bit down hard. The green dragon let out a wheeze, then slackened. Throm let him go, and the lifeless body plummeted the ground. Aidan's father hovered there for a moment, recovering his breath. He had fought well that time, but how long could he keep it up?

Unwilling to let his father out of his sight, Aidan resigned himself to following Throm around the battle. He would watch the pendragon's back and confront any warrior who threatened him. His father may have hardly spoken a word to Aidan since he turned down the nomination for the Bitkal, but he would not give up on the dragon that had raised him. It wasn't Throm's time yet, and Aidan did not want to lose him before they had resolved their differences.

34

BAILEY

Phoebe and I paced around a parking lot about a mile from the airport, waiting impatiently. We didn't dare get any closer until the battle reached full scale, and all the green dragons in the hangars left to go fight Aidan and his clan. Earl leaned against his car, smoking one of his precious cigarettes. We'd decided to bring several vehicles since we couldn't be certain how many children Matrika currently held. As evidenced by Christine's daughter being taken the other night after our recon, there might be more than we last counted.

Conrad was in charge of my truck while I was off rescuing the kids, and Danae had brought Norma's car. Hopefully, that would be more than enough. It was hard to sit still when I knew the children were so close. Phoebe had set her mouth in a grim line that made me think she felt the same way—or maybe she was only itching to fight. I couldn't be sure with her.

Movement in the sky caught my attention. Numerous red shapes were heading toward the airport, growing larger as they came closer. They weren't flying very high or I might have seen them sooner—maybe five hundred feet above the ground.

I looked at Conrad. "Wait until fifteen minutes after we leave and then move the truck up to the YMCA. Park behind the building and stay hidden until you see Phoebe and I come out with the children. Got it?"

He crossed his arms. "You told me this three times already, but yeah, I got it."

"Sorry," I said, rubbing my face. "I just don't want anything to go wrong."

Conrad sighed. "I know. Just watch your own ass, too."

"The battle is beginning." Phoebe drew our attention back to the sky.

The red dragons had formed a line and a dozen or so green were flying up to attack. That couldn't be close to all of the Shadowan, but then I spotted a stream of them exiting the hangars and flying up—a whole lot more. In the space of two minutes, the two clans were almost evenly matched with just a slight advantage on the Taugud side.

I frowned. "Isn't that more dragons living there than we thought?"

"Shifitt," Phoebe cursed. "Yes. I have never seen a den with so many of them living together. Usually, only a jakhal holds more than twenty or so."

She and Aidan had explained to me that a jakhal was sort of like a clan capital. Who knew the beasts could be so organized? I continued pondering that, trying to keep myself distracted. With so many dragons a short distance away, my slayer instincts were beginning to rise. I was doing my best to keep them tamped down. For the past few days while waiting for this battle, I had been practicing getting near green dragons without attacking them. Conrad had helped with that, working to keep me in check. If I was going to get the children to safety, I could not afford to get distracted. I'd steadily built up a tolerance with each sighting, only killing one dragon when we first started the exercises. Oddly, I had been seeing more of the Shadowan than normal in the central part of Norman.

Then a thought occurred to me. "Do you think they've been ramping up their numbers in this area because they plan to attack your clan soon?"

Phoebe's mouth set in a grim line. "We believe so. It is one of the reasons my father did not hesitate to call for this battle when we informed him of the den."

"What did he think about you rescuing the children?" I asked.

She gave me a confident smile. "I told him it would help win over the humans if they could see we are not their enemy."

"I'll make sure they know your clan is the main reason their kids are safe," I said.

Phoebe dipped her chin. "I would appreciate that."

Glancing back toward the airport, which I had avoided doing to keep myself calm, I saw the battle was now in full swing. That's what we had been waiting for. "It's time to go."

Danae pointed a finger at me. "Be careful. I don't want to be healing more of your wounds after this. You've already tested my skills enough."

"You've got to have someone to practice on, right?" I asked, giving her a teasing smile.

She just glared at me.

During our conversation, Phoebe kept quiet. Aidan had warned her one of my friends was a sorceress, and he'd told her to leave Danae alone. Shifters weren't fans of the magic users, but the brother and sister were tolerating my friend out of respect for me.

Earl tossed me a black t-shirt. "You told me not to let you forget this."

Oh, right. It was a little too warm outside to be wearing an extra layer, but I needed to at least try to hide my camrium outfit in case we got close enough to any other shifters for them to notice. I didn't want to risk getting Phoebe and Aidan in trouble for helping a slayer.

"Thanks." I pulled it over my head.

"You can thank me by coming back alive with those children," Earl said in a gruff voice.

I gave a final nod to Conrad. "See you in about fifteen minutes."

"You bet you will." He made a shooing gesture. "Now, get out of here."

Phoebe and I took off at a sprint down the street. Most of the green dragons would have left the hangars by this point, giving us the perfect opportunity to sneak into their den. We ran quickly enough it only took us about six minutes to reach the airport. Phoebe and I slowed down and headed along the row of hangars with the female shifter scenting the air.

Her brows drew together. "I can hardly smell the children here. Their scent is faint."

"What does that mean?" I had heightened senses but nothing like a dragon. At the moment, all I could pick up was the acrid stench of burning grass where part of the battle took place on the ground.

"They are not in that building anymore." Phoebe nodded at the one where we'd seen the children last.

I froze. "You mean they moved the kids?"

"Yes."

Damn it all to hell. "Think you can find them?"

"We will see." She picked up the pace to a slow jog, moving down the line of hangars. We passed several before she came to a sudden halt and waved me closer to her. "I believe they are in the structure up ahead, but I smell two other dragons there as well."

Since she spoke in a low tone, I followed her example and whispered, "Matrika?"

"I do not know her scent, but we will find out soon enough."

We crept alongside the building, heading toward the hangar where Phoebe had indicated the children would be. The sounds of battle about five hundred feet away made it difficult to listen for any other noises, but I thought I heard a huff and snort. Dragons made all sorts of strange noises when they were just standing around. I had noticed that when I was practicing getting near them without killing them.

Phoebe held up a hand, and we stopped just before going around the corner, then she lifted her index finger. I took a wild stab in the dark and figured she meant only one dragon sat outside. She handed me my blade, which she had kept in shiggara in case we ran into any shifters first. Then we leaped into view.

A giant green dragon sat before the closed hangar doors. It spotted us right away and charged toward us. Phoebe and I separated, silently agreeing to take the dragon from opposite sides.

The beast let out a snarl and went for the female shifter first, lashing out at her. She dodged the strike and slashed at the creature's face with her sword. While Phoebe kept the dragon distracted, I leaped onto its back and straddled it. The beast bucked once, but it had to keep moving on its feet to dodge the shifter's quick and painful strikes.

I brought my sword down, aiming for the vulnerable spot on the beast's back. The weapon pushed through the scales and into the body. Partway through, the dragon growled and tried bucking me off again, but I squeezed with my thighs and held my position. The sword sunk deep. With a hard jerk, I brought it back and sliced into the heart. The dragon shuddered once and slumped beneath me, wheezing out its last breath.

"Good work." Phoebe nodded.

"You too."

We jogged over to the hangar, and she frowned at the large doors. "You understand these human constructions better than I do. How do we get inside?"

I thought about asking if she could burn her way through, but we had no way of knowing where Matrika or the children were located. It was too big of a risk to use that trick yet.

"There's got to be a smaller entrance somewhere." I ran my gaze around, not seeing one. "Let's try the other side."

As we rushed to find the door, my heart pounded in my chest. Killing the dragon had helped ease some of the tension I'd been feeling since I stopped fighting them as much these last few days. Aidan had said with each kill my battle lust would grow. I hadn't understood what he meant at the time, still being new to the slayer business, but I was beginning to get it now.

We located a regular-sized door at the far end of the building. It was locked, so we kicked it until we busted the frame enough to pull it away. Then we paused, gazing into the darkness beyond. It was still bright enough outside we needed a moment for our eyes to adjust. I drew in deep breaths, smelling the fear of the children and the rage of the dragon inside. That told me all I needed to know. To hell with waiting for full night vision, I went racing inside.

Phoebe followed on my heels. "Bailey, to your left!"

I turned in that direction and almost came face-to-face with Matrika. It had seemed dark when I'd first entered, but now I spotted a hole in the roof that shed some light on this side of the building. If not for the setting sun, it might have been brighter.

The dragon stood in front of the children, who made soft sounds of distress behind her. She snorted, huffed, and puffed as her red eyes narrowed on us. Like a mother protecting her brood, she didn't back down.

I breathed through my instant rage at seeing her and forced myself to calm down. One wrong move on my part and the children could get hurt. It would be easier if I could draw Matrika away from them.

Lifting my sword in a threatening manner, I met her gaze. "We can do this the easy way or the hard way, but I will get those children back to their parents."

She growled in answer.

"Phoebe," I said, taking a quick glance at her where she stood next to me. "Think you can talk to her the dragon way?"

Aidan's sister worked her jaw. "I can try."

I knew when she started speaking telepathically because the dragon turned her gaze to the female shifter. There was no telling what Phoebe said, but Matrika's response was a fierce snarl. Well, at least it was worth a shot.

"You know I almost killed you once. I will finish you this time if you don't get out of my way," I warned.

A young girl crept around the dragon, little ringlets of blond hair shining in the soft light. "Are you here to take me back to my mommy?"

I recognized her. "Yes, Lacy. Your mommy misses you very much, and she's worried about you. Are you okay?"

"Yeah, I'm okay. Just hungry. She—" the girl pointed at Matrika, "gives us awful things to eat like burned meat and stuff."

Just like Aidan could light a candle if he set his mind to it, he'd said dragons could cook their food if they liked it that way. It was just easier for them to blow destructive flames, rather than slightly cooler ones.

"You see, Matrika. They aren't happy here. You have to let them go home to their human parents who know how to take care of them." I wanted to resolve this peacefully for the children's sake. They had been through enough without me killing a dragon in front of their eyes. While they appeared scared, that fear didn't seem to be directed at Matrika. Rather, at the situation in general. There was a loud battle raging outside, and the sounds of it filtered into the hangar.

Phoebe glanced at me. "Matrika says the kids are hers now, and we can't have them."

Dammit. I gave Aidan's sister an inquiring brow, and she nodded. We had no choice but to battle this out with the children here or not. While we'd waited with Earl and the others down the street, we'd run through a few strategies of attack, so we were prepared for almost anything.

I turned my gaze to the little girl, who still stood just beyond the dragon. "Lacy, I need you and the other kids to back away as far as you can, alright?"

"Are you going to kill her?" this came from a little boy who came within view.

"Just turn around and don't watch." God, how I hated being in this position. I had no way of knowing what Matrika had said or done since she'd taken the children. For all I knew, they had Stockholm syndrome. The two I'd seen so far appeared mostly clean with no obvious signs of injury. She might have given them crappy food, but she hadn't hurt them.

Some of the children sniffled. Matrika glanced back at them and they quieted, moving farther away. I was surprised. She was actually getting them to cooperate and do what I asked. Then she turned her gaze back to me and growled, leaping forward.

Phoebe and I broke apart. This time, I took the dragon head on, slashing at Matrika and dodging her attempts to bite at my legs. As the dragon kept forcing me backward, Phoebe worked her way around toward the children. Matrika swatted her tail at the shifter, but Aidan's sister leaped up in time to miss the strike. I sliced the green dragon's nose, and she returned her attention to me. We took turns slashing at each other. Her talons gouged my upper left arm in almost the same spot as she'd injured before, but then I returned the favor with a strike to one of her eyes, cutting right through it.

Meanwhile, Phoebe was blowing flames into the side of the building, making a hole for the children to escape. It took longer in her human form because she couldn't billow the fire out as big as when she was a dragon. I was grateful for her resourcefulness. Aidan's sister understood how much I didn't want the little ones to see this fight, which I had made clear beforehand.

I cut Matrika's paw when she lashed out at me again. She let out a strangled cry that sounded almost like a dog when it got hurt. I kicked her in the head next, doing all I could to delay the kill. The kids were watching, and several of them cried, calling her name. Damn the dragon for getting them attached to her.

Phoebe finished burning the hole, and she began guiding the children through it, careful to only touch them where their clothes covered their skin. As I angled Matrika to the side a little farther away, I caught a quick view of the rest of the kids. There were six more, making seven of them altogether. Lacy had been the only new addition.

Matrika and I continued battling it out, neither of us going for the killing blow. It was beginning to bother me that she wasn't trying that hard to kill me. If I didn't know better, I would have thought her heart wasn't into it.

The last child made it through the hole. Phoebe took a final glance back at me, and I silently willed her to follow the kids. Maybe she read the message in my eyes because she did as I wanted. Matrika caught my diverted attention and looked back. She let out a frustrated snarl when she saw the children were gone. Before I could go for the kill, she lifted into the air, escaping through the hole in the roof.

Oh, for crying out loud. I scowled at her escape hatch, then ran for the hole in the wall. Leaping through it, I found Phoebe and the children running away. She held one little girl who was wrapped in a camrium blanket she must have pulled from shiggara, and the other kids moved on their own ahead of her.

I glanced up at the sky. Matrika hovered a hundred feet overhead, gazing longingly at the children. She jerked her attention to me, and a look of resignation came over her eyes. She turned and flew away. Not toward the battle, but toward the north.

With that threat out of the way, I sheathed my sword and ran up to Phoebe and the kids, picking up a young boy who straggled behind. Together, we hurried south toward the main road leading to the airport. Just before we reached it, Conrad pulled up in the truck.

"Hurry!" he yelled, hopping out of the vehicle to help.

I pulled the back door open and slid the boy inside, then I took the girl from Phoebe and put her in there next. The rest of the kids climbed into the back of the truck with Conrad's help. Sounds of the battle in the field nearby spurred us. The hundreds of dragons fighting over there couldn't see us from this side of the building, but all it took was one of them coming overhead to blow our cover.

"Dear, Zorya," Phoebe said, a look of horror coming over her face.

I followed her gaze, and my heart skipped a beat. At least fifty green dragons were coming from the north—fresh, new arrivals. The battle had been in the shifters' favor before, but it wouldn't anymore.

"Ah, shit," Conrad cursed, forgetting about the children in the truck.

I could hardly yell at him for it now, especially since those were my thoughts exactly.

"I have to go fight with my toriq," Phoebe said.

"No." I shook my head. "We have to go to plan B."

When she and Aidan had stopped by a couple of days ago to update me on the battle plans, I'd told them of an idea I had if the situation became dire. Conrad and I had gone back to the Thamaran nest and retrieved the eggs left behind after my father and I killed the parents. Phoebe had confirmed the baby dragons inside were still fine and would likely hatch in the next couple of weeks. They were currently in the trunk of the car Danae brought, carefully wrapped and cushioned. My initial instincts were to kill them before they were hatched, but I had decided to keep them alive just in case we needed them. Now I was glad I did.

"Drop the children off and get the eggs," I ordered Conrad.

He rubbed his head. "I knew you were going to say that."

"Go!"

He climbed into the truck and drove off, though not too fast since the kids were in the back. I watched him get away, making sure no dragons came along to attack. Thankfully, they were still too busy fighting over on the airfield.

"Phoebe," I said, turning to her. "You have to track down Matrika and drag her scaly ass back here as a hostage—hurt her a little if necessary. The last I saw, she flew north heading away from the battle. If we're lucky, we can work out a trade to make the Shadowan leave Norman if we don't kill her and let her have the eggs."

Aidan's sister scowled. "Would you like me to grab the moon for you while I am out, too?"

She hadn't been too hot on this idea when I first brought it up, and I'd had to revise it a little since things didn't go quite like I expected. "Do you have any better ideas?"

From the way Aidan described it, the Shadowan loved Matrika. She was their only known weakness, though I still couldn't understand why she held such a lofty position. Even when the rest of their clan went out to fight Aidan and the shifters, they still spared a guard for their little princess. If there was any chance we could broker a deal, this was the way.

"Fine. I'll do it," Phoebe said, then her gaze hardened. "But you're going to go out there and kill some of those zishkat while I'm getting Matrika."

I'd heard the term zishkat once before and asked Aidan what it meant. He said it was dragon dung.

"I thought you all didn't want me getting into this fight." I glanced down at my oversized t-shirt. The first time a dragon sent flames my way, the camrium clothes underneath would be exposed.

"This is an emergency." She looked toward the sky where some of the red dragons were now fighting multiple opponents. "I'd rather get into trouble for associating with you than see more of my toriq dead."

I pulled my sword out of its sheath. "Then you can count on me to help."

"Take down as many as you can," Phoebe said, then she began to shift.

35

AIDAN

Aidan stood on the ground, bloody and wounded from his last battle with a rather vicious opponent. Three dragons circled him, preparing to attack. He had lost track of his father about ten minutes ago. It worried him deeply, but he needed to deal with his current situation before he could locate Throm again. The pendragon had been wounded several times, and he was in no shape to fight anymore.

The beast directly in front of Aidan lashed out at him. He sidestepped to avoid it, bumping into another Shadowan. That one took advantage and leaped on top of him. Sharp talons dug into his sides. Aidan twisted and turned, trying to buck his attacker off, but the dragon just dug his claws deeper.

Then he heard a voice he hadn't expected to hear. "Get off of him, you damn zishkat!"

The beast within him was elated to see the slayer, but Aidan was not so pleased. This wasn't the time or the place for Bailey to be making an appearance. Not only would she have difficulty stopping once she began killing, but she would draw the notice of his toriq.

She cut her way through the third Shadowan, finishing him with a sword through his back. It was faster than he had ever seen Bailey kill a dragon before. There was a wild look in her eyes as she finished. She was in full slayer mode now, and her bloodlust was high. Bailey ran forward with her sword out and shoved the blade through the side of the beast on top of him, her aim surprisingly accurate. The dragon slumped, and Aidan shook him off.

He went for the final one before she could reach it. The Shadowan was so surprised to find a slayer in their midst that the beast had his eyes on her, rather than him. Aidan leaped forward and bit into the dragon's throat, wasting no time crushing it. He fell dead on the ground.

You should not be here, Aidan said telepathically, unsure if it would work with him speaking instead of his beast.

"You're outnumbered, and your sister told me to help even the odds until she can carry out plan B," Bailey hissed, careful of the other Taugud who fought nearby and might hear her.

Ah, plan B. He'd hoped they would not have to resort to that. It must mean Matrika was still alive somewhere, and Bailey wouldn't be here unless she had successfully rescued the children. Though he was certain the Shadowan valued their princess, he didn't know if it would be enough of a trade. He supposed they'd find out soon enough.

Very well, but take care not to kill my people, he said, grateful that he could at least communicate with her in dragon form. Aidan did not want to speculate too much on how that was possible. It meant there was a far deeper connection between them than he had yet acknowledged.

Bailey didn't answer. Instead, she spun on her feet and attacked the first green dragon she could find. Aidan supposed that was answer enough, considering she had to move around one of his brethren to get to the Shadowan. Somehow, she had gained even greater control since he last tested her. She had said she would continue to work on it, but Bailey had achieved a greater level than he dared hope for.

Feeling a renewed surge of energy, Aidan sought out his own foe and attacked. One after another, he took green dragons down until it seemed all he saw was a sea of blood. Still bodies from both toriqan lay strewn across the earth—some dead and some dying. In his search for his father between bouts of fighting, he spotted Donar. His cousin was covered in wounds but still battling his enemies with a touch of crazed zeal. He also caught Falcon take down two opponents within moments of each other.

After killing what must have been the tenth dragon Aidan had faced, he ran into Bailey again. She was bloodier than before and wounded in several places, but still standing and fighting with a vengeance. He couldn't have been prouder of her. Then the scene just beyond her caught his attention. Two green dragons tore into Throm as he attempted to fight them off, but he lacked the strength to do any real damage. The right side of his body gaped wide open, revealing his ribs, and one of his legs hung at an odd angle. If he were to survive, he would need a healer right away.

Aidan raced across the ground, desperate to save his father before it was too late. Bailey was finishing off her opponent as he ran past her. He could not stop to explain. Aidan kept going, watching with horror as one of the dragons rammed into Throm's side, knocking him over. The other Shadowan went for his neck.

Only a few more paces and Aidan would be there.

The green dragon chomped hard on Throm's throat while the other tore deep into his belly. Aidan roared his anger, but the Shadowan paid no attention to him. They knew who they were killing and wanted the glory of taking the pendragon's life. As Aidan reached them, the first released Throm's neck and stepped away. He caught a glimpse of his father's eyes and watched the light go out of them. The pendragon—the male who had inspired and guided him for more than two centuries—had just breathed his last breath.

Noooo! This could not be happening.

Aidan had meant to protect his father and see him alive through the end of the battle. Anguish unlike anything he had felt before ran through him. Now he would never be able to speak to his sire again or gain his forgiveness. Aidan let out a mournful wail for all his toriq to hear, letting them know what had happened. They echoed it with their own sounds of sorrow.

You will die for this! Aidan said to the one who crushed Throm's throat.

He leaped on top of the dragon, ripping and tearing into him with his teeth. Aidan's pain and anger fueled him. In moments, there was little left of the Shadowan to identify. He would be claiming no glory for himself today. Aidan twisted to find the other dragon who had attacked Throm, but he found Bailey had already finished him off. As she hovered over the beast's with her bloody sword in hand, she gave him a respectful nod.

While he had been distracted with killing his father's murderer, she had protected his back and fended off his would-be attacker. Some shifter males might be ashamed to have a female—especially a slayer—aid them in battle. He took pride in the fact that she was capable of doing it, and for him.

Stop fighting if you want your princess to live! Phoebe called out. Aidan turned to find his sister standing on the rooftop of a hangar, gripping Matrika's throat with her teeth.

Within seconds, the battlefield went still. Shadowan and Taugud alike stopped and turned to look at Phoebe and their princess. Though she was smaller than Matrika, she looked the part of a vengeful warrior. Aidan noted that Bailey quietly slipped away while everyone had their attention elsewhere. Her fists were clenched and her expression tight as she fought to maintain control, but she managed to walk past a dozen dragons before clearing the battlefield.

Once she was out of sight, Aidan sat next to his dead father and guarded his body while listening to his sister propose the terms for Matrika's release. She made it clear the Shadowan must withdraw to the north, citing a human interstate they called I-240, though she described it in terms the pure dragons could understand. That was much farther north than they had discussed, but it could not hurt to ask for more than they expected.

She also told the Shadowan about the eggs, pulling one from shiggara for everyone to see and stating there was one more like it, both almost ready to hatch. They came from the Thamaran, but the parents were killed by a slayer so the eggs would not be missed. It would allow Matrika a chance to be the mother she wished to be so desperately. All the Shadowan had to do was give up a bit of territory—or they could continue to fight and lose the princess and the eggs. It was their choice.

Volker, the pendragon and Matrika's father, came forward. *You ask for too much.*

I think not. Phoebe said, maintaining her tight hold on the female dragon's throat. It was just as well she did not need her mouth to talk. *You are the one who clearly planned to invade our territory, and it is your warrior who just killed our pendragon. I could take my revenge on your daughter, or I could make her very happy. The decision is yours.*

Volker called two dragons to him. They spoke through private communications for several minutes before he addressed Phoebe again. *Perhaps we can redefine the territorial boundaries you have proposed.*

Absolutely not, she growled and bit harder into Matrika, who made a pain-filled sound. *You have five seconds to consider before I finish her.*

The Shadowan pendragon took a step forward, but then remembered the imminent threat to his daughter and stopped. *Very well, we accept your offer.*

Aidan was shocked. That had taken very little convincing, even with Matrika's life at stake. The Shadowan must value her even more than anyone guessed.

Ruari appeared at the base of the building. *We must prepare for the ritual of agreement.*

Why was Aidan not surprised his brother showed up so quickly now? With the pendragon dead and the successor not present, it fell on one of Throm's children to perform the blood ritual that would seal the accord. Ruari wouldn't want to miss a chance in the spotlight, though Aidan noted his brother didn't appear all that worse for wear from the battle. He had likely hidden for most of the fighting, only revealing himself long enough for the toriq to see him participating. Aidan might have argued against letting his brother perform the ritual, but it was rather painful. Let Ruari be the one to experience a stab through the gut—he certainly deserved it.

Very well, produce the blades and let us get on with this, Volker said. The pure dragons had a different tradition they used amongst each other, but this was the method they used when shifters were involved.

Aidan ordered one of his clansmen to watch over Throm's body, then made his way forward to assist his brother and sister. No matter his inner turmoil, his family needed to present a united force to the Shadowan and show them that despite the loss of their pendragon, they remained strong. Though inside, Aidan felt himself falling apart. He would deal with his pain later when he could be alone. For now, he held his head high and showed none of his despair.

36

BAILEY

I weaved my way around the dragons crowding the airfield. Though I averted my gaze from the beasts as best I could, the wild scent of them assailed my nose. My body thrummed with the need to fight and kill more of them. I concentrated on the pain of my wounds, letting that be my focus. One dragon had taken a bite of my ankle just before I ran my sword through its heart. I didn't think any bones were broken, but the punctures from its sharp teeth throbbed, and the skin swelled inside my boot.

A round of growls sounded as I neared the edge of the field, I glanced up at the hangar roof where Phoebe had a stranglehold on Matrika. She must have told the Shadowan the terms of the deal we'd discussed beforehand. I wished I could have heard her speech, but it appeared telepathy only worked on me with Aidan.

The last time I looked his way there had been deep pain and sorrow in his eyes. I didn't recognize the dragon he had tried to save and reached too late, but the beast's worn scales and softer body gave the impression it was older. Could it have been his father? I couldn't recall Aidan ever mentioning any other older male that he might mourn so heavily. All I knew was that his grief had been palpable. Under other circumstances, I might have tried comforting him, but all I was able to do was protect his back by killing the beast eyeing him. Aidan had no idea how close he came to the green dragon taking him down while he fought the other one.

I made it past the row of airport hangars and onto the main road. Some of the tension eased inside me. The scent of the hundreds of dragons behind me was slowly fading. I began to jog down the street, ignoring the pain in my ankle and other wounds, just wanting to put as much distance as I could from the battlefield. After a few minutes, Conrad pulled up alongside me. Had he been lurking somewhere nearby?

He rolled down the truck window. "Looking for a ride?"

"I thought I told you to go back with the children," I said, giving him a disapproving look.

"I did. They're back at Earl's eatin' their way through the candy stash." He grinned. "But I wouldn't be much of a sidekick if I let you walk home wounded now would I?"

"I suppose not." I worked my way around to the passenger side of the truck and got in. Normally, I insisted on driving if we were together, but I was in too much pain to bother at the moment. "But sidekicks should obey orders."

"Uh huh, show me one example of a sidekick who always obeyed orders."

I mulled that over and saw that he had a point.

"There's a first time for everything," I replied instead.

Conrad turned the truck around and started driving toward Earl's neighborhood. With the conditions of the roads these days, it would take about fifteen to twenty minutes. I pulled a miniature first aid kit from the glove compartment and started cleaning up the slash wounds on my arms, chest, and face. The blood was dried, but I was rather certain I could make zombies look good.

I pulled down the visor mirror, noting half my braid had been torn out and my hair hung in all directions. There were three slash marks across my left cheek— one of them a mere half inch from my eye. It didn't hurt as much as it should. Was I just getting used to being wounded and the minor injuries didn't bother me anymore? Sometimes, I wondered how much becoming a slayer had changed me. If I ever saw my mother again, would she even be able to recognize her own daughter? That was a scary thought.

I'd just finished tending my visible injuries when Conrad pulled up to the neighborhood "gate" where Justin and Miles opened it right away for us. The sun had set, leaving a fading pink haze on the horizon. We usually didn't come in around this time, but we didn't see any dragons on the way back. If Phoebe got the Shadowan to agree to the terms we discussed, the green beasts wouldn't be a problem anymore in this part of Norman. We would only have the Thamaran on the west side of town to worry about.

Justin and Miles gave me a salute as we passed by them. Though I was no soldier, I returned the gesture since it seemed like the thing to do. Then I turned my gaze ahead where I caught sight of a white cargo van parked along the street with antennas and a small satellite dish jutting from the top. That had to be Hank, the radio guy. Earl had promised to get him here if we rescued the children. Like any good reporter, this was the kind of opportunity he wouldn't want to miss.

We parked in Earl's driveway. I caught sight of the mother and daughter scene on the porch, and tears misted my eyes. Christine was holding Lacy, rocking her back and forth. Age notwithstanding, they looked so much alike with their fair skin and wavy blond hair. Even if reuniting them was all I could have accomplished today, it would have made it worth every single injury I got.

Conrad and I walked up to them, and he took a seat beside Christine. "So how much of my candy did she eat?"

Lacy held up her hand, splaying her fingers. "Five."

"You little goblin." Conrad reached over and tickled her belly, making her giggle.

Christine smiled at the banter, then looked up at me. "Thank you for this."

"No problem," I said, shrugging. It was always kind of awkward on the rare occasion someone took the time to thank me. I never knew how to respond. "I'm just glad she's safe and okay."

Christine shook her head. "I can't believe there isn't a scratch on her. She told me the dragon never hurt any of the children and that they could even touch its scales without getting burned. I didn't think that was possible."

I frowned. "It's not supposed to be."

"She could heal our booboos, too!" Lacy added.

"She did?" I asked, surprised.

The little girl jerked her head up and down. "Yep. I had a scratch, and she made it go away."

Aidan hadn't mentioned Matrika was a healer. That put things in a whole new perspective because as I understood it, a dragon with such a gift was extremely rare—like one in a thousand. I was willing to bet Phoebe would get whatever she asked for in return for not killing the princess.

"Bailey!" a man called from behind me.

I turned and spotted a guy who appeared to be in his early forties with tan skin, shaggy brown hair, and a thick mustache. He wore a pair of loose-fitting jeans and a blue t-shirt with a yellow smiley face on it. The man had come from the direction of the white van.

"Yeah," I said, bracing myself for whatever questions he might ask.

"I'm Hank." He held out a hand, and I shook it. "I've been told you are the one we have to thank for returning the town's missing children."

Speaking of which, I gazed around not seeing the other six. "Where are the rest of them?"

Hank gestured toward Trish's house. "They're in there with your friends Trish and Danae, getting snacks."

"Oh. Well, maybe I should go check on them," I said, starting to turn away.

"Wait. I'd like you to answer a few questions for my listeners before you go."

I knew he was going to say that. Despite being tired and injured, I supposed I had to do it. There was a message I'd promised to deliver to the citizens of Norman if things went well.

"Alright," I agreed.

He led me over to the van, opening the side door where I caught sight of an array of equipment inside. Electronics weren't my specialty, but I assumed this was how he managed to keep his radio station up and running. He must have installed extra batteries or something to keep it all powered. There were a lot of gadgets and wires in there.

Hank had me sit on a short stool and lean into a microphone set on a narrow table. He took control of another one. Nervously, I watched as he switched off the music he had been playing and informed listeners that he had another update for them.

"Right here next to me, I've got Bailey Monzac. She is the dragon slayer many of you have reported sighting around Norman, battling those dangerous beasts who I certainly wouldn't want to go near. She has just returned from her latest battle after rescuing the missing children. And I've gotta tell you, she didn't walk away from that fight unscathed."

Hank paused to glance over at me. "Would you like to tell us how you found the children and got them away from the dragons, Bailey?"

"Um, sure," I said, not feeling like the confident slayer I should be at all. "I had a lot of help."

"From who?" he asked, drawing his brows together.

"Well, I had to track down the children's location first before I could do anything." I paused for a moment and decided not to mention Javier. His help didn't come for free, so I wasn't about to give him any credit. "Then I had to scout out the den where the kids were being kept, which turned out to have about a hundred dragons living there."

Hank's eyes rounded. "Surely even you can't fight that many!"

"No, I can't." I shook my head. "But I knew how to contact a source with the red dragons to get their help. For those of you who don't know, they are shapeshifters and unlike the green dragons, they can take on human form."

He let out a nervous laugh. "You're joking, right?"

This was my best chance to put all the information out there. I had no idea how much Aidan would approve of me revealing, but I had to say enough to help convince the people listening. If his clan was going to

425

find a peaceful way to work with humans, there had to be a first step, and this was it.

"I know what I'm saying sounds crazy, but it's true. After everything else we've seen in recent months, you've gotta realize there is even more out there that we don't know about yet. The red dragons are shape-shifters, and they have a fortress near Lake Thunderbird. There are humans living with them who accidentally crossed over to the other dimension before it collided with ours. I've met one of those people, and I can testify that they are happy and safe there. Now, the red dragons want to extend their territory farther out and protect the people in this town, too."

Hank was so stunned that it took him a moment to respond. "So I take it they helped you rescue the kids."

"Yes." I nodded. "While their warriors battled the green dragons, a shifter and I fought our way to the kids and got them out."

"Wow, so you don't kill just any dragon."

I gave him a rueful smile, thinking of my father and what he would think of this. "No, but it's not easy. Something in my genetics more or less drives me to attack all dragons. I can't really take credit for choosing to fight them because I don't actually get a choice."

Hank's gaze ran up and down me. "How many did you kill today?"

"Um." I had to stop and think about it. "Five or six, I think." There were so many of them around me during the battle that I'd literally gotten lost in the melee.

It could have been more, but my blood lust had been so high that my memories of that time were a little hazy.

"The fact that you don't know for sure is amazing." Hank's voice was filled with admiration. "I think I'd remember each one just so I could brag about it."

I forced myself to laugh. "Anytime you want to take over for me, just let me know."

"I believe I'll let you keep that job and stick with working the radio," he replied, amused.

Through the open van door, I caught the flash of lights near the gate. Though it had grown dark in the last few minutes since the sun set, I could make out enough of the car to know I didn't recognize it. Miles jogged alongside the vehicle, guiding it in the direction of Trish's house. It was risky letting strangers inside, but Justin was supposed to verify everyone by asking for a name and description of their child before allowing them to enter. They'd also be allowed to stay the night so they wouldn't have to travel the danger-ous streets again to get back home. Even if Phoebe got the Shadowan to go along with the deal, it might take a few days or so for the green dragons to clear out of Norman.

"I believe one of the parents is here to pick up their kid, Hank. Time to go." I got off the stool, not waiting for his permission to leave.

"Thanks for your time, Bailey," he said, hurriedly. "I should wrap this up as well…"

I hurried away, not caring to listen any further. The car stopped in front of Trish's house and a black man and woman got out. I estimated them to be in their early thirties. As soon as they started their way across the lawn, a little boy with dark skin and a big smile on his face went running toward his parents.

The father scooped him up and hugged him close, before handing him to his crying mother. She kissed the little boy's cheeks over and over, between saying how much she loved and missed him. I moved over to my truck to lean against it to watch. There was something truly amazing about seeing a family back together again, despite all that had happened recently that could have torn them apart forever. It made me miss my own parents and siblings that much more, but it also gave me hope that I would be with them again someday. Sort of like that song by Carrie Underwood "See You Again."

A black and tan German shepherd came running up to me. I leaned down and petted the retired police dog. "Hey, Bomber. Haven't seen you in a while."

He panted and lolled his tongue at me.

"I think he's missed you," Jennifer said, walking up.

The curvy woman with short, brown hair was the current owner of the dog, though it was her husband who had worked with Bomber until dragons killed him shortly after D-day. Now she took care of the dog and used him to help keep the neighborhood safe. Jennifer lived on the next block over, so I'd missed seeing her during my last few visits.

"How are you doing?" I asked.

She raised her brows. "Better than you. Has Danae looked you over yet?"

"No. I don't have any injuries that won't heal on their own in a day or two." I leaned down to pet Bomber again. "I'll be fine."

"You did a good thing here," she said, nodding toward the family with the little boy.

I straightened and looked at the smiling parents. "It's my job."

"Killing dragons is your job. Saving the children was something you chose to do. I heard all about the trouble you went through just to find them." She gave me an amused look. "Don't sell yourself short, Bailey."

I was saved from the trouble of answering her when the sound of motorcycles rumbling down the street drew our attention. Turning around, I spotted Miles pointing three bikers toward Trish's house. Since I knew about them from our previous meeting, I'd warned him and Justin they'd probably be showing up.

The men continued down the street, pulling up behind the car of the first family to arrive. Larry quickly shut off his bike and ran up to his son, who had come out of the house as soon as he heard the engines rumbling. I watched as the man dropped to his knees and wrapped his arms around his son. His shoulders were shaking as he buried his face in the boy's neck.

One of the other bikers turned his gaze in my direction—it was the boss who hadn't liked me all that much the last time I saw him. He stared at me for a moment, then gave me a nod. It was as close to a thank you as I was probably going to get out of him. I nodded back.

He and the other man waited for a couple of minutes before joining Larry with his son. They patted the boy on the shoulder and started talking to him. I'd worried the kids would be horribly traumatized after their stay with the dragons, but so far they'd handled it better than expected. Maybe it was the excitement of seeing their families again or maybe the nightmares would come later. I just hoped they would be able to move past it and be happy again—or as happy as anyone could be these days.

One by one, more cars pulled up. Jennifer and Bomber left me to talk to the new arrivals, and kids excitedly petted the dog. As much as I enjoyed seeing the reunions, I was beginning to think I was going to choke on my emotions if I watched them for much longer. I shouted at Conrad that I was heading out. He still sat with Christine on the porch, talking to her and her daughter. When he started to get up, I waved him away and got in the truck. My job was done here.

37

BAILEY

A noise awoke me—footsteps on the porch. I sat up on the couch and grabbed my pistol from the coffee table. The door opened slowly, and Aidan poked his head inside. I let out a sigh of relief, lowering the gun.

He ran his gaze up and down me. "Did I wake you?"

I glanced at the wall clock and saw it was almost midnight. After getting back here around ten o'clock, I'd washed up and put on a tank top and shorts. It hadn't been my intention to fall asleep yet, but at some point while waiting to see if Aidan would stop by, I'd passed out on the couch.

"Yeah, but it's okay."

Aidan moved into the house, shutting the door behind him. "Are you well?"

"Just a few light injuries," I said, lifting my ankle for him to see. It was still red and swollen, but the gashes on my face were already scabbed over. "How about you?"

The cuts I remembered seeing on his arms were already gone, but his camrium uniform—which he'd apparently changed to a cleaner one since I saw him last—covered any other wounds he might have.

"Nothing serious." He moved over to sit in a chair across from me.

There was a pensive expression on Aidan's face. He was doing his best to hide his emotions, but it was clear he wasn't doing all that well emotionally. Tonight had been rough, but I suspected it was worse for him. He sat there not saying anything. It was all I could do to stay put and not go to him.

"So what happened after I left?" I asked, breaking the tense silence.

"The Shadowan agreed to the terms. They require one week to clear their dragons from the area, but after that, we should not be seeing them around anymore," he said, his voice so matter-of-fact that it drove me nuts. When I'd first met Aidan, he was a lot livelier. As time had gone on, he'd begun to close up. It was driving me crazy that his beast was more open to me than him.

"Does that mean I can move back to Earl's in a week?" It was something I'd been considering. If there weren't any green dragons in that part of town, there was no risk of drawing them to Trish and the others.

"You could," he paused and worked his throat. "But I would rather you stayed. It is easier for me to meet with you here where my toriq's patrols usually do not pass. The area where your friends live will become part of their route."

While he made a fair point, I got the impression there was more to it. "That's the only reason?"

He stared at me for a moment. "I am asking you to live here, in my private lair. Would you do that for me?"

There was a whole lot more to this than he wanted to admit—maybe even to himself. I hadn't been all that happy to stay in his house at first. It was far out of town and away from my friends, but the longer I stayed here, the more I liked the privacy. Plus, everyone kept bringing me food, so I didn't even have to scrounge for it anymore, and Earl hooked me up with fuel every time I stopped by from a tanker truck they'd somehow acquired. I would be fine living in Aidan's lair for now.

"If that's what you want..." I finished with a shrug.

"It is."

I couldn't explain why I didn't argue the point further. Maybe because I could see the deep emotions in Aidan's gaze—pain, fear, and frustration. He was hurting badly inside. It didn't make a huge difference where I lived as long as I could keep going out to fight dragons. There were still plenty of Thamarans left for me to hunt down. Once we got them cleared out, we could finally look at getting me home to my family.

"Alright. I'll live here for now," I said, then I remembered the thing I'd been wanting to tell him. "By the way, I think I know why the Shadowan are so protective of Matrika, and it's not just because she's the pendragon's daughter."

He lifted a brow. "What is it then?"

"She's a healer. One of the children told me she healed her wound—and apparently, Matrika's touch didn't burn any of the kids."

Aidan appeared stunned. "That would explain a lot."

"But how is it that she doesn't burn them?" I asked.

"Healers can control their temperatures better than other dragons." He sat back in his seat, still reeling from my news. "It is the only reason our healer can tend humans."

"Wow. Well, that's interesting."

He nodded. "Yes, and it is a very good reason for them to want to protect her. I am guessing the only reason she was living away from her jakhal was to act as the healer for the contingent down here. We are certain they would have attacked our toriq soon if we had not made the first move."

"I am surprised they would have let her out by herself to take those kids then," I said, shaking my head.

Aidan gave me an ironic smile. "Even princesses enjoy getting into a little trouble every once in a while. I got the impression that her father was not pleased with her at all, but he would never reveal the full extent of their problems in front of us."

"True," I agreed.

Aidan shifted in his chair. "There is something else I would like to discuss with you—something that I mentioned before but did not have the time to explain."

I frowned. "What is it?"

"When I was helping my sister investigate the murder..." he stopped and let out a snort. I'd already heard about what really happened with their captain, so I understood the irony in his tone. "Anyway, I spoke with each of the weapons makers in the fortress. One of them mentioned being very interested in human firearms. He is hoping to acquire a gun that he can study and attempt to improve upon for fighting dragons."

"Really?" I asked.

Aidan nodded. "I know I told you before that there was nothing I could do to help you with your ammunition problem, but if this weapons maker were to design a firearm for our warriors to use, that would be different. I could provide you with one of them and a supply of bullets."

"What about gun powder?" That was one of the other problems that held us back. It wasn't easy to acquire more, and no one wanted to sacrifice their regular ammunition they used against human looters and street thugs.

"He believes he might be able to find a suitable alternative through our own supplies," Aidan said, managing a small smile. "It could take months for him to craft the first firearm and there will be testing after that before he perfects it enough to make more of them, but I believe it will be worth the wait."

Considering how long it took humans to make prototypes for new weaponry, I wasn't surprised by that estimate. Better to have some hope we'd have a dragon-killing weapon in the future than none at all.

"Whenever it's ready, I'll be happy to test it." I got up and headed toward the weapons closet where I kept my spare rifle stored. Conrad and I had found a cache of them in the basement of a house that had been burned down. It was pure luck that the guns weren't damaged and that we'd discovered them.

"Thank you," Aidan said when I returned and handed the rifle to him. A moment later it disappeared into shiggara.

I stood there, shifting from foot to foot. "Aidan, who was the dragon who died?"

He stiffened. "Many dragons died tonight."

It was rather crass of me that I hadn't asked about his clan losses before. "How many?"

"Counting my father?" He didn't meet my gaze. "Nineteen lost their lives in the battle."

I fell to my knees in front of him and took hold of his hands where they rested in his lap. "I'm so sorry."

"It might have been more if you had not helped us," he said, squeezing my hands in return.

I swallowed. "But I didn't see those green dragons attacking your father in time to save him."

"Neither did I." Aidan shut his eyes.

"Is there anything I can do?" I ached to see him this way.

He shook his head. "We will hold his funeral to-morrow afternoon, and then his successor will become the official new pendragon."

"And that's the captain who faked his death?" I asked.

Aidan and Phoebe both told me he was a good man, but I didn't know him. Would things become much different with a new leader? And with Aidan not being the pendragon's son any longer, I imagined some of the freedoms he had before would be gone.

"Yes, his name is Nanoq," he replied.

I leaned closer. "Whatever you need—I am here."

Aidan stared long and hard at me, then jerked away. Before I could say anything, he was on his feet, pacing the room. I watched helplessly as he muttered things in the dragon language that I could not understand. It was like he was fighting some inner battle.

"Would you please stop?" I begged.

He turned to face me. "You have no idea what is going on in my head right now."

"Then tell me."

Aidan clenched his fists and let me see his emotions, pure and unfiltered. "Are you certain you wish to know?"

I recognized the rage, sadness, and lust all mixed together like a hurricane swirling in his yellow eyes. Aidan wasn't really asking if I wanted to know. He was asking if I wanted to experience all there was to him.

"Show me," I said.

"I can't promise you forever."

"Nobody can." I took a step forward. "But we can promise each other tonight and that is enough for me."

"Is it?"

I swallowed. "If that is all we can take for ourselves, it's still more than we've got now."

He drew in a ragged breath. "You have no idea how tempting you are."

And he had no idea that I was falling for him, but I didn't dare say that. "One night, Aidan. Even with everything working against us—we can have that much."

"And how do I know you won't hate me in the morning when I must leave?" he asked.

"I could never hate you."

His gaze was a deep pool of emotion. "Nor could I hate you."

We met each other halfway, and he pulled me into his arms. I wrapped my legs around his waist, feeling like I couldn't get close enough to him. Ever since the battle, I'd been feeling a kind of restless energy that had nothing to do with the need to kill more dragons. No, I craved a dragon for an entirely different reason. We kissed like two lovers who knew this night could never be anything more than a brief moment of happiness that would have to hold us over for a long time to come. He pulled and yanked at my clothes while I did the same thing to his.

Then he laid me on the couch and stopped, hovering over me. "Are you certain about this?"

I lay there naked and unafraid. Who cared what the future brought as long as I had him right now. This moment could last me for eternity—it would have to. "Yes."

He crushed his lips to mine and I sunk into the heat of his skin.

38

AIDAN

It would be dawn in an hour, and though he had left Bailey fast asleep—albeit reluctantly—he did not wish to return home yet. Now he had a new kind of restless energy. It was the kind that came with the realization that he cared deeply for a woman and had consummated a relationship that could go no further.

At least, not on a permanent basis.

Aidan did not regret what happened between them. Those precious few hours with the slayer had felt too right for him to find fault with their union. Bailey had said the same, afterward when they lay resting in each other's arms. They could make no promises, but neither did they wish to hide their feelings anymore. It was a useless exercise anyway that had made him miserable for the past few months. Even his beast was rumbling his happiness deep in the recesses of Aidan's mind.

He swooped toward the lake, knowing he must wash the scent of Bailey from him whether he liked it or not. His toriq must never know what he had done. It was bad enough they may have seen him fighting alongside the slayer for a portion of the battle. Aidan had no idea what kind of ramifications would come of that, but he had warned Bailey that he may not be able to return for a while. If it came to it, he could send his sister or Kayla to check on her once or twice a week until he felt it safe to return.

Aidan dipped into the deepest part of the lake, submerging himself. Dragons could swim quite well. It was only a matter of keeping one's wings tucked closely to prevent too much drag. He worked his way to the shore and rolled in the mud, allowing it to cover as much of him as possible before moving back into deeper water again to rinse.

Once he was certain none of Bailey's scent remained, he left the lake. Aidan let the cool breeze whisk the water from his body as he soared through the sky. He flew in lazy circles until hints of dawn colored the sky to the east. As much as it pained him to return to the fortress, he knew he must. It was not that Aidan feared what he might face from his toriq once he arrived, but that his father would not be alive and waiting for him. Throm had been such a strong presence for his whole life that it didn't seem comprehensible that the pendragon was gone.

Aidan landed at the front of the fortress, shifted into his human form, and headed toward the gate. He

noted that the guards were now wearing dark gray—
the color of mourning for shifters. Everyone in the toriq would wear it for one moon cycle, and then they
would return to their usual attire. Aidan would need
to change into his after he reached his rooms. He had
not worn the gray since his mother passed so he did not
keep a set in shiggara.

When he entered the great hall, Phoebe spotted
him right away. She grabbed him and pulled him aside.
Then she hugged him, uncaring of her open display of
affection. They had lost their father and most would
not judge.

"I was worried about you," she said, pulling away.
"Where did you go?"

After the agreement with the Shadowan had been
resolved, and he'd ensured warriors would take the
pendragon's body back to the fortress, he had left without another word. Aidan should have known she would
worry, but at the time he had not been thinking clearly.
His only thoughts had been to fly as fast and as hard as
he could. He had done that for almost two hours when
he eventually found himself in the clearing next to his
lair. Bailey had been inside—he knew—and he could
not stop himself from seeing her.

"I needed time to think," Aidan replied.

Phoebe narrowed her eyes. *You went to see the slayer,
didn't you?*

I did. There was no point in denying it. His sister
could see through him better than anyone.

"Did it help?" she asked, speaking aloud again.

He nodded.

"Then that is all that matters." She gave him a soft smile.

Aidan was surprised at her response. "Truly?"

"Just be careful. That's all I ask." She gave him a stern look, which was closer to the response he had been expecting.

"I will," he said.

She ran her gaze around the great hall where shifters were steadily leaving to find their beds. They normally went to sleep a couple of hours before sunrise, but the battle that night and the loss of the pendragon had kept them up later than usual. There were many tired and worn faces, though Aidan noted half of them cast him curious gazes and the other half suspicious ones.

Ruari crossed the hall to join them. "Nanoq wishes to speak with you."

"Now?" Aidan lifted a brow. He wasn't the pendragon yet and would not begin his duties until after Throm's funeral.

"I'm afraid word has reached him about the slayer you were seen fighting alongside." Ruari put his hands up in an innocent gesture. "But I swear it wasn't me. I never even saw her until she walked off the battlefield."

Aidan sighed. "I suppose I should get it over with."

"Don't worry." Phoebe patted him on the arm. "He has no authority yet so if he wishes to see you now it can't be that bad."

Nanoq was a rather rigid man who tended to see things in black and white. Aidan didn't hold out much hope, but he had carefully crafted arguments should it come to needing a defense.

"I will see you both at noon meal," he said, clasping both their arms. He did not usually show affection to Ruari, but in the wake of their father's death, he would make an exception this time. There was grief shadowing his brother's eyes as well. Perhaps he had a heart in there somewhere after all.

"Nanoq is in the pendragon's office," Ruari called out as Aidan walked away.

He had already assumed as much and headed straight for it. Once he reached the door, he stood there for a moment and took a deep breath. Phoebe had a point. The soon-to-be pendragon could not level any serious punishments on Aidan yet, which left him with a reprimand at most.

"Enter," Nanoq replied with a muffled voice.

Aidan stepped inside and found the former captain behind the pendragon's desk. It would soon belong to Nanoq, which still didn't seem real to him. So much had changed recently, and it had all happened rather quickly. Aidan had adapted to much of it without much difficulty, but this would be the hardest adjustment of all.

"You wished to see me." He stood stiffly before Nanoq.

"Yes." The former captain looked up. "I have been told you were seen with a dragon slayer during the battle. It is unclear whether you happened to come close to her a few times or if you were fighting alongside her. I wish to hear your side of the story."

Aidan hesitated, knowing that Nanoq would learn the truth eventually. Kade had foreseen that the to-riq would need Bailey in the future, and their people would have to accept her at that time if they were to be saved from whatever dangers lay ahead. If he lied now, as soon as Nanoq found out the truth, he would never trust Aidan again. There was no choice except to tell the future pendragon what really occurred, or at least an abbreviated version of it.

"The slayer was only supposed to take the human children away once the battle began, but when she saw we were in trouble, she joined the fight. I admit that I allowed her to be there," Aidan said, keeping his tone even.

Nanoq lifted a brow. "And your sister? Wasn't she the one who took on the task of rescuing the children?"

"Yes, but someone had to get the kids to the humans. The slayer was the only person who could get near the battle without risking getting burned to death. I asked her to do it, and Phoebe did not know her true identity." Though Aidan would not lie to protect himself, he would do so for his sister. He could not afford for Phoebe to be in trouble as well.

Nanoq leaned forward, his expression unreadable. "How long have you known this slayer?"

"A few months."

"Months?" the future pendragon's eyes widened.

Aidan clasped his hands behind him. "When I found her, she had just survived a dragon attempting to burn her, and she had no idea what she was. I took it upon myself to train her and make her an ally."

"Why?" Nanoq asked.

"For the same reason we made rescuing the children part of our mission. Winning over the humans will help bring them to our side, which will allow us to live more peacefully within our territory. The slayer is a link between us and them," Aidan explained. He refrained from using Bailey's name. That would be seen as too personal and might raise suspicions further.

Nanoq's jaw hardened. "The humans who live here could be our emissaries."

"Perhaps, but the ones in the human city see the slayer fighting the green dragons, and they respect her more. If she tells her people that we can be trusted, they are more likely to believe it."

"Will she do that for us?" Nanoq asked.

Aidan lifted his chin, knowing the answer. "She already has."

The former captain rubbed his face. "By our law, I should punish you for associating with her."

"That law only applies if a slayer kills one of our people. We do not seek out those who do not harm us," Aidan argued. His uncle had prepared him for this, using old texts from the library to formulate a defense should this particular circumstance come up.

"I admit that all the witness testimonies agree. She was never seen attacking a member of our toriq, and she may have saved your life, but slayers are not able to control themselves. It is a small miracle none of our people were harmed by her." Nanoq narrowed his eyes. "You brought great risk upon our warriors by allowing that woman to fight in the battle."

Aidan didn't flinch. "If she were any other slayer, that might be true, but *I* trained her. She has built up her tolerance to us, and she can control herself—which last night's battle proved."

"I will have to look into this further." Nanoq sighed. "In the meantime, you are not to see her. I have much to do in the coming weeks, but when the time is right I will speak with her myself and find out if what you say is true."

Aidan almost couldn't believe his ears. "You would give her a chance?"

"I must see for myself whether she is a threat or not. Once I have ascertained her disposition, I will consider how to handle her from there." Nanoq narrowed his eyes. "But you will stay away from the slayer until then, is that clear?"

"Yes," Aidan said. Though there was no guarantee everything would work out, this was a better response than he could have hoped for. Perhaps the old captain wasn't as rigid as everyone thought after all.

"Good." Nanoq gestured at him. "You are dismissed."

Aidan didn't waste time leaving the room. With most of the toriq now in their beds, the halls were quiet. He took a chance and headed toward the library. Aidan's uncle would likely have heard about the pendragon's death through his personal servant, but it would be up to Nanoq to decide if Kade's outcast status would continue or finally end. That was one of the many things that would keep the new pendragon busy. Aidan held no illusion that they would meet with Bailey soon due to the busy schedule Nanoq would have ahead, but he took comfort that it would eventually happen.

He slipped through the backdoor and listened for any sounds of his uncle moving around. Nothing stirred except an old clock at the front of the library, which ticked at regular intervals. The overpowering odors of old texts and tomes, as well as Kade's unique scent drifting everywhere, prevented Aidan from finding his uncle with his nose. A slight shuffling to his left drew him in that direction. He weaved his way around stacks of books on the floor until he reached the far wall, lined with rows of scrolls.

Kade stood on a ladder, perusing a text. He glanced over at Aidan with a gleam in his eyes. "I was hoping I would see you soon."

"You heard?" Aidan asked, though he knew the answer.

"Yes. The old man let himself get killed in battle." Kade clucked his tongue. "I should have known he would insist on dying that way."

Aidan masked his annoyance. He might understand his uncle's position, but he still loved his father and would miss him. "The slayer participated in the battle as well. She was seen fighting close to me, and I was forced to admit I had allied with her."

"How did that go over with Nanoq?" Kade lifted an inquiring brow.

"He is undecided. I have been told not to see the slayer for now until Nanoq can meet with Bailey and decide for himself whether she is a threat to us or not."

Aidan's uncle nodded. "Nanoq is even wiser than most people think."

"I had expected him to take a harder stance," Aidan said, still surprised his meeting with the future pendragon went as well as it did.

"Nanoq faces an uncertain future where every ally could mean the difference in our survival. I am certain he will come to see the value of Bailey with time." Kade climbed down from the ladder and stopped before Aidan. "For now, do as he asks and avoid seeing the slayer."

"That is what I planned." As much as Aidan hated the idea, he would do whatever it took to build Nanoq's trust and protect Bailey.

"Good. Now come see this." Kade gestured at Aidan to follow.

They moved to the front of the library where a row of stone tables were set for visitors to use. His uncle led him to the nearest one and pointed at a single sheet of yellowed parchment lying there.

Aidan squinted at it. "I cannot read the script."

"Neither can I," Kade said, shaking his head. "But it is from the missing tome."

"You found it?" Aidan asked, surprised.

"No, but it appears I separated this page from the rest for some reason. It was hidden in an old text having to do with ancient artifacts." Kade traced his fingers lightly over the parchment. "I am certain it is not a coincidence I put it there, but it will take me time to figure out how the page and the text are related."

Aidan could not begin to decipher the words. The letters were written in a smooth scrawl that he had never seen before. "And the language?"

"I must determine that as well, but my instincts tell me once I do, there will be a journey involved." Amusement danced in Kade's eyes. "I am certain it will be great fun for you and the slayer."

"To where?" Aidan asked, pleased to hear that Bailey would be involved, but confused as to what his uncle was implying.

"I will inform you as soon as I know."

DRAGON LANGUAGE GLOSSARY

Alefire: Thick and potent ale with a spicy aftertaste that the dragons drink (more than two mugs will make them drunk).

Bitkal: Ritual which decides who will become the next pendragon.

Camrium: Leather or suede-like clothing worn by shifters and the humans living with them that is fireproof and spelled with magic for protection.

Cryas: Soul.

Fushka (pl.- fushkan): Fool, idiot.

Jakhal: The clan seat of power—their capital.

Kederrawien: Dimension the dragons lived in for the past thousand years.

Petroes: Dragonflies (not the ones native to earth) who only come for a short period each summer. They can breathe tiny flames that will harm humans much like being sunburned.

Shifitt: Dragon curse word similar to damn or shit.

Shiggara: Stasis or limbo (an invisible place for dragons to store a small amount of supplies).

Stinguise: A foul smelling juice that can temporarily cover up other scents.

Sude camria: Black Camria, the plant used to manufacture the garments worn by dragon shifters while in human form. The end result can have a leather or suede-like appearance, depending on the process used to weave the cloth together.

Toriq (pl.- toriqan): Clan/Tribe.

Zaphiriam: A fire-proof metal with qualities similar to steel that dragons use to forge weaponry. It is black with red veins running through it.

Zishkat: Dragon dung.

Zorya: The dragon goddess.

DRAGON CLAN NAMES

SHAPE-SHIFTER CLANS:

Taugud- Clan in mid-western U.S. (southeast Oklahoma) that Aidan belongs to.

Straegud- Clan in eastern U.S.

Craegud- Clan in western U.S.

Faegud- Clan in north/northeast Texas with a mixture of pure and shape-shifter dragons.

PURE DRAGON CLANS:

Shadowan- Dragon clan in Oklahoma that holds the *northeast* part of the state, as well as parts of Arkansas and Kansas.

Thamaran- Dragon clan in Oklahoma that holds the *west* side of the state and the Texas panhandle.

Ghastanan- Dragon clan in Texas that holds the central portion, including Dallas.

Don't want to miss Susan Illene's next novel? Sign up for her book release alerts here: http://eepurl.com/-pb-L

Dragon's Breath Series
Stalked by Flames
Dancing with Flames
Forged by Flames (coming late October 2016)

Other Works by Susan
Darkness Haunts
Darkness Taunts
Chained by Darkness (novella)
Darkness Divides
Playing with Darkness (novella)
Darkness Clashes
Darkness Shatters
Darkness Wanes

ACKNOWLEDGMENTS

As always, I have a lot of people to thank. My family has been a huge support this time around. I spent many weekends at my father's house writing, and he helped read over chapters, providing a quick second opinion when I needed it. My Aunt Connie and Uncle Jerry also graciously allowed me to write at their house when I needed a quiet place to go (I've gotten tired of writing at home and needed to change my venues up to keep me motivated). They fed me many great dinners while I was over there on weekdays and they gave me a hard time if I wasn't working on the book enough. Though I told them to do that, it was nice that they really stuck to it! This book might have been late if not for all my family pushing me to get it done.

My husband has also been great about making sure I have everything I need (often running to the store so I am stocked up on energy drinks) and he is a semi-willing listener to my story ideas. For all that I harass him about his lack of help, he truly is there for me when I need him.

Special thanks to my editor, Angela, and to all my beta readers. This book would have all sorts of issues without the helpful input and edits I've gotten from you all. Thanks to my cousin-in-law, Caleb, for continuing to hound me for so long about having a garrote for a weapon in one of my books. I know it felt like I've been ignoring you for a couple of years now about that, but you finally got your wish once I had a good use for it! Also, to Crystal

Shannon, who won the contest for picking the name of a new shifter character (Lorcan) in Dancing with Flames.

A huge thanks to my cover artists. The list is long for how many people it takes to produce the Dragon's Breath Series covers, but it includes: Claudia at Phat Puppy Art, Catie (the Font Diva), Teresa Yeh (photographer), Isabella Capri (Model), and last but not least Jeff Brown for the beautiful background on the cover. Also to my design brain storming team- Rachel, Kristy, Sarah, and Heather. They help give me great concept ideas and feedback for my covers and track down the best places to get the model's wardrobe.

For research on the book, I have to thank the folks over at the Moore-Lindsey Historical House Museum for helping me with research material. Various businesses and/or their employees in the downtown Norman area were kind enough to answer as many of my questions as they could about the buildings there. Thanks to Trevor at 107.7 radio for stepping away from a broadcast he was doing at Homeland grocery store so that I could ask him how his station transmits from various locations around town and how complicated it could be in an apocalyptic situation. He was kind enough to not look at me like I was too crazy.

The list goes on and I can't possibly thank (or remember) everyone who has contributed in some way. There are so many of you, but that doesn't mean I don't appreciate your help. And last but not least, thanks to all my readers. Your motivation and love for my books are what helps keep me going.

ABOUT SUSAN ILLENE

Instead of making the traditional post high school move and attending college, Susan joined the U.S. Army. She spent her eighteenth birthday in the gas chamber—an experience she is sure is best left for criminals. For eleven years she served first as a human resources specialist and later as an Arabic linguist (mostly in Airborne units). Though all her duty assignments were stateside, she did make two deployments to Iraq where her language skills were put to regular use.

After leaving the service in 2009, Susan returned to school to study history with a focus on the Middle East at the University of Oklahoma. She no longer finds many opportunities to test her fighting abilities in real life, unless her husband is demanding she cook him a real meal (macaroni and cheese apparently doesn't count), but she's found a new outlet in writing urban fantasy heroines who can.

Made in the USA
Lexington, KY
30 December 2016